PUDD'NHEAD WILSON

AND

THOSE EXTRAORDINARY TWINS

MARK TWAIN

PUDD'NHEAD WILSON

AND

THOSE EXTRAORDINARY TWINS

Introduction by Ron Powers

Illustrations by F. M. Senior and C. H. Warren

themes
- racism
- satirizing the ignorance of racists
- ideals within small communities
- appearance vs. racism
- appearance vs. reality
- nature vs. nurture

THE MODERN LIBRARY

NEW YORK

2002 Modern Library Paperback Edition

Introduction copyright © 2002 by Ron Powers
Biographical note © 1993 by Random House, Inc.
Reading group guide © 2002 by Random House, Inc.

LIBRARY OF CONGRESS CATALOGING-IN-PUBLICATION DATA
Twain, Mark, 1835–1910.
Pudd'nhead Wilson; and, Those extraordinary twins / Mark Twain; introduction by Ron Powers;
illustrations by F. M. Senior and C. H. Warren.
p.   cm.
ISBN 0-8129-6622-8 (trade pbk.)
1. Infants switched at birth—Fiction. 2. Impostors and imposture—Fiction. 3. Passing
(Identity)—Fiction. 4. Trials (Murder)—Fiction. 5. Race relations—Fiction. I. Title:
Pudd'nhead Wilson; and, Those extraordinary twins. II. Twain, Mark, 1835–1910.
Those extraordinary twins.   III. Title: Extraordinary twins.   IV. Title.

PS1317 .A1 2002
813'.4—dc21   2002066002

Modern Library website address: www.modernlibrary.com

Printed in the United States of America

4 6 8 9 7 5 3

MARK TWAIN

Mark Twain was born Samuel Langhorne Clemens on November 30, 1835, in Florida, Missouri. His family moved to the Mississippi River port town of Hannibal four years later. His father—who failed as a storekeeper, worked as a clerk, and was finally appointed justice of the peace—died when Sam was eleven. Soon afterward the boy began working as an apprentice printer, and by age sixteen he was occasionally writing newspaper sketches. He left Hannibal at eighteen to work as an itinerant printer in New York, Philadelphia, St. Louis, and Cincinnati. From 1857 to 1861 he worked on Mississippi River steamboats, advancing from cub pilot to licensed pilot.

When the Civil War interrupted river traffic, Sam headed west with his brother Orion, who had been appointed secretary of the Nevada Territory. Settling at first in Carson City, he left his brother's employ and tried his luck at prospecting. He was unsuccessful at mining, but his humorous contributions to regional periodicals attracted notice, and in September 1862 he accepted a job with the *Virginia City Territorial Enterprise*. There he came under the influence of Sagebrush School writers, especially Joseph T. Goodman and Dan De Quille, and his writing career began.

His first pen name was Josh, but in January 1863 he changed it to Mark Twain, originally a river term indicating safe water. He left Virginia City in May 1864 for San Francisco, from where he continued to send columns to the *Enterprise,* but he also wrote for several local newspapers, including the *San Francisco Call.* The *Sacramento Union* sent him on a five-month trip to the Sandwich Islands (Hawaii) in 1866, from which he wrote articles that were soon adapted for a lecture tour, and later for chapters of *Roughing It.* The *Alta California* paid for his passage in 1867 on an organized tour of Europe and the Near East. His growing fame as a humorous writer and lecturer was enhanced by *The Celebrated Jumping Frog of Calaveras County and Other Sketches* (1867).

After his marriage to Olivia Louis (Livy) Langdon in 1870, Twain settled first in Buffalo, New York, and then for two decades in Hartford, Connecticut. His newspaper sketches from his European trip were expanded into *The Innocents Abroad* (1869), and his Western and Sandwich Island adventures were transformed into *Roughing It* (1872). *The Gilded Age*, written with Charles Dudley Warner, followed in 1873. Twain subsequently mined his childhood experiences for three of his masterpieces: *The Adventures of Tom Sawyer* (1876), *Life on the Mississippi* (1883), and, finally, *Adventures of Huckleberry Finn* (1884–85), on which he worked for nearly a decade. Another vein, historical fiction, resulted in *The Prince and the Pauper* (1882), *A Connecticut Yankee in King Arthur's Court* (1889), and *Personal Recollections of Joan of Arc* (1896). He continued his travel writing with *A Tramp Abroad* (1880) and *Following the Equator* (1897). Literary associates during these years included Bret Harte, George Washington Cable, Joel Chandler Harris, and the most important and long-lasting of them all, William Dean Howells.

During these years, Twain embarked on numerous unsuccessful business ventures. A notable exception was his undertaking to publish the memoirs of the terminally ill Ulysses S. Grant in 1885. His most disastrous investment was in a typesetting machine designed by James W. Paige. Twain lost a fortune in that project, and its failure contributed to his declaration of bankruptcy in 1894.

Despite Twain's public image as a humorist and the genial author of heartwarming tales of an idyllic American boyhood, there is ample evidence in his writings of deepening pessimism. The deaths of two of his daughters, Susy and Jean, added to the bitterness of his reflections. His novel *The Tragedy of Pudd'nhead Wilson* (1894), an indictment of slavery, was followed by such late works as "To the Person Sitting in Darkness" (1901), "The War Prayer" (1905), and "King Leopold's Soliloquy" (1905), which were overtly critical of imperialism and colonialism. The privately published *What Is Man?* (1906) is a bleak expression of determinism, and the posthumously published *Mysterious Stranger* fragments and *Letters from the Earth,* both criticisms of religious teachings, are among his darkest writings. In his last years, his financial troubles finally resolved, Twain settled near Redding, Connecticut, with his daughter Clara, and died in his mansion, Stormfield, on April 21, 1910.

Contents

Contents

INTRODUCTION

OUT OF SLAPSTICK, GENIUS:
MARK TWAIN, MEET DR. HACKENBUSH

Ron Powers

Mark Twain would have loved Groucho Marx's famous "snapper," "I don't want to belong to any club that would accept me as a member." In fact, he himself came pretty close to the essence of the sentiment when he declared that "high and fine literature is wine, and mine is only water; but everybody likes water." Both of these cigar-puffing comic anarchists (whose lives overlapped by fifteen years) were striking a uniquely American pose against the pretenses of High Art and its limiting regulations—a pose that each man, in his way, helped create and legitimize.

In his strange two-headed mutant of a tragicomic tour de force, "The Tragedy of Pudd'nhead Wilson" and "Those Extraordinary Twins," published under one cover in 1894, Mark Twain at times seems to be the entire Marx Brothers troupe all rolled into one, hell-bent on breaking every aesthetic rule in sight. He romps madly here and there around the drawing room of literary decorum, upsetting furniture, slapping a lampshade on the bust of Ralph Waldo Emerson, while throwing together a kind of anti-novel fashioned from spare genre parts, newsprint, circus handbills, and a large pot of glue.

Only when the dust has settled, the cat stops shrieking, and the resident men of letters dare peep out from behind their couches does anyone notice something exalted in the debris: there, on the trickster's pages, amid the cheap melodrama and the set-piece plot turns, shimmers one transcendent character, the third-greatest that Twain ever created, after Jim and Huckleberry Finn: the Shakespearean Roxana, the redeeming glory of Mark Twain's rambling tome.

Roxana: lionhearted maternal life force suffering her destiny as slavewoman in the pre–Civil War river town of Dawson's Landing, Missouri. Perpetrator of the baby-switching scheme that sets the "Pudd'nhead Wilson" narrative in motion. Trapped thereafter by her good-bad act of betrayal in an ever-tightening web of humiliations, abuse, and risky actions. A shattered avatar, finally, of all the violations upon motherhood inflicted over more than two centuries by the institution of American slavery.

Yet even more than all that: a lacerating symbol of the racial-identity issue that still disrupted the nation even in the year the book was published, 1893. For Roxana was "Negro," and thus a slave, chiefly via her society's arbitrary, damning definition: only one-sixteenth of her lineage contained African blood.

Typically of her creator's capacity to drive his legions of learned scholars and critics to head-smacking distraction, Roxana's stature as a literary figure was pretty much lost on Mark Twain. (Nothing new here: he also shrugged off "The Celebrated Jumping Frog of Calaveras County," his humorous tall tale that would change the course of American comic storytelling, as "a villainous backwoods sketch"; considered the cloying "Personal Recollections of Joan of Arc" to be the greatest thing he ever wrote; and remained essentially clueless about the enduring merits of his masterpiece, "Adventures of Huckleberry Finn.") From his own correspondence and early drafts, we know that he was far more absorbed—consciously, at least—in the two-headed minor characters and the detective-novel subplots that flew in and out of his various revisions.

He was even more absorbed in *the* classic impediment, and sometimes conduit, to High Art: the need to make a lot of money as fast as he could. More than absorbed; he was desperate. It was this desperation, as much as comic insouciance, that fueled the delirious assemblage, separation, and bizarre reconstruction of "The Tragedy of Pudd'nhead Wilson" and "Those Extraordinary Twins."

In the early 1890s, Mark Twain, the erratically brilliant man of letters, was deeply at war with his alter ego, Samuel L. Clemens, social climber and risk-addicted businessman. Twain's marriage into Eastern gentility and his early free-spirited travel books (*Innocents Abroad, Roughing It*) had made the onetime Sammy Clemens, kidhood shirttail Missouri dreamer, a wealthy public figure by age forty. But his compulsion for lavish household spending and his weakness for catastrophic investments (chiefly the Paige typesetting machine) soon launched him and his family on a two-decade spiral toward bankruptcy, which he would declare in the year *Pudd'nhead* was published.

In 1893, then, Twain was scribbling for survival. Writing obsessively from his penury-induced exile in a villa near Florence, his labors interrupted by eight Atlantic crossings in a series of futile fundraising schemes, the fifty-eight-year-old author foraged through topical themes that might yield up fungible story material. Even at his *Huckleberry Finn* best, Mark Twain was never much for elegant narrative structure or unity in, say, the Henry James tradition. ("I would rather be damned to John Bunyan's heaven than read that," was his take on *The Bostonians.*) At less than his best, he tended to shake out the whole of his mental musings onto the page and keep whatever tickled his fancy, whether it fit in with any other scraps of theme or not.

Only by understanding these pressures and tics of writing habit is it possible to see how Mark Twain could have produced "Pudd'nhead Wilson" and "Those Extraordinary Twins." Could have produced, that is, a novel—well, two novels, or a novel-and-a-half—that drew variously upon: (a) his longstanding fascination with twins, and in particular a pair of Siamese twins that had toured America during his boyhood; (b) a landmark segregation case then making its way toward the U.S. Supreme Court; (c) the nascent science of fingerprinting as a forensic tool and its usefulness as a device in detective fiction, which he loved; (d) dueling; (e) babies switched at birth; (f) the manners and speaking habits of people in antebellum river towns; and, finally, the theme least intentional yet most inevitable, enriched as it was by a lifetime of morally charged recollection and critical thought: (g) the American stain—the *twin* stains, let us stipulate—of slavery and racism as they pervert human identity and besmirch slave and master, black and white, alike.

———

Mark Twain began drafting his novel on a jaunty note in the early summer of 1892. He seems to have had in mind (cash aside) nothing more freighted than a farce, an accelerating romp of slapstick dysfunction. His device was the arrival in tiny Dawson's Landing of an Italian traveler with two heads and four arms. (Twain had been intrigued by the physically conjoined Chang and Eng Bunker, Chinese twins whom he had encountered during their stint with Phineas T. Barnum's circus in 1869.) Under the working title "Those Extraordinary Twins," he dashed off a series of over-the-top predicaments suffered by the uni-stemmed counts Luigi and Angelo as they collide with the characters, folkways, and politics of a remote Missouri river town. Propelled largely via pitch-perfect dialogue (a gift that Twain seems often to have undervalued; he replaced much of it with blocky exposition as the "Pudd'nhead" revision took form), the "Twins" story reads as affable nonsense, a sly but forgettable set-piece comedy of manners.

Evidently Mark Twain felt the same way. In a letter from Florence to the manager of his publishing firm, Fred J. Hall, dated December 12, 1892, he wrote:

"I finished 'Those Extraordinary Twins' night before last—makes 60 or 80,000 words—haven't counted.

"The last third of it suits me to a dot. I begin, today, to entirely recast and re-write the first two-thirds—new plan, with two minor characters, made very prominent, one major character cropped out, and the Twins subordinated to a minor but not insignificant place.

"*The* minor character will now become the chiefest, and I will name the story after him—'*Pudd'nhead Wilson*.'"

It is here that Twain's conscious sense of design seems to grow murky, while at the same time his powerful unconscious grows eversharper and more insistent. Granted, Pudd'nhead—a gaffe-prone but shrewd, if client-starved, lawyer in the village—figures decisively in the plot's convoluted courtroom climax. But to call him "chiefest" is peculiar. Far more prominent in the narrative is the saturnine Tom Driscoll. Tom, spoiled son of the prominent Judge Driscoll, is the blond, blue-eyed wastrel whose debauchery and scheming introduce a knife-edge of menace entirely lacking from the genial "Twins" draft.

At least everyone in Dawson's Landing *thinks* Tom is the judge's son, including Tom. In fact he is someone else entirely: he is Valet de Chambre, or "Chambers," the offspring of the slavewoman Roxana, who secretly switched him in his infancy with the judge's real son Thomas à Becket, a blond, blue-eyed Chambers lookalike.

In this rather melodramatic plot device, Mark Twain accidentally unleashed the "chiefest" character of his whole sprawling narrative, and one of the chiefest in nineteenth-century American literature. The suffering, the dangers, the filial heartbreak that Roxana endures as a consequence of her desperate treachery are matched, in the story, only by her towering willpower and the flow of impassioned, if coarsely phrased, language that pours from her. (Though white-skinned, she speaks the rough argot of the illiterate black slave society.) No other woman character in Twain's works can approach Roxana for psychological depth. None can match the anguished aria that, in Chapter XVIII, strains against her limiting patois. Few of his men can. Even Jim himself, in the early and the late chapters of *Huckleberry Finn,* can come off as something of a stock character in a minstrel routine or as a handy foil for Tom Sawyer's manic brain-storms. Not so Roxana. After her first bantering exchange with another slave in Chapter II, she ascends to serious purpose, and remains on that plane throughout.

It may be useful here to clarify her baby-switching motive, given the fast-receding nuances of the pre–Civil War slave universe she inhabited. Roxana shares a daily terror with her peers in the small-farm upper reaches of the slaveholding states: that she or her kin might at any time be "sold down the river," to one of the brutal, sweltering plantation gulags of the Deep South.

This terror propels Roxana to her fateful, morally compromised action and all its consequences. Entrusted by the newly widowed Judge Driscoll to supervise his infant son along with her own, she seizes a chance to place each baby in the other's cradle. She has now ensured a live of ease and privilege for her blood kin, at the price of sharing the daily joys of mother and child. And she has consigned an innocent baby to a lifetime in bondage.

The topical sources of Roxana and her plight are not hard to trace. In the ruins of Reconstruction, racial resegregation—"Jim Crow"—swept virulently through the defeated Confederacy. In 1892 Homer Plessy, a "Negro" by dint of being one-eighth African-American, was jailed for entering a whites-only railroad car in New Orleans. His case drew national attention as it made its way to the Supreme Court (which in 1896 ruled against him), not only for its test of black citizens' rights, but for raising the issue of how "race" is defined. A connoisseur of race-based travesties in America, Twain followed the case closely; Roxana was his literary response to it.

But having set this remarkable creature into action, Mark Twain appears to forget, for long stretches, that she exists. His attention keeps straying to those other scraps of plot recipe he has assembled; like a frugal cook, he seems incapable of throwing any of them out.

What are those weird Italian twins doing in this reconstituted stew? Well, adding a little side flavor, apparently, although their intrinsic function has by now nearly vanished. "I have pulled the twins apart and made two individuals of them," Twain advised Fred Hall on July 30, 1893; "I have sunk them out of sight, they are mere flitting shadows now, and of no importance." Well, then, why...? But wait! a new enthusiasm has overtaken the frantic storyteller: detective fiction! "Tom Driscoll," Roxana's secret demon-seed, swells in his depravity as the redrafted plot progresses until, in a fit of money-lust, he blackens his face, lays out a woman's dress for himself (don't ask; just read the story), and stabs to death the judge—who has recently survived a wild pistol duel with the twin Luigi, of whom he is actually rather fond, but never mind.

"The whole story is centered on the murder and the trial," Twain exulted a little misleadingly to the ever-patient Hall; "from the first chapter the movement is straight ahead without divergence or side-play to the murder and the trial."

The murder, for which Luigi is indicted, gives purpose to the long-idle Pudd'nhead, the title character, who at the story's outset got himself ostracized from polite Dawson's Landing society with an inane comment about killing half a dog, and spent the next two decades wondering, one might speculate, just how the hell he was going to get himself back into Mark Twain's extravaganza. No problem: it turns out that Pudd'nhead, an aspiring lawyer, is pretty adept at the forensic science of fingerprinting, even though that science would not emerge in America until about half a century after the novel's time-frame. (Twain to Hall: "[T]he finger-prints in this one is virgin ground— absolutely *fresh,* and mighty curious and interesting to everybody.")

It turns out also that Wilson has killed his twenty years of idle time by collecting the fingerprints of just about every man, woman, and child in the village. And since "Tom Driscoll" left his telltale fingerprints on the fatal knife, then obligingly leaves the knife at the scene, the stage is set for Pudd'nhead, in an eleventh-hour display of court-room sworl-matching, to—but you're way ahead of me. Suffice it to say that Luigi is vindicated, "Tom" is dispatched down the river, and justice reigns—except for poor Roxy, who, Twain confides rather briskly to us in the "Conclusion," finishes her years a heartbroken, life-less wreck.

Not until the book's publication in December 1894 did Twain re-veal the fullest extent of his feverish reconfiguring.

In an extraordinary preface to "Those Extraordinary Twins," Twain, describing himself as "a man who is not born with the novel-writing gift," opens his heart to the reader about how his original light-hearted draft had "changed itself from a farce to a tragedy while I was going along with it...not one story, but two stories tangled together; and they obstructed and interrupted each other at every turn."

What is a self-confessed "jackleg" novelist to do in a situation like that? Mark Twain tells us what: "I pulled one of the stories out by the roots, and left the other one—a kind of literary Caesarean operation."

"A kind of leftover omelet" might be closer to the point, but let us not quibble. What follows the introduction is the excised "Twins" farce, or most of it, complete with chatty little bracketed asides that compress certain plotlines or refer the reader back to the previous "Tragedy" for transplanted exposition. ("Then they went to Wilson's house, and Chapter XI of 'Pudd'nhead Wilson' follows, which tells of the girl seen in Tom Driscoll's room; and closes with the kicking of Tom by Luigi at the anti-temperance mass meeting of the Sons of Liberty.")

All in all, it is enough to make a proto-postmodernist out of the most hidebound Victorian. (A dirty little secret here: line by raffish line, "Twins" is more enjoyable as a sheer read than "Pudd'nhead," with its long blocks of dryly summarized development.) It is curious, and oddly touching, then, to read how several critics of the day strug-gled to take this self-conscious bundle of scattershot plotlines in stride. "The author gives us an interesting glimpse into his workshop," the *Springfield* (Massachusetts) *Republican* gamely murmured, "and lets us see that his ideas grow in precisely the erratic manner that we should expect." Many reviews took note of Roxana's singular power. "Her gusts of passion and despair," noted *The Athenaeum*, "her vanity, her motherly love, and the glimpses of nobler feelings...make her very human, and create a sympathy for her in spite of her unscrupulous actions."

It remained for the *Critic* of May 11, 1895, to play the role of pompous, out-of-it Margaret DuMont to Mark Twain's anarchic Groucho: "A work may be infinitely amusing," its reviewer trilled, "it may abound even with flashes and touches of genius, and yet the form in which it comes into the world may be so crude, so coarse, so erring from the ways of true classicism, so offensive to immemorial canons of taste, that the critic, in spite of his enjoyment and wonder, puts it reluctantly down in the category of unclassifiable literary things only to take it up and enjoy it again!"

After alluding loftily to such "exquisite" humorists as Aristophanes, Cervantes, Molière and Swift, *The Critic*'s critic gathered himself for his withering finale:

"The irksome question comes up: What *is* this? is it literature? is Mr. Clemens a 'writer' at all? must he not after all be described as an admirable after-dinner storyteller... who, in an evil moment, urged by admiring friends, has put pen to paper and written down his stories?"

To which Mark Twain, with Groucho rotating his cigar in rapt approval from the sidelines, might have shot back: "I *told* you my writing was water! I never said I wanted to belong to your club. And by the way—could you advance me a few thousand dollars till payday?"

———

RON POWERS, a Pulitzer Prize–winning author and native of Hannibal, Missouri, has written twelve books, including *Dangerous Water: A Biography of the Boy Who Became Mark Twain*. He lives in Middlebury, Vermont.

A Note on the Text

Pudd'nhead Wilson was first serialized in the *Century Magazine* from December 1893 through June 1894. The text for this Modern Library Paperback Classic, as well as the selected illustrations by F. M. Senior and C. H. Warren, was taken from the first American edition, published by the American Publishing Company in 1894. The original title of the 1894 American edition was *The Tragedy of Pudd'nhead Wilson And the Comedy Those Extraordinary Twins*. Minor obvious typographical errors have been corrected for this edition.

Mark Twain

The Tragedy of

PUDD'NHEAD WILSON

And the Comedy

THOSE EXTRAORDINARY TWINS

BY

MARK TWAIN
(SAMUEL L. CLEMENS)

With Marginal Illustrations.

1894
HARTFORD, CONN.
AMERICAN PUBLISHING COMPANY.

PUDD'NHEAD

WILSON

A Whisper to the Reader

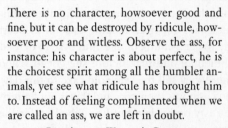

There is no character, howsoever good and fine, but it can be destroyed by ridicule, howsoever poor and witless. Observe the ass, for instance: his character is about perfect, he is the choicest spirit among all the humbler animals, yet see what ridicule has brought him to. Instead of feeling complimented when we are called an ass, we are left in doubt.

PUDD'NHEAD WILSON'S CALENDAR

A person who is ignorant of legal matters is always liable to make mistakes when he tries to photograph a court scene with his pen; and so I was not willing to let the law chapters in this book go to press without first subjecting them to rigid and exhausting revision and correction by a trained barrister—if that is what they are called. These chapters are right, now, in every detail, for they were rewritten under the immediate eye of William Hicks, who studied law part of a while in southwest Missouri thirty-five years ago and then came over here to Florence for his health and is still helping for exercise and board in Macaroni Vermicelli's horsefeed shed which is up the back alley as you turn around the corner out of the Piazza del Duomo just beyond the house where that stone that Dante used to sit on six hundred years ago is let into the wall when he let on to be watching them build Giotto's campanile and yet always got tired looking as soon as Beatrice passed along on her way to get a chunk of chestnut cake to defend herself with in case of a Ghibelline outbreak before she got to school, at the same old stand where they sell the same old cake to this day and it is just as light and good as it was then, too, and this is not flattery, far from it. He was a little rusty on his law, but he rubbed up for this book, and those two or three legal chapters are right and straight, now. He told me so himself.

Given under my hand this second day of January, 1893, at the Villa Viviani, village of Settignano, three miles back of Florence, on the hills—the same certainly affording the most charming view to be found on this planet, and with it the most dreamlike and enchanting sunsets to be found in any planet or even in any solar system—and given, too, in the swell room of the house, with the busts of Cerretani senators and other grandees of this line looking approvingly down upon me as they used to look down upon Dante, and mutely asking me to adopt them into my family, which I do with pleasure, for my remotest ancestors are but spring chickens compared with these robed and stately antiques, and it will be a great and satisfying lift for me, that six hundred years will.

Mark Twain

CHAPTER I

Tell the truth or trump—but get the trick.
PUDD'NHEAD WILSON'S CALENDAR

The scene of this chronicle is the town of Dawson's Landing, on the Missouri side of the Mississippi, half a day's journey, per steamboat, below St. Louis.

In 1830 it was a snug little collection of modest one- and two-story frame dwellings whose whitewashed exteriors were almost concealed from sight by climbing tangles of rose-vines, honeysuckles and morning-glories. Each of these pretty homes had a garden in front fenced with white palings and opulently stocked with hollyhocks, marigolds, touch-me-nots, prince's-feathers and other old-fashioned flowers; while on the window-sills of the houses stood wooden boxes containing moss-rose plants and terra-cotta pots in which grew a breed of geranium whose spread of intensely red blossoms accented the prevailing pink tint of the rose-clad house-front like an explosion of flame. When there was room on the ledge outside of the pots and boxes for a cat, the cat was there—in sunny weather—stretched at full length, asleep and blissful, with her furry belly to the sun and a paw curved over her nose. Then that house was complete, and its contentment and peace were made manifest to the world by this symbol, whose testimony is infallible. A home without a cat—and a well-fed, well-petted and properly revered cat—may be a perfect home, perhaps, but how can it prove title?

All along the streets, on both sides, at the outer edge of the brick sidewalks, stood locust-trees with trunks protected by wooden boxing, and these furnished shade for summer and a sweet fragrance in spring when the clusters of buds came forth. The main street, one block back from the river, and running parallel with it, was the sole business street. It was six blocks long, and in each block two or three brick stores three stories high towered above interjected bunches of little frame shops. Swinging signs creaked in the wind, the street's whole length.

The candy-striped pole which indicates nobility proud and ancient along the palace-bordered canals of Venice, indicated merely the humble barbershop along the main street of Dawson's Landing. On a chief corner stood a lofty unpainted pole wreathed from top to bottom with tin pots and pans and cups, the chief tinmonger's noisy notice to the world (when the wind blew) that his shop was on hand for business at that corner.

The hamlet's front was washed by the clear waters of the great river; its body stretched itself rearward up a gentle incline; its most rearward border fringed itself out and scattered its houses about the base-line of the hills; the hills rose high, inclosing the town in a half-moon curve, clothed with forests from foot to summit.

Steamboats passed up and down every hour or so. Those belonging to the little Cairo line and the little Memphis line always stopped; the big Orleans liners stopped for hails only, or to land passengers or freight; and this was the case also with the great flotilla of "transients." These latter came out of a dozen rivers—the Illinois, the Missouri, the Upper Mississippi, the Ohio, the Monongahela, the Tennessee, the Red River, the White River, and so on; and were bound every whither and stocked with every imaginable comfort or necessity which the Mississippi's communities could want, from the frosty Falls of St. Anthony down through nine climates to torrid New Orleans.

Dawson's Landing was a slaveholding town, with a rich slave-worked grain and pork country back of it. The town was sleepy and comfortable and contented. It was fifty years old, and was growing slowly—very slowly, in fact, but still it was growing.

The chief citizen was York Leicester Driscoll, about forty years old, judge of the county court. He was very proud of his old Virginian ancestry, and in his hospitalities and his rather formal and stately manners he kept up its traditions. He was fine and just and generous. To be a gentleman—a gentleman without stain or blemish—was his only religion, and to it he was always faithful. He was respected, esteemed and beloved by all the community. He was well off, and was gradually adding to his store. He and his wife were very nearly happy, but not quite, for they had no children. The longing for the treasure of a child had grown stronger and stronger as the years slipped away, but the blessing never came—and was never to come.

With this pair lived the Judge's widowed sister, Mrs. Rachel Pratt, and she also was childless—childless, and sorrowful for that reason, and not to be comforted. The women were good and commonplace people, and did their duty and had their reward in clear consciences and the community's approbation. They were Presbyterians, the Judge was a free-thinker.

Pembroke Howard, lawyer and bachelor, aged about forty, was another old Virginian grandee with proved descent from the First Families. He was a fine, brave, majestic creature, a gentleman according to the nicest requirements of the Virginia rule, a devoted Presbyterian, an authority on the "code," and a man always courteously ready to stand up before you in the field if any act or word of his had seemed doubtful or suspicious to you, and explain it with any weapon you might prefer from brad-awls to artillery. He was very popular with the people, and was the Judge's dearest friend.

Then there was Colonel Cecil Burleigh Essex, another F.F.V. of formidable caliber—however, with him we have no concern.

Percy Northumberland Driscoll, brother to the Judge, and younger than he by five years, was a married man, and had had children around his hearthstone; but they were attacked in detail by measles, croup and scarlet fever, and this had given the doctor a chance with his effective antediluvian methods; so the cradles were empty. He was a prosperous man, with a good head for speculations, and his fortune was growing. On the 1st of February, 1830, two boy babes were born in his house: one to him, the other to one of his slave girls, Roxana by name. Roxana was twenty years old. She was up and around the same day, with her hands full, for she was tending both babies.

Mrs. Percy Driscoll died within the week. Roxy remained in charge of the children. She had her own way, for Mr. Driscoll soon absorbed himself in his speculations and left her to her own devices.

In that same month of February, Dawson's Landing gained a new citizen. This was Mr. David Wilson, a young fellow of Scotch parentage. He had wandered to this remote region from his birthplace in the interior of the State of New York, to seek his fortune. He was twenty-five years old, college-bred, and had finished a post-college course in an Eastern law school a couple of years before.

He was a homely, freckled, sandy-haired young fellow, with an intelligent blue eye that had frankness and comradeship in it and a covert twinkle of a pleasant sort. But for an unfortunate remark of his, he would no doubt have entered at once upon a successful career at Dawson's Landing. But he made his fatal remark the first day he spent in the village, and it "gaged" him. He had just made the acquaintance of a group of citizens when an invisible dog began to yelp and snarl and howl and make himself very comprehensively disagreeable, whereupon young Wilson said, much as one who is thinking aloud—

"I wish I owned half of that dog."

"Why?" somebody asked.

"Because I would kill my half."

The group searched his face with curiosity, with anxiety even, but found no light there, no expression that they could read. They fell away from him as from something uncanny, and went into privacy to discuss him. One said:

"'Pears to be a fool."

"'Pears?" said another. "*Is*, I reckon you better say."

"Said he wished he owned *half* of the dog, the idiot," said a third. "What did he reckon would become of the other half if he killed his half? Do you reckon he thought it would live?"

"Why, he must have thought it, unless he *is* the downrightest fool in the world; because if he hadn't thought it, he would have wanted to own the whole dog, knowing that if he killed his half and the other half died, he would be responsible for that half just the same as if he had killed that half instead of his own. Don't it look that way to you, gents?"

"Yes, it does. If he owned one half of the general dog, it would be so; if he owned one end of the dog and another person owned the other end, it would be so, just the same; particularly in the first case, because if you kill one half of a general dog, there ain't any man that can tell whose half it was, but if he owned one end of the dog, maybe he could kill his end of it and——"

"No, he couldn't either; he couldn't and not be responsible if the other end died, which it would. In my opinion the man ain't in his right mind."

"In my opinion he hain't *got* any mind."

No. 3 said: "Well, he's a lummox, anyway."

"That's what he is," said No. 4, "he's a labrick—just a Simon-pure labrick, if ever there was one."

"Yes, sir, he's a dam fool, that's the way I put him up," said No. 5. "Anybody can think different that wants to, but those are my sentiments."

"I'm with you, gentlemen," said No. 6. "Perfect jackass—yes, and it ain't going too far to say he is a pudd'nhead. If he ain't a pudd'nhead, I ain't no judge, that's all."

Mr. Wilson stood elected. The incident was told all over the town, and gravely discussed by everybody. Within a week he had lost his first name; Pudd'nhead took its place. In time he came to be liked, and well liked too; but by that time the nickname had got well stuck on, and it stayed. That first day's verdict made him a fool, and he was not able to get it set aside, or even modified. The nickname soon ceased to carry any harsh or unfriendly feeling with it, but it held its place, and was to continue to hold its place for twenty long years.

Chapter II

Adam was but human—this explains it all. He did not want the apple for the apple's sake, he wanted it only because it was forbidden. The mistake was in not forbidding the serpent; then he would have eaten the serpent.

PUDD'NHEAD WILSON'S CALENDAR

Pudd'nhead Wilson had a trifle of money when he arrived, and he bought a small house on the extreme western verge of the town. Between it and Judge Driscoll's house there was only a grassy yard, with a paling fence dividing the properties in the middle. He hired a small office down in the town and hung out a tin sign with these words on it:

DAVID WILSON
ATTORNEY AND COUNSELOR-AT-LAW.
SURVEYING, CONVEYANCING, ETC.

But his deadly remark had ruined his chance—at least in the law. No clients came. He took down his sign, after a while, and put it up on his own house with the law features knocked out of it. It offered his services now in the humble capacities of land-surveyor and expert accountant. Now and then he got a job of survey-ing to do, and now and then a merchant got him to straighten out his books. With Scotch patience and pluck he resolved to live down his reputation and work his way into the legal field yet. Poor fellow, he could not foresee that it was going to take him such a weary long time to do it.

He had a rich abundance of idle time, but it never hung heavy on his hands, for he interested himself in every new thing that was born into the universe of ideas, and studied it and experimented upon it at his house. One of his pet fads was palmistry. To another one he gave no name, neither would he explain to anybody what its purpose was, but merely said it was an amusement. In fact he had found that his fads added to his reputation as a pudd'nhead; therefore he was growing chary of being too communicative about them. The fad without a name was one which dealt with people's finger-marks. He carried in his coat pocket a shallow box with grooves in it, and in the grooves strips of glass five inches long and three inches wide. Along the lower edge of each strip was pasted a slip of white paper. He asked people to pass their hands through their hair (thus collecting upon them a thin coating of the natural oil) and then make a thumb-mark on a glass strip, following it with the mark of the ball of each finger in succession. Under this row of faint grease-prints he would write a record on the strip of white paper—thus:

JOHN SMITH, *right hand*—

and add the day of the month and the year, then take Smith's left hand on another glass strip, and add name and date and the words "left hand." The strips were now returned to the grooved box, and took their place among what Wilson called his "records."

He often studied his records, examining and poring over them with absorbing interest until far into the night; but what he found there—if he found anything—he revealed to no one. Sometimes he copied on paper the involved and delicate pattern left by the ball of a finger, and then vastly enlarged it with a pantograph so that he could examine its web of curving lines with ease and convenience.

One sweltering afternoon—it was the first day of July, 1830—he was at work over a set of tangled account-books in his work-room, which looked westward over a stretch of vacant lots, when a conversation outside disturbed him. It was carried on in yells, which showed that the people engaged in it were not close together:

"Say, Roxy, how does yo' baby come on?" This from the distant voice.

"Fust-rate; how does *you* come on, Jasper?" This yell was from close by.

"Oh, I's middlin'; hain't got noth'n' to complain of. I's gwine to come a-court'n' you bimeby, Roxy."

"*You* is, you black mud-cat! Yah—yah—yah! I got somep'n' better to do den 'sociat'n' wid niggers as black as you is. Is ole Miss Cooper's Nancy done give you de mitten?" Roxy followed this sally with another discharge of care-free laughter.

"You's jealous, Roxy, dat's what's de matter wid *you*, you hussy— yah—yah—yah! Dat's de time I got you!"

"Oh, yes, *you* got me, hain't you. 'Clah to goodness if dat conceit o' yo'n strikes in, Jasper, it gwine to kill you sho'. If you b'longed to me I'd sell you down de river 'fo' you git too fur gone. Fust time I runs acrost yo' marster, I's gwine to tell him so."

This idle and aimless jabber went on and on, both parties enjoying the friendly duel and each well satisfied with his own share of the wit exchanged—for wit they considered it.

Wilson stepped to the window to observe the combatants; he could not work while their chatter continued. Over in the vacant lots was Jasper, young, coal-black and of magnificent build, sitting on a wheel-barrow in the pelting sun—at work, supposably, whereas he was in fact only preparing for it by taking an hour's rest before beginning. In front of Wilson's porch stood Roxy, with a local hand-made baby-wagon, in which sat her two charges—one at each end and facing each other. From Roxy's manner of speech, a stranger would have expected her to be black, but she was not. Only one sixteenth of her was black, and that sixteenth did not show. She was of majestic form and stature, her attitudes were imposing and statuesque, and her gestures and movements distinguished by a noble and stately grace. Her complexion was very fair, with the rosy glow of vigorous health in the cheeks, her face was full of character and expression, her eyes were brown and liquid, and she had a heavy suit of fine soft hair which was also brown, but the fact was not apparent because her head was bound about with a checkered handkerchief and the hair was concealed under it. Her face was shapely, intelligent and comely—even beautiful. She had an easy, independent carriage—when she was among her own caste—and a high and "sassy" way, withal; but of course she was meek and humble enough where white people were.

To all intents and purposes Roxy was as white as anybody, but the one sixteenth of her which was black outvoted the other fifteen parts and made her a negro. She was a slave, and salable as such. Her child was thirty-one parts white, and he, too, was a slave, and by a fiction of law and custom a negro. He had blue eyes and flaxen curls like his white comrade, but even the father of the white child was able to tell the children apart—little as he had commerce with them—by their clothes: for the white babe wore ruffled soft muslin and a coral necklace, while the other wore merely a coarse tow-linen shirt which barely reached to its knees, and no jewelry.

The white child's name was Thomas à Becket Driscoll, the other's name was Valet de Chambre: no surname—slaves hadn't the privilege. Roxana had heard that phrase somewhere, the fine sound of it had pleased her ear, and as she had supposed it was a name, she loaded it on to her darling. It soon got shortened to "Chambers," of course.

Wilson knew Roxy by sight, and when the duel of wit began to play out, he stepped outside to gather in a record or two. Jasper went to work energetically, at once, perceiving that his leisure was observed. Wilson inspected the children and asked—

"How old are they, Roxy?"

"Bofe de same age, sir—five months. Bawn de fust o' Feb'uary."

"They're handsome little chaps. One's just as handsome as the other, too."

A delighted smile exposed the girl's white teeth, and she said:

"Bless yo' soul, Misto Wilson, it's pow'ful nice o' you to say dat, 'ca'se one of 'em ain't on'y a nigger. Mighty prime little nigger, *I* al'ays says, but dat's ca'se it's mine, o' course."

"How do you tell them apart, Roxy, when they haven't any clothes on?"

Roxy laughed a laugh proportioned to her size, and said:

"Oh, *I* kin tell 'em 'part, Misto Wilson, but I bet Marse Percy couldn't, not to save his life."

Wilson chatted along for awhile, and presently got Roxy's finger-

prints for his collection—right hand and left—
on a couple of his glass strips; then labeled and
dated them, and took the "records" of both
children, and labeled and dated them also.

Two months later, on the 3d of September,
he took this trio of finger-marks again. He
liked to have a "series," two or three "takings"
at intervals during the period of childhood,
these to be followed by others at intervals of
several years.

The next day—that is to say, on the 4th of
September—something occurred which profoundly impressed Roxana. Mr. Driscoll
missed another small sum of money—which
is a way of saying that this was not a new
thing, but had happened before. In truth it
had happened three times before. Driscoll's
patience was exhausted. He was a fairly humane man toward slaves and other animals;
he was an exceedingly humane man toward
the erring of his own race. Theft he could
not abide, and plainly there was a thief in his
house. Necessarily the thief must be one of
his negroes. Sharp measures must be taken.
He called his servants before him. There
were three of these, besides Roxy: a man, a

woman, and a boy twelve years old. They were not related. Mr. Driscoll said:

"You have all been warned before. It has done no good. This time I will teach you a lesson. I will sell the thief. Which of you is the guilty one?"

They all shuddered at the threat, for here they had a good home, and a new one was likely to be a change for the worse. The denial was general. None had stolen anything—not money, anyway—a little sugar, or cake, or honey, or something like that, that "Marse Percy wouldn't mind or miss," but not money—never a cent of money. They were eloquent in their protestations, but Mr. Driscoll was not moved by them. He answered each in turn with a stern "Name the thief!"

The truth was, all were guilty but Roxana; she suspected that the others were guilty, but she did not know them to be so. She was horrified to think how near she had come to being guilty herself; she had been saved in the nick of time by a revival in the colored Methodist Church, a fortnight before, at which time and place she "got religion." The very next day after that gracious experience, while her change of style was fresh upon her and she was vain of her purified condition, her master left a couple of dollars lying unprotected on his desk, and she happened upon that temptation when she was polishing around with a dust-rag. She looked at the money awhile with a steadily rising resentment, then she burst out with—

"Dad blame dat revival, I wisht it had 'a' be'n put off till to-morrow!"

Then she covered the tempter with a book, and another member of the kitchen cabinet got it. She made this sacrifice as a matter of religious etiquette; as a thing necessary just now, but by no means to be wrested into a precedent; no, a week or two would limber up her piety, then she would be rational again, and the next two dollars that got left out in the cold would find a comforter—and she could name the comforter.

Was she bad? Was she worse than the general run of her race? No. They had an unfair show in the battle of life, and they held it no sin to take military advantage of the enemy—in a small way; in a small way, but not in a large one. They would smouch provisions from the pantry whenever they got a chance; or a brass thimble, or a cake of wax, or an emery-bag, or a paper of needles, or a silver spoon, or a dollar bill, or small articles of clothing, or any other property of light value; and so far were they from considering such reprisals sinful, that they would go to church and shout and pray the loudest and sincerest with their plunder in their pockets. A farm smoke-house had to be kept heavily padlocked, for even the colored deacon himself could not resist a ham when Providence showed him in a dream, or otherwise, where such a thing hung lonesome and longed for some one to love. But with a hundred hanging before him the deacon would not take two—that is, on the same night. On frosty nights the humane negro prowler would warm the end of a plank and put it up under the cold claws of chickens roosting in a tree; a drowsy hen would step on to the comfortable board, softly clucking her gratitude, and the prowler would dump her into his bag, and later into his stomach, perfectly sure that in taking this trifle from the man who daily robbed him of an inestimable treasure—his liberty—he was not committing any sin that God would remember against him in the Last Great Day.

"Name the thief!"

For the fourth time Mr. Driscoll had said it, and always in the same hard tone. And now he added these words of awful import:

"I give you one minute"—he took out his watch. "If at the end of that time you have not confessed, I will not only sell all four of you, *but*—I will sell you DOWN THE RIVER!"

It was equivalent to condemning them to hell! No Missouri negro doubted this. Roxy reeled in her tracks and the color vanished out of her face; the others dropped to their knees as if they had been shot;

tears gushed from their eyes, their supplicating hands went up, and three answers came in the one instant:

"I done it!"

"I done it!"

"I done it!—have mercy, marster—Lord have mercy on us po' niggers!"

"Very good," said the master, putting up his watch, "I will sell you *here* though you don't deserve it. You ought to be sold down the river."

The culprits flung themselves prone, in an ecstasy of gratitude, and kissed his feet, declaring that they would never forget his goodness and never cease to pray for him as long as they lived. They were sincere, for like a god he had stretched forth his mighty hand and closed the gates of hell against them. He knew, himself, that he had done a noble and gracious thing, and was privately well pleased with his magnanimity; and that night he set the incident down in his diary, so that his son might read it in after years, and be thereby moved to deeds of gentleness and humanity himself.

Chapter III

Whoever has lived long enough to find out what life is, knows how deep a debt of gratitude we owe to Adam, the first great benefactor of our race. He brought death into the world.

PUDD'NHEAD WILSON'S CALENDAR

Percy Driscoll slept well the night he saved his house-minions from going down the river, but no wink of sleep visited Roxy's eyes. A profound terror had taken possession of her. Her child could grow up and be sold down the river! The thought crazed her with horror. If she dozed and lost herself for a moment, the next moment she was on her feet flying to her child's cradle to see if it was still there. Then she would gather it to her heart and pour out her love upon it in a frenzy

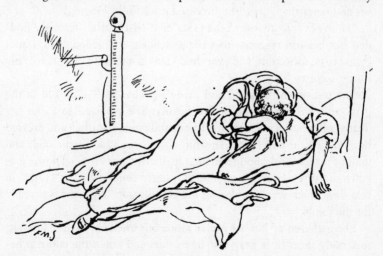

of kisses, moaning, crying, and saying "Dey sha'n't, oh, dey *sha'n't!*—yo' po' mammy will kill you fust!"

Once, when she was tucking it back in its cradle again, the other child nestled in its sleep and attracted her attention. She went and stood over it a long time communing with herself:

"What has my po' baby done, dat he couldn't have yo' luck? He hain't done noth'n'. God was good to you; why warn't he good to him? Dey can't sell *you* down de river. I hates yo' pappy; he hain't got no heart—for niggers he hain't, anyways. I hates him, en I could kill him!" She paused awhile, thinking; then she burst into wild sobbings again, and turned away, saying, "Oh, I got to kill my chile, dey ain't no yuther way,—killin' *him* wouldn't save de chile fum goin' down de river. Oh, I got to do it, yo' po' mammy's got to kill you to save you, honey"—she gathered her baby to her bosom, now, and began to smother it with caresses—"Mammy's got to kill you—how *kin* I do it! But yo' mammy ain't gwine to desert you—no, no; *dah,* don't cry—she gwine *wid* you, she gwine to kill herself too. Come along, honey, come along wid mammy; we gwine to jump in de river, den de troubles o' dis worl' is all over—dey don't sell po' niggers down the river over *yonder.*"

She started toward the door, crooning to the child and hushing it; midway she stopped, suddenly. She had caught sight of her new Sunday gown—a cheap curtain-calico thing, a conflagration of gaudy colors and fantastic figures. She surveyed it wistfully, longingly.

"Hain't ever wore it yet," she said, "en it's jist lovely." Then she nodded her head in response to a pleasant idea, and added, "No, I ain't gwine to be fished out, wid everybody lookin' at me, in dis mis'able ole linsey-woolsey."

She put down the child and made the change. She looked in the glass and was astonished at her beauty. She resolved to make her death-toilet perfect. She took off her handkerchief-turban and dressed her glossy wealth of hair "like white folks"; she added some odds and ends of rather lurid ribbon and a spray of atrocious artificial flowers; finally she threw over her shoulders a fluffy thing called a "cloud" in that day, which was of a blazing red complexion. Then she was ready for the tomb.

She gathered up her baby once more; but when her eye fell upon its miserably short little gray tow-linen shirt and noted the contrast between its pauper shabbiness and her own volcanic irruption of infernal splendors, her mother-heart was touched, and she was ashamed.

"No, dolling, mammy ain't gwine to treat you so. De angels is gwine to 'mire you jist as much as dey does yo' mammy. Ain't gwine to have 'em putt'n' dey han's up 'fo' dey eyes en sayin' to David en Goliah en dem yuther prophets, 'Dat chile is dress' too indelicate fo' dis place.' "

By this time she had stripped off the shirt. Now she clothed the naked little creature in one of Thomas à Becket's snowy long baby-gowns, with its bright blue bows and dainty flummery of ruffles.

"Dah—now you's fixed." She propped the child in a chair and stood off to inspect it. Straightway her eyes began to widen with astonishment and admiration, and she clapped her hands and cried out, "Why, it do beat all!—I *never* knowed you was so lovely. Marse Tommy ain't a bit puttier—not a single bit."

She stepped over and glanced at the other infant; she flung a glance back at her own; then one more at the heir of the house. Now a strange light dawned in her eyes, and in a moment she was lost in thought. She seemed in a trance; when she came out of it she muttered, "When I 'uz a-washin' 'em in de tub, yistiddy, his own pappy asked me which of 'em was his'n."

She began to move about like one in a dream. She undressed Thomas à Becket, stripping him of everything, and put the tow-linen shirt on him. She put his coral necklace on her own child's neck. Then she placed the children side by side, and after earnest inspection she muttered—

"Now who would b'lieve clo'es could do de like o' dat? Dog my cats if it ain't all *I* kin do to tell t' other fum which, let alone his pappy."

She put her cub in Tommy's elegant cradle and said—

"You's young Marse *Tom* fum dis out, en I got to practise and git used to 'memberin' to call you dat, honey, or I's gwine to make a mistake some time en git us bofe into trouble. Dah—now you lay still en don't fret no mo', Marse Tom—oh, thank de good Lord in heaven, you's saved, you's saved!—dey ain't no man kin ever sell mammy's po' little honey down de river now!"

She put the heir of the house in her own child's unpainted pine cradle, and said, contemplating its slumbering form uneasily—

"I's sorry for you, honey; I's sorry, God knows I is,—but what *kin* I do, what *could* I do? Yo' pappy would sell him to somebody, some time, en den he'd go down de river, sho', en I couldn't, couldn't, *couldn't* stan' it."

She flung herself on her bed and began to think and toss, toss and think. By and by she sat suddenly upright, for a comforting thought had flown through her worried mind—

"'Tain't no sin—*white* folks has done it! It ain't no sin, glory to goodness it ain't no sin! *Dey's* done it—yes, en dey was de biggest quality in de whole bilin', too—*kings!*"

She began to muse; she was trying to gather out of her memory the dim particulars of some tale she had heard some time or other. At last she said—

"Now I's got it; now I 'member. It was dat ole nigger preacher dat tole it, de time he come over here fum Illinois en preached in de nigger church. He said dey ain't nobody kin save his own self—can't do it by faith, can't do it by works, can't do it no way at all. Free grace is de *on'y* way, en dat don't come fum nobody but jis' de Lord; en *he* kin give it to anybody he please, saint or sinner—*he* don't kyer. He do jis' as he's a mineter. He s'lect out anybody dat suit him, en put another one in his place, en make de fust one happy forever en leave t'other one to burn wid Satan. De preacher said it was jist like dey done in Englan' one time, long time ago. De queen she lef' her baby layin' aroun' one day, en went out callin'; en one o' de niggers roun'-'bout de place dat was 'mos' white, she come in en see de chile layin' aroun', en tuck en put her own chile's clo'es on de queen's chile, en put de queen's chile's clo'es on her own chile, en den lef' her own chile layin' aroun' en tuck en toted de queen's chile home to de nigger-quarter, en nobody ever foun' it out, en her chile was de king bimeby, en sole de queen's chile down de river one time when dey had to settle up de estate. Dah, now—de preacher said it his own self, en it ain't no sin, 'ca'se white folks done it. *Dey* done it—yes, *dey* done it; en not on'y jis' common white folks nuther, but de biggest quality dey is in de whole bilin'. Oh, I's *so* glad I 'member 'bout dat!"

She got up light-hearted and happy, and went to the cradles and spent what was left of the night "practising." She would give her own child a light pat and say humbly, "Lay still, Marse Tom," then give the real Tom a pat and say with severity, "Lay *still*, Chambers!—does you want me to take somep'n' *to* you?"

As she progressed with her practice, she was surprised to see how steadily and surely the awe which had kept her tongue reverent and her manner humble toward her young master was transferring itself to her speech and manner toward the usurper, and how similarly handy she was becoming in transferring her motherly curtness of speech and peremptoriness of manner to the unlucky heir of the ancient house of Driscoll.

She took occasional rests from practising, and absorbed herself in calculating her chances.

"Dey'll sell dese niggers to-day fo' stealin' de money, den dey'll buy some mo' dat don't know de chillen—so *dat's* all right. When I takes de chillen out to git de air, de minute I's roun' de corner I's gwine to gaum dey mouths all roun' wid jam, den dey can't *nobody* notice dey's changed. Yes, I gwineter do dat till I's safe, if it's a year.

"Dey ain't but one man dat I's afeard of, en dat's dat Pudd'nhead Wilson. Dey calls him a pudd'nhead, en says he's a fool. My lan', dat man ain't no mo' fool den I is! He's de smartes' man in dis town, less'n it's Jedge Driscoll or maybe Pem Howard. Blame dat man, he worries me wid dem ornery glasses o' hisn; *I* b'lieve he's a witch. But nemmine, I's gwine to happen aroun' dah one o' dese days en let on dat I reckon he wants to print de chillen's fingers ag'in; en if *he* don't notice dey's changed, I bound dey ain't nobody gwine to notice it, en den I's safe, sho'. But I reckon I'll tote along a hoss-shoe to keep off de witch-work."

The new negroes gave Roxy no trouble, of course. The master gave her none, for one of his speculations was in jeopardy, and his mind was so occupied that he hardly saw the children when he looked at them, and all Roxy had to do was to get them both into a gale of laughter when he came about; then their faces were mainly cavities exposing gums, and he was gone again before the spasm passed and the little creatures resumed a human aspect.

Within a few days the fate of the speculation became so dubious that Mr. Percy went away with his brother the Judge, to see what could be done with it. It was a land speculation as usual, and it had gotten complicated with a lawsuit. The men were gone seven weeks. Before they got back Roxy had paid her visit to Wilson, and was satisfied. Wilson took the finger-prints, labeled them with the names and with the date—October the first—put them carefully away and continued his chat with Roxy, who seemed very anxious that he should admire the great advance in flesh and beauty which the babies had made since he

took their finger-prints a month before. He complimented their improvement to her contentment; and as they were without any disguise of jam or other stain, she trembled all the while and was miserably frightened lest at any moment he—

But he didn't. He discovered nothing; and she went home jubilant, and dropped all concern about the matter permanently out of her mind.

Chapter IV

Adam and Eve had many advantages, but the principal one was, that they escaped teething.

PUDD'NHEAD WILSON'S CALENDAR

There is this trouble about special providences—namely, there is so often a doubt as to which party was intended to be the beneficiary. In the case of the children, the bears and the prophet, the bears got more real satisfaction out of the episode than the prophet did, because they got the children.

PUDD'NHEAD WILSON'S CALENDAR

This history must henceforth accommodate itself to the change which Roxana has consummated, and call the real heir "Chambers" and the usurping little slave "Thomas à Becket"—shortening this latter name to "Tom," for daily use, as the people about him did.

"Tom" was a bad baby, from the very beginning of his usurpation. He would cry for nothing; he would burst into storms of devilish temper without notice, and let go scream after scream and squall after squall, then climax the thing with "holding his breath"—

that frightful specialty of the teething nursling, in the throes of which the creature exhausts its lungs, then is convulsed with noiseless squirmings and twistings and kickings in the effort to get its breath, while the lips turn blue and the mouth stands wide and rigid, offering for inspection one wee tooth set in the lower rim of a hoop of red gums; and when the appalling stillness has endured until one is sure the lost breath will never return, a nurse comes flying, and dashes water in the child's face, and—presto! the lungs fill, and instantly discharge a shriek, or a yell, or a howl which bursts the listening ear and surprises the owner of it into saying words which would not go well with a halo if he had one. The baby Tom would claw anybody who came within reach of his nails, and pound anybody he could reach with his rattle. He would scream for water until he got it, and then throw cup and all on the floor and scream for more. He was indulged in all his caprices, howsoever troublesome and exasperating they might be; he was allowed to eat anything he wanted, particularly things that would give him the stomach-ache.

When he got to be old enough to begin to toddle about and say broken words and get an idea of what his hands were for, he was a more consummate pest than ever. Roxy got no rest while he was awake. He would call for anything and everything he saw, simply saying "Awnt it!" (want it), which was a command. When it was brought, he said in a frenzy, and motioning it away with his hands, "Don't awnt it! don't awnt it!" and the moment it was gone he set up frantic yells of "Awnt it! awnt it! awnt it!" and Roxy had to give wings to her heels to get that thing back to him again before he could get time to carry out his intention of going into convulsions about it.

What he preferred above all other things was the tongs. This was because his "father" had forbidden him to have them lest he break windows and furniture with them. The moment Roxy's back was turned he would toddle to the presence of the tongs and say "Like it!" and cock his eye to one side to see if Roxy was observing; then, "Awnt it!" and cock his eye again; then, "Hab it!" with another furtive glance; and finally, "Take it!"—and the prize was his. The next moment the heavy implement was raised aloft; the next, there was a crash and a squall, and the cat was off on three legs to meet an engagement; Roxy would arrive just as the lamp or a window went to irremediable smash.

Tom got all the petting, Chambers got none. Tom got all the delicacies, Chambers got mush and milk, and clabber without sugar. In consequence Tom was a sickly child and Chambers wasn't. Tom was "fractious," as Roxy called it, and overbearing; Chambers was meek and docile.

With all her splendid common sense and practical every-day ability, Roxy was a doting fool of a mother. She was this toward her child—and she was also more than this: by the fiction created by herself, he was become her master; the necessity of recognizing this relation outwardly and of perfecting herself in the forms required to express the recognition, had moved her to such diligence and faithfulness in practicing these forms that this exercise soon concreted itself into habit; it became automatic and unconscious; then a natural result followed: deceptions intended solely for others gradually grew practically into self-deceptions as well; the mock reverence became real reverence, the mock obsequiousness real obsequiousness, the mock homage real homage; the little counterfeit rift of separation between imitation-slave and imitation-master widened and widened, and became an abyss, and a very real one—and on one side of it stood Roxy, the dupe of her own deceptions, and on the other stood her child, no longer a usurper to her, but her accepted and recognized master. He was her darling, her master, and her deity all in one, and in her worship of him she forgot who she was and what he had been.

In babyhood Tom cuffed and banged and scratched

Chambers unrebuked, and Chambers early learned that between meekly bearing it and resenting it, the advantage all lay with the former policy. The few times that his persecutions had moved him beyond control and made him fight back had cost him very dear at headquarters; not at the hands of Roxy, for if she ever went beyond scolding him sharply for "forgitt'n' who his young marster was," she at least never extended her punishment beyond a box on the ear. No, Percy Driscoll was the person. He told Chambers that under no provocation whatever was he privileged to lift his hand against his little master. Chambers overstepped the line three times, and got three such convincing canings from the man who was his father and didn't know it, that he took Tom's cruelties in all humility after that, and made no more experiments.

Outside of the house the two boys were together all through their boyhood. Chambers was strong beyond his years, and a good fighter; strong because he was coarsely fed and hard worked about the house, and a good fighter because Tom furnished him plenty of practice—on white boys whom he hated and was afraid of. Chambers was his constant body-guard, to and from school; he was present on the playground at recess to protect his charge. He fought himself into such a formidable reputation, by and by, that Tom could have changed clothes with him, and "ridden in peace," like Sir Kay in Launcelot's armor.

He was good at games of skill, too. Tom staked him with marbles to play "keeps" with, and then took all the winnings away from him. In the winter season Chambers was on hand, in Tom's worn-out clothes, with "holy" red mittens, and "holy" shoes, and pants "holy" at the knees and seat, to drag a sled up the hill for Tom, warmly clad, to ride down on; but he never got a ride himself. He built snow men and snow fortifications under Tom's directions. He was Tom's patient target when Tom wanted to do some snowballing, but the target couldn't fire back. Chambers carried Tom's skates to the river and strapped them on him, then trotted around after him on the ice, so as to be on hand when wanted; but he wasn't ever asked to try the skates himself.

In summer the pet pastime of the boys of Dawson's Landing was to steal apples, peaches, and melons from the farmers' fruitwagons,— mainly on account of the risk they ran of getting their heads laid open with the butt of the farmer's whip. Tom was a distinguished adept at these thefts—by proxy. Chambers did his stealing, and got the peach-stones, apple-cores, and melon-rinds for his share.

Tom always made Chambers go in swimming with him, and stay by him as a protection. When Tom had had enough, he would slip out and tie knots in Chambers's shirt, dip the knots in the water to make them hard to undo, then dress himself and sit by and laugh while the naked shiverer tugged at the stubborn knots with his teeth.

Tom did his humble comrade these various ill turns partly out of native viciousness, and partly because he hated him for his superiorities of physique and pluck, and for his manifold clevernesses. Tom couldn't dive, for it gave him splitting headaches. Chambers could dive without inconvenience, and was fond of doing it. He excited so much admiration, one day, among a crowd of white boys, by throwing back somersaults from the stern of a canoe, that it wearied Tom's spirit, and at last he shoved the canoe underneath Chambers while he was in the air—so he came down on his head in the canoe-bottom; and while he lay unconscious, several of Tom's ancient adversaries saw that their long-desired opportunity was come, and they gave the false heir such a drubbing that with Chambers's best help he was hardly able to drag himself home afterward.

When the boys were fifteen and upward, Tom was "showing off" in the river one day, when he was taken with a cramp, and shouted for help. It was a common trick with the boys—particularly if a stranger was present—to pretend a cramp and howl for help; then when the stranger came tearing hand over hand to the rescue, the howler would go on struggling and howling till he was close at hand, then replace the howl with a sarcastic smile and swim blandly away, while the town boys assailed the dupe with a volley of jeers and laughter. Tom had never tried this joke as yet, but was supposed to be trying it now, so the boys held warily back; but Chambers believed his master was in earnest, therefore he swam out, and arrived in time, unfortunately, and saved his life.

This was the last feather. Tom had managed to endure everything else, but to have to remain publicly and permanently under such an obligation as this to a nigger, and to this nigger of all niggers—this was too much. He heaped insults upon Chambers for "pretending to think he was in earnest in calling for help," and said that anybody but a block-headed nigger would have known he was funning and left him alone.

Tom's enemies were in strong force here, so they came out with their opinions quite freely. They laughed at him, and called him coward, liar, sneak, and other sorts of pet names, and told him they meant to call Chambers by a new name after this, and make it common in the town—"Tom Driscoll's niggerpappy,"—to signify that he had had a second birth into this life, and that Chambers was the author of his new being. Tom grew frantic under these taunts, and shouted—

"Knock their heads off, Chambers! knock their heads off! What do you stand there with your hands in your pockets for?"

Chambers expostulated, and said, "But, Marse Tom, dey's too many of 'em—dey's—"

"Do you hear me?"

"Please, Marse Tom, don't make me! Dey's so many of 'em dat———"

Tom sprang at him and drove his pocketknife into him two or three times before the boys could snatch him away and give the wounded lad a chance to escape. He was considerably hurt, but not seriously. If the blade had been a little longer his career would have ended there.

Tom had long ago taught Roxy "her place." It had been many a day now since she had ventured a caress or a fondling epithet in his quarter. Such things, from a "nigger," were repulsive to him, and she had been warned to keep her distance and remember who she was. She saw her darling gradually cease from being her son, she saw *that* detail perish utterly; all that was left was master—master, pure and simple, and it was not a gentle mastership, either. She saw herself sink from the sublime height of motherhood to the somber depths of unmodified slavery. The abyss of separation between her and her boy was complete. She was merely his chattel, now, his convenience, his dog, his

cringing and helpless slave, the humble and unresisting victim of his capricious temper and vicious nature.

Sometimes she could not go to sleep, even when worn out with fatigue, because her rage boiled so high over the day's experiences with her boy. She would mumble and mutter to herself—

"He struck me, en I warn't no way to blame—struck me in de face, right before folks. En he's al'ays callin' me nigger-wench, en hussy, en all dem mean names, when I's doin' de very bes' I kin. Oh, Lord, I done so much for him—I lif' him away up to what he is—en dis is what I git for it."

Sometimes when some outrage of peculiar offensiveness stung her to the heart, she would plan schemes of vengeance and revel in the fancied spectacle of his exposure to the world as an impostor and a slave; but in the midst of these joys fear would strike her: she had made him too strong; she could prove nothing, and—heavens, she might get sold down the river for her pains! So her schemes always went for nothing, and she laid them aside in impotent rage against the fates, and against herself for playing the fool on that fatal September day in not providing herself with a witness for use in the day when such a thing might be needed for the appeasing of her vengeance-hungry heart.

And yet the moment Tom happened to be good to her, and kind,—and this occurred every now and then,—all her sore places were healed, and she was happy; happy and proud, for this was her son, her nigger son, lording it among the whites and securely avenging their crimes against her race.

There were two grand funerals in Dawson's Landing that fall—the fall of 1845. One was that of Colonel Cecil Burleigh Essex, the other that of Percy Driscoll.

On his death-bed Driscoll set Roxy free and delivered his idolized ostensible son solemnly into the keeping of his brother, the Judge and his wife. Those childless people were glad to get him. Childless people are not difficult to please.

Judge Driscoll had gone privately to his brother, a month before, and bought Chambers. He had heard that Tom had been trying to get his father to sell the boy down the river, and he wanted to prevent the scandal—for public sentiment did not approve of that way of treating family servants for light cause or for no cause.

Percy Driscoll had worn himself out in trying to save his great speculative landed estate, and had died without succeeding. He was hardly in his grave before the boom collapsed and left his hitherto envied young devil of an heir a pauper. But that was nothing; his uncle told him he should be his heir and have all his fortune when he died; so Tom was comforted.

Roxy had no home, now; so she resolved to go around and say goodby to her friends and then clear out and see the world—that is to say, she would go chambermaiding on a steamboat, the darling ambition of her race and sex.

Her last call was on the black giant, Jasper. She found him chopping Pudd'nhead Wilson's winter provision of wood.

Wilson was chatting with him when Roxy arrived. He asked her how she could bear to go off chambermaiding and leave her boys; and chaffingly offered to copy off a series of their finger-prints, reaching up to their twelfth year, for her to remember them by; but she sobered in a moment, wondering if he suspected anything; then she said she believed she didn't want them. Wilson said to himself, "The drop of black blood in her is superstitious; she thinks there's some devilry, some witch-business about my glass mystery somewhere; she used to come here with an old horseshoe in her hand; it could have been an accident, but I doubt it."

CHAPTER V

Training is everything. The peach was once a bitter almond; cauliflower is nothing but cabbage with a college education.

PUDD'NHEAD WILSON'S CALENDAR

Remark of Dr. Baldwin's, concerning upstarts: We don't care to eat toadstools that think they are truffles.

PUDD'NHEAD WILSON'S CALENDAR

Mrs. York Driscoll enjoyed two years of bliss with that prize, Tom—bliss that was troubled a little at times, it is true, but bliss nevertheless; then she died, and her husband and his childless sister, Mrs. Pratt, continued the bliss-business at the old stand. Tom was petted and indulged and spoiled to his entire content—or nearly that. This went on till he was nineteen, then he was sent to Yale. He went handsomely equipped with "conditions," but otherwise he was not an object of distinction there. He remained at Yale two years, and then threw up the struggle. He came home with his manners a good deal improved; he had lost his surliness and brusqueness, and was rather pleasantly soft and smooth, now; he was furtively, and sometimes openly, ironical of speech, and given to gently touching people on the raw, but he did it with a good-natured semiconscious air that carried it off safely, and kept him from getting into trouble. He was as indolent as ever and showed no very strenuous desire to hunt up an occupation. People argued from this that he preferred to be supported by his uncle until his uncle's shoes should become vacant. He brought back one or two new habits with him, one of which he rather openly practised—tippling—but concealed another which was gambling. It would not do to gamble where his uncle could hear of it; he knew that quite well.

Tom's Eastern polish was not popular among the young people. They could have endured it, perhaps, if Tom had stopped there; but he wore gloves, and that they couldn't stand, and wouldn't; so he was mainly without society. He brought home with him a suit of clothes of such exquisite style and cut and fashion,—Eastern fashion, city fashion,—that it filled everybody with anguish and was regarded as a peculiarly wanton affront. He enjoyed the feeling which he was exciting, and paraded the town serene and happy all day; but the young fellows set a tailor to work that night, and when Tom started out on his parade next morning he found the old deformed negro bell-ringer straddling along in his wake tricked out in a flamboyant curtain-calico exaggeration of his finery, and imitating his fancy Eastern graces as well as he could.

Tom surrendered, and after that clothed himself in the local fashion. But the dull country town was tiresome to him, since his acquaintanceship with livelier regions, and it grew daily more and more so. He began to make little trips to St. Louis for refreshment. There he found companionship to suit him, and pleasures to his taste, along with more freedom, in some particulars, than he could have at home. So, during the next two years his visits to the city grew in frequency and his tarryings there grew steadily longer in duration.

He was getting into deep waters. He was taking chances, privately, which might get him into trouble some day—in fact, *did*.

Judge Driscoll had retired from the bench and from all business activities in 1850, and had now been comfortably idle three years. He was president of the Free-thinkers' Society, and Pudd'nhead Wilson was the other member. The society's weekly discussions were now the old lawyer's main interest in life. Pudd'nhead was still toiling in obscurity at the bottom of the ladder, under the blight of that unlucky remark which he had let fall twenty-three years before about the dog.

Judge Driscoll was his friend, and claimed that he had a mind above the average, but that was regarded as one of the Judge's whims, and it failed to modify the public opinion. Or rather, that was one of the reasons why it failed, but there was another and better one. If the Judge had stopped with bare assertion, it would have had a good deal of effect; but he made the mistake of trying to prove his position. For some years Wilson had been privately at work on a whimsical almanac, for his amusement—a calendar, with a little dab of ostensible philosophy, usually in ironical form, appended to each date; and the Judge thought that these quips and fancies of Wilson's were neatly turned and cute; so he carried a handful of them around, one day, and read them to some of the chief citizens. But irony was not for those people; their mental vision was not focussed for it. They read those playful trifles in the solidest earnest, and decided without hesitancy that if there had ever been any doubt that Dave Wilson was a pudd'nhead—which there hadn't—this revelation removed that doubt for good and all. That is just the way in this world; an enemy can partly ruin a man, but it takes a good-natured injudicious friend to complete the thing and make it perfect. After this the Judge felt tenderer than ever toward Wilson, and surer than ever that his calendar had merit.

Judge Driscoll could be a free-

thinker and still hold his place in society because he was the person of most consequence in the community, and therefore could venture to go his own way and follow out his own notions. The other member of his pet organization was allowed the like liberty because he was a cipher in the estimation of the public, and nobody attached any importance to what he thought or did. He was liked, he was welcome enough all around, but he simply didn't count for anything.

The widow Cooper—affectionately called "aunt Patsy" by everybody—lived in a snug and comely cottage with her daughter Rowena, who was nineteen, romantic, amiable, and very pretty, but otherwise of no consequence. Rowena had a couple of young brothers—also of no consequence.

The widow had a large spare room which she let to a lodger, with board, when she could find one, but this room had been empty for a year now, to her sorrow. Her income was only sufficient for the family support, and she needed the lodging-money for trifling luxuries. But now, at last, on a flaming June day, she found herself happy; her tedious wait was ended; her year-worn advertisement had been answered; and not by a village applicant, oh, no!—this letter was from away off yonder in the dim great world to the North: it was from St. Louis. She sat on her porch gazing out with unseeing eyes upon the shining reaches of the mighty Mississippi, her thoughts steeped in her good fortune. Indeed it was specially good fortune, for she was to have two lodgers instead of one.

She had read the letter to the family, and Rowena had danced away to see to the cleaning and airing of the room by the slave woman Nancy, and the boys had rushed abroad in the town to spread the great news, for it was matter of public interest, and the public would wonder and not be pleased if not informed. Presently Rowena returned, all ablush with joyous excitement, and begged for a re-reading of the letter. It was framed thus:

HONORED MADAM: My brother and I have seen your advertisement, by chance, and beg leave to take the room you offer. We are twenty-four years of age and twins. We are Italians by birth, but have lived long in the various countries of Europe, and several years in the United States. Our names are Luigi and Angelo Capello. You desire but one guest; but dear Madam, if you will allow us to pay for two, we will not incommode you. We shall be down Thursday.

"Italians! How romantic! Just think, ma—there's never been one in this town, and everybody will be dying to see them, and they're all *ours!* Think of that!"

"Yes, I reckon they'll make a grand stir."

"Oh, indeed they will. The whole town will be on its head! Think— they've been in Europe and everywhere! There's never been a traveler in this town before. Ma, I shouldn't wonder if they've seen kings!"

"Well, a body can't tell; but they'll make stir enough, without that."

"Yes, that's of course. Luigi—Angelo. They're lovely names; and so grand and foreign—not like Jones and Robinson and such. Thursday they are coming, and this is only Tuesday; it's a cruel long time to wait. Here comes Judge Driscoll in at the gate. He's heard about it. I'll go and open the door."

The Judge was full of congratulations and curiosity. The letter was read and discussed. Soon Justice Robinson arrived with more congratulations, and there was a new reading and a new discussion. This was the beginning. Neighbor after neighbor, of both sexes, followed, and the procession drifted in and out all day and evening and all Wednesday and Thursday. The letter was read and re-read until it was nearly worn out; everybody admired its courtly and gracious tone, and smooth and practised style, everybody was sympathetic and excited, and the Coopers were steeped in happiness all the while.

The boats were very uncertain in low water, in these primitive times. This time the Thursday boat had not arrived at ten at night—so the people had waited at the landing all day for nothing; they were driven to their homes by a heavy storm without having had a view of the illustrious foreigners.

Eleven o'clock came; and the Cooper house was the only one in the town that still had lights burning. The rain and thunder were booming yet, and the anxious family were still waiting, still hoping. At last there was a knock at the door and the family jumped to open it. Two negro men entered, each carrying a trunk, and proceeded up-stairs toward the guest-room. Then entered the twins—the handsomest, the best dressed, the most distinguished-looking pair of young fellows the West had ever seen. One was a little fairer than the other, but otherwise they were exact duplicates.

Chapter VI

Let us endeavor so to live that when we come to die even the undertaker will be sorry.

PUDD'NHEAD WILSON'S CALENDAR

Habit is habit, and not to be flung out of the window by any man, but coaxed down-stairs a step at a time.

PUDD'NHEAD WILSON'S CALENDAR

At breakfast in the morning the twins' charm of manner and easy and polished bearing made speedy conquest of the family's good graces. All constraint and formality quickly disappeared, and the friendliest feeling succeeded. Aunt Patsy called them by their Christian names almost from the beginning. She was full of the keenest curiosity about

them, and showed it; they responded by talking about themselves, which pleased her greatly. It presently appeared that in their early youth they had known poverty and hardship. As the talk wandered along the old lady watched for the right place to drop in a question or two concerning that matter, and when she found it she said to the blond twin who was now doing the biographies in his turn while the brunette one rested—

"If it ain't asking what I ought not to ask, Mr. Angelo, how did you come to be so friendless and in such trouble when you were little? Do you mind telling? But don't if you do."

"Oh, we don't mind it at all, madam; in our case it was merely misfortune, and nobody's fault. Our parents were well to do, there in Italy, and we were their only child. We were of the old Florentine nobility"—Rowena's heart gave a great bound, her nostrils expanded, and a fine light played in her eyes—"and when the war broke out my father was on the losing side and had to fly for his life. His estates were confiscated, his personal property seized, and there we were, in Germany, strangers, friendless, and in fact paupers. My brother and I were ten years old, and well educated for that age, very studious, very fond of our books, and well grounded in the German, French, Spanish, and English languages. Also, we were marvelous musical prodigies—if you will allow me to say it, it being only the truth.

"Our father survived his misfortunes only a month, our mother soon followed him, and we were alone in the world. Our parents could have made themselves comfortable by exhibiting us as a show, and they had many and large offers; but the thought revolted their pride, and they said they would starve and die first. But what they wouldn't consent to do we had to do without the formality of consent. We were seized for the debts occasioned by their illness and their funerals, and placed among the attractions of a cheap museum in Berlin to earn the liquidation money. It took us two years to get out of that slavery. We traveled all about Germany receiving no wages, and not even our keep. We had to be exhibited for nothing, and beg our bread.

"Well, madam, the rest is not of much consequence. When we escaped from that slavery at twelve years of age, we were in some respects men. Experience had taught us some valuable things; among others, how to take care of ourselves, how to avoid and defeat sharks and sharpers, and how to conduct our own business for our own profit and without other people's help. We traveled everywhere—years and years—picking up smatterings of strange tongues, familiarizing ourselves with strange sights and strange customs, accumulating an education of a wide and varied and curious sort. It was a pleasant life. We went to Venice—to London, Paris, Russia, India, China, Japan——"

At this point Nancy the slave woman thrust her head in at the door and exclaimed:

"Ole Missus, de house is plum' jam full o' people, en dey's jes a-spi'lin' to see de gen'lmen!" She indicated the twins with a nod of her head, and tucked it back out of sight again.

It was a proud occasion for the widow, and she promised herself high satisfaction in showing off her fine foreign birds before her neighbors and friends—simple folk who had hardly ever seen a foreigner of any kind, and never one of any distinction or style. Yet her feeling was moderate indeed when contrasted with Rowena's. Rowena was in the clouds, she walked on air; this was to be the greatest day, the most romantic episode, in the colorless history of that dull country town. She was to be familiarly near the source of its glory and feel the full flood of it pour over her and about her; the other girls could only gaze and envy, not partake.

The widow was ready, Rowena was ready, so also were the foreigners.

The party moved along the hall, the twins in advance, and entered the open parlor door, whence issued a low hum of conversation. The twins took a position near the door; the widow stood at Luigi's side, Rowena stood beside Angelo, and the march-past and the introductions began. The widow was all smiles and contentment. She received the procession and passed it on to Rowena.

"Good mornin', Sister Cooper"—hand-shake.

"Good morning, Brother Higgins—Count Luigi Capello, Mr. Higgins"—hand-shake, followed by a devouring stare and "I'm glad to see ye," on the part of Higgins, and a courteous inclination of the head and a pleasant "Most happy!" on the part of Count Luigi.

"Good mornin', Roweny"—hand-shake.

"Good morning, Mr. Higgins—present you to Count Angelo Capello." Hand-shake, admiring stare, "Glad to see ye,"—courteous nod, smily "Most happy!" and Higgins passes on.

None of these visitors was at ease, but, being honest people, they didn't pretend to be. None of them had ever seen a person bearing a title of nobility before, and none had been expecting to see one now, consequently the title came upon them as a kind of pile-driving surprise and caught them unprepared. A few tried to rise to the emergency, and got out an awkward "My lord," or "Your lordship," or something of that sort, but the great majority were overwhelmed by the unaccustomed word and its dim and awful associations with gilded courts and stately ceremony and anointed kingship, so they only fumbled through the hand-shake and passed on, speechless. Now and then, as happens at all receptions everywhere, a more than ordinarily friendly soul blocked the procession and kept it waiting while he inquired how the brothers liked the village, and how long they were going to stay, and if their families were well, and dragged in the weather, and hoped it would get cooler soon, and all that sort of thing, so as to be able to say, when they got home, "I had quite a long talk with them"; but nobody did or said anything of a regrettable kind, and so the great affair went through to the end in a creditable and satisfactory fashion.

General conversation followed, and the twins drifted about from group to group, talking easily and fluently and winning approval, compelling admiration and achieving favor from all.

The widow followed their conquering march with a proud eye, and every now and then Rowena said to herself with deep satisfaction, "And to think they are ours—all ours!"

There were no idle moments for mother or daughter. Eager inquiries concerning the twins were pouring into their enchanted ears all the time; each was the constant center of a group of breathless listeners; each recognized that she knew now for the first time the real meaning of that great word Glory, and perceived the stupendous value of it, and understood why men in all ages had been willing to throw away meaner happinesses, treasure, life itself, to get a taste of its sublime and supreme joy. Napoleon and all his kind stood accounted for—and justified.

When Rowena had at last done all her duty by the people in the parlor, she went up-stairs to satisfy the longings of an overflow-meeting there, for the parlor was not big enough to hold all the comers. Again she was besieged by eager questioners and again she swam in sunset seas of glory. When the forenoon was nearly gone, she recognized with a pang that this most splendid episode of her life was almost over, that nothing could prolong it, that nothing quite its equal could ever fall to her fortune again. But never mind, it was sufficient unto itself, the grand occasion had moved on an ascending scale from the start, and was a noble and memorable success. If the twins could but do some crowning act, now, to climax it, something unusual, some-

thing startling, something to concentrate upon themselves the company's loftiest admiration, something in the nature of an electric surprise—

Here a prodigious slam-banging broke out below, and everybody rushed down to see. It was the twins knocking out a classic four-handed piece on the piano, in great style. Rowena was satisfied—satisfied down to the bottom of her heart.

The young strangers were kept long at the piano. The villagers were astonished and enchanted with the magnificence of their performance, and could not bear to have them stop. All the music that they had ever heard before seemed spiritless prentice-work and barren of grace or charm when compared with these intoxicating floods of melodious sound. They realized that for once in their lives they were hearing masters.

CHAPTER VII

One of the most striking differences between a cat
and a lie is that a cat has only nine lives.

PUDD'NHEAD WILSON'S CALENDAR

The company broke up reluctantly, and
drifted toward their several homes, chatting
with vivacity, and all agreeing that it would
be many a long day before Dawson's Landing would see the equal of this one again.
The twins had accepted several invitations
while the reception was in progress, and
had also volunteered to play some duets at
an amateur entertainment for the benefit of

a local charity. Society was eager to receive them to its bosom. Judge Driscoll had the good fortune to secure them for an immediate drive, and to be the first to display them in public. They entered his buggy with him, and were paraded down the main street, everybody flocking to the windows and sidewalks to see.

The Judge showed the strangers the new graveyard, and the jail, and where the richest man lived, and the Freemasons' hall, and the Methodist church, and the Presbyterian church, and where the Baptist church was going to be when they got some money to build it with, and showed them the town hall and the slaughter-house, and got out the independent fire company in uniform and had them put out an imaginary fire; then he let them inspect the muskets of the militia company, and poured out an exhaustless stream of enthusiasm over all these splendors, and seemed very well satisfied with the responses he got, for the twins admired his admiration, and paid him back the best they could, though they could have done better if some fifteen or sixteen hundred thousand previous experiences of this sort in various countries had not already rubbed off a considerable part of the novelty of it.

The Judge laid himself out hospitably to make them have a good time, and if there was a defect anywhere it was not his fault. He told them a good many humorous anecdotes, and always forgot the nub, but they were always able to furnish it, for these yarns were of a pretty early vintage, and they had had many a rejuvenating pull at them before. And he told them all about his several dignities, and how he had held this and that and the other place of honor or profit, and had once been to the legislature, and was now president of the Society of Free-thinkers. He said the society had been in existence four years, and already had two members, and was firmly established. He would call for the brothers in the evening if they would like to attend a meeting of it.

Accordingly he called for them, and on the way he told them all about Pudd'nhead Wilson, in order that they might get a favorable impression of him in advance and be prepared to like him. This scheme succeeded—the favorable impression was achieved. Later it was confirmed and solidified when Wilson proposed that out of courtesy to the strangers the usual topics be put aside and the hour be devoted to

conversation upon ordinary subjects and the cultivation of friendly
relations and good-fellowship,—a proposition which was put to vote
and carried.

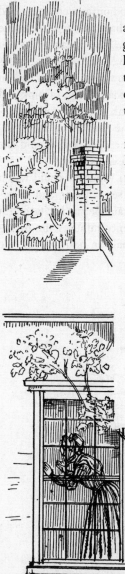

The hour passed quickly away in lively talk,
and when it was ended the lonesome and neglected Wilson was richer by two friends than
he had been when it began. He invited the
twins to look in at his lodgings, presently, after
disposing of an intervening engagement, and
they accepted with pleasure.

Toward the middle of the evening they
found themselves on the road to his house.
Pudd'nhead was at home waiting for them and
putting in his time puzzling over a thing which
had come under his notice that morning. The
matter was this: He happened to be up very
early—at dawn, in fact; and he crossed the
hall which divided his cottage through the
center, and entered a room to get something
there. The window of the room had no curtains, for that side of the house had long been
unoccupied, and through this window he
caught sight of something which surprised
and interested him. It was a young woman—a
young woman where properly no young
woman belonged; for she was in Judge
Driscoll's house, and in the bedroom over the

Judge's private study or sitting-room. This was young Tom Driscoll's bedroom. He and the Judge, the Judge's widowed sister Mrs. Pratt and three negro servants were the only people who belonged in the house. Who, then, might this young lady be? The two houses were separated by an ordinary yard, with a low fence running back through its middle from the street in front to the lane in the rear. The distance was not great, and Wilson was able to see the girl very well, the window-shades of the room she was in being up, and the window also. The girl had on a neat and trim summer dress, patterned in broad stripes of pink and white, and her bonnet was equipped with a pink veil. She was practising steps, gaits and attitudes, apparently; she was doing the thing gracefully, and was very much absorbed in her work. Who could she be, and how came she to be in young Tom Driscoll's room?

Wilson had quickly chosen a position from which he could watch the girl without running much risk of being seen by her, and he remained there hoping she would raise her veil and betray her face. But she disappointed him. After a matter of twenty minutes she disappeared, and although he stayed at his post half an hour longer, she came no more.

Toward noon he dropped in at the Judge's and talked with Mrs. Pratt about the great event of the day, the levee of the distinguished foreigners at Aunt Patsy Cooper's. He asked after her nephew Tom, and she said he was on his way home, and that she was expecting him to arrive a little before night; and added that she and the Judge were gratified to gather from his letters that he was conducting himself very nicely and creditably—at which Wilson winked to himself privately. Wilson did not ask if there was a newcomer in the house, but he asked questions that would have brought light-throwing answers as to that matter if Mrs. Pratt had had any light to throw; so he went away satisfied that he knew of things that were going on in her house of which she herself was not aware.

He was now waiting for the twins, and still puzzling over the problem of who that girl might be, and how she happened to be in that young fellow's room at daybreak in the morning.

Chapter VIII

The holy passion of Friendship is of so sweet and steady
and loyal and enduring a nature that it will last through a
whole lifetime, if not asked to lend money.

PUDD'NHEAD WILSON'S CALENDAR

Consider well the proportions of things. It is
better to be a young June-bug than an old bird
of paradise.

PUDD'NHEAD WILSON'S CALENDAR

It is necessary now, to hunt up Roxy.

At the time she was set free and went
away chambermaiding, she was thirty-
five. She got a berth as second chambermaid
on a Cincinnati boat in the New Orleans
trade, the *Grand Mogul*. A couple of trips made
her wonted and easy-going at the work, and infatuated her with the stir and adventure and independence of steamboat life. Then she was
promoted and became head chambermaid. She was a favorite
with the officers, and exceedingly proud of
their joking
and
friendly
ways
with
her.

During eight years she served three parts of the year on that boat, and the winters on a Vicksburg packet. But now for two months she had had rheumatism in her arms, and was obliged to let the wash-tub alone. So she resigned. But she was well fixed—rich, as she would have described it; for she had lived a steady life, and had banked four dollars every month in New Orleans as a provision for her old age. She said in the start that she had "put shoes on one bar'footed nigger to tromple on her with," and that one mistake like that was enough; she would be independent of the human race thenceforth forevermore if hard work and economy could accomplish it. When the boat touched the levee at New Orleans she bade good-by to her comrades on the *Grand Mogul* and moved her kit ashore.

But she was back in an hour. The bank had gone to smash and carried her four hundred dollars with it. She was a pauper, and homeless. Also disabled bodily, at least for the present. The officers were full of sympathy for her in her trouble, and made up a little purse for her. She resolved to go to her birthplace; she had friends there among the negroes, and the unfortunate always help the unfortunate, she was well aware of that; those lowly comrades of her youth would not let her starve.

She took the little local packet at Cairo, and now she was on the home-stretch. Time had worn away her bitterness against her son, and she was able to think of him with serenity. She put the vile side of him out of her mind, and dwelt only on recollections of his occasional acts of kindness to her. She gilded and otherwise decorated these, and made them very pleasant to contemplate. She began to long to see him. She would go and fawn upon him, slave-like—for this would have to be her attitude, of course—and maybe she would find that time had modified him, and that he would be glad to see his long-forgotten old nurse and treat her gently. That would be lovely; that would make her forget her woes and her poverty.

Her poverty! That thought inspired her to add another castle to her dream: maybe he would give her a trifle now and then—maybe a dollar, once a month, say; any little thing like that would help, oh, ever so much.

By the time she reached Dawson's Landing she was her old self again; her blues were gone, she was in high feather. She would get along, surely; there were many kitchens where the servants would share their meals with her, and also steal sugar and apples and other dainties for her to carry home—or give her a chance to pilfer them herself, which would answer just as well. And there was the church. She was a more rabid and devoted Methodist than ever, and her piety was no sham, but was strong and sincere. Yes, with plenty of creature comforts and her old place in the amen-corner in her possession again, she would be perfectly happy and at peace thenceforward to the end.

She went to Judge Driscoll's kitchen first of all. She was received there in great form and with vast enthusiasm. Her wonderful travels, and the strange countries she had seen and the adventures she had had, made her a marvel, and a heroine of romance. The negroes hung enchanted upon the great story of her experiences, interrupting her all along with eager questions, with laughter, exclamations of delight and expressions of applause; and she was obliged to confess to herself that if there was anything better in this world than steamboating, it was the glory to be got by telling about it. The audience loaded her stomach with their dinners, and then stole the pantry bare to load up her basket.

Tom was in St. Louis. The servants said he had spent the best part of his time there during the previous two years. Roxy came every day, and had many talks about the family and its affairs. Once she asked why Tom was away so much. The ostensible "Chambers" said:

"De fac' is, ole marster kin git along better when young marster's away den he kin when he's in de town; yes, en he love him better, too; so he gives him fifty dollahs a month——"

"No, is dat so? Chambers, you's a-jokin', ain't you?"

"'Clah to goodness I ain't, mammy; Marse Tom tole me so his own self. But nemmine, 't ain't enough."

"My lan', what de reason 't ain't enough?"

"Well, I's gwine to tell you, if you gimme a chanst, mammy. De reason it ain't enough is 'ca'se Marse Tom gambles."

Roxy threw up her hands in astonishment and Chambers went on—

"Ole marster found it out, 'ca'se he had to pay two hundred dollahs for Marse Tom's gamblin' debts, en dat's true, mammy, jes as dead certain as you's bawn."

"Two—hund'd—dollahs! Why, what is you talkin' 'bout? Two—hund'd—dollahs. Sakes alive, it's 'mos' enough to buy a tol'able good second-hand nigger wid. En you ain't lyin', honey?—you wouldn't lie to yo' ole mammy?"

"It's God's own truth, jes as I tell you—two hund'd dollahs—I wisht I may never stir outen my tracks if it ain't so. En, oh, my lan', ole Marse was jes a-hoppin'! he was b'ilin' mad, I tell you! He tuck 'n' dissenhurrit him."

He licked his chops with relish after that stately word. Roxy struggled with it a moment, then gave it up and said—

"Dissen*whiched* him?"

"Dissenhurrit him."

"What's dat? What do it mean?"

"Means he bu'sted de will."

"Bu's—ted de will! He wouldn't *ever* treat him so! Take it back, you mis'able imitation nigger dat I bore in sorrow en tribbilation."

Roxy's pet castle—an occasional dollar from Tom's pocket—was tumbling to ruin before her eyes. She could not abide such a disaster as that; she couldn't endure the thought of it. Her remark amused Chambers:

"Yah-yah-yah! jes listen to dat! If I's imitation, what is you? Bofe of us is imitation *white*—dat's what we is—en pow'ful good imitation, too—yah-yah-yah!—we don't 'mount to noth'n as imitation *niggers*; en as for——"

"Shet up yo' foolin', 'fo' I knock you side de head, en tell me 'bout de will. Tell me 't ain't bu'sted—do, honey, en I'll never forgit you."

"Well, *'tain't*—'ca'se dey's a new one made, en Marse Tom's all right ag'in. But what is you in sich a sweat 'bout it for, mammy? 'Tain't none o' your business I don't reckon."

"'Tain't none o' my business? Whose business is it den, I'd like to know? Wuz I his mother tell he was fifteen years old, or wusn't I?—you answer me dat. En you speck I could see him turned out po' en ornery on de worl' en never care noth'n' 'bout it? I reckon if you'd ever be'n a mother yo'self, Valet de Chambers, you wouldn't talk sich foolishness as dat."

"Well, den, ole Marse forgive him en fixed up de will ag'in—do dat satisfy you?"

Yes, she was satisfied now, and quite happy and sentimental over it. She kept coming daily, and at last she was told that Tom had come home. She began to tremble with emotion, and straightway sent to beg him to let his "po' ole nigger mammy have jes one sight of him en die for joy."

Tom was stretched at his lazy ease on a sofa when Chambers brought the petition. Time had not modified his ancient detestation of the humble drudge and protector of his boyhood; it was still bitter and uncompromising. He sat up and bent a severe gaze upon the fair face of the young fellow whose name he was unconsciously using and whose family rights he was enjoying. He maintained the gaze until the victim of it had become satisfactorily pallid with terror, then he said—

"What does the old rip want with me?"

The petition was meekly repeated.

"Who gave you permission to come and disturb me with the social attentions of niggers?"

Tom had risen. The other young man was trembling now, visibly. He saw what was coming, and bent his head sideways, and put up his left arm to shield it. Tom rained cuffs upon the head and its shield, saying no word: the victim received each blow with a beseeching "Please, Marse Tom!—oh, please, Marse Tom!" Seven blows—then Tom said, "Face the door—march!" He followed behind with one, two, three solid kicks. The last one helped the pure-white slave over the door-sill, and he limped away mopping his eyes with his old ragged sleeve. Tom shouted after him, "Send her in!"

Then he flung himself panting on the sofa again, and rasped out the remark, "He arrived just at the right moment; I was full to the brim with bitter thinkings, and nobody to take it out of. How refreshing it was! I feel better."

Tom's mother entered now, closing the door behind her, and approached her son with all the wheedling and supplicating servilities that fear and interest can impart to the words and attitudes of the born slave. She stopped a yard from her boy and made two or three admiring exclamations over his manly stature and general handsomeness, and Tom put an arm under his head and hoisted a leg over the sofa-back in order to look properly indifferent.

"My lan', how you is growed, honey! 'Clah to goodness, I wouldn't a-knowed you, Marse Tom! 'deed I wouldn't! Look at me good; does you 'member old Roxy?—does you know yo' old nigger mammy, honey? Well now, I kin lay down en die in peace, 'ca'se I'se seed——"

"Cut it short, —— it, cut it short! What is it you want?"

"You heah dat? Jes de same old Marse Tom, al'ays so gay and funnin' wid de ole mammy. I 'uz jes as shore——"

"Cut it short, I tell you, and get along! What do you want."

This was a bitter disappointment. Roxy had for so many days nourished and fondled and petted her notion that Tom would be glad to see his old nurse, and would make her proud and happy to the marrow with a cordial word or two, that it took two rebuffs to convince her that he was not funning, and that her beautiful dream was a fond and foolish vanity, a shabby and pitiful mistake. She was hurt to the heart, and so ashamed that for a moment she did not quite know what to do or how to act. Then her breast began to heave, the tears came, and in her forlornness she was moved to try that other dream of hers—an appeal to her boy's charity; and so, upon the impulse, and without reflection, she offered her supplication:

"Oh, Marse Tom, de po' ole mammy is in sich hard luck dese days; en she's kinder crippled in de arms en can't work, en if you could gimme a dollah—on'y jes one little dol——"

Tom was on his feet so suddenly that the supplicant was startled into a jump herself.

"A dollar!—give you a dollar! I've a notion to strangle you! Is *that* your errand here? Clear out! and be quick about it!"

Roxy backed slowly toward the door. When she was half-way she stopped, and said mournfully:

"Marse Tom, I nussed you when you was a little baby, en I raised you all by myself tell you was 'most a young man; en now you is young en rich, en I is po' en gitt'n ole, en I come heah b'lievin' dat you would he'p de ole mammy 'long down de little road dat's lef' 'twix' her en de grave, en——"

Tom relished this tune less than any that had preceded it, for it began to wake up a sort of echo in his conscience; so he interrupted and said with decision, though without asperity, that he was not in a situation to help her, and wasn't going to do it.

"Ain't you ever gwine to he'p me, Marse Tom?"

"No! Now go away and don't bother me any more."

Roxy's head was down, in an attitude of humility. But now the fires of her old wrongs flamed up in her breast and began to burn fiercely. She raised her head slowly, till it was well up, and at the same time her great frame unconsciously assumed an erect and masterful attitude, with all the majesty and grace of her vanished youth in it. She raised her finger and punctuated with it:

"You has said de word. You has had yo' chance, en you has trompled it under yo' foot. When you git another one, you'll git down on yo' knees en *beg* for it!"

A cold chill went to Tom's heart, he didn't know why; for he did not reflect that such words, from such an incongruous source, and so solemnly delivered, could not easily fail of that effect. However, he did the natural thing: he replied with bluster and mockery:

"*You'll* give me a chance—*you!* Perhaps I'd better get down on my knees now! But in case I don't—just for argument's sake—what's going to happen, pray?"

"Dis is what is gwine to happen. I's gwine as straight to yo' uncle as I·kin walk, en tell him every las' thing I knows 'bout you."

Tom's cheek blenched, and she saw it. Disturbing thoughts began to chase each other through his head. "How can she know? And yet she must have found out—she looks it. I've had the will back only three months, and am already deep in debt again, and moving heaven and earth to save myself from exposure and destruction, with a reasonably fair show of getting the thing covered up if I'm let alone, and now this fiend has gone and found me out somehow or other. I wonder how much she knows? Oh, oh, oh, it's enough to break a body's heart! But I've got to humor her—there's no other way."

Then he worked up a rather sickly sample of a gay laugh and a hollow chipperness of manner, and said:

"Well, well, Roxy dear, old friends like you and me mustn't quarrel. Here's your dollar—now tell me what you know."

He held out the wild-cat bill; she stood as she was, and made no movement. It was her turn to scorn persuasive foolery, now, and she did not waste it. She said, with a grim implacability in voice and manner which made Tom almost realize that even a former slave can remember for ten minutes insults and injuries returned for compliments and flatteries received, and can also enjoy taking revenge for them when the opportunity offers:

"What does I know? I'll tell you what I knows. I knows enough to bu'st dat will to flinders—en more, mind you, *more!*"

Tom was aghast.

"More?" he said. "What do you call more? Where's there any room for more?"

Roxy laughed a mocking laugh, and said scoffingly, with a toss of her head, and her hands on her hips—

"Yes!—oh, I reckon! *Co'se* you'd like to know—wid yo' po' little ole rag dollah. What you reckon I's gwine to tell *you* for?—you ain't got no money. I's gwine to tell yo' uncle—en I'll do it dis minute, too—he'll gimme *five* dollahs for de news, en mighty glad, too."

She swung herself around disdainfully, and started away. Tom was in a panic. He seized her skirts, and implored her to wait. She turned and said, loftily—

"Look-a-heah, what 'uz it I tole you?"

"You—you—I don't remember anything. What was it you told me?"

"I tole you dat de next time I give you a chance you'd git down on yo' knees en beg for it."

Tom was stupefied for a moment. He was panting with excitement. Then he said:

"Oh, Roxy, you wouldn't require your young master to do such a horrible thing. You can't mean it."

"I'll let you know mighty quick whether I means it or not! You call me names, en as good as spit on me when I comes here po' en ornery en 'umble, to praise you for bein' growed up so fine en handsome, en tell you how I used to nuss you en tend you en watch you when you 'uz sick en hadn't no mother but me in de whole worl', en beg you to give de po' ole nigger a dollah for to git her som'n' to eat, en you call me names—*names,* dad blame you! Yassir, I gives you jes one chance mo', and dat's *now,* en it las' on'y a half a second—you hear?"

Tom slumped to his knees and began to beg, saying—

"You see I'm begging, and it's honest begging, too! Now tell me, Roxy, tell me."

The heir of two centuries of unatoned insult and outrage looked down on him and seemed to drink in deep draughts of satisfaction. Then she said—

"Fine nice young white gen'l'man kneelin' down to a nigger-wench! I's wanted to see dat jes once befo' I's called. Now, Gabr'el, blow de hawn, I's ready...Git up!"

Tom did it. He said, humbly—

"Now, Roxy, don't punish me any more. I deserved what I've got, but be good and let me off with that. Don't go to uncle. Tell me—I'll give you the five dollars."

"Yes, I bet you will; en you won't stop dah, nuther. But I ain't gwine to tell you heah——"

"Good gracious, no!"

"Is you 'feared o' de ha'nted house?"

"N-no."

"Well, den, you come to de ha'nted house 'bout ten or 'leven tonight, en climb up de ladder, 'ca'se de sta'r-steps is broke down, en you'll find me. I's a-roostin' in de ha'nted house 'ca'se I can't 'ford to roos' nowhers' else." She started toward the door, but stopped and said, "Gimme de dollah bill!" He gave it to her. She examined it and said, "H'm—like enough de bank's bu'sted." She started again, but halted again. "Has you got any whisky?"

"Yes, a little."

"Fetch it!"

He ran to his room overhead and brought down a bottle which was two-thirds full. She tilted it up and took a drink. Her eyes sparkled with satisfaction, and she tucked the bottle under her shawl, saying, "It's prime. I'll take it along."

Tom humbly held the door for her, and she marched out as grim and erect as a grenadier.

CHAPTER IX

Why is it that we rejoice at a birth and grieve at a funeral? It is because we are not the person involved.

It is easy to find fault, if one has that disposition. There was once a man who, not being able to find any other fault with his coal, complained that there were too many prehistoric toads in it.

Tom flung himself on the sofa, and put his throbbing head in his hands, and rested his elbows on his knees. He rocked himself back and forth and moaned.

"I've knelt to a nigger wench!" he muttered. "I thought I had struck the deepest depths of degradation before, but oh, dear, it was nothing to this.... Well, there is one consolation, such as it is—I've struck bottom this time; there's nothing lower."

But that was a hasty conclusion.

At ten that night he climbed the ladder in the haunted house, pale, weak and wretched. Roxy was standing in the door of one of the rooms, waiting, for she had heard him.

This was a two-story log house which had acquired the reputation a few years before of being haunted, and that was the end of its usefulness. Nobody would live in it afterward, or go near it by night, and most people even gave it a wide berth in the daytime. As it had no competition, it was called *the* haunted house. It was getting crazy and ruinous, now, from long neglect. It stood three hundred yards beyond Pudd'nhead Wilson's house, with nothing between but vacancy. It was the last house in the town at that end.

Tom followed Roxy into the room. She had a pile of clean straw in the corner for a bed, some cheap but well-kept clothing was hanging on the wall, there was a tin lantern freckling the floor with little spots of light, and there were various soap-and-candle boxes scattered about, which served for chairs. The two sat down. Roxy said—

"Now den, I'll tell you straight off, en I'll begin to k'leck de money later on; I ain't in no hurry. What does you reckon I's gwine to tell you?"

"Well, you—you—oh, Roxy, don't make it too hard for me! Come right out and tell me you've found out somehow what a shape I'm in on account of dissipation and foolishness."

"Disposition en foolishness! *No* sir, dat ain't it. Dat jist ain't nothin' at all, 'longside o' what *I* knows."

Tom stared at her, and said—

"Why, Roxy, what do you mean?"

She rose, and gloomed above him like a Fate.

"I means dis—en it's de Lord's truth. You ain't no more kin to ole Marse Driscoll den I is!—*dat's* what I means!" and her eyes flamed with triumph.

"What!"

"Yassir, en *dat* ain't all! You's a *nigger!*—*bawn* a nigger en a *slave!*—en you's a nigger en a slave dis minute; en if I opens my mouf ole Marse Driscoll'll sell you down de river befo' you is two days older den what you is now!"

"It's a thundering lie, you miserable old blatherskite!"

"It ain't no lie, nuther. It's jes de truth, en nothin' *but* de truth, so he'p me. Yassir—you's my *son*—"

"You devil!"

"En dat po' boy dat you's be'n a-kickin' en a-cuffin' to-day is Percy Driscoll's son en yo' *marster*——"

"You beast!"

"En *his* name's Tom Driscoll, en *yo'* name's Valet de Chambers, en you ain't *got* no fambly name, beca'se niggers don't *have* em!"

Tom sprang up and seized a billet of wood and raised it; but his mother only laughed at him, and said—

"Set down, you pup! Does you think you kin skyer me? It ain't in you, nor de likes of you. I reckon you'd shoot me in de back, maybe, if you got a chance, for dat's jist yo' style—*I* knows you, throo en throo—but I don't mind gitt'n killed, beca'se all dis is down in writin' en it's in safe hands, too, en de man dat's got it knows whah to look for de right man when I gits killed. Oh, bless yo' soul, if you puts yo' mother up for as big a fool as *you* is, you's pow'ful mistaken, I kin tell you! Now den, you set still en behave yo'self; en don't you git up ag'in till I tell you!"

Tom fretted and chafed awhile in a whirlwind of disorganizing sensations and emotions, and finally said, with something like settled conviction—

"The whole thing is moonshine; now then, go ahead and do your worst; I'm done with you."

Roxy made no answer. She took the lantern and started toward the door. Tom was in a cold panic in a moment.

"Come back, come back!" he wailed. "I didn't mean it, Roxy; I take it all back, and I'll never say it again! Please come back, Roxy!"

The woman stood a moment, then she said gravely:

"Dat's one thing you's got to stop, Valet de Chambers. You can't call me *Roxy,* same as if you was my equal. Chillen don't speak to dey mammies like dat. You'll call me ma or mammy, dat's what you'll call me—least-ways when dey ain't nobody aroun'. *Say* it!"

It cost Tom a struggle, but he got it out.

"Dat's all right. Don't you ever forget it ag'in, if you knows what's good for you. Now den, you has said you wouldn't ever call it lies en moonshine ag'in. I'll tell you dis, for a warnin': if you ever does say it ag'in, it's de *las'* time you'll ever say it to me; I'll tramp as straight to de Judge as I kin walk, en tell him who you is, en *prove* it. Does you b'lieve me when I says dat?"

"Oh," groaned Tom, "I more than believe it; I *know* it."

Roxy knew her conquest was complete. She could have proved nothing to anybody, and her threat about the writings was a lie; but she knew the person she was dealing with, and had made both statements without any doubt as to the effect they would produce.

She went and sat down on her candle-box, and the pride and pomp of her victorious attitude made it a throne. She said—

"Now den, Chambers, we's gwine to talk business, en dey ain't gwine to be no mo' foolishness. In de fust place, you gits fifty dollahs a month; you's gwine to han' over half of it to yo' ma. Plank it out!"

But Tom had only six dollars in the world. He gave her that, and promised to start fair on next month's pension.

"Chambers, how much is you in debt?"

Tom shuddered, and said—

"Nearly three hundred dollars."

"How is you gwine to pay it?"

Tom groaned out—"Oh, I don't know; don't ask me such awful questions."

But she stuck to her point until she wearied a confession out of him: he had been prowling about in disguise, stealing small valuables from private houses; in fact, had made a good deal of a raid on his fellow-villagers a fortnight before, when he was supposed to be in St. Louis; but he doubted if he had sent away enough stuff to realize the required amount, and was afraid to make a further venture in the present excited state of the town. His mother approved of his conduct, and offered to help, but this frightened him. He tremblingly ventured to say that if she would retire from the town he should feel better and safer, and could hold his head higher—and was going on to make an argument, but she interrupted and surprised him pleasantly by saying she was ready; it didn't make any difference to her where she stayed, so that she got her share of the pension regularly. She said she would not go far, and would call at the haunted house once a month for her money. Then she said—

"I don't hate you so much now, but I've hated you a many a year—and anybody would. Didn't I change you off, en give you a good fambly en a good name, en made you a white gen'l'man en rich, wid store clothes on—en what did I git for it? You despised me all de time, en was al'ays sayin' mean hard things to me befo' folks, en wouldn't ever let me forgit I's a nigger—en—en———"

She fell to sobbing, and broke down. Tom said—"But you know I didn't know you were my mother; and besides———"

"Well, nemmine 'bout dat, now; let it go. I's gwine to fo'git it." Then she added fiercely, "En don't ever make me remember it ag'in, or you'll be sorry, *I* tell you."

When they were parting, Tom said, in the most persuasive way he could command—

"Ma, would you mind telling me who was my father?"

He had supposed he was asking an embarrassing question. He was mistaken. Roxy drew herself up with a proud toss of her head, and said—

"Does I mine tellin' you? No, dat I don't! You ain't got no 'casion to be shame' o' yo' father, *I* kin tell you. He wuz de highest quality in dis whole town—ole Virginny stock. Fust famblies, he wuz. Jes as good stock as de Driscolls en de Howards, de bes' day dey ever seed." She put on a little prouder air, if possible, and added impressively: "Does you 'member Cunnel Cecil Burleigh Essex, dat died de same year yo' young Marse Tom Driscoll's pappy died, en all de Masons en Odd Fellers en Churches turned out en give him de bigges' funeral dis town ever seed? Dat's de man."

Under the inspiration of her soaring complacency the departed graces of her earlier days returned to her, and her bearing took to it-

self a dignity and state that might have passed for queenly if her surroundings had been a little more in keeping with it.

"Dey ain't another nigger in dis town dat's as high-bawn as you is.
Now den, go 'long! En jes you hold yo' head up as high as you want
to—you has de right, en dat I kin swah."

CHAPTER X

All say, "How hard it is that we have to die"—a strange complaint to come from the mouths of people who have had to live.
PUDD'NHEAD WILSON'S CALENDAR

When angry, count four; when very angry, swear.
PUDD'NHEAD WILSON'S CALENDAR

Every now and then, after Tom went to bed, he had sudden wakings out of his sleep, and his first thought was, "Oh, joy, it was all a dream!" Then he laid himself heavily down again, with a groan and the muttered words, "A nigger! I am a nigger! Oh, I wish I was dead!"

He woke at dawn with one more repetition of this horror, and then he resolved to meddle no more with that treacherous sleep. He began to think. Sufficiently bitter thinkings they were. They wandered along something after this fashion:

"Why were niggers *and* whites made? What crime did the uncreated first nigger commit that the curse of birth was decreed for him? And why is this awful difference made between white and black? ... How hard the nigger's fate seems, this morning!—yet until last night such a thought never entered my head."

He sighed and groaned an hour or more away. Then "Chambers" came humbly in to say that breakfast was nearly ready. "Tom" blushed scarlet to see this aristocratic white youth cringe to him, a nigger, and call him "Young Marster." He said roughly—

"Get out of my sight!" and when the youth was gone, he muttered, "He has done me no harm, poor wretch, but he is an eyesore to me now, for he is Driscoll the young gentleman, and I am a—oh, I wish I was dead!"

A gigantic irruption, like that of Krakatoa a few years ago, with the accompanying earthquakes, tidal waves, and clouds of volcanic dust, changes the face of the surrounding landscape beyond recognition, bringing down the high lands, elevating the low, making fair lakes where deserts had been, and deserts where green prairies had smiled before. The tremendous catastrophe which had befallen Tom had changed his moral landscape in much the same way. Some of his low places he found lifted to ideals, some of his ideals had sunk to the valleys, and lay there with the sackcloth and ashes of pumice-stone and sulphur on their ruined heads.

For days he wandered in lonely places, thinking, thinking, thinking— trying to get his bearings. It was new work. If he met a friend, he found that the habit of a lifetime had in some mysterious way vanished—his arm hung limp, instead of involuntarily extending the hand for a shake. It was the "nigger" in him asserting its humility, and he blushed and was abashed. And the "nigger" in him was surprised when the white friend put out his hand for a shake with him. He found the "nigger" in him involuntarily giving the road, on the sidewalk, to the white rowdy and loafer. When Rowena, the dearest thing his heart knew, the idol of his secret worship, invited him in, the "nigger" in him made an embarrassed excuse and was afraid to enter and sit with the dread white folks on equal terms. The "nigger" in him went shrinking and skulking here and there and yonder, and fancying it saw suspicion and maybe detection in all faces, tones, and gestures. So strange and un-characteristic was Tom's conduct that people noticed it, and turned to look after him when he passed on; and when he glanced back—as he could not help doing, in spite of his best resistance—and caught that puzzled expression in a person's face, it gave him a sick feeling, and he took himself out of view as quickly as he could. He presently came to have a hunted sense and a hunted look, and then he fled away to the hill-tops and the solitudes. He said to himself that the curse of Ham was upon him.

He dreaded his meals; the "nigger" in him was ashamed to sit at the white folks' table, and feared discovery all the time; and once when Judge Driscoll said, "What's the matter with you? You look as meek as a nigger," he felt as secret murderers are said to feel when the accuser says, "Thou art the man!" Tom said he was not well, and left the table.

His ostensible "aunt's" solicitudes and endearments were become a terror to him, and he avoided them.

And all the time, hatred of his ostensible "uncle" was steadily growing in his heart; for he said to himself, "He is white; and I am his chattel, his property, his goods, and he can sell me, just as he could his dog."

For as much as a week after this, Tom imagined that his character had undergone a pretty radical change. But that was because he did not know himself.

In several ways his opinions were totally changed, and would never go back to what they were before, but the main structure of his character was not changed, and could not be changed. One or two very important features of it were altered, and in time effects would result from this, if opportunity offered—effects of a quite serious nature, too. Under the influence of a great mental and moral upheaval his character and habits had taken on the appearance of complete change, but after a while with the subsidence of the storm both began to settle toward their former places. He dropped gradually back into his old frivolous and easy-going ways and conditions of feeling and manner of speech, and no familiar of his could have detected anything in him that differentiated him from the weak and careless Tom of other days.

The theft-raid which he had made upon the village turned out better than he had ventured to hope. It produced the sum necessary to pay his gaming-debts, and saved him from exposure to his uncle and another smashing of the will. He and his mother learned to like each other fairly well. She couldn't love him, as yet, because there "warn't nothing *to* him," as she expressed it, but her nature needed something or somebody to rule over, and he was better than nothing. Her strong character and aggressive and commanding ways compelled Tom's admiration in spite of the fact that he got more illustrations of them than he needed for his comfort. However, as a rule her conversation was made up of racy tattle about the privacies of the chief families of the town (for she went harvesting among their kitchens every time she came to the village), and Tom enjoyed this. It was just in his line. She always collected her half of his pension punctually, and he was always at the haunted house to have a chat with her on these occasions. Every now and then she paid him a visit there on between-days also.

Occasionally he would run up to St. Louis for a few weeks, and at last temptation caught him again. He won a lot of money, but lost it, and with it a deal more besides, which he promised to raise as soon as possible.

For this purpose he projected a new raid on his town. He never meddled with any other town, for he was afraid to venture into houses whose ins and outs he did not know and the habits of whose households he was not acquainted with. He arrived at the haunted house in disguise on the Wednesday before the advent of the twins—after writing his aunt Pratt that he would not arrive until two days after—and lay in hiding there with his mother until toward daylight Friday morning, when he went to his uncle's house and entered by the back way with his own key, and slipped up to his room, where he could have the use of mirror and toilet articles. He had a suit of girl's clothes with him in a bundle as a disguise for his raid, and was wearing a suit of his mother's clothing, with black gloves and veil. By dawn he was tricked out for his raid, but he caught a glimpse of Pudd'nhead Wilson through the window over the way, and knew that Pudd'nhead had caught a glimpse of him. So he entertained Wilson with some airs and graces and attitudes for a while, then stepped out of sight and resumed the other disguise, and by and by went down and out the back way and started down town to reconnoiter the scene of his intended labors.

But he was ill at ease. He had changed back to Roxy's dress, with the stoop of age added to the disguise, so that Wilson would not bother himself about a humble old woman leaving a neighbor's house by the back way in the early morning, in case he was still spying. But supposing Wilson had seen him leave, and had thought it suspicious, and had also followed him? The thought made Tom cold. He gave up the raid for the day, and hurried back to the haunted house by the obscurest route he knew. His mother was gone; but she came back, by and by, with the news of the grand reception at Patsy Cooper's, and soon persuaded him that the opportunity was like a special providence, it was so inviting and perfect. So he went raiding, after all, and made a nice success of it while everybody was gone to Patsy Cooper's. Success gave him nerve and even actual intrepidity; insomuch, indeed, that after he had conveyed his harvest to his mother in a back alley, he went to the reception himself, and added several of the valuables of that house to his takings.

After this long digression we have how arrived once more at the
point where Pudd'nhead Wilson, while waiting for the arrival of the
twins on that same Friday evening, sat puzzling over the strange apparition of that morning—a girl in young Tom Driscoll's bedroom;
fretting, and guessing, and puzzling over it, and wondering who the
shameless creature might be.

Chapter XI

There are three infallible ways of pleasing an author, and the three form a rising scale of compliment: 1, to tell him you have read one of his books; 2, to tell him you have read all of his books; 3, to ask him to let you read the manuscript of his forthcoming book. No. 1 admits you to his respect; No. 2 admits you to his admiration; No. 3 carries you clear into his heart.

PUDD'NHEAD WILSON'S CALENDAR

As to the Adjective: when in doubt, strike it out.

PUDD'NHEAD WILSON'S CALENDAR

The twins arrived presently, and talk began. It flowed along chattily and sociably, and under its influence the new friendship gathered ease and strength. Wilson got out his Calendar, by request, and read a passage or two from it, which the twins praised quite cordially. This pleased the author so much that he complied gladly when they asked him to lend them a batch of the work to read at home. In the course of their wide travels they had found out that there are three sure ways of pleasing an author; they were now working the best of the three.

There was an interruption, now. Young Tom Driscoll appeared, and joined the party. He pretended to be seeing the distinguished strangers for the first time when they rose to shake hands; but this was only a blind, as he had already had a glimpse of them, at the reception, while robbing the house. The twins made mental note that he was smooth-faced and rather handsome, and

smooth and undulatory in his movements—graceful, in fact. Angelo
thought he had a good eye; Luigi thought there was something veiled
and sly about it. Angelo thought he had a pleasant free-and-easy way
of talking; Luigi thought it was more so than was agreeable. Angelo
thought he was a sufficiently nice young man; Luigi reserved his decision. Tom's first contribution to the conversation was a question which
he had put to Wilson a hundred times before. It was always cheerily
and good-naturedly put, and always inflicted a little pang, for it
touched a secret sore; but this time the pang was sharp, since strangers
were present.

"Well, how does the law come on? Had a case yet?"

Wilson bit his lip, but answered, "No—not yet," with as much indifference as he could assume. Judge Driscoll had generously left the
law feature out of the Wilson biography which he had furnished to the
twins. Young Tom laughed pleasantly, and said:

"Wilson's a lawyer, gentlemen, but he doesn't practise now."

The sarcasm bit, but Wilson kept himself under control, and said
without passion:

"I don't practise, it is true. It is true that I have never had a case, and
have had to earn a poor living for twenty years as an expert accountant
in a town where I can't get hold of a set of books to untangle as often
as I should like. But it is also true that I did fit myself well for the practice of the law. By the time I was your age, Tom, I had chosen a profession, and was soon competent to enter upon it." Tom winced. "I
never got a chance to try my hand at it, and I may never get a chance;

and yet if I ever do get it I shall be found ready, for I have kept up my law-studies all these years."

"That's it; that's good grit! I like to see it. I've a notion to throw all my business your way. My business and your law-practice ought to make a pretty gay team, Dave," and the young fellow laughed again.

"If you will throw—" Wilson had thought of the girl in Tom's bedroom, and was going to say, "If you will throw the surreptitious and disreputable part of your business my way, it may amount to something;" but thought better of it and said, "However, this matter doesn't fit well in a general conversation."

"All right, we'll change the subject; I guess you were about to give me another dig, anyway, so I'm willing to change. How's the Awful Mystery flourishing these days? Wilson's got a scheme for driving plain window-glass out of the market by decorating it with greasy finger-marks, and getting rich by selling it at famine prices to the crowned heads over in Europe to outfit their palaces with. Fetch it out, Dave."

Wilson brought three of his glass strips, and said—

"I get the subject to pass the fingers of his right hand through his hair, so as to get a little coating of the natural oil on them, and then press the balls of them on the glass. A fine and delicate print of the lines in the skin results, and is permanent, if it doesn't come in contact with something able to rub it off. You begin, Tom."

"Why, I think you took my finger-marks once or twice before."

"Yes; but you were a little boy the last time, only about twelve years old."

"That's so. Of course I've changed entirely since then, and variety is what the crowned heads want, I guess."

He passed his fingers through his crop of short hair, and pressed them one at a time on the glass. Angelo made a print of his fingers on another glass, and Luigi followed with the third. Wilson marked the glasses with names and date, and put them away. Tom gave one of his little laughs, and said—

"I thought I wouldn't say anything, but if variety is what you are after, you have wasted a piece of glass. The hand-print of one twin is the same as the hand-print of the fellow-twin."

"Well, it's done now, and I like to have them both, anyway," said Wilson, returning to his place.

"But look here, Dave," said Tom, "you used to tell people's fortunes, too, when you took their finger-marks. Dave's just an all-round genius—a genius of the first water, gentlemen; a great scientist running to seed here in this village, a prophet with the kind of honor that prophets generally get at home—for here they don't give shucks for his scientifics, and they call his skull a notion-factory—hey, Dave, ain't it so? But never mind; he'll make his mark some day—finger-mark, you know, he-he! But really, you want to let him take a shy at your palms once; it's worth twice the price of admission or your money's returned at the door. Why, he'll read your wrinkles as easy as a book, and not only tell you fifty or sixty things that's going to happen to you, but fifty or sixty thousand that ain't. Come, Dave, show the gentlemen what an inspired Jack-at-all-science we've got in this town, and don't know it."

Wilson winced under this nagging and not very courteous chaff, and the twins suffered with him and for him. They rightly judged, now, that the best way to relieve him would be to take the thing in earnest and treat it with respect, ignoring Tom's rather overdone raillery; so Luigi said—

"We have seen something of palmistry in our wanderings, and know very well what astonishing things it can do. If it isn't a science, and one of the greatest of them, too, I don't know what its other name ought to be. In the Orient——"

Tom looked surprised and incredulous. He said—

"That juggling a science? But really, you ain't serious, are you?"

"Yes, entirely so. Four years ago we had our hands read out to us as if our palms had been covered with print."

"Well, do you mean to say there was actually anything in it?" asked Tom, his incredulity beginning to weaken a little.

"There was this much in it," said Angelo: "what was told us of our characters was minutely exact—we could not have bettered it ourselves. Next, two or three memorable things that had happened to us were laid bare—things which no one present but ourselves could have known about."

"Why, it's rank sorcery!" exclaimed Tom, who was now becoming very much interested. "And how did they make out with what was going to happen to you in the future?"

"On the whole, quite fairly," said Luigi. "Two or three of the most striking things foretold have happened since; much the most striking one of all happened within that same year. Some of the minor prophecies have come true; some of the minor and some of the major ones have not been fulfilled yet, and of course may never be: still, I should be more surprised if they failed to arrive than if they didn't."

Tom was entirely sobered, and profoundly impressed. He said, apologetically—

"Dave, I wasn't meaning to belittle that science; I was only chaffing—chattering, I reckon I'd better say. I wish you would look at their palms. Come, won't you?"

"Why, certainly, if you want me to; but you know I've had no chance to become an expert, and don't claim to be one. When a past event is somewhat prominently recorded in the palm I can generally detect that, but minor ones often escape me,—not always, of course, but often,—but I haven't much confidence in myself when it comes to reading the future. I am talking as if palmistry was a daily study with me, but that is not so. I haven't examined half a dozen hands in the last half dozen years; you see, the people got to joking about it, and I stopped to let the talk die down. I'll tell you what we'll do, Count Luigi: I'll make a try at your past, and if I have any success there—no, on the whole, I'll let the future alone; that's really the affair of an expert."

He took Luigi's hand. Tom said—

"Wait—don't look yet, Dave! Count Luigi, here's paper and pencil. Set down that thing that you said was the most striking one that was foretold to you, and happened less than a year afterward, and give it to me so I can see if Dave finds it in your hand."

Luigi wrote a line privately, and folded up the piece of paper, and handed it to Tom, saying—

"I'll tell you when to look at it, if he finds it."

Wilson began to study Luigi's palm, tracing life lines, heart lines, head lines, and so on, and noting carefully their relations with the cobweb of finer and more delicate marks and lines that enmeshed them on all sides; he felt of the fleshy cushion at the base of the thumb, and noted its shape; he felt of the fleshy side of the hand between the wrist and the base of the little finger, and noted its shape also; he painstakingly examined the fingers, observing their form, proportions, and natural manner of disposing themselves when in repose. All this process was watched by the three spectators with absorbing interest, their heads

bent together over Luigi's palm, and nobody disturbing the stillness with a word. Wilson now entered upon a close survey of the palm again, and his revelations began.

He mapped out Luigi's character and disposition, his tastes, aversions, proclivities, ambitions, and eccentricities in a way which sometimes made Luigi wince and the others laugh, but both twins declared that the chart was artistically drawn and was correct.

Next, Wilson took up Luigi's history. He proceeded cautiously and with hesitation, now, moving his finger slowly along the great lines of the palm, and now and then halting it at a "star" or some such landmark, and examining that neighborhood minutely. He proclaimed one or two past events, Luigi confirmed his correctness, and the search went on. Presently Wilson glanced up suddenly with a surprised expression—

"Here is record of an incident which you would perhaps not wish me to——"

"Bring it out," said Luigi, good-naturedly; "I promise you it sha'n't embarrass me."

But Wilson still hesitated, and did not seem quite to know what to do. Then he said—

"I think it is too delicate a matter to—to—I believe I would rather write it or whisper it to you, and let you decide for yourself whether you want it talked out or not."

"That will answer," said Luigi; "write it."

Wilson wrote something on a slip of paper and handed it to Luigi, who read it to himself and said to Tom—

"Unfold your slip and read it, Mr. Driscoll."

Tom read:

"It was prophesied that I would kill a man. It came true before the year was out."

Tom added, "Great Scott!"

Luigi handed Wilson's paper to Tom, and said—

"Now read this one."

Tom read:

"You have killed someone, but whether man, woman or child, I do not make out."

"Cæsar's ghost!" commented Tom, with astonishment. "It beats anything that was ever heard of! Why, a man's own hand is his deadliest enemy! Just think of that—a man's own hand keeps a record of the deepest and fatalest secrets of his life, and is treacherously ready to expose him to any black-magic stranger that comes along. But what do you let a person look at your hand for, with that awful thing printed in it?"

"Oh," said Luigi, reposefully, "I don't mind it. I killed the man for good reasons, and I don't regret it."

"What were the reasons?"

"Well, he needed killing."

"I'll tell you why he did it, since he won't say himself," said Angelo, warmly. "He did it to save my life, that's what he did it for. So it was a noble act, and not a thing to be hid in the dark."

"So it was, so it was," said Wilson; "to do such a thing to save a brother's life is a great and fine action."

"Now come," said Luigi, "it is very pleasant to hear you say these things, but for unselfishness, or heroism, or magnanimity, the circumstances won't stand scrutiny. You overlook one detail; suppose I hadn't saved Angelo's life, what would have become of mine? If I had let the man kill him, wouldn't he have killed me, too? I saved my own life, you see."

"Yes; that is your way of talking," said Angelo, "but I know you—I don't believe you thought of yourself at all. I keep that weapon yet that Luigi killed the man with, and I'll show it to you sometime. That incident makes it interesting, and it had a history before it came into Luigi's hands which adds to its interest. It was given to Luigi by a great Indian prince, the Gaikowar of Baroda, and it had been in his family two or three centuries. It killed a good many disagreeable people who troubled that hearthstone at one time and another. It isn't much to look at, except that it isn't shaped like other knives, or

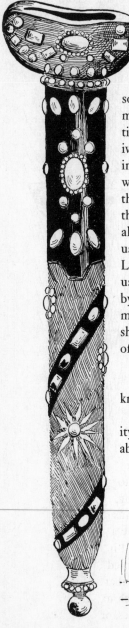

dirks, or whatever it may be called—here, I'll draw it for you." He took a sheet of paper and made a rapid sketch. "There it is—a broad and murderous blade, with edges like a razor for sharpness. The devices engraved on it are the ciphers or names of its long line of possessors—I had Luigi's name added in Roman letters myself with our coat of arms, as you see. You notice what a curious handle the thing has. It is solid ivory, polished like a mirror, and is four or five inches long—round, and as thick as a large man's wrist, with the end squared off flat, for your thumb to rest on; for you grasp it, with your thumb resting on the blunt end—so—and lift it aloft and strike downward. The Gaikowar showed us how the thing was done when he gave it to Luigi, and before that night was ended Luigi had used the knife, and the Gaikowar was a man short by reason of it. The sheath is magnificently ornamented with gems of great value. You will find the sheath more worth looking at than the knife itself, of course."

Tom said to himself—

"It's lucky I came here. I would have sold that knife for a song; I supposed the jewels were glass."

"But go on; don't stop," said Wilson. "Our curiosity is up now, to hear about the homicide. Tell us about that."

"Well, briefly, the knife was to blame for that, all around. A native servant slipped into our room in the palace in the night, to kill us and steal the knife on account of the fortune incrusted on its sheath, without a doubt. Luigi had it under his pillow; we were in bed together. There was a dim night-light burning. I was asleep, but Luigi was awake, and he thought he detected a vague form nearing the bed. He slipped the knife out of the sheath and was ready, and unembarrassed by hampering bed-clothes, for the weather was hot and we hadn't any. Suddenly that native rose at the bedside, and bent over me with his right hand lifted and a dirk in it aimed at my throat; but Luigi grabbed his wrist, pulled him downward, and drove his own knife into the man's neck. That is the whole story."

Wilson and Tom drew deep breaths, and after some general chat about the tragedy, Pudd'nhead said, taking Tom's hand—

"Now, Tom, I've never had a look at your palms, as it happens; perhaps you've got some little questionable privacies that need—hel-lo!"

Tom had snatched away his hand, and was looking a good deal confused.

"Why, he's blushing!" said Luigi.

Tom darted an ugly look at him, and said sharply—

"Well, if I am, it ain't because I'm a murderer!" Luigi's dark face flushed, but before he could speak or move, Tom added with anxious haste: "Oh, I beg a thousand pardons. I didn't mean that; it was out before I thought, and I'm very, very sorry—you must forgive me!"

Wilson came to the rescue, and smoothed things down as well as he could; and in fact was entirely successful as far as the twins were concerned, for they felt sorrier for the affront put upon him by his guest's outburst of ill manners than for the insult offered to Luigi. But the success was not so pronounced with the offender. Tom tried to seem at his ease, and he went through the motions fairly well, but at bottom he felt resentful toward all the three witnesses of his exhibition; in fact, he felt so annoyed at them for having witnessed it and noticed it that he almost forgot to feel annoyed at himself for placing it before them. However, something presently happened which made him almost comfortable, and brought him nearly back to a state of charity and friendliness. This was a little spat between the twins; not much of a spat, but still a spat; and before they got far with it they were in a decided condition of irritation with each other. Tom was charmed; so pleased, indeed, that he cautiously did what he could to increase the irritation while pretending to be actuated by more respectable motives. By his help the fire got warmed up to the blazing-point, and he might have had the happiness of seeing the flames show up, in another moment, but for the interruption of a knock on the door—an interruption which fretted him as much as it gratified Wilson. Wilson opened the door.

The visitor was a good-natured, ignorant, energetic, middle-aged Irishman named John Buckstone, who was a great politician in a small way, and always took a large share in public matters of every sort. One of the town's chief excitements, just now, was over the matter of rum. There was a strong rum party and a strong anti-rum party. Buckstone was training with the rum party, and he had been sent to hunt up the twins and invite them to attend a mass-meeting of that faction. He delivered his errand, and said the clans were already gathering in the big hall over the market-house. Luigi accepted the invitation cordially, Angelo less cordially, since he disliked crowds, and did not drink the powerful intoxicants of America. In fact, he was even a teetotaler sometimes—when it was judicious to be one.

The twins left with Buckstone, and Tom Driscoll joined company with them uninvited.

In the distance one could see a long wavering line of torches drifting down the main street, and could hear the throbbing of the bass drum, the clash of cymbals, the squeaking of a fife or two, and the faint roar of remote hurrahs. The tail-end of this procession was climbing the market-house stairs when the twins arrived in its neighborhood; when they reached the hall it was full of people, torches, smoke, noise and enthusiasm. They were conducted to the platform by Buckstone—Tom Driscoll still following—and were delivered to the chairman in the midst of a prodigious explosion of welcome. When the noise had moderated a little, the chair proposed that "our illustrious guests be at once elected, by complimentary acclamation, to membership in our ever-glorious organization, the paradise of the free and the perdition of the slave."

This eloquent discharge opened the floodgates of enthusiasm again, and the election was carried with thundering unanimity. Then arose a storm of cries:

"Wet them down! Wet them down! Give them a drink!"

Glasses of whisky were handed to the twins. Luigi waved his aloft, then brought it to his lips; but Angelo set his down. There was another storm of cries:

"What's the matter with the other one?" "What is the blond one going back on us for?" "Explain! Explain!"

The chairman inquired, and then reported—

"We have made an unfortunate mistake, gentlemen. I find that the Count Angelo Cappello is opposed to our creed—is a teetotaler, in fact, and was not intending to apply for membership with us. He desires that we reconsider the vote by which he was elected. What is the pleasure of the house?"

There was a general burst of laughter, plentifully accented with whistlings and cat-calls, but the energetic use of the gavel presently restored something like order. Then a man spoke from the crowd, and said that while he was very sorry that the mistake had been made, it would not be possible to rectify it at the present meeting. According to the by-laws it must go over to the next regular meeting for action. He would not offer a motion, as none was required. He desired to apologize to the gentleman in the name of the house, and begged to assure him that as far as it might lie in the power of the Sons of Liberty, his temporary membership in the order would be made pleasant to him.

This speech was received with great applause, mixed with cries of— "That's the talk!" "He's a good fellow, anyway, if he *is* a teetotaler!" "Drink his health!" "Give him a rouser, and no heel-taps!"

Glasses were handed around, and everybody on the platform drank Angelo's health, while the house bellowed forth in song:

> For he's a jolly good fel-low,
> For he's a jolly good fel-low,
> For he's a jolly good fe-el-low,—
> Which nobody can deny.

Tom Driscoll drank. It was his second glass, for he had drunk Angelo's the moment that Angelo had set it down. The two drinks made him very merry—almost idiotically so—and he began to take a most lively and prominent part in the proceedings, particularly in the music and cat-calls and side-remarks.

The chairman was still standing at the front, the twins at his side. The extraordinarily close resemblance of the brothers to each other suggested a witticism to Tom Driscoll, and just as the chairman began a speech he skipped forward and said with an air of tipsy confidence to the audience—

"Boys, I move that he keeps still and lets this human philopena snip you out a speech."

The descriptive aptness of the phrase caught the house, and a mighty burst of laughter followed.

Luigi's southern blood leaped to the boiling-point in a moment under the sharp humiliation of this insult delivered in the presence of four hundred strangers. It was not in the young man's nature to let the matter pass, or to delay the squaring of the account. He took a couple of strides and halted behind the unsuspecting joker. Then he drew back and delivered a kick of such titanic vigor that it lifted Tom clear over the footlights and landed him on the heads of the front row of the Sons of Liberty.

Even a sober person does not like to have a human being emptied on him when he is not doing any harm; a person who is not sober cannot endure such an attention at all. The nest of Sons of Liberty that Driscoll landed in had not a sober bird in it; in fact there was probably not an entirely sober one in the auditorium. Driscoll was promptly and indignantly flung on to the heads of Sons in the next row, and these Sons passed him on toward the rear, and then immediately began to pummel the front-row Sons who had passed him to them. This course was strictly followed by bench after bench as Driscoll traveled in his tumultuous and airy flight toward the door; so he left behind him an ever lengthening wake of raging and plunging and fighting and swearing humanity. Down went group after group of torches, and presently above the deafening clatter of the gavel, roar of angry voices, and crash of succumbing benches, rose the paralyzing cry of "FIRE!"

The fighting ceased instantly; the cursing ceased; for one distinctly defined moment there was a dead hush, a motionless calm, where the tempest had been; then with one impulse the multitude awoke to life and energy again, and went surging and struggling and swaying, this way and that, its outer edges melting away through windows and doors and gradually lessening the pressure and relieving the mass.

The fire-boys were never on hand so suddenly before; for there was no distance to go, this time, their quarters being in the rear end of the market-house. There was an engine company and a hook-and-ladder company. Half of each was composed of rummies and the other half of anti-rummies, after the moral and political share-and-share-alike fashion of the frontier town of the period. Enough anti-rummies were loafing in quarters to man the engine and the ladders. In two minutes they had their red shirts and helmets on—they never stirred officially in unofficial costume—and as the mass meeting overhead smashed through the long row of windows and poured out upon the roof of the arcade, the deliverers were ready for them with a powerful stream of water which washed some of them off the roof and nearly drowned the rest. But water was preferable to fire, and still the stampede from the windows continued, and still the pitiless drenchings assailed it until the building was empty; then the fire-boys mounted to the hall and flooded it with water enough to annihilate forty times as much fire as there was there; for a village fire-company does not often get a chance to show off, and so when it does get a chance it makes the most of it. Such citizens of that village as were of a thoughtful and judicious temperament did not insure against fire; they insured against the fire-company.

Chapter XII

Courage is resistance to fear, mastery of fear—not absence of fear. Except a creature be part coward it is not a compliment to say it is brave; it is merely a loose misapplication of the word. Consider the flea!—incomparably the bravest of all the creatures of God, if ignorance of fear were courage. Whether you are asleep or awake he will attack you, caring nothing for the fact that in bulk and strength you are to him as are the massed armies of the earth to a sucking child; he lives both day and night and all days and nights in the very lap of peril and the immediate presence of death, and yet is no more afraid than is the man who walks the streets of a city that was threatened by an earthquake ten centuries before. When we speak of Clive, Nelson, and Putnam as men who "didn't know what fear was," we ought always to add the flea—and put him at the head of the procession.

PUDD'NHEAD WILSON'S CALENDAR

Judge Driscoll was in bed and asleep by ten o'clock on Friday night, and he was up and gone a-fishing before daylight in the morning with his friend Pembroke Howard. These two had been boys together in Virginia when that State still ranked

as the chief and most imposing member of the Union, and they still coupled the proud and affectionate adjective "old" with her name when they spoke of her. In Missouri a recognized superiority attached to any person who hailed from Old Virginia; and this superiority was exalted to supremacy when a person of such nativity could also prove descent from the First Families of that great commonwealth. The Howards and Driscolls were of this aristocracy. In their eyes it was a nobility. It had its unwritten laws, and they were as clearly defined and as strict as any that could be found among the printed statutes of the land. The F.F.V. was born a gentleman; his highest duty in life was to watch over that great inheritance and keep it unsmirched. He must keep his honor spotless. Those laws were his chart; his course was marked out on it; if he swerved from it by so much as half a point of the compass it meant shipwreck to his honor; that is to say, degradation from his rank as a gentleman. These laws required certain things of him which his religion might forbid: then his religion must yield—the laws could not be relaxed to accommodate religions or anything else. Honor stood first; and the laws defined what it was and wherein it differed in certain details from honor as defined by church creeds and by the social laws and customs of some of the minor divisions of the globe that had got crowded out when the sacred boundaries of Virginia were staked out.

If Judge Driscoll was the recognized first citizen of Dawson's Landing, Pembroke Howard was easily its recognized second citizen. He was called "the great lawyer"—an earned title. He and Driscoll were of the same age—a year or two past sixty.

Although Driscoll was a free-thinker and Howard a strong and determined Presbyterian, their warm intimacy suffered no impairment in consequence. They were men whose opinions were their own property and not subject to revision and amendment, suggestion or criticism, by anybody, even their friends.

The day's fishing finished, they came floating down stream in their skiff, talking national politics and other high matters, and presently met a skiff coming up from town, with a man in it who said:

"I reckon you know one of the new twins gave your nephew a kicking last night, Judge?"

"Did *what?*"

"Gave him a kicking."

The old Judge's lips paled, and his eyes began to flame. He choked with anger for a moment, then he got out what he was trying to say—

"Well—well—go on! give me the details."

The man did it. At the finish the Judge was silent a minute, turning over in his mind the shameful picture of Tom's flight over the foot-lights; then he said, as if musing aloud—"H'm—I don't understand it. I was asleep at home. He didn't wake me. Thought he was competent to manage his affair without my help, I reckon." His face lit up with pride and pleasure at that thought, and he said with a cheery complacency, "I like that—it's the true old blood—hey, Pembroke?"

Howard smiled an iron smile, and nodded his head approvingly. Then the news-bringer spoke again—

"But Tom beat the twin on the trial."

The Judge looked at the man wonderingly, and said—

"The trial? What trial?"

"Why, Tom had him up before Judge Robinson for assault and battery."

The old man shrank suddenly together like one who has received a death-stroke. Howard sprang for him as he sank forward in a swoon, and took him in his arms, and bedded him on his back in the boat. He sprinkled water in his face, and said to the startled visitor—

"Go, now—don't let him come to and find you here. You see what an effect your heedless speech has had; you ought to have been more considerate than to blurt out such a cruel piece of slander as that."

"I'm right down sorry I did it now, Mr. Howard, and I wouldn't have done it if I had thought: but it ain't slander; it's perfectly true, just as I told him."

He rowed away. Presently the old Judge came out of his faint and looked up piteously into the sympathetic face that was bent over him.

"Say it ain't true, Pembroke; tell me it ain't true!" he said in a weak voice.

There was nothing weak in the deep organtones that responded—

"You know it's a lie as well as I do, old friend. He is of the best blood of the Old Dominion."

"God bless you for saying it!" said the old gentleman, fervently. "Ah, Pembroke, it was such a blow!"

Howard stayed by his friend, and saw him home, and entered the house with him. It was dark, and past supper-time, but the Judge was not thinking of supper; he was eager to hear the slander refuted from headquarters, and as eager to have Howard hear it, too. Tom was sent for, and he came immediately. He was bruised and lame, and was not a happy-looking object. His uncle made him sit down, and said—

"We have been hearing about your adventure, Tom, with a handsome lie added to it for embellishment. Now pulverize that lie to dust! What measures have you taken? How does the thing stand?"

Tom answered guilelessly: "It don't stand at all; it's all over. I had him up in court and beat him. Pudd'nhead Wilson defended him—first case he ever had, and lost it. The judge fined the miserable hound five dollars for the assault."

Howard and the Judge sprang to their feet with the opening sentence—why, neither knew; then they stood gazing vacantly at each other. Howard stood a moment, then sat mournfully down without saying anything. The Judge's wrath began to kindle, and he burst out—

"You cur! You scum! You vermin! Do you mean to tell me that blood of my race has suffered a blow and crawled to a court of law about it? Answer me!"

Tom's head drooped, and he answered with an eloquent silence. His uncle stared at him with a mixed expression of amazement and shame and incredulity that was sorrowful to see. At last he said—

"Which of the twins was it?"

"Count Luigi."

"You have challenged him?"

"N—no," hesitated Tom, turning pale.

"You will challenge him to-night. Howard will carry it."

Tom began to turn sick, and to show it. He turned his hat round and round in his hand, his uncle glowering blacker and blacker upon him as the heavy seconds drifted by; then at last he began to stammer, and said piteously—

"Oh, please don't ask me to do it, uncle! He is a murderous devil— I never could—I—I'm afraid of him!"

Old Driscoll's mouth opened and closed three times before he could get it to perform its office; then he stormed out—

"A coward in my family! A Driscoll a coward! Oh, what have I done to deserve this infamy!" He tottered to his secretary in the corner repeating that lament again and again in heartbreaking tones, and got out of a drawer a paper, which he slowly tore to bits, scattering the bits absently in his track as he walked up and down the room, still grieving and lamenting. At last he said—

"There it is, shreds and fragments once more—my will. Once more you have forced me to disinherit you, you base son of a most noble father! Leave my sight! Go—before I spit on you!"

The young man did not tarry. Then the Judge turned to Howard:

"You will be my second, old friend?"

"Of course."

"There is pen and paper. Draft the cartel, and lose no time."

"The Count shall have it in his hands in fifteen minutes," said Howard.

Tom was very heavy-hearted. His appetite was gone with his property and his self-respect. He went out the back way and wandered down the obscure lane grieving, and wondering if any course of future conduct, however discreet and carefully perfected and watched over, could win back his uncle's favor and persuade him to reconstruct once more that generous will which had just gone to ruin before his eyes. He finally concluded that it could. He said to himself that he had accomplished this sort of triumph once already, and that what had been done once could be done again. He would set about it. He would bend every energy to the task, and he would score that triumph once more, cost what it might to his convenience, limit as it might his frivolous and liberty-loving life.

"To begin," he said to himself, "I'll square up with the proceeds of my raid, and then gambling has got to be stopped—and stopped short

off. It's the worst vice I've got—from my standpoint, anyway, because it's the one he can most easily find out, through the impatience of my creditors. He thought it expensive to have to pay two hundred dollars to them for me once. Expensive—*that!* Why, it cost me the whole of his fortune—but of course he never thought of that; some people can't think of any but their own side of a case. If he had known how deep I am in, now, the will would have gone to pot without waiting for a duel to help. Three hundred dollars! It's a pile! But he'll never hear of it, I'm thankful to say. The minute I've cleared it off, I'm safe; and I'll never touch a card again. Anyway, I won't while he lives, I make oath to that. I'm entering on my last reform—I know it—yes, and I'll win; but after that, if I ever slip again I'm gone."

CHAPTER XIII

When I reflect upon the number of disagreeable people who I know
have gone to a better world, I am moved to lead a different life.

PUDD'NHEAD WILSON'S CALENDAR

October. This is one of the peculiarly dangerous months to speculate in
stocks in. The others are July, January, September, April, November,
May, March, June, December, August, and February.

PUDD'NHEAD WILSON'S CALENDAR

Thus mournfully communing with himself, Tom
moped along the lane past Pudd'nhead Wilson's
house, and still on and on between fences inclosing vacant country on each hand till he neared
the haunted house, then he came moping back
again, with many sighs and heavy with trouble.
He sorely wanted cheerful company. Rowena!
His heart gave a bound at the thought, but the
next thought quieted it—the detested twins
would be there.

He was on the inhab-
ited side of Wilson's
house, and now as he
approached it he no-
ticed that the sitting-
room was lighted.
This would do; oth-
ers made him feel
unwelcome some-
times, but Wilson
never failed in
courtesy toward

him, and a kindly courtesy does at least save one's feelings, even if it is not professing to stand for a welcome. Wilson heard footsteps at his threshold, then the clearing of a throat.

"It's that fickle-tempered, dissipated young goose—poor devil, he finds friends pretty scarce to-day, likely, after the disgrace of carrying a personal-assault case into a law-court."

A dejected knock. "Come in!"

Tom entered, and drooped into a chair, without saying anything. Wilson said kindly—

"Why, my boy, you look desolate. Don't take it so hard. Try and forget you have been kicked."

"Oh, dear," said Tom, wretchedly, "it's not that, Pudd'nhead—it's not that. It's a thousand times worse than that—oh, yes, a million times worse."

"Why, Tom, what do you mean? Has Rowena—"

"Flung me? No, but the old man has."

Wilson said to himself, "Aha!" and thought of the mysterious girl in the bedroom. "The Driscolls have been making discoveries!" Then he said aloud, gravely:

"Tom, there are some kinds of dissipation which——"

"Oh, shucks, this hasn't got anything to do with dissipation. He wanted me to challenge that derned Italian savage, and I wouldn't do it."

"Yes, of course he would do that," said Wilson in a meditative matter-of-course way, "but the thing that puzzled me was, why he didn't look to that last night, for one thing, and why he let you carry such a matter into a court of law at all, either before the duel or after it. It's no place for it. It was not like him. I couldn't understand it. How did it happen?"

"It happened because he didn't know anything about it. He was asleep when I got home last night."

"And you didn't wake him? Tom, is that possible?"

Tom was not getting much comfort here. He fidgeted a moment, then said:

"I didn't choose to tell him—that's all. He was going a-fishing before dawn, with Pembroke Howard, and if I got the twins into the common calaboose—and I thought sure I could—I never dreamed of their slipping out on a paltry fine for such an outrageous offense— well, once in the calaboose they would be disgraced, and uncle wouldn't want any duels with that sort of characters, and wouldn't allow any."

"Tom, I am ashamed of you! I don't see how you could treat your good old uncle so. I am a better friend of his than you are; for if I had known the circumstances I would have kept that case out of court until I got word to him and let him have a gentleman's chance."

"You would?" exclaimed Tom, with lively surprise. "And it your first case! And you know perfectly well there never would have *been* any case if he had got that chance, don't you? And you'd have finished your days a pauper nobody, instead of being an actually launched and recognized lawyer to-day. And you would really have done that, would you?"

"Certainly."

Tom looked at him a moment or two, then shook his head sorrowfully and said—

"I believe you—upon my word I do. I don't know why I do, but I do. Pudd'nhead Wilson, I think you're the biggest fool I ever saw."

"Thank you."

"Don't mention it."

"Well, he has been requiring you to fight the Italian and you have refused. You degenerate remnant of an honorable line! I'm thoroughly ashamed of you, Tom!"

"Oh, that's nothing! I don't care for anything, now that the will's torn up again."

"Tom, tell me squarely—didn't he find any fault with you for anything but those two things—carrying the case into court and refusing to fight?"

He watched the young fellow's face narrowly, but it was entirely reposeful, and so also was the voice that answered:

"No, he didn't find any other fault with me. If he had had any to find, he would have begun yesterday, for he was just in the humor for it. He drove that jack-pair around town and showed them the sights, and when he came home he couldn't find his father's old silver watch that don't keep time and he thinks so much of, and couldn't remember what he did with it three or four days ago when he saw it last, and so when I arrived he was all in a sweat about it, and when I suggested that it probably wasn't lost but stolen, it put him in a regular passion and he said I was a fool—which convinced me, without any trouble, that that was just what he was afraid *had* happened, himself, but did not want to believe it, because lost things stand a better chance of being found again than stolen ones."

"Whe-ew!" whistled Wilson; "score another on the list."

"Another what?"

"Another theft!"

"Theft?"

"Yes, theft. That watch isn't lost, it's stolen. There's been another raid on the town—and just the same old mysterious sort of thing that has happened once before, as you remember."

"You don't mean it!"

"It's as sure as you are born! Have you missed anything yourself?"

"No. That is, I did miss a silver pencil-case that Aunt Mary Pratt gave me last birthday——"

"You'll find it stolen—that's what you'll find."

"No, I sha'n't; for when I suggested theft about the watch and got such a rap, I went and examined my room, and the pencil-case was missing, but it was only mislaid, and I found it again."

"You are sure you missed nothing else?"

"Well, nothing of consequence. I missed a small plain gold ring worth two or three dollars, but that will turn up. I'll look again."

"In my opinion you'll not find it. There's been a raid, I tell you, Come *in!*"

Mr. Justice Robinson entered, followed by Buckstone and the town-constable, Jim Blake. They sat down, and after some wandering and aimless weather-conversation Wilson said—

"By the way, we've just added another to the list of thefts, maybe two. Judge Driscoll's old silver watch is gone, and Tom here has missed a gold ring."

"Well, it is a bad business," said the Justice, "and gets worse the further it goes. The Hankses, the Dobsons, the Pilligrews, the Ortons, the Grangers, the Hales, the Fullers, the Holcombs, in fact everybody that lives around about Patsy Cooper's has been robbed of little things like trinkets and teaspoons and such-like small valuables that are easily carried off. It's perfectly plain that the thief took advantage of the reception at Patsy Cooper's when all the neighbors were in her house and all their niggers hanging around her fence for a look at the show, to raid the vacant houses undisturbed. Patsy is miserable about it; miserable on account of the neighbors, and particularly miserable on account of her foreigners, of course; so miserable on their account that she hasn't any room to worry about her own little losses."

"It's the same old raider," said Wilson. "I suppose there isn't any doubt about that."

"Constable Blake doesn't think so."

"No, you're wrong there," said Blake; "the other times it was a man; there was plenty of signs of that, as we know, in the profession, though we never got hands on him; but this time it's a woman."

Wilson thought of the mysterious girl straight off. She was always in his mind now. But she failed him again. Blake continued:

"She's a stoop-shouldered old woman with a covered basket on her arm, in a black veil, dressed in mourning. I saw her going aboard the ferry-boat yesterday. Lives in Illinois, I reckon; but I don't care where she lives, I'm going to get her—she can make herself sure of that."

"What makes you think she's the thief?"

"Well, there ain't any other, for one thing; and for another, some of the nigger draymen that happened to be driving along saw her coming out of or going into houses, and told me so—and it just happens that they was *robbed* houses, every time."

It was granted that this was plenty good enough circumstantial evidence. A pensive silence followed, which lasted some moments, then Wilson said—

"There's one good thing, anyway. She can't either pawn or sell Count Luigi's costly Indian dagger."

"My!" said Tom, "is *that* gone?"

"Yes."

"Well, that was a haul! But why can't she pawn it or sell it?"

"Because when the twins went home from the Sons of Liberty meeting last night, news of the raid was sifting in from everywhere, and Aunt Patsy was in distress to know if they had lost anything. They found that the dagger was gone, and they notified the police and pawnbrokers everywhere. It was a great haul, yes, but the old woman won't get anything out of it, because she'll get caught."

"Did they offer a reward?" asked Buckstone.

"Yes; five hundred dollars for the knife, and five hundred more for the thief."

"What a leather-headed idea!" exclaimed the constable. "The thief da'sn't go near them, nor send anybody. Whoever goes is going to get himself nabbed, for there ain't any pawnbroker that's going to lose the chance to——"

If anybody had noticed Tom's face at that time, the gray-green color of it might have provoked curiosity; but nobody did. He said to himself: "I'm gone! I never can square up; the rest of the plunder won't pawn or sell for half of the bill. Oh, I know it—I'm gone, I'm gone—and this time it's for good. Oh, this is awful—I don't know what to do, nor which way to turn!"

"Softly, softly," said Wilson to Blake. "I planned their scheme for them at midnight last night, and it was all finished up ship-shape by two this morning. They'll get their dagger back, and then I'll explain to you how the thing was done."

There were strong signs of a general curiosity, and Buckstone said—

"Well, you have whetted us up pretty sharp, Wilson, and I'm free to say that if you don't mind telling us in confidence——"

"Oh, I'd as soon tell as not, Buckstone, but as long as the twins and I agreed to say nothing about it, we must let it stand so. But you can take my word for it you won't be kept waiting three days. Somebody will apply for that reward pretty promptly, and I'll show you the thief and the dagger both very soon afterward."

The constable was disappointed, and also perplexed. He said—

"It may all be—yes, and I hope it will, but I'm blamed if I can see my way through it. It's too many for yours truly."

The subject seemed about talked out. Nobody seemed to have anything further to offer. After a silence the justice of the peace informed Wilson that he and Buckstone and the constable had come as a committee, on the part of the Democratic party, to ask him to run for mayor—for the little town was about to become a city and the first charter election was approaching. It was the first attention which Wilson had ever received at the hands of any party; it was a sufficiently humble one, but it was a recognition of his début into the town's life and activities at last; it was a step upward, and he was deeply gratified. He accepted, and the committee departed, followed by young Tom.

Chapter XIV

The true Southern watermelon is a boon apart, and not to be mentioned with commoner things. It is chief of this world's luxuries, king by the grace of God over all the fruits of the earth. When one has tasted it, he knows what the angels eat. It was not a Southern watermelon that Eve took: we know it because she repented.

Pudd'nhead Wilson's Calendar

About the time that Wilson was bowing the committee out, Pembroke Howard was entering the next house to report. He found the old Judge sitting grim and straight in his chair, waiting.

"Well, Howard—the news?"

"The best in the world."

"Accepts, does he?" and the light of battle gleamed joyously in the Judge's eye.

"Accepts? Why, he jumped at it."

"Did, did he? Now that's fine—that's very fine. I like that. When is it to be?"

"Now! Straight off! To-night! An admirable fellow—admirable!"

"Admirable? He's a darling! Why, it's an honor as well as a pleasure to stand up before such a man. Come—off with you! Go and arrange everything—and give him my heartiest compliments. A rare fellow, indeed; an admirable fellow, as you have said!"

Howard hurried away, saying—

"I'll have him in the vacant stretch between Wilson's and the haunted house within the hour, and I'll bring my own pistols."

Judge Driscoll began to walk the floor in a state of pleased excitement; but presently he stopped, and began to think—began to think of Tom. Twice he moved toward the secretary, and twice he turned away again; but finally he said—

"This may be my last night in the world— I must not take the chance. He is worthless and unworthy, but it is largely my fault. He was intrusted to me by my brother on his dying bed, and I have indulged him to his hurt, instead of training him up severely, and making a man of him. I have violated my trust, and I must not add the sin of desertion to that. I have forgiven him once already, and would subject him to a long and hard trial before forgiving him again, if I could live; but I must not run that risk. No, I must restore the will. But if I survive the duel, I will hide it away, and he will not know, and I will not tell him until he reforms, and I see that his reformation is going to be permanent."

He re-drew the will, and his ostensible nephew was heir to a fortune again. As he was finishing his task, Tom, wearied with another brooding tramp, entered the house and went tiptoeing past the sitting-room door. He glanced in, and hurried on, for the sight of his uncle had nothing but terrors for him to-night. But his uncle was writing! That was unusual at this late hour. What could he be writing? A chill of anxiety settled down upon Tom's heart. Did that writing concern him? He was afraid so. He reflected that when ill luck begins, it does not come in sprinkles, but in showers. He said he would get a glimpse of that document or know the reason why. He heard some one coming, and stepped out of sight and hearing. It was Pembroke Howard. What could be hatching?

Howard said, with great satisfaction:

"Everything's right and ready. He's gone to the battle-ground with his second and the surgeon—also with his brother. I've arranged it all with Wilson—Wilson's his second. We are to have three shots apiece."

"Good! How is the moon?"

"Bright as day, nearly. Perfect, for the distance—fifteen yards. No wind—not a breath; hot and still."

"All good; all first-rate. Here, Pembroke, read this, and witness it."

Pembroke read and witnessed the will, then gave the old man's hand a hearty shake and said:

"Now that's right, York—but I knew you would do it. You couldn't leave that poor chap to fight along without means or profession, with certain defeat before him, and I knew you wouldn't, for his father's sake if not for his own."

"For his dead father's sake I couldn't, I know; for poor Percy—but you know what Percy was to me. But mind—Tom is not to know of this unless I fall to-night."

"I understand. I'll keep the secret."

The Judge put the will away, and the two started for the battle-ground. In another minute the will was in Tom's hands. His misery vanished, his feelings underwent a tremendous revulsion. He put the will carefully back in its place, and spread his mouth and swung his hat once, twice, three times around his head, in imitation of three rousing huzzas, no sound issuing from his lips. He fell to communing with himself excitedly and joyously, but every now and then he let off another volley of dumb hurrahs.

He said to himself: "I've got the fortune again, but I'll not let on that I know about it. And this time I'm going to hang on to it. I take no more risks. I'll gamble no more, I'll drink no more, because—well, because I'll not go where there is any of that sort of thing going on, again. It's the sure way, and the only sure way; I might have thought of that sooner—well, yes, if I had wanted to. But now—dear me, I've had a scare this time, and I'll take no more chances. Not a single chance more. Land! I persuaded myself this evening that I could fetch him around without any great amount of effort, but I've been getting more and more heavy-hearted and doubtful straight along, ever since. If he tells me about this thing, all right; but if he doesn't, I sha'n't let on. I—well, I'd like to tell Pudd'nhead Wilson, but—no, I'll think about that; perhaps I won't." He whirled off another dead huzza, and said, "I'm reformed, and this time I'll stay so, sure!"

He was about to close with a final grand silent demonstration, when he suddenly recollected that Wilson had put it out of his power to pawn or sell the Indian knife, and that he was once more in awful peril of exposure by his creditors for that reason. His joy collapsed utterly, and he turned away and moped toward the door moaning and lamenting over the bitterness of his luck. He dragged himself up-stairs, and brooded in his room a long time disconsolate and forlorn, with Luigi's Indian knife for a text. At last he sighed and said:

"When I supposed these stones were glass and this ivory bone, the thing hadn't any interest for me because it hadn't any value, and couldn't help me out of my trouble. But now—why, now it is full of interest; yes, and of a sort to break a body's heart. It's a bag of gold that has turned to dirt and ashes in my hands. It could save me, and save me so easily, and yet I've got to go to ruin. It's like drowning with a life-preserver in my reach. All the hard luck comes to me, and all the good luck goes to other people—Pudd'nhead Wilson, for instance; even his career has got a sort of a little start at last, and what has he done to deserve it, I should like to know? Yes, he has opened his own road, but he isn't content with that, but must block mine. It's a sordid, selfish world, and I wish I was out of it." He allowed the light of the candle to play upon the jewels of the sheath, but the flashings and sparklings had no charm for his eye; they were only just so many pangs to his heart. "I must not say anything to Roxy about this thing," he said, "she is too daring. She would be for digging these stones out and selling them, and then—why, she would be arrested and the stones traced, and then—" The thought made him quake, and he hid the knife away, trembling all over and glancing furtively about, like a criminal who fancies that the accuser is already at hand.

Should he try to sleep? Oh, no, sleep was not for him; his trouble was too haunting, too afflicting for that. He must have somebody to mourn with. He would carry his despair to Roxy.

He had heard several distant gunshots, but that sort of thing was not uncommon, and they had made no impression upon him. He went out at the back door, and turned westward. He passed Wilson's house and proceeded along the lane, and presently saw several figures approaching Wilson's place through the vacant lots. These were the duelists returning from the fight; he thought he recognized them, but as he had no desire for white people's company, he stooped down behind the fence until they were out of his way.

Roxy was feeling fine. She said:

"Whah was you, child? Warn't you in it?"

"In what?"

"In de duel."

"Duel? Has there been a duel?"

"'Co'se dey has. De ole Jedge has be'n havin' a duel wid one o' dem twins."

"Great Scott!" Then he added to himself: "That's what made him re-make the will; he thought he might get killed, and it softened him toward me. And that's what he and Howard were so busy about.... Oh dear, if the twin had only killed him, I should be out of my——"

"What is you mumblin' bout, Chambers? Whah was you? Didn't you know dey was gwyne to be a duel?"

"No, I didn't. The old man tried to get me to fight one with Count Luigi, but he didn't succeed, so I reckon he concluded to patch up the family honor himself."

He laughed at the idea, and went rambling on with a detailed account of his talk with the Judge, and how shocked and ashamed the Judge was to find that he had a coward in his family. He glanced up at last, and got a shock himself. Roxana's bosom was heaving with suppressed passion, and she was glowering down upon him with measureless contempt written in her face.

"En you refuse' to fight a man dat kicked you, 'stid o' jumpin' at de chance! En you ain't got no mo' feelin' den to come en tell me, dat fetched sich a po' low-down ornery rabbit into de worl'! Pah! it make me sick! It's de nigger in you, dat's what it is. Thirty-one parts o' you is white, en on'y one part nigger, en dat po' little one part is yo' *soul*. Tain't wuth savin'; tain't wuth totin' out on a shovel en throwin' in de gutter. You has disgraced yo' birth. What would yo' pa think o' you? It's enough to make him turn in his grave."

The last three sentences stung Tom into a fury, and he said to himself that if his father were only alive and in reach of assassination his mother would soon find that he had a very clear notion of the size of his indebtedness to that man, and was willing to pay it up in full, and would do it too, even at risk of his life; but he kept his thought to himself; that was safest in his mother's present state.

"Whatever has come o' yo' Essex blood? Dat's what I can't understan'. En it ain't on'y jist Essex blood dat's in you, not by a long sight—'deed it ain't! My great-great-great-gran'father en yo' great-great-great-great-gran'father was Ole Cap'n John Smith, de highest blood dat Ole Virginny ever turned out, en *his* great-great-gran'mother or somers along back dah, was Pocahontas de Injun queen, en her husbun' was a nigger king outen Africa—en yit here you is, a slinkin' outen a duel en disgracin' our whole line like a ornery lowdown hound! Yes, it's de nigger in you!"

She sat down on her candle-box and fell into a reverie. Tom did not disturb her; he sometimes lacked prudence, but it was not in circumstances of this kind. Roxana's storm went gradually down, but it died hard, and even when it seemed to be quite gone, it would now and then break out in a distant rumble, so to speak, in the form of muttered ejaculations. One of these was, "Ain't nigger enough in him to show in his finger-nails, en dat takes mighty little—yit dey's enough to paint his soul."

Presently she muttered. "Yassir, enough to paint a whole thimbleful of 'em." At last her ramblings ceased altogether, and her countenance began to clear—a welcome sign to Tom, who had learned her moods, and knew she was on the threshold of good-humor, now. He noticed that from time to time she unconsciously carried her finger to the end of her nose. He looked closer and said:

"Why, mammy, the end of your nose is skinned. How did that come?"

She sent out the sort of whole-hearted peal of laughter which God has vouchsafed in its perfection to none but the happy angels in heaven and the bruised and broken black slave on the earth, and said:

"Dad fetch dat duel, I be'n in it myself."

"Gracious! did a bullet do that?"

"Yassir, you bet it did!"

"Well, I declare! Why, how did that happen?"

"Happened dis-away. I 'uz a-sett'n' here

kinder dozin' in de dark, en *che-bang!* goes a gun, right out dah. I skips along out towards t'other end o' de house to see what's gwyne on, en stops by de ole winder on de side towards Pudd'nhead Wilson's house dat ain't got no sash in it,—but dey ain't none of 'em got any sashes, fur as dat's concerned,—en I stood dah in de dark en look out, en dar in de moonlight, right down under me 'uz one o' de twins a-cussin'—not much, but jist a-cussin' soft—it 'uz de brown one dat 'uz cussin', 'ca'se he 'uz hit in de shoulder. En Doctor Claypool he 'uz a-workin' at him, en Pudd'nhead Wilson he 'uz a-he'pin', en ole Jedge Driscoll en Pem Howard 'uz a-standin' out yonder a little piece waitin' for 'em to git ready agin. En treckly dey squared off en give de word, en *bang-bang* went de pistols, en de twin he say, 'Ouch!'—hit him on de han' dis time,—en I hear dat same bullet go *spat!* ag'in, de logs under de winder; en de nex' time dey shoot, de twin say, 'Ouch!' ag'in, en I done it too, 'ca'se de bullet glance' on his cheek-bone en skip up here en glance on de side o' de winder en whiz right acrost my face en tuck de hide off'n my nose—why, if I'd 'a 'be'n jist a inch or a inch en a half furder 't would 'a' tuck de whole nose en disfiggered me. Here's de bullet; I hunted her up."

"Did you stand there all the time?"

"Dat's a question to ask, ain't it! What else would I do? Does I git a chance to see a duel every day?"

"Why, you were right in range! Weren't you afraid?"

The woman gave a sniff of scorn.

"'Fraid! De Smith-Pocahontases ain't 'fraid o' nothin', let alone bullets."

"They've got pluck enough, I suppose; what they lack is judgment. *I* wouldn't have stood there."

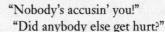

"Nobody's accusin' you!"

"Did anybody else get hurt?"

"Yes, we all got hit 'cep' de blon' twin en de doctor en de seconds. De Jedge didn't git hurt, but I hear Pudd'n-head say de bullet snip some o' his ha'r off."

"'George!" said Tom to himself, "to come so near being out of my trouble, and miss it by an inch. Oh dear, dear, he will live to find me out and sell me to some nigger-trader yet—yes, and he would do it in a minute." Then he said aloud, in a grave tone—

"Mother, we are in an awful fix."

Roxana caught her breath with a spasm, and said—

"Chile! What you hit a body so sudden for, like dat? What's be'n en gone en happen'?"

"Well, there's one thing I didn't tell you. When I wouldn't fight, he tore up the will again, and—

Roxana's face turned a dead white, and she said—

"Now you's *done!*—done forever! Dat's de end. Bofe un us is gwyne to starve to—"

"Wait and hear me through, can't you! I reckon that when he resolved to fight, himself, he thought he might get killed and not have a chance to forgive me any more in this life, so he made the will again, and I've seen it, and it's all right. But——"

"Oh, thank goodness, den we's safe ag'in!—safe! en so what did you want to come here en talk sich dreadful——"

"Hold *on,* I tell you, and let me finish. The swag I gathered won't half square me up, and the first thing we know, my creditors—well, you know what'll happen."

Roxana dropped her chin, and told her son to leave her alone—she must think this matter out. Presently she said impressively:

"You got to go mighty keerful now, I tell you! En here's what you got to do. He didn't git killed, en if you gives him de least reason, he'll bust de will ag'in, en dat's de *las'* time, now you hear me! So—you's got to show him what you kin do in de nex' few days. You's got to be pison good, en let him see it; you got to do everything dat'll make him b'lieve in you, en you got to sweeten aroun' ole Aunt Pratt, too,—she's pow'-ful strong wid de Jedge, en de bes' frien' you got. Nex', you'll go 'long away to Sent Louis, en dat'll *keep* him in yo' favor. Den you go en make a bargain wid dem people. You tell 'em he ain't gwyne to live long—en dat's de fac', too,—en tell 'em you'll pay 'em intrust, en big intrust, too,—ten per—what you call it?"

"Ten per cent a month?"

"Dat's it. Den you take and sell yo' truck aroun', a little at a time, en pay de intrust. How long will it las'?"

"I think there's enough to pay the interest five or six months."

"Den you's all right. If he don't die in six months, dat don't make no diff'rence—Providence'll provide. You's gwyne to be safe—if you be-haves." She bent an austere eye on him and added, "En you *is* gwyne to behave—does you know dat?"

He laughed and said he was going to try, anyway. She did not un-bend. She said gravely:

"Tryin' ain't de thing. You's gwyne to *do* it. You ain't gwyne to steal a pin—'ca'se it ain't safe no mo'; en you ain't gwyne into no bad com-p'ny—not even once, you understand; en you ain't gwyne to drink a drop—nary single drop; en you ain't gwyne to gamble one single gam-ble—not one! Dis ain't what you's gwyne to *try* to do, it's what you's gwyne to *do.* En I'll tell you how I knows it. Dis is how. I's gwyne to foller along to Sent Louis my own self; en you's gwyne to come to me every day o' yo' life, en I'll look you over; en if you fails in one single one o' dem things—jist *one*—I take my oath I'll come straight down to dis town en tell de Jedge you's a nigger en a slave—en *prove* it!" She paused to let her words sink home. Then she added, "Chambers, does you b'lieve me when I says dat?"

Tom was sober enough now. There was no levity in his voice when he answered:

"Yes, mother, I know, now, that I am reformed—and permanently. Permanently—and beyond the reach of any human temptation.

"Den g' long home en begin!"

CHAPTER XV

Nothing so needs reforming as other people's habits.
—PUDD'NHEAD WILSON'S CALENDAR

Behold, the fool saith, "Put not all thine eggs in the one basket"—which is but a manner of saying, "Scatter your money and your attention;" but the wise man saith, "Put all your eggs in the one basket and—WATCH THAT BASKET."
—PUDD'NHEAD WILSON'S CALENDAR

What a time of it Dawson's Landing was having! All its life it had been asleep, but now it hardly got a chance for a nod, so swiftly did big events and crashing surprises come along in one another's wake: Friday morning, first glimpse of Real Nobility, also grand reception at Aunt Patsy Cooper's, also great robber-raid; Friday evening, dramatic kicking of the heir of the chief citizen in presence of four hundred people; Saturday morning, emergence as practising lawyer of the long-submerged Pudd'nhead Wilson; Saturday night, duel between chief citizen and titled stranger.

The people took more pride in the duel than in

all the other events put together, perhaps. It was a glory to their town to have such a thing happen there. In their eyes the principals had reached the summit of human honor. Everybody paid homage to their names; their praises were in all mouths. Even the duelists' subordinates came in for a handsome share of the public approbation: wherefore Pudd'nhead Wilson was suddenly become a man of consequence. When asked to run for the mayoralty Saturday night he was risking defeat, but Sunday morning found him a made man and his success assured.

The twins were prodigiously great, now; the town took them to its bosom with enthusiasm. Day after day, and night after night, they went dining and visiting from house to house, making friends, enlarging and solidifying their popularity, and charming and surprising all with their musical prodigies, and now and then heightening the effects with samples of what they could do in other directions, out of their stock of rare and curious accomplishments. They were so pleased that they gave the regulation thirty days' notice, the required preparation for citizenship, and resolved to finish their days in this pleasant place. That was the climax. The delighted community rose as one man and applauded; and when the twins were asked to stand for seats in the forthcoming aldermanic board, and consented, the public contentment was rounded and complete.

Tom Driscoll was not happy over these things; they sunk deep, and hurt all the way down. He hated the one twin for kicking him, and the other one for being the kicker's brother.

Now and then the people wondered why nothing was heard of the raider, or of the stolen knife or the other plunder, but nobody was able to throw any light on that matter. Nearly a week had drifted by, and still the thing remained a vexed mystery.

On Saturday Constable Blake and Pudd'nhead Wilson met on the street, and Tom Driscoll joined them in time to open their conversation for them. He said to Blake—"You are not looking well, Blake; you seem to be annoyed about something. Has anything gone wrong in the detective business? I believe you fairly and justifiably claim to have a pretty good reputation in that line, isn't it so?"—which made Blake feel good, and look it; but Tom added, "for a country detective"—which made Blake feel the other way, and not only look it, but betray it in his voice—

"Yes, sir, I *have* got a reputation; and it's as good as anybody's in the profession, too, country or no country."

"Oh, I beg pardon; I didn't mean any offense. What I started out to ask was only about the old woman that raided the town—the stoop-shouldered old woman, you know, that you said you were going to catch; and I knew you would, too, because you have the reputation of never boasting, and—well, you—you've caught the old woman?"

"D—— the old woman!"

"Why, sho! you don't mean to say you haven't caught her?"

"No; I haven't caught her. If anybody could have caught her, I could; but nobody couldn't, I don't care who he is."

"I am sorry, real sorry—for your sake; because, when it gets around that a detective has expressed himself so confidently, and then——"

"Don't you worry, that's all—don't you worry; and as for the town, the town needn't worry, either. She's my meat—make yourself easy about that. I'm on her track; I've got clues that——"

"That's good! Now if you could get an old veteran detective down from St. Louis to help you find out what the clues mean, and where they lead to, and then——"

"I'm plenty veteran enough myself, and I don't need anybody's help. I'll have her inside of a we—inside of a month. That I'll swear to!"

Tom said carelessly—

"I suppose that will answer—yes, that will answer. But I reckon she is pretty old, and old people don't often outlive the cautious pace of the professional detective when he has got his clues together and is out on his still-hunt."

Blake's dull face flushed under this gibe, but before he could set his retort in order Tom had turned to Wilson, and was saying, with placid indifference of manner and voice—

"Who got the reward, Pudd'nhead?"

Wilson winced slightly, and saw that his own turn was come.

"What reward?"

"Why, the reward for the thief, and the other one for the knife."

Wilson answered—and rather uncomfortably, to judge by his hesitating fashion of delivering himself—

"Well, the—well, in fact, nobody has claimed it yet."

Tom seemed surprised.

"Why, is that so?"

Wilson showed a trifle of irritation when he replied—

"Yes, it's so. And what of it?"

"Oh, nothing. Only I thought you had struck out a new idea, and invented a scheme that was going to revolutionize the time-worn and ineffectual methods of the——" He stopped, and turned to Blake, who was happy now that another had taken his place on the gridiron: "Blake, didn't you understand him to intimate that it wouldn't be necessary for you to hunt the old woman down?"

"B'George, he said he'd have thief and swag both inside of three days—he did, by hokey! and that's just about a week ago. Why, I said at the time that no thief and no thief's pal was going to try to pawn or sell a thing where he knowed the pawnbroker could get both rewards by taking *him* into camp *with* the swag. It was the blessedest idea that ever *I* struck!"

"You'd change your mind," said Wilson, with irritated bluntness, "if you knew the entire scheme instead of only part of it."

"Well," said the constable, pensively, "I had the idea that it wouldn't work, and up to now I'm right anyway."

"Very well, then, let it stand at that, and give it a further show. It has worked at least as well as your own methods, you perceive."

The constable hadn't anything handy to hit back with, so he discharged a discontented sniff, and said nothing.

After the night that Wilson had partly revealed his scheme at his house, Tom had tried for several days to guess out the secret of the rest of it, but had failed. Then it occurred to him to give Roxana's smarter head a chance at it. He made up a supposititious case, and laid it before her. She thought it over, and delivered her verdict upon it. Tom said to himself, "She's hit it, sure!" He thought he would test that verdict, now, and watch Wilson's face; so he said reflectively—

"Wilson, you're not a fool—a fact of recent discovery. Whatever your scheme was, it had sense in it, Blake's opinion to the contrary notwithstanding. I don't ask you to reveal it, but I will suppose a case— a case which will answer as a starting-point for the real thing I am going to come at, and that's all I want. You offered five hundred dollars for the knife, and five hundred for the thief. We will suppose, for argument's sake, that the first reward is *advertised* and the second offered by *private letter* to pawnbrokers and——"

Blake slapped his thigh, and cried out—

"By Jackson, he's got you, Puddn'head! Now why couldn't I or *any* fool have thought of that?"

Wilson said to himself, "Anybody with a reasonably good head would have thought of it. I am not surprised that Blake didn't detect it; I am only surprised that Tom did. There is more to him than I supposed." He said nothing aloud, and Tom went on:

"Very well. The thief would not suspect that there was a trap, and he would bring or send the knife, and say he bought it for a song, or found it in the road, or something like that, and try to collect the reward, and be arrested—wouldn't he?"

"Yes," said Wilson.

"I think so," said Tom. "There can't be any doubt of it. Have you ever seen that knife?"

"No."

"Has any friend of yours?"

"Not that I know of."

"Well, I begin to think I understand why your scheme failed."

"What do you mean, Tom? What are you driving at?" asked Wilson, with a dawning sense of discomfort.

"Why, that there *isn't* any such knife."

"Look here, Wilson," said Blake, "Tom Driscoll's right, for a thousand dollars—if I had it."

Wilson's blood warmed a little, and he wondered if he had been played upon by those strangers; it certainly had something of that look. But what could they gain by it? He threw out that suggestion. Tom replied:

"Gain? Oh, nothing that you would value, maybe. But they are strangers making their way in a new community. Is it nothing to them to appear as pets of an Oriental prince—at no expense? Is it nothing to them to be able to dazzle this poor little town with thousand-dollar rewards—at no expense? Wilson, there isn't any such knife, or your scheme would have fetched it to light. Or if there is any such knife, they've got it yet. I believe, myself, that they've seen such a knife, for Angelo pictured it out with his pencil too swiftly and handily for him to have been inventing it, and of course I can't swear that they've never had it; but this I'll go bail for—if they had it when they came to this town, they've got it yet."

Blake said—

"It looks mighty reasonable, the way Tom puts it; it most certainly does."

Tom responded, turning to leave—

"You find the old woman, Blake, and if she can't furnish the knife, go and search the twins!"

Tom sauntered away. Wilson felt a good deal depressed. He hardly knew what to think. He was loth to withdraw his faith from the twins, and was resolved not to do it on the present indecisive evidence; but—well, he would think, and then decide how to act.

"Blake, what do you think of this matter?"

"Well, Pudd'nhead, I'm bound to say I put it up the way Tom does. They hadn't the knife; or if they had it, they've got it yet."

The men parted. Wilson said to himself:

"I believe they had it; if it had been stolen, the scheme would have restored it, that is certain. And so I believe they've got it yet."

Tom had no purpose in his mind when he encountered those two men. When he began his talk he hoped to be able to gall them a little and get a trifle of malicious entertainment out of it. But when he left, he left in great spirits, for he perceived that just by pure luck and no troublesome labor he had accomplished several delightful things: he had touched both men on a raw spot and seen them squirm; he had modified Wilson's sweetness for the twins with one small bitter taste that he wouldn't be able to get out of his mouth right away; and, best of all, he had taken the hated twins down a peg with the community; for Blake would gossip around freely, after the manner of detectives, and within a week the town would be laughing at them in its sleeve for offering a gaudy reward for a bauble which they either never possessed or hadn't lost. Tom was very well satisfied with himself.

Tom's behavior at home had been perfect during the entire week. His uncle and aunt had seen nothing like it before. They could find no fault with him anywhere.

Saturday evening he said to the Judge—

"I've had something preying on my mind, uncle, and as I am going away, and might never see you again, I can't bear it any longer. I made you believe I was afraid to fight that Italian adventurer. I had to get out of it on some pretext or other, and maybe I chose badly, being taken unawares, but no honorable person could consent to meet him in the field, knowing what I knew about him."

"Indeed? What was that?"

"Count Luigi is a confessed assassin."

"Incredible!"

"It is perfectly true. Wilson detected it in his hand, by palmistry, and charged him with it, and cornered him up so close that he had to confess; but both twins begged us on their knees to keep the secret, and swore they would lead straight lives here; and it was all so pitiful that we gave our word of honor never to expose them while they kept that promise. You would have done it yourself, uncle."

"You are right, my boy; I would. A man's secret is still his own property, and sacred, when it has been surprised out of him like that. You did well, and I am proud of you." Then he added mournfully, "But I wish I could have been saved the shame of meeting an assassin on the field of honor."

"It couldn't be helped, uncle. If I had known you were going to challenge him I should have felt obliged to sacrifice my pledged word in order to stop it, but Wilson couldn't be expected to do otherwise than keep silent."

"Oh no; Wilson did right, and is in no way to blame. Tom, Tom, you have lifted a heavy load from my heart; I was stung to the very soul when I seemed to have discovered that I had a coward in my family."

"You may imagine what it cost *me* to assume such a part, uncle."

"Oh, I know it, poor boy, I know it. And I can understand how much it has cost you to remain under that unjust stigma to this time. But it is all right now, and no harm is done. You have restored my comfort of mind, and with it your own; and both of us had suffered enough."

The old man sat awhile plunged in thought; then he looked up with a satisfied light in his eye, and said: "That this assassin should have put the affront upon me of letting me meet him on the field of honor as if he were a gentleman is a matter which I will presently settle—but not now. I will not shoot him until after election. I see a way to ruin them both before; I will attend to that first. Neither of them shall be elected, that I promise. You are sure that the fact that he is an assassin has not got abroad?"

"Perfectly certain of it, sir."

"It will be a good card. I will fling a hint at it from the stump on the polling-day. It will sweep the ground from under both of them."

"There's not a doubt of it. It will finish them."

"That and outside work among the voters will, to a certainty. I want you to come down here by and by and work privately among the rag-tag and bobtail. You shall spend money among them; I will furnish it."

Another point scored against the detested twins! Really it was a great day for Tom. He was encouraged to chance a parting shot, now, at the same target, and did it.

"You know that wonderful Indian knife that the twins have been making such a to-do about? Well, there's no track or trace of it yet; so the town is beginning to sneer and gossip and laugh. Half the people believe they never had any such knife, the other half believe they had it and have got it still. I've heard twenty people talking like that today."

Yes, Tom's blemishless week had restored him to the favor of his aunt and uncle.

His mother was satisfied with him, too. Privately, she believed she was coming to love him, but she did not say so. She told him to go along to St. Louis, now, and she would get ready and follow. Then she smashed her whisky bottle and said—

"Dah now! I's a-gwyne to make you walk as straight as a string, Chambers, en so I's bown' you ain't gwyne to git no bad example out o' yo' mammy. I tole you you couldn't go into no bad comp'ny. Well, you's gwyne into my comp'ny, en I's gwyne to fill de bill. Now, den, trot along, trot along!"

Tom went aboard one of the big transient boats that night with his heavy satchel of miscellaneous plunder, and slept the sleep of the unjust, which is serener and sounder than the other kind, as we know by the hanging-eve history of a million rascals. But when he got up in the morning, luck was against him again: A brother-thief had robbed him while he slept, and gone ashore at some intermediate landing.

Chapter XVI

If you pick up a starving dog and make him prosperous, he will not bite you. This is the principal difference between a dog and a man.

PUDD'NHEAD WILSON'S CALENDAR

We know all about the habits of the ant, we know all about the habits of the bee, but we know nothing at all about the habits of the oyster. It seems almost certain that we have been choosing the wrong time for studying the oyster.

PUDD'NHEAD WILSON'S CALENDAR

When Roxana arrived, she found her son in such despair and misery that her heart was touched and her motherhood rose up strong in her. He was ruined past hope, now; his destruction would be immediate and sure, and he would be an outcast and friendless. That was reason enough for a mother to love a child; so she loved him, and told him so. It made him wince, secretly—for she was a "nigger." That he was one himself was far from reconciling him to that despised race.

Roxana poured out endearments upon him, to which he responded uncomfortably, but as well as he could. And she tried to comfort him, but that was not possible. These intimacies quickly became horrible to him, and within the hour he began to try to get up courage enough to tell her so, and require that they be discontinued or very considerably modified. But he was afraid of her; and besides, there came a lull, now, for she had begun to think. She was trying to invent a saving plan. Finally she started up, and said she had found a

way out. Tom was almost suffocated by the joy of this sudden good news. Roxana said:

"Here is de plan, en she'll win, sure. I's a nigger, en nobody ain't gwyne to doubt it dat hears me talk. I's wuth six hund'd dollahs. Take en sell me, en pay off dese gamblers."

Tom was dazed. He was not sure he had heard aright. He was dumb for a moment; then he said:

"Do you mean that you would be sold into slavery to save me?"

"Ain't you my chile? En does you know anything dat a mother won't do for her chile? Dey ain't nothin' a white mother won't do for her chile. Who made 'em so? De Lord done it. En who made de niggers? De Lord made 'em. In de inside, mothers is all de same. De good Lord he made 'em so. I's gwyne to be sole into slavery, en in a year you's gwyne to buy yo' ole mammy free ag'in. I'll show you how. Dat's de plan."

Tom's hopes began to rise, and his spirits along with them. He said—

"It's lovely of you, mammy—it's just—"

"Say it ag'in! En keep on sayin' it? It's all de pay a body kin want in dis worl', en it's mo' den enough. Laws bless you, honey, when I's slavin' aroun', en dey 'buses me, if I knows you's a-sayin' dat, 'way off yonder somers, it'll heal up all de sore places, en I kin stan' 'em."

"I *do* say it again, mammy, and I'll keep on saying it, too. But how am I going to sell you? You're free, you know."

"Much diff'rence dat make! White folks ain't partic'lar. De law kin sell me now if dey tell me to leave de State in six months en I don't go. You draw up a paper—bill o' sale—en put it 'way off yonder, down in de middle 'o Kaintuck somers, en sign some names to it, en say you'll sell me cheap 'ca'se you's hard up; you'll find you ain't gwyne to have no trouble. You take me up de country a piece, en sell me on a farm; dem people ain't gwyne to ask no questions if I's a bargain."

Tom forged a bill of sale and sold his mother to an Arkansas cotton-planter for a trifle over six hundred dollars. He did not want to commit this treachery, but luck threw the man in his way, and this saved him the necessity of going up country to hunt up a purchaser, with the added risk of having to answer a lot of questions, whereas this planter was so pleased with Roxy that he asked next to none at all. Besides, the planter insisted that Roxy wouldn't know where she was, at first, and that by the time she found out she would already have become contented. And Tom argued with himself that it was an immense advantage for Roxy to have a master who was so pleased with her, as this planter manifestly was. In almost no time his flowing reasonings carried him to the point of even half believing he was doing Roxy a splendid surreptitious service in selling her "down the river." And then he kept diligently saying to himself all the time: "It's for only a year. In a year I buy her free again; she'll keep that in mind, and it'll reconcile her." Yes; the little deception could do no harm, and everything would come out right and pleasant in the end, any way. By agreement, the conversation in Roxy's presence was all about the man's "upcountry" farm, and how pleasant a place it was, and how happy the slaves were there; so poor Roxy was entirely deceived; and easily, for she was not dreaming that her own son could

be guilty of treason to a mother who, in voluntarily going into slavery—slavery of any kind, mild or severe, or of any duration, brief or long—was making a sacrifice for him compared with which death would have been a poor and commonplace one. She lavished tears and loving caresses upon him privately, and then went away with her owner—went away broken-hearted, and yet proud of what she was doing, and glad that it was in her power to do it.

Tom squared his accounts, and resolved to keep to the very letter of his reform, and never to put that will in jeopardy again. He had three hundred dollars left. According to his mother's plan, he was to put that safely away, and add her half of his pension to it monthly. In one year this fund would buy her free again.

For a whole week he was not able to sleep well, so much the villainy which he had played upon his trusting mother preyed upon his rag of a conscience; but after that he began to get comfortable again, and was presently able to sleep like any other miscreant.

———

The boat bore Roxy away from St. Louis at four in the afternoon, and she stood on the lower guard abaft the paddle-box and watched Tom

through a blur of tears until he melted into the throng of people and disappeared; then she looked no more, but sat there on a coil of cable crying till far into the night. When she went to her foul steerage-bunk at last, between the clashing engines, it was not to sleep, but only to wait for the morning, and, waiting, grieve.

It had been imagined that she "would not know," and would think she was traveling up stream. She! Why, she had been steamboating for years. At dawn she got up and went listlessly and sat down on the cable-coil again. She passed many a snag whose "break" could have told her a thing to break her heart, for it showed a current moving in the same direction that the boat was going; but her thoughts were elsewhere, and she did not notice. But at last the roar of a bigger and nearer break than usual brought her out of her torpor, and she looked up, and her practised eye fell upon that telltale rush of water. For one moment her petrified gaze fixed itself there. Then her head dropped upon her breast, and she said—

"Oh, de good Lord God have mercy on po' sinful me—*I's sole down de river!*"

CHAPTER XVII

Even popularity can be overdone. In Rome, along at first, you are full of regrets that Michelangelo died; but by and by you only regret that you didn't see him do it.

PUDD'NHEAD WILSON'S CALENDAR

July 4. Statistics show that we lose more fools on this day than in all the other days of the year put together. This proves, by the number left in stock, that one Fourth of July per year is now inadequate, the country has grown so.

PUDD'NHEAD WILSON'S CALENDAR

The summer weeks dragged by, and then the political campaign opened—opened in pretty warm fashion, and waxed hotter and hotter daily. The twins threw themselves into it with their whole heart, for their self-love was engaged. Their popularity, so general at first, had suffered afterward; mainly because they had been *too* popular, and so a natural reaction had followed. Besides, it had been diligently whispered around that it was curious—indeed, *very* curious—that that wonderful knife of theirs did not turn up—*if* it was so valuable, or *if* it had ever existed. And with the whisperings went chucklings and nudgings and winks, and such things have an effect. The twins considered that success in the election would reinstate them, and that defeat would work them irreparable damage. Therefore they worked hard, but not harder than Judge Driscoll and Tom worked against them in the closing days of the canvas.

Tom's conduct had remained so letter-perfect during two whole months, now, that his uncle not only trusted him with money with which to persuade voters, but trusted him to go and get it himself out of the safe in the private sitting-room.

The closing speech of the campaign was made by Judge Driscoll, and he made it against both of the foreigners. It was disastrously effective. He poured out rivers of ridicule upon them, and forced the big mass-meeting to laugh and applaud. He scoffed at them as adventurers, mountebanks, sideshow riff-raff, dime museum freaks; he assailed their showy titles with measureless derision; he said they were back-alley barbers disguised as nobilities, peanut pedlers masquerading as gentlemen, organ-grinders bereft of their brother monkey. At last he stopped and stood still. He waited until the place had become absolutely silent and expectant, then he delivered his deadliest shot; delivered it with ice-cold seriousness and deliberation, with a significant emphasis upon the closing words: he said he believed that the reward offered for the lost knife was humbug and buncombe, and that its owner would know where to find it whenever he should have occasion *to assassinate somebody.*

Then he stepped from the stand, leaving a startled and impressive hush behind him instead of the customary explosion of cheers and party cries.

The strange remark flew far and wide over the town and made an extraordinary sensation. Everybody was asking, "What could he mean by that?" And everybody went on asking that question, but in vain; for the Judge only said he knew what he was talking about, and stopped there; Tom said he hadn't any idea what his uncle meant, and Wilson, whenever he was asked what he thought it meant, parried the question by asking the questioner what *he* thought it meant.

Wilson was elected, the twins were defeated—crushed, in fact, and left forlorn and substantially friendless. Tom went back to St. Louis happy.

Dawson's Landing had a week of repose, now, and it needed it. But it was in an expectant state, for the air was full of rumors of a new duel. Judge Driscoll's election labors had prostrated him, but it was said that as soon as he was well enough to entertain a challenge he would get one from Count Luigi.

The brothers withdrew entirely from society, and nursed their humiliation in privacy. They avoided the people, and went out for exercise only late at night, when the streets were deserted.

CHAPTER XVIII

Gratitude and treachery are merely the
two extremities of the same procession.
You have seen all of it that is worth staying
for when the band and the gaudy officials
have gone by.

PUDD'NHEAD WILSON'S CALENDAR

Thanksgiving Day. Let all give humble,
hearty, and sincere thanks, now, but the
turkeys. In the island of Fiji they do not use
turkeys; they use plumbers. It does not become you and me to sneer at Fiji.

PUDD'NHEAD WILSON'S CALENDAR

The Friday after the election was a rainy
one in St. Louis. It rained all day long, and
rained hard, apparently trying its best to
wash that soot-blackened town white, but of
course not succeeding. Toward midnight
Tom Driscoll arrived at his lodgings from

the theatre in the heavy downpour, and closed his umbrella and let himself in; but when he would have shut the door, he found that there was another person entering—doubtless another lodger; this person closed the door and tramped up-stairs behind Tom. Tom found his door in the dark, and entered it and turned up the gas. When he faced about, lightly whistling, he saw the back of a man. The man was closing and locking his door for him. His whistle faded out and he felt uneasy. The man turned around, a wreck of shabby old clothes, sodden with rain and all a-drip, and showed a black face under an old slouch hat. Tom was frightened. He tried to order the man out, but the words refused to come, and the other man got the start. He said, in a low voice—

"Keep still—I's yo' mother!"

Tom sunk in a heap on a chair, and gasped out—

"It was mean of me, and base—I know it; but I meant it for the best, I did indeed—I can swear it."

Roxana stood awhile looking mutely down on him while he writhed in shame and went on incoherently babbling self-accusations mixed with pitiful attempts at explanation and palliation of his crime; then she seated herself and took off her hat, and her unkempt masses of long brown hair tumbled down about her shoulders.

"It ain't no fault o' yo'n dat dat ain't gray," she said sadly, noticing the hair.

"I know it, I know it! I'm a scoundrel. But I swear I meant it for the best. It was a mistake, of course, but I thought it was for the best, I truly did."

Roxy began to cry softly, and presently words began to find their way out between her sobs. They were uttered lamentingly, rather than angrily—

"Sell a pusson down de river—*down de river!*—for de bes'! I wouldn't treat a dog so! I is all broke down en wore out, now, en so I reckon it ain't in me to storm aroun' no mo', like I used to when I 'uz trompled on en 'bused. I don't know—but maybe it's so. Leastways, I's suffered so much dat mournin' seem to come mo' handy to me now den stormin'."

These words should have touched Tom Driscoll, but if they did, that effect was obliterated by a stronger one—one which removed the heavy weight of fear which lay upon him, and gave his crushed spirit a most grateful rebound, and filled all his small soul with a deep sense of relief. But he kept prudently still, and ventured no comment. There was a voiceless interval of some duration, now, in which no sounds were heard but the beating of the rain upon the panes, the sighing and complaining of the winds, and now and then a muffled sob from Roxana. The sobs became more and more infrequent, and at last ceased. Then the refugee began to talk again:

"Shet down dat light a little. More. More yit. A pusson dat is hunted don't like de light. Dah—dat'll do. I kin see whah you is, en dat's enough. I's gwine to tell you de tale, en cut it jes as short as I kin, en den I'll tell you what you's got to do. Dat man dat bought me ain't a bad man; he's good enough, as planters goes; en if he could'a' had his way I'd 'a' be'n a house servant in his fambly en be'n comfortable: but his wife she was a Yank, en not right down good lookin', en she riz up agin me straight off; so den dey sent me out to de quarter 'mongst de common fiel' han's. Dat woman warn't satisfied even wid dat, but she worked up de overseer ag'in' me, she 'uz dat jealous en hateful; so de overseer he had me out befo' day in de mawnin's en worked me de whole long day as long as dey'uz any light to see by; en many's de lashin's I got 'ca'se I couldn't come up to de work o' de stronges'. Dat overseer wuz a Yank, too, outen New Englan', en anybody down South kin tell you what dat mean. *Dey* knows how to work a nigger to death, en day knows how to whale 'em, too—whale 'em till dey backs is welted like a washboard. 'Long at fust my marster say de good word for me to de overseer, but dat 'uz bad for me; for de mistis she fine it out, en arter dat I jist ketched it at every turn—dey warn't no mercy for me no mo'."

Tom's heart was fired—with fury 'against the planter's wife; and he said to himself, "But for that meddlesome fool, everything would have gone all right." He added a deep and bitter curse against her.

The expression of this sentiment was fiercely written in his face, and stood thus revealed to Roxana by a white glare of lightning which turned the somber dusk of the room into dazzling day at that moment. She was pleased—pleased and grateful; for did not that expression show that her child was capable of grieving for his mother's wrongs and of feeling resentment toward her persecutors?—a thing which she had been doubting. But her flash of happiness was only a flash, and went out again and left her spirit dark; for she said to herself, "He sole me down de river—he can't feel for a body long: dis'll pass en go." Then she took up her tale again.

"'Bout ten days ago I 'uz sayin' to myself dat I couldn't
las' many mo' weeks I 'uz so wore out wid de awful work
en de lashin's, en so downhearted en misable. En I
didn't care no mo', nuther—life warn't wuth noth'n'
to me, if I got to go on like dat. Well, when a body is
in a frame o' mine like dat, what do a body care
what a body do? Dey was a little sickly nigger wench 'bout ten year ole dat 'uz good to
me, en hadn't no mammy, po' thing, en I
loved her en she loved me; en she come out
whah I 'uz workin 'en she had a roasted
tater, en tried to slip it to me,—rob-
bin' herself, you see, 'ca'se she knowed
de overseer didn't gimme enough to
eat,—en he ketched her at it, en give her
a lick acrost de back wid his stick,
which 'uz as thick as a broom-handle,
en she drop' screamin' on de groun', en
squirmin' en wallerin' aroun' in de dust like a spider dat's got crippled.
I couldn't stan' it. All de hell-fire dat 'uz ever in my heart flame' up, en
I snatch de stick outen his han' en laid him flat. He laid dah moanin' en
cussin', en all out of his head,
you know, en de niggers 'uz
plumb sk'yerd to death. Dey
gathered roun' him to hep' him, en I
jumped on his hoss en took out for
de river as tight as I could go. I
knowed what dey would do
wid me. Soon as he got well
he would start in en work
me to death if marster let
him; en if dey didn't do
dat, they'd sell me furder
down de river, en dat's
de same thing. So I 'lowed
to drown myself en git out
o' my troubles. It 'uz gitt'n'
towards dark. I 'uz at de

river in two minutes. Den I see a canoe, en I says dey ain't no use to drown myself tell I got to; so I ties de hoss in de edge o' de timber en shove out down de river, keepin' in under de shelter o' de bluff bank en prayin' for de dark to shet down quick. I had a pow'ful good start, 'ca'se de big house 'uz three mile back f'om de river en on'y de work-mules to ride dah on, en on'y niggers to ride 'em, en *day* warn't gwine to hurry—dey'd gimme all de chance dey could. Befo' a body could go to de house en back it would be long pas' dark, en dey couldn't track de hoss en fine out which way I went tell mawnin', en de niggers would tell 'em all de lies dey could 'bout it.

"Well, de dark come, en I went on a-spinnin' down de river. I paddled mo'n two hours, den I warn't worried no mo', so I quit paddlin, en floated down de current, considerin' what I 'uz gwine to do if I didn't have to drown myself. I made up some plans, en floated along, turnin' 'em over in my mine. Well, when it 'uz a little pas' midnight, as I reckoned, en I had come fifteen or twenty mile, I see de lights o' a steamboat layin' at de bank, whah dey warn't no town en no woodyard, en putty soon I ketched de shape o' de chimbly-tops ag'in' de stars, en de good gracious me, I 'most jumped out o' my skin for joy! It 'uz de *Gran' Mogul*—I 'uz chambermaid on her for eight seasons in de Cincinnati en Orleans trade. I slid 'long pas'—don't see nobody stirrin' nowhah—hear 'em a-hammerin' away in de engine-room, den I knowed what de matter was—some o' de machinery's broke. I got asho' below de boat and turn' de canoe loose, den I goes 'long up, en dey 'uz jes one plank out, en I step' 'board de boat. It 'uz pow'ful hot, deckhan's en roustabouts 'uz sprawled aroun' asleep on de fo'cas'l, de second mate, Jim Bangs, he sot dah on de bitts wid his head down,

asleep—'ca'se dat's de way de second mate stan' de cap'n's watch!—en de ole watchman, Billy Hatch, he 'uz a-noddin' on de companionway;—en I knowed 'em all; 'en, lan', but dey did look good! I says to myself, I wished old marster'd come along *now* en try to take me—bless yo' heart, I's 'mong frien's, I is. So I tromped right along 'mongst 'em, en went up on de b'iler deck en 'way back aft to de ladies' cabin guard, en sot down dah in de same cheer dat I'd sot in 'mos' a hund'd million times, I reckon; en it 'uz jist home ag'in, I tell you!

"In 'bout an hour I heard de ready-bell jingle, en den de racket begin. Putty soon I hear de gong strike. 'Set her back on de outside,' I says to myself—'I reckon I knows dat music!' I hear de gong ag'in. 'Come ahead on de inside,' I says. Gong ag'in. 'Stop de outside.' Gong ag'in. 'Come ahead on de outside—now we's pinted for Sent Louis, en I's outer de woods en ain't got to drown myself at all.' I knowed de *Mogul* 'uz in de Sent Louis trade now, you see. It 'uz jes fair daylight when we passed our plantation, en I seed a gang o' niggers en white folks huntin' up en down de sho', en troublin' deyselves a good deal 'bout me; but I warn't troublin' myself none 'bout dem.

"'Bout dat time Sally Jackson, dat used to be my second chambermaid en 'uz head chambermaid now, she come out on de guard, en 'uz pow'ful glad to see me, en so 'uz all de officers; en I tole 'em I'd got kidnapped en sole down de river, en dey made me up twenty dollahs en give it to me, en Sally she rigged me out wid good clo'es, en when I got here I went straight to whah you used to wuz, en den I come to dis house, en dey say you's away but 'spected back every day; so I didn't dast to go down de river to Dawson's, 'ca'se I might miss you.

"Well, las' Monday I 'uz pass'n' by one o' dem places in Fourth street whah deh sticks up runaway-nigger bills, en he'ps to ketch 'em, en I seed my marster! I 'mos' flopped down on de groun', I felt so gone. He had his back to me, en 'uz talkin' to de man en givin' him some bills—nigger-bills, I reckon, en I'se de nigger. He's offerin' a reward—dat's it. Ain't I right, don't you reckon?"

Tom had been gradually sinking into a state of ghastly terror, and he said to himself, now: "I'm lost, no matter what turn things take! This man has said to me that he thinks there was something suspicious about that sale. He said he had a letter from a passenger on the *Grand Mogul* saying that Roxy came here on that boat and that everybody on board knew all about the case; so he says that her coming here instead of flying to a free State looks bad for me, and that if I don't find her for him, and that pretty soon, he will make trouble for me. I never believed that story; I couldn't believe she would be so dead to all motherly instincts as to come here, knowing the risk she would run of getting me into irremediable trouble. And after all, here she is! And I stupidly swore I would help him find her, thinking it was a perfectly safe thing to promise. If I venture to deliver her up, she— she—but how can I help myself? I've got to do that or pay the money, and where's the money to come from? I—I—well, I should think that if he would swear to treat her kindly hereafter—and she says, herself, that he is a good man—and if he would swear to never allow her to be overworked, or ill fed, or——"

A flash of lightning exposed Tom's pallid face, drawn and rigid with these worrying thoughts. Roxana spoke up sharply now, and there was apprehension in her voice—

"Turn up dat light! I want to see yo' face better. Dah now—lemme look at you. Chambers, you's as white as yo' shirt! Has you seen dat man? Has he be'n to see you?"

"Ye-s."

"When?"

"Monday noon."

"Monday noon! Was he on my track?"

"He—well, he thought he was. That is, he hoped he was. This is the bill you saw." He took it out of his pocket.

"Read it to me!"

She was panting with excitement, and there was a dusky glow in her eyes that Tom could not translate with certainty, but there seemed to be something threatening about it. The handbill had the usual rude woodcut of a turbaned negro woman running, with the customary bundle on a stick over her shoulder, and the heading in bold type, "$100 REWARD." Tom read the bill aloud—at least the part that described Roxana and named the master and his St. Louis address and the address of the Fourth-street agency; but he left out the item that applicants for the reward might also apply to Mr. Thomas Driscoll.

"Gimme de bill!"

Tom had folded it and was putting it in his pocket. He felt a chilly streak creeping down his back, but said as carelessly as he could—

"The bill? Why, it isn't any use to you, you can't read it. What do you want with it?"

"Gimme de bill!" Tom gave it to her, but with a reluctance which he could not entirely disguise. "Did you read it *all* to me?"

"Certainly I did."

"Hole up yo' han' en swah to it."

Tom did it. Roxana put the bill carefully away in her pocket, with her eyes fixed upon Tom's face all the while; then she said—

"Yo's lyin'!"

"What would I want to lie about it for?"

"I don't know—but you is. Dat's my opinion, anyways. But nemmine 'bout dat. When I seed dat man I 'uz dat sk'yerd dat I could sca'cely wobble home. Den I give a nigger man a dollar for dese clo'es, en I ain't be'n in a house sense, night ner day, till now. I blacked my face en laid hid in de cellar of a ole house dat's burnt down, daytimes, en robbed de sugar hogsheads en grain sacks on de wharf, nights, to git somethin' to eat, en never dast to try to buy noth'n', en I's 'mos' starved. En I never dast to come near dis place till dis rainy night, when dey ain't no people roun' sca'cely. But to-night I be'n a-stannin' in de dark alley ever since night come, waitin' for you to go by. En here I is."

She fell to thinking. Presently she said—

"You seed dat man at noon, las' Monday?"

"Yes."

"I seed him de middle o' dat arternoon. He hunted you up, didn't he?"

"Yes."

"Did he give you de bill dat time?"

"No, he hadn't got it printed yet."

Roxana darted a suspicious glance at him.

"Did you he'p him fix up de bill?"

Tom cursed himself for making that stupid blunder, and tried to rectify it by saying he remembered, now, that it *was* at noon Monday that the man gave him the bill. Roxana said—

"You's lyin' ag'in, sho." Then she straightened up and raised her finger:

"Now den! I's gwine to ask you a question, en I wants to know how you's gwine to git aroun' it. You knowed he 'uz arter me; en if you run off, 'stid o' stayin' here to he'p him, he'd know dey 'uz somethin' wrong 'bout dis business, en den he would inquire 'bout you, en dat would take him to yo' uncle, en yo' uncle would read de bill en see dat you be'n sellin' a free nigger down de river, en you know *him,* I reckon! He'd t'ar up de will en kick you outen de house. Now, den, you answer me dis question: hain't you tole dat man dat I would be sho' to come here, en den you would fix it so he could set a trap en ketch me?"

Tom recognized that neither lies nor arguments could help him any longer—he was in a vise, with the screw turned on, and out of it there was no budging. His face began to take on an ugly look, and presently he said, with a snarl—

"Well, what could I do? You see, yourself, that I was in his grip and couldn't get out."

Roxy scorched him with a scornful gaze awhile, then she said—

"What could you do? You could be Judas to yo' own mother to save yo' wuthless hide! Would anybody b'lieve it? No—a dog couldn't! You is de low-downest orneriest hound dat was ever pup'd into dis worl'—en I's 'sponsible for it!"—and she spat on him.

He made no effort to resent this. Roxy reflected a moment, then she said—

"Now I'll tell you what you's gwine to do. You's gwine to give dat man de money dat you's got laid up, en make him wait till you kin go to de Jedge en git de res' en buy me free agin."

"Thunder! what are you thinking of? Go and ask him for three hundred dollars and odd? What would I tell him I want with it, pray?"

Roxy's answer was delivered in a serene and level voice—

"You'll tell him you's sole me to pay yo' gamblin' debts en dat you lied to me en was a villain, en dat I 'quires you to git dat money en buy me back ag'in."

"Why, you've gone stark mad! He would tear the will to shreds in a minute—don't you know that?"

"Yes, I does."

"Then you don't believe I'm idiot enough to go to him, do you?"

"I don't b'lieve nothin' 'bout it—I *knows* you's a-goin'. I knows it 'ca'se you knows dat if you don't raise dat money I'll go to him myself, en den he'll sell *you* down de river, en you kin see how you like it!"

Tom rose, trembling and excited, and there was an evil light in his eye. He strode to the door and said he must get out of this suffocating place for a moment and clear his brain in the fresh air so that he could determine what to do. The door wouldn't open. Roxy smiled grimly, and said—

"I's got de key, honey—set down. You needn't cle'r up yo' brain none to fine out what you gwine to do—*I* knows what you's gwine to do." Tom sat down and began to pass his hands through his hair with a helpless and desperate air. Roxy said, "Is dat man in dis house?"

Tom glanced up with a surprised expression, and asked—

"What gave you such an idea?"

"You done it. Gwine out to cle'r yo' brain! In de fust place you ain't got none to cle'r, en in de second place yo' ornery eye tole on you.

You's de low-downest hound dat ever—but I done tole you dat befo'. Now den, dis is Friday. You kin fix it up wid dat man, en tell him you's gwine away to git de res' o' de money, en dat you'll be back wid it nex' Tuesday, or maybe Wednesday. You understan'?"

Tom answered sullenly—

"Yes."

"En when you gits de new bill o' sale dat sells me to my own self, take en send it in de mail to Mr. Pudd'nhead Wilson, en write on de back dat he's to keep it tell I come. You understan'?"

"Yes."

"Dat's all den. Take yo' umbreller, en put on yo' hat."

"Why?"

"Beca'se you's gwine to see me home to de wharf. You see dis knife? I's toted it aroun' sense de day I seed dat man en bought dese clo'es en it. If he ketch me, I's gwine to kill myself wid it. Now start along, en go sof', en lead de way; en if you gives a sign in dis house, or if anybody comes up to you in de street, I's gwine to jam it right into you. Chambers, does you b'lieve me when I says dat?"

"It's no use to bother me with that question. I know your word's good."

"Yes, it's diff'rent from yo'n! Shet de light out en move along—here's de key."

They were not followed. Tom trembled every time a late straggler brushed by them on the street, and half expected to feel the cold steel

in his back. Roxy was right at his heels and always in reach. After tramping a mile they reached a wide vacancy on the deserted wharves, and in this dark and rainy desert they parted.

As Tom trudged home his mind was full of dreary thoughts and wild plans; but at last he said to himself, wearily—

"There is but the one way out. I must follow her plan. But with a variation—I will not ask for the money and ruin myself; I will *rob* the old skinflint."

CHAPTER XIX

Few things are harder to put up with than the annoyance of a good example.

PUDD'NHEAD WILSON'S CALENDAR

It were not best that we should all think alike; it is difference of opinion that makes horse-races.

PUDD'NHEAD WILSON'S CALENDAR

Dawson's Landing was comfortably finishing its season of dull repose and waiting patiently for the duel. Count Luigi was waiting, too; but not patiently, rumor said. Sunday came, and Luigi insisted on having his challenge conveyed. Wilson carried it. Judge Driscoll declined to fight with an assassin—"that is," he added significantly, "in the field of honor."

Elsewhere, of course, he would be ready. Wilson tried to convince him that if he had been present himself when Angelo told about the homicide committed by Luigi, he would not have considered the act discreditable to Luigi; but the obstinate old man was not to be moved.

Wilson went back to his principal and reported the failure of his mission. Luigi was incensed, and asked how it could be that the old gentleman, who was by no means dull-witted, held his trifling nephew's evidence and inferences to be of more value than Wilson's. But Wilson laughed, and said—

"That is quite simple; that is easily explicable. I am not his doll—his baby—his infatuation: his nephew is. The Judge and his late wife never had any children. The Judge and his wife were past middle age when this treasure fell into their lap. One must make allowances for a parental instinct that has been starving for twenty-five or thirty years. It is famished, it is crazed with hunger by that time, and will be entirely satisfied with anything that comes handy; its taste is atrophied, it can't tell mud-cat from shad. A devil born to a young couple is measurably recognizable by them as a devil before long, but a devil adopted by an old couple is an angel to them, and remains so, through thick and thin. Tom is this old man's angel; he is infatuated with him. Tom can persuade him into things which other people can't—not all things; I don't mean that, but a good many—particularly one class of things: the things that create or abolish personal partialities or prejudices in the old man's mind. The old man liked both of you. Tom conceived a hatred for you. That was enough; it turned the old man around at once. The oldest and strongest friendship must go to the ground when one of these late-adopted darlings throws a brick at it."

"It's a curious philosophy," said Luigi.

"It ain't a philosophy at all—it's a fact. And there is something pathetic and beautiful about it, too. I think there is nothing more pathetic than to see one of these poor old childless couples taking a menagerie of yelping little worthless dogs to their hearts; and then adding some cursing and squawking parrots and a jackass-voiced macaw; and next a couple of hundred screeching songbirds, and presently some fetid guinea-pigs and rabbits, and a howling colony of cats. It is all a groping and ignorant effort to construct out of base metal and brass filings, so to speak, something to take the place of that golden treasure denied them by Nature, a child. But this is a digression. The unwritten law of this region requires you to kill Judge Driscoll on sight, and he and the community will expect that attention at your hands—though of course your own death by his bullet will answer every purpose. Look out for him! Are you heeled—that is, fixed?"

"Yes; he shall have his opportunity. If he attacks me I will respond."

As Wilson was leaving, he said—

"The Judge is still a little used up by his campaign work, and will not get out for a day or so; but when he does get out, you want to be on the alert."

About eleven at night the twins went out for exercise, and started on a long stroll in the veiled moonlight.

Tom Driscoll had landed at Hackett's Store, two miles below Dawson's, just about half an hour earlier, the only passenger for that lonely spot, and had walked up the shore road and entered Judge Driscoll's house without having encountered any one either on the road or under the roof.

He pulled down his window-blinds and lighted his candle. He laid off his coat and hat and began his preparations. He unlocked his trunk and got his suit of girl's clothes out from under the male attire in it, and laid it by. Then he blacked his face with burnt cork and put the

cork in his pocket. His plan was, to slip down to his uncle's private sitting-room below, pass into the bedroom, steal the safe-key from the old gentleman's clothes, and then go back and rob the safe. He took up his candle to start. His courage and confidence were high, up to this point, but both began to waver a little, now. Suppose he should make a noise, by some accident, and get caught—say, in the act of opening the safe? Perhaps it would be well to go armed. He took the Indian knife from its hiding-place, and felt a pleasant return of his wandering courage. He slipped stealthily down the narrow stair, his hair rising and his pulses halting at the slightest creak. When he was half-way down, he was disturbed to perceive that the landing below was touched by a faint glow of light. What could that mean? Was his uncle still up? No, that was not likely; he must have left his night-taper there when he went to bed. Tom crept on down, pausing at every step to listen. He found the door standing open, and glanced in. What he saw pleased him beyond measure. His uncle was asleep on the sofa; on a small table at the head of the sofa a lamp was burning low, and by it stood the old man's small tin cash-box, closed. Near the box was a pile of bank-notes and a piece of paper covered with figures in pencil. The safe-door was not open. Evidently the sleeper had wearied himself with work upon his finances, and was taking a rest.

Tom set his candle on the stairs, and began to make his way toward the pile of notes, stooping low as he went. When he was passing his uncle, the old man stirred in his sleep, and Tom stopped instantly—stopped, and softly drew the knife from its sheath, with his heart thumping, and his eyes fastened upon his benefactor's face. After a moment or two he ventured forward again—one step—reached for his prize and seized it, dropping the knife-sheath. Then he felt the old man's strong grip upon him, and a wild cry of "Help! help!" rang in his ear. Without hesitation he drove the knife home—and was free. Some of the notes escaped from his left hand and fell in the blood on the floor. He dropped the knife and snatched them up and started to fly; transferred them to his left hand, and seized the knife again, in his fright and confusion, but remembered himself and flung it from him, as being a dangerous witness to carry away with him.

He jumped for the stair-foot, and closed the door behind him; and as he snatched his candle and fled upward, the stillness of the night was broken by the sound of urgent footsteps approaching the house. In another moment he was in his room and the twins were standing aghast over the body of the murdered man!

Tom put on his coat, buttoned his hat under it, threw on his suit of girl's clothes, dropped the veil, blew out his light, locked the room door by which he had just entered, taking the key, passed through his other door into the back hall, locked that door and kept the key, then worked his way along in the dark and descended the back stairs. He was not expecting to meet anybody, for all interest was centered in the other part of the house, now; his calculation proved correct. By the time he was passing through the backyard, Mrs. Pratt, her servants, and a dozen half-dressed neighbors had joined the twins and the dead, and accessions were still arriving at the front door.

As Tom, quaking as with a palsy, passed out at the gate, three women came flying from the house on the opposite side of the lane. They rushed by him and in at the gate, asking him what the trouble was there, but not waiting for an answer. Tom said to himself, "Those old maids waited to dress—they did the same thing the night Stevens's house burned down next door." In a few minutes he was in the haunted house. He lighted a candle and took off his girl-clothes. There was blood on him all down his left side, and his right hand was red with the stains of the blood-soaked notes which he had crushed in it; but other-wise he was free from this sort of evidence. He cleansed his hand on the straw, and cleaned most of the smut from his face. Then he burned his male and female attire to ashes, scattered the ashes, and put on a disguise proper for a tramp. He blew out his light, went below, and was soon loafing down the river road with the intent to borrow and use one of Roxy's devices. He found a canoe and paddled off down-stream, setting the canoe adrift as dawn approached, and making his way by land to the next village, where he kept out of sight till a transient steamer came along, and then took deck passage for St. Louis. He was ill at ease until Dawson's Landing was behind him; then he said to himself, "All the detectives on earth couldn't trace me now; there's not a vestige of a clue left in the world; that homicide will take its place with the permanent mysteries, and people won't get done trying to guess out the secret of it for fifty years."

In St. Louis, next morning, he read this brief telegram in the pa-pers—dated at Dawson's Landing:

> Judge Driscoll, an old and respected citizen, was assassinated here about midnight by a profligate Italian nobleman or barber on account of a quarrel growing out of the recent election. The assassin will prob-ably be lynched.

"One of the twins!" soliloquized Tom; "how lucky! It is the knife that has done him this grace. We never know when fortune is trying to favor us. I actually cursed Pudd'nhead Wilson in my heart for putting it out of my power to sell that knife. I take it back, now."

Tom was now rich and independent. He arranged with the planter, and mailed to Wilson the new bill of sale which sold Roxana to herself; then he telegraphed his Aunt Pratt:

Have seen the awful news in the papers and am almost prostrated with grief. Shall start by packet to-day. Try to bear up till I come.

When Wilson reached the house of mourning and had gathered such details as Mrs. Pratt and the rest of the crowd could tell him, he took command as mayor, and gave orders that nothing should be touched, but everything left as it was until Justice Robinson should arrive and take the proper measures as coroner. He cleared everybody out of the room but the twins and himself. The sheriff soon arrived and took the twins away to jail. Wilson told them to keep heart, and promised to do his best in their defense when the case should come to trial. Justice Robinson came presently, and with him Constable Blake. They examined the room thoroughly. They found the knife and the sheath. Wilson noticed that there were finger-prints on the knife-handle. That pleased him, for the twins had re-quired the earliest comers to make a scrutiny of their hands and clothes, and neither these people nor Wilson himself had found any blood-stains upon them. Could there be a possibility that the twins had spoken the truth when they said they found the man dead when they ran into the house in answer to the cry for help? He thought of that mysterious girl at once. But this was not the sort of work for a girl to be engaged in. No matter; Tom Driscoll's room must be examined.

After the coroner's jury had viewed the body and its surroundings, Wilson suggested a search up-stairs, and he went along. The jury forced an entrance to Tom's room, but found nothing, of course.

The coroner's jury found that the homicide was committed by Luigi, and that Angelo was accessory to it.

The town was bitter against the unfortunates, and for the first few days after the murder they were in constant danger of being lynched. The grand jury presently indicted Luigi for murder in the first degree, and Angelo as accessory before the fact. The twins were transferred from the city jail to the county prison to await trial.

Wilson examined the finger-marks on the knife-handle and said to himself, "Neither of the twins made those marks." Then manifestly there was another person concerned, either in his own interest or as hired assassin.

But who could it be? That, he must try to find out. The safe was not open, the cash-box was closed, and had three thousand dollars in it. Then robbery was not the motive, and revenge was. Where had the murdered man an enemy except Luigi? There was but that one person in the world with a deep grudge against him.

The mysterious girl! The girl was a great trial to Wilson. If the motive had been robbery, the girl might answer; but there wasn't any girl that would want to take this old man's life for revenge. He had no quarrels with girls; he was a gentleman.

Wilson had perfect tracings of the finger-marks of the knife-handle; and among his glass-records he had a great array of the finger-prints of women and girls, collected during the last fifteen or eighteen years, but he scanned them in vain, they successfully withstood every test; among them were no duplicates of the prints on the knife.

The presence of the knife on the stage of the murder was a worrying circumstance for Wilson. A week previously he had as good as admitted to himself that he believed Luigi had possessed such a knife, and that he still possessed it notwithstanding his pretense that it had been stolen. And now here was the knife, and with it the twins. Half the town had said the twins were humbugging when they claimed that they had lost their knife, and now these people were joyful, and said, "I told you so!"

If their finger-prints had been on the handle—but it was useless to bother any further about that; the finger-prints on the handle were *not* theirs—that he knew perfectly.

Wilson refused to suspect Tom; for first, Tom couldn't murder any-body—he hadn't character enough; secondly, if he could murder a person he wouldn't select his doting benefactor and nearest relative; thirdly, self-interest was in the way; for while the uncle lived, Tom was sure of a free support and a chance to get the destroyed will revived again, but with the uncle gone, that chance was gone, too. It was true the will had really been revived, as was now discovered, but Tom could not have been aware of it, or he would have spoken of it, in his native talky, unsecretive way. Finally, Tom was in St. Louis when the murder was done, and got the news out of the morning journals, as was shown by his telegram to his aunt. These speculations were unemphasized sensations rather than articulated thoughts, for Wilson would have laughed at the idea of seriously connecting Tom with the murder.

Wilson regarded the case of the twins as desperate—in fact, about hopeless. For he argued that if a confederate was not found, an en-lightened Missouri jury would hang them, sure; if a confederate was found, that would not improve the matter, but simply furnish one more person for the sheriff to hang. Nothing could save the twins but the discovery of a person who did the murder on his sole personal ac-count—an undertaking which had all the aspect of the impossible. Still, the person who made the finger-prints must be sought. The twins might have no case *with* him, but they certainly would have none with-out him.

So Wilson mooned around, thinking, thinking, guessing, guessing, day and night, and arriving nowhere. Whenever he ran across a girl or a woman he was not acquainted with, he got her finger-prints, on one pretext or another; and they always cost him a sigh when he got home, for they never tallied with the finger-marks on the knife-handle.

As to the mysterious girl, Tom swore he knew no such girl, and did not remember ever seeing a girl wearing a dress like the one described by Wilson. He admitted that he did not always lock his room, and that sometimes the servants forgot to lock the house doors; still, in his opinion the girl must have made but few visits or she would have been discovered. When Wilson tried to connect her with the stealing-raid, and thought she might have been the old woman's confederate, if not the very thief herself disguised as an old woman, Tom seemed struck, and also much interested, and said he would keep a sharp eye out for this person or persons, although he was afraid that she or they would be too smart to venture again into a town where everybody would now be on the watch for a good while to come.

Everybody was pitying Tom, he looked so quiet and sorrowful, and seemed to feel his great loss so deeply. He was playing a part, but it was not all a part. The picture of his alleged uncle, as he had last seen him, was before him in the dark pretty frequently, when he was awake, and called again in his dreams, when he was asleep. He wouldn't go into the room where the tragedy had happened. This charmed the doting Mrs. Pratt, who realized now, "as she had never done before," she said, what a sensitive and delicate nature her darling had, and how he adored his poor uncle.

CHAPTER XX

Even the clearest and most perfect circumstantial
evidence is likely to be at fault, after all, and
therefore ought to be received with great caution.
Take the case of any pencil, sharpened
by any woman: if you have witnesses, you
will find she did it with a knife; but if
you take simply the aspect of the pencil,
you will say she did it with her teeth.

PUDD'NHEAD WILSON'S CALENDAR

The weeks dragged along, no friend visiting the jailed twins but their counsel and
Aunt Patsy Cooper, and the day of trial
came at last—the heaviest day in Wilson's life;
for with all his tireless diligence he had discovered no sign or trace of
the missing confederate. "Confederate" was the term he had long ago
privately accepted for that person—not as being unquestionably the
right term, but as being at least possibly the
right one, though he was never able to understand why the twins did
not vanish and es-
cape, as the confed-

erate had done, instead of remaining by the murdered man and getting caught there.

The court-house was crowded, of course, and would remain so to the finish, for not only in the town itself, but in the country for miles around, the trial was the one topic of conversation among the people. Mrs. Pratt, in deep mourning, and Tom with a weed on his hat, had seats near Pembroke Howard, the public prosecutor, and back of them sat a great array of friends of the family. The twins had but one friend present to keep their counsel in countenance, their poor old sorrowing landlady. She sat near Wilson, and looked her friendliest. In the "nigger corner" sat Chambers; also Roxy, with good clothes on, and her bill of sale in her pocket. It was her most precious possession, and she never parted with it, day or night. Tom had allowed her thirty-five dollars a month ever since he came into his property, and had said that he and she ought to be grateful to the twins for making them rich; but had roused such a temper in her by this speech that he did not repeat the argument afterward. She said the old Judge had treated her child a thousand times better than he deserved, and had never done her an unkindness in his life; so she hated these outlandish devils for killing him, and shouldn't ever sleep satisfied till she saw them hanged for it. She was here to watch the trial, now, and was going to lift up just one "hooraw" over it if the County Judge put her in jail a year for it. She gave her turbaned head a toss and said, "When dat verdic' comes, I's gwine to lif' dat *roof*, now, I *tell* you."

Pembroke Howard briefly sketched the State's case. He said he would show by a chain of circumstantial evidence without break or fault in it anywhere, that the principal prisoner at the bar committed the murder; that the motive was partly revenge, and partly a desire to take his own life out of jeopardy, and that his brother, by his presence, was a consenting accessory to the crime; a crime which was the basest known to the calendar of human misdeeds—assassination; that it was conceived by the blackest of hearts and consummated by the cowardliest of hands; a crime which had broken a loving sister's heart, blighted the happiness of a young nephew who was as dear as a son, brought inconsolable grief to many friends, and sorrow and loss to the whole community. The utmost penalty of the outraged law would be exacted, and upon the accused, now present at the bar, that penalty would unquestionably be executed. He would reserve further remark until his closing speech.

He was strongly moved, and so also was the whole house; Mrs. Pratt and several other women were weeping when he sat down, and many an eye that was full of hate was riveted upon the unhappy prisoners.

Witness after witness was called by the State, and questioned at length; but the cross-questioning was brief. Wilson knew they could furnish nothing valuable for his side. People were sorry for Pudd'n-head; his budding career would get hurt by this trial.

Several witnesses swore they heard Judge Driscoll say in his public speech that the twins would be able to find their lost knife again when they needed it to assassinate somebody with. This was not news, but now it was seen to have been sorrowfully prophetic, and a profound sensation quivered through the hushed court-room when those dismal words were repeated.

The public prosecutor rose and said that it was within his knowl-edge, through a conversation held with Judge Driscoll on the last day of his life, that counsel for the defense had brought him a challenge from the person charged at this bar with murder; that he had refused to fight with a confessed assassin—"that is, on the field of honor," but had added significantly, that he would be ready for him elsewhere. Presum-ably the person here charged with murder was warned that he must kill or be killed the first time he should meet Judge Driscoll. If counsel for the defense chose to let the statement stand so, he would not call him to the witness stand. Mr. Wilson said he would offer no denial. [Murmurs in the house—"It is getting worse and worse for Wilson's case."]

Mrs. Pratt testified that she heard no outcry, and did not know what woke her up, unless it was the sound of rapid footsteps approaching the front door. She jumped up and ran out in the hall just as she was, and heard the footsteps flying up the front steps and then following be-hind her as she ran to the sitting-room. There she found the accused standing over her murdered brother. [Here she broke down and sobbed. Sensation in the court.] Resuming, she said the persons enter-ing behind her were Mr. Rogers and Mr. Buckstone.

Cross-examined by Wilson, she said the twins proclaimed their in-nocence; declared that they had been taking a walk, and had hurried to the house in response to a cry for help which was so loud and strong that they had heard it at a considerable distance; that they begged her and the gentlemen just mentioned to examine their hands and clothes—which was done, and no blood stains found.

Confirmatory evidence followed from Rogers and Buckstone.

The finding of the knife was verified, the advertisement minutely describing it and offering a reward for it was put in evidence, and its exact correspondence with that description proved. Then followed a few minor details, and the case for the State was closed.

Wilson said that he had three witnesses, the Misses Clarkson, who would testify that they met a veiled young woman leaving Judge Driscoll's premises by the back gate a few minutes after the cries for help were heard, and that their evidence, taken with certain circumstantial evidence which he would call the court's attention to, would in his opinion convince the court that there was still one person concerned in this crime who had not yet been found, and also that a stay of proceedings ought to be granted, in justice to his clients, until that person should be discovered. As it was late, he would ask leave to defer the examination of his three witnesses until the next morning.

The crowd poured out of the place and went flocking away in excited groups and couples, talking the events of the session over with vivacity and consuming interest, and everybody seemed to have had a satisfactory and enjoyable day except the accused, their counsel, and their old-lady friend. There was no cheer among these, and no substantial hope.

In parting with the twins Aunt Patsy did attempt a good-night with a gay pretense of hope and cheer in it, but broke down without finishing.

Absolutely secure as Tom considered himself to be, the opening solemnities of the trial had nevertheless oppressed him with a vague uneasiness, his being a nature sensitive to even the smallest alarms; but from the moment that the poverty and weakness of Wilson's case lay exposed to the court, he was comfortable once more, even jubilant. He left the court-room sarcastically sorry for Wilson. "The Clarksons met an unknown woman in the back lane," he said to himself—"*that* is his case! I'll give him a century to find her in—a couple of them if he likes. A woman who doesn't exist any longer, and the clothes that gave her her sex burnt up and the ashes thrown away— oh, certainly, he'll find *her* easy enough!" This reflection set him to admiring, for the hundredth time, the shrewd ingenuities by which he had insured himself against detection—more, against even suspicion.

"Nearly always in cases like this there is some little detail or other overlooked, some wee little track or trace left behind, and detection follows; but here there's not even the faintest suggestion of a trace left. No more than a bird leaves when it flies through the air—yes, through the night, you may say. The man that can track a bird through the air in the dark and find that bird is the man to track me out and find the Judge's assassin—no other need apply. And that is the job that has been laid out for poor Pudd'nhead Wilson, of all people in the world! Lord, it will be pathetically funny to see him grubbing and groping after that woman that don't exist, and the right person sitting under his very nose all the time!" The more he thought the situation over, the more the humor of it struck him. Finally he said, "I'll never let him hear the last of that woman. Every time I catch him in company, to his dying day, I'll ask him in the guileless affectionate way that used to gravel him so when I inquired how his unborn law-business was coming along, 'Got on her track yet—hey, Pudd'nhead?' " He wanted to laugh, but that would not have answered; there were people about, and he was mourning for his uncle. He made up his mind that it would be good entertainment to look in on Wilson that night and watch him worry over his barren law-case and goad him with an exasperating word or two of sympathy and commiseration now and then.

Wilson wanted no supper, he had no appetite. He got out all the finger-prints of girls and women in his collection of records and pored gloomily over them an hour or more, trying to convince himself that

that troublesome girl's marks were there somewhere and had been overlooked. But it was not so. He drew back his chair, clasped his hands over his head, and gave himself up to dull and arid musings.

Tom Driscoll dropped in, an hour after dark, and said with a pleasant laugh as he took a seat—

"Hello, we've gone back to the amusements of our days of neglect and obscurity for consolation, have we?" and he took up one of the glass strips and held it against the light to inspect it. "Come, cheer up, old man; there's no use in losing your grip and going back to this child's-play merely because this big sunspot is drifting across your shiny new disk. It'll pass, and you'll be all right again,"—and he laid the glass down. "Did you think you could win always?"

"Oh, no," said Wilson, with a sigh, "I didn't expect that, but I can't believe Luigi killed your uncle, and I feel very sorry for him. It makes me blue. And you would feel as I do, Tom, if you were not prejudiced against those young fellows."

"I don't know about that," and Tom's countenence darkened, for his memory reverted to his kicking; "I owe them no good will, considering the brunette one's treatment of me that night. Prejudice or no prejudice, Pudd'nhead, I don't like them, and when they get their deserts you're not going to find me sitting on the mourner's bench."

He took up another strip of glass, and exclaimed—

"Why, here's old Roxy's label! Are you going to ornament the royal palaces with nigger paw-marks, too? By the date here, I was seven months old when this was done, and she was nursing me and her little nigger cub. There's a line straight across her thumb-print. How comes that?" and Tom held out the piece of glass to Wilson.

"That is common," said the bored man, wearily. "Scar of a cut or a scratch, usually"—and he took the strip of glass indifferently, and raised it toward the lamp.

All the blood sunk suddenly out of his face; his hand quaked, and he gazed at the polished surface before him with the glassy stare of a corpse.

"Great Heavens, what's the matter with you, Wilson? Are you going to faint?"

Tom sprang for a glass of water and offered it, but Wilson shrank shuddering from him and said—

"No, no!—take it away!" His breast was rising and falling, and he moved his head about in a dull and wandering way, like a person who has been stunned. Presently he said, "I shall feel better when I get to bed; I have been overwrought to-day; yes, and over-worked for many days."

"Then I'll leave you and let you to get to your rest. Good-night, old man." But as Tom went out he couldn't deny himself a small parting gibe: "Don't take it so hard; a body can't win every time; you'll hang somebody yet."

Wilson muttered to himself, "It is no lie to say I am sorry I have to begin with you, miserable dog though you are!"

He braced himself up with a glass of cold whisky, and went to work again. He did not compare the new finger-marks unintentionally left by Tom a few minutes before on Roxy's glass with the tracings of the marks left on the knife-handle, there being no need of that (for his trained eye), but busied himself with another matter, muttering from time to time, "Idiot that I was!—Nothing but a *girl* would do me—a man in girl's clothes never occurred to me." First, he hunted out the plate containing the finger-prints made by Tom when he was twelve years old, and laid it by itself; then he brought forth the marks made by Tom's baby fingers when he was a suckling of seven months, and placed these two plates with the one containing this subject's newly (and unconsciously) made record.

"Now the series is complete," he said with satisfaction, and sat down to inspect these things and enjoy them.

But his enjoyment was brief. He stared a considerable time at the three strips, and seemed stupefied with astonishment. At last he put them down and said, "I can't make it out at all—hang it, the baby's don't tally with the others!"

He walked the floor for half an hour puzzling over his enigma, then he hunted out two other glass plates.

He sat down and puzzled over these things a good while, but kept muttering, "It's no use; I can't understand it. They don't tally right, and yet I'll swear the names and dates are right, and so of course they *ought* to tally. I never labeled one of these things carelessly in my life. There is a most extraordinary mystery here."

He was tired out, now, and his brains were beginning to clog. He said he would sleep himself fresh, and then see what he could do with this riddle. He slept through a troubled and unrestful hour, then unconsciousness began to shred away, and presently he rose drowsily to a sitting posture. "Now what was that dream?" he said, trying to recall it; "what was that dream?—it seemed to unravel that puz——"

He landed in the middle of the floor at a bound, without finishing the sentence, and ran and turned up his light and seized his "records." He took a single swift glance at them and cried out—

"It's so! Heavens, what a revelation! And for twenty-three years no man has ever suspected it!"

Chapter XXI

He is useless on top of the ground; he ought to be under it, inspiring the cabbages.

April 1. This is the day upon which we are reminded of what we are on the other three hundred and sixty-four.

Wilson put on enough clothes for business purposes and went to work under a high pressure of steam. He was awake all over. All sense of weariness had been swept away by the invigorating refreshment of the great and hopeful discovery which he had made. He made fine and accurate reproductions of a number of his "records," and then enlarged them on a scale of ten to one with his pantograph. He did these pantograph enlargements on sheets of white cardboard, and made each individual line of the bewildering maze of whorls or curves or loops which constituted the "pattern," of a "record" stand out bold and black by reinforcing it with ink. To the untrained eye the collection of delicate originals made by the human finger on the glass plates looked about alike; but when enlarged ten times they resembled the markings of a block of wood that has been sawed across the grain, and the dullest eye could detect at a glance, and at a distance of many feet, that no two of the patterns were alike. When Wilson had at last finished his tedious and

difficult work, he arranged its results according to a plan in which a progressive order and sequence was a principal feature; then he added to the batch several pantograph enlargements which he had made from time to time in bygone years.

The night was spent and the day well advanced, now. By the time he had snatched a trifle of breakfast it was nine o'clock, and the court was ready to begin its sitting. He was in his place twelve minutes later with his "records."

Tom Driscoll caught a slight glimpse of the records, and nudged his nearest friend and said, with a wink, "Pudd'nhead's got a rare eye to business—thinks that as long as he can't win his case it's at least a noble good chance to advertise his palace-window decorations without any expense." Wilson was informed that his witnesses had been delayed, but would arrive presently; but he rose and said he should probably not have occasion to make use of their testimony. [An amused murmur ran through the room—"It's a clean backdown! he gives up without

hitting a lick!"] Wilson continued—"I have other testimony—and better. [This compelled interest, and evoked murmurs of surprise that had a detectible ingredient of disappointment in them.] If I seem to be springing this evidence upon the court, I offer as my justification for this, that I did not discover its existence until late last night, and have been engaged in examining and classifying it ever since, until half an hour ago. I shall offer it presently; but first I wish to say a few preliminary words.

"May it please the Court, the claim given the front place, the claim most persistently urged, the claim most strenuously and I may even say aggressively and defiantly insisted upon by the prosecution, is this—that the person whose hand left the blood-stained finger-prints upon the handle of the Indian knife is the person who committed the murder." Wilson paused, during several moments, to give impressiveness to what he was about to say, and then added tranquilly, "*We grant that claim.*"

It was an electrical surprise. No one was prepared for such an admission. A buzz of astonishment rose on all sides, and people were heard to intimate that the overworked lawyer had lost his mind. Even the veteran judge, accustomed as he was to legal ambushes and masked batteries in criminal procedure, was not sure that his ears were not deceiving him, and asked counsel what it was he had said. Howard's impassive face betrayed no sign, but his attitude and bearing lost something of their careless confidence for a moment. Wilson resumed:

"We not only grant that claim, but we welcome it and strongly endorse it. Leaving that matter for the present, we will now proceed to consider other points in the case which we propose to establish by evidence, and shall include that one in the chain in its proper place."

He had made up his mind to try a few hardy guesses, in mapping out his theory of the origin and motive of the murder—guesses designed to fill up gaps in it—guesses which could help if they hit, and would probably do no harm if they didn't.

"To my mind, certain circumstances of the case before the court seem to suggest a motive for the homicide quite different from the one insisted on by the State. It is my conviction that the motive was not revenge, but robbery. It has been urged that the presence of the accused brothers in that fatal room, just after notification that one of them must take the life of Judge Driscoll or lose his own the moment the parties should meet, clearly signifies that the natural instinct of self-preservation moved my clients to go there secretly and save Count Luigi by destroying his adversary.

"Then why did they stay there, after the deed was done? Mrs. Pratt had time, although she did not hear the cry for help, but woke up some moments later, to run to that room—and there she found these men standing and making no effort to escape. If they were guilty, they ought to have been running out of the house at the same time that she was running to that room. If they had had such a strong instinct toward self-preservation as to move them to kill that unarmed man, what had become of it now, when it should have been more alert than ever? Would any of us have remained there? Let us not slander our intelligence to that degree.

"Much stress has been laid upon the fact that the accused offered a very large reward for the knife with which this murder was done; that no thief came forward to claim that extraordinary reward; that the latter fact was good circumstantial evidence that the claim that the knife had been stolen was a vanity and a fraud; that these details taken in connection with the memorable and apparently prophetic speech of the deceased concerning that knife, and the final discovery of that very knife in the fatal room where no living person was found present with the slaughtered man but the owner of the knife and his brother, form an indestructible chain of evidence which fixes the crime upon those unfortunate strangers.

"But I shall presently ask to be sworn, and shall testify that there was a large reward offered for the *thief,* also; that it was offered secretly and not advertised; that this fact was indiscreetly mentioned—or at least tacitly admitted—in what was supposed to be safe circumstances, but may *not* have been. The thief may have been present himself. [Tom Driscoll had been looking at the speaker, but dropped his eyes at this point.] In that case he would retain the knife in his possession, not daring to offer it for sale, or for pledge in a pawn-shop. [There was a nodding of heads among the audience by way of admission that this was not a bad stroke.] I shall prove to the satisfaction of the jury that there *was* a person in Judge Driscoll's room several minutes before the accused entered it. [This produced a strong sensation; the last drowsy-head in the court-room roused up, now, and made preparation to listen.] If it shall seem necessary, I will prove by the Misses Clarkson that they met a veiled person—ostensibly a woman—coming out of the back gate a few minutes after the cry for help was heard. This person was not a woman, but a man dressed in woman's clothes." Another sensation. Wilson had his eye on Tom when he hazarded this guess, to see what effect it would produce. He was satisfied with the result, and said to himself, "It was a success—he's hit!"

"The object of that person in that house was robbery, not murder. It is true that the safe was not open, but there was an ordinary tin cashbox on the table, with three thousand dollars in it. It is easily supposable that the thief was concealed in the house; that he knew of this box, and of its owner's habit of counting its contents and arranging his accounts at night—if he had that habit, which I do not assert, of course;—that he tried to take the box while its owner slept, but made a noise and was seized, and had to use the knife to save himself from capture; and that he fled without his booty because he heard help coming.

"I have now done with my theory, and will proceed to the evidences by which I propose to try to prove its soundness." Wilson took up several of his strips of glass. When the audience recognized these familiar mementoes of Pudd'nhead's old-time childish "puttering" and folly, the tense and funereal interest vanished out of their faces, and the house burst into volleys of relieving and refreshing laughter, and Tom chirked up and joined in the fun himself; but Wilson was apparently not disturbed. He arranged his records on the table before him, and said—

"I beg the indulgence of the court while I make a few remarks in explanation of some evidence which I am about to introduce, and which I shall presently ask to be allowed to verify under oath on the witness stand. Every human being carries with him from his cradle to his grave certain physical marks which do not change their character, and by which he can always be identified—and that without shade of doubt or question. These marks are his signature, his physiological autograph, so to speak, and this autograph can not be counterfeited, nor can he disguise it or hide it away, nor can it become illegible by the wear and mutations of time. This signature is not his face—age can change that beyond recognition; it is not his hair, for that can fall out; it is not his height, for duplicates of that exist; it is not his form, for duplicates of that exist also, whereas this signature is each man's very own—there is no duplicate of it among the swarming populations of the globe! [The audience were interested once more.]

"This autograph consists of the delicate lines or corrugations with which Nature marks the insides of the hands and the soles of the feet. If you will look at the balls of your fingers,—you that have very sharp eyesight,—you will observe that these dainty curving lines lie close together, like those that indicate the borders of oceans in maps, and that they form various clearly defined patterns, such as arches, circles, long curves, whorls, etc., and that these patterns differ on the different fingers. [Every man in the room had his hand up to the light, now, and his head canted to one side, and was minutely scrutinizing the balls of his fingers; there were whispered ejaculations of "Why, it's so—I never noticed that before!"] The patterns on the right hand are not the same as those on the left. [Ejaculations of "Why, that's so, too!"] Taken finger for finger, your patterns differ from your neighbor's. [Comparisons were made all over the house—even the judge and jury were absorbed in this curious work.] The patterns of a twin's right hand are not the same as those on his left. One twin's patterns are never the same as his fellow-twin's patterns—the jury will find that the patterns upon the finger-balls of the accused follow this rule. [An examination of the twins' hands was begun at once.] You have often heard of twins who were so exactly alike that when dressed alike their own parents could not tell them apart. Yet there was never a twin born into this world that did not carry from birth to death a sure identifier in this mysterious and marvelous natal autograph. That once known to you, his fellow-twin could never personate him and deceive you."

Wilson stopped and stood silent. Inattention dies a quick and sure death when a speaker does that. The stillness gives warning that something is coming. All palms and finger-balls went down, now, all slouching forms straightened, all heads came up, all eyes were fastened upon Wilson's face. He waited yet one, two, three moments, to let his pause complete and perfect its spell upon the house; then, when through the profound hush he could hear the ticking of the clock on the wall, he put out his hand and took the Indian knife by the blade and held it aloft where all could see the sinister spots upon its ivory handle; then he said, in a level and passionless voice—

"Upon this haft stands the assassin's natal autograph, written in the blood of that helpless and unoffending old man who loved you and whom you all loved. There is but one man in the whole earth whose hand can duplicate that crimson sign,"—he paused and raised his eyes to the pendulum swinging back and forth,—"and please God we will produce that man in this room before the clock strikes noon!"

Stunned, distraught, unconscious of its own movement, the house half rose, as if expecting to see the murderer appear at the door, and a breeze of muttered ejaculations swept the place. "Order in the court!— sit down!" This from the sheriff. He was obeyed, and quiet reigned again. Wilson stole a glance at Tom, and said to himself, "He is flying signals of distress, now; even people who despise him are pitying him; they think this is a hard ordeal for a young fellow who has lost his benefactor by so cruel a stroke—and they are right." He resumed his speech:

"For more than twenty years I have amused my compulsory leisure with collecting these curious physical signatures in this town. At my house I have hundreds upon hundreds of them. Each and every one is labelled with name and date; not labelled the next day or even the next hour, but in the very minute that the impression was taken. When I go upon the witness stand I will repeat under oath the things which I am now saying. I have the finger-prints of the court, the sheriff, and every member of the jury. There is hardly a person in this room, white or black, whose natal signature I cannot produce, and not one of them can so disguise himself that I cannot pick him out from a multitude of his fellow-creatures and unerringly identify him by his hands. And if he and I should live to be a hundred I could still do it. [The interest of the audience was steadily deepening, now.]

"I have studied some of these signatures so much that I know them as well as the bank cashier knows the autograph of his oldest customer. While I turn my back now, I beg that several persons will be so good as to pass their fingers through their hair, and then press them upon one of the panes of the window near the jury, and that among them the accused may set *their* finger-marks. Also, I beg that these experimenters, or others, will set their finger-marks upon another pane, and add again the marks of the accused, but not placing them in the same order or relation to the other signatures as before—for, by one chance in a million, a person might happen upon the right marks by pure guess-work *once*, therefore I wish to be tested twice."

He turned his back, and the two panes were quickly covered with delicately-lined oval spots, but visible only to such persons as could get a dark background for them—the foliage of a tree, outside, for instance. Then, upon call, Wilson went to the window, made his examination, and said—

"This is Count Luigi's right hand; this one, three signatures below, is his left. Here is Count Angelo's right; down here is his left. Now for the other pane: here and here are Count Luigi's, here and here are his brother's." He faced about. "Am I right?"

A deafening explosion of applause was the answer. The Bench said—

"This certainly approaches the miraculous!"

Wilson turned to the window again and remarked, pointing with his finger—

"This is the signature of Mr. Justice Robinson. [Applause.] This, of Constable Blake. [Applause.] This, of John Mason, juryman. [Applause.] This, of the sheriff. [Applause.] I cannot name the others, but I have them all at home, named and dated, and could identify them all by my finger-print records."

He moved to his place through a storm of applause—which the sheriff stopped, and also made the people sit down, for they were all standing and struggling to see, of course. Court, jury, sheriff, and everybody had been too absorbed in observing Wilson's performance to attend to the audience earlier.

"Now, then," said Wilson, "I have here the natal autographs of two children—thrown up to ten times the natural size by the pantograph, so that any one who can see at all can tell the markings apart at a glance. We will call the children *A* and *B*. Here are *A's* finger-marks, taken at the age of five months. Here they are again, taken at seven months. [Tom started.] They are alike, you see. Here are *B's* at five months, and also at seven months. They, too, exactly copy each other, but the patterns are quite different from *A's*, you observe. I shall refer to these again presently, but we will turn them face down, now.

"Here, thrown up ten sizes, are the natal autographs of the two persons who are here before you accused of murdering Judge Driscoll. I made these pantograph copies last night, and will so swear when I go upon the witness stand. I ask the jury to compare them with the finger-marks of the accused upon the window panes, and tell the court if they are the same."

He passed a powerful magnifying-glass to the foreman.

One juryman after another took the cardboard and the glass and made the comparison. Then the foreman said to the judge—

"Your honor, we are all agreed that they are identical."

Wilson said to the foreman—

"Please turn that cardboard face down, and take this one, and compare it searchingly, by the magnifier, with the fatal signature upon the knife-handle, and report your finding to the court."

Again the jury made minute examinations, and again reported—

"We find them to be exactly identical, your honor."

Wilson turned toward the counsel for the prosecution, and there was a clearly recognizable note of warning in his voice when he said—

"May it please the court, the State has claimed, strenuously and persistently, that the blood-stained finger-prints upon that knife-handle were left there by the assassin of Judge Driscoll. You have heard us grant that claim, and welcome it." He turned to the jury: "Compare the finger-prints of the accused with the finger-prints left by the assassin—and report."

The comparison began. As it proceeded, all movement and all sound ceased, and the deep silence of an absorbed and waiting suspense settled upon the house; and when at last the words came—

"*They do not even resemble,*" a thundercrash of applause followed and the house sprang to its feet, but was quickly repressed by official force and brought to order again. Tom was altering his position every few minutes, now, but none of his changes brought repose nor any small trifle of comfort. When the house's attention was become fixed once more, Wilson said gravely, indicating the twins with a gesture—

"These men are innocent—I have no further concern with them. [Another outbreak of applause began, but was promptly checked.] We will now proceed to find the guilty. [Tom's eyes were starting from their sockets—yes, it was a cruel day for the bereaved youth, everybody thought.] We will return to the infant autographs of *A* and *B*. I will ask the jury to take these large pantograph facsimiles of *A's* marked five months and seven months. Do they tally?"

The foreman responded—

"Perfectly."

"Now examine this pantograph, taken at eight months, and also marked *A*. Does it tally with the other two?"

The surprised response was—

"*No—they differ widely!*"

"You are quite right. Now take these two pantographs of *B's* autograph, marked five months and seven months. Do they tally with each other?"

"Yes—perfectly."

"Take this third pantograph marked *B,* eight months. Does it tally with *B's* other two?"

"*By no means!*"

"Do you know how to account for those strange discrepancies? I will tell you. For a purpose unknown to us, but probably a selfish one, somebody changed those children in the cradle."

This produced a vast sensation, naturally; Roxana was astonished at this admirable guess, but not disturbed by it. To guess the exchange was one thing, to guess who did it quite another. Pudd'nhead Wilson could do wonderful things, no doubt, but he couldn't do impossible ones. Safe? She was perfectly safe. She smiled privately.

"Between the ages of seven months and eight months those children were changed in the cradle"—he made one of his effect-collecting pauses, and added—"and the person who did it is in this house!"

Roxy's pulses stood still! The house was thrilled as with an electric shock, and the people half rose as if to seek a glimpse of the person who had made that exchange. Tom was growing limp; the life seemed oozing out of him. Wilson resumed:

"*A* was put into *B's* cradle in the nursery; *B* was transferred to the kitchen and became a negro and a slave, [Sensation—confusion of angry ejaculations]—but within a quarter of an hour he will stand before you white and free! [Burst of applause, checked by the officers.] From seven months onward until now, *A* has still been a usurper, and in my finger-record he bears *B's* name. Here is his pantograph at the age of twelve. Compare it with the assassin's signature upon the knife-handle. Do they tally?"

The foreman answered—

"To the minutest detail!"

Wilson said, solemnly—

"The murderer of your friend and mine—York Driscoll of the generous hand and the kindly

spirit—sits in among you. Valet de Chambre, negro and slave,—falsely called Thomas à Becket Driscoll,—make upon the window the finger-prints that will hang you!"

Tom turned his ashen face imploringly toward the speaker, made some impotent move-ments with his white lips, then slid limp and life-less to the floor.

Wilson broke the awed silence with the words—

"There is no need. He has confessed."

Roxy flung herself upon her knees, covered her face with her hands, and out through her sobs the words struggled—

"De Lord have mercy on me, po' misable sinner dat I is!"

The clock struck twelve.

The court rose; the new prisoner, handcuffed, was removed.

CONCLUSION

It is often the case that the man who can't tell a lie thinks he is the best judge of one.

PUDD'NHEAD WILSON'S CALENDAR

October 12, the Discovery. It was wonderful to find America, but it would have been more wonderful to miss it.

PUDD'NHEAD WILSON'S CALENDAR

The town sat up all night to discuss the amazing events of the day and swap guesses as to when Tom's trial would begin. Troop after troop of citizens came to serenade Wilson, and require a speech, and shout themselves hoarse over every sentence that fell from his lips—for all his sentences were golden, now, all were marvelous. His long fight against hard luck and prejudice was ended; he was a made man for good.

And as each of these roaring gangs of enthusiasts marched away, some remorseful member of it was quite sure to raise his voice and say—

"And this is the man the likes of us have called a pudd'nhead for more than twenty years. He has resigned from that position, friends."

"Yes, but it isn't vacant—we're elected."

———

The twins were heroes of romance, now, and with rehabilitated reputations. But they were weary of Western adventure, and straightway retired to Europe.

Roxy's heart was broken. The young fellow upon whom she had inflicted twenty-three years of slavery continued the false heir's pension of thirty-five dollars a month to her, but her hurts were too deep for money to heal; the spirit in her eye was quenched, her martial bearing departed with it, and the voice of her laughter ceased in the land. In her church and its affairs she found her only solace.

The real heir suddenly found himself rich and free, but in a most embarrassing situation. He could neither read nor write, and his speech was the basest dialect of the negro quarter. His gait, his attitudes, his gestures, his bearing, his laugh—all were vulgar and uncouth; his manners were the manners of a slave. Money and fine clothes could not mend these defects or cover them up; they only made them the more glaring and the more pathetic. The poor fellow could not endure the terrors of the white man's parlor, and felt at home and at peace nowhere but in the kitchen. The family pew was a misery to him, yet he could nevermore enter into the solacing refuge of the "nigger gallery"—that was closed to him for good and all. But we cannot follow his curious fate further—that it would be a long story.

The false heir made a full confession and was sentenced to imprisonment for life. But now a complication came up. The Percy Driscoll estate was in such a crippled shape when its owner died that it could pay only sixty per cent of its great indebtedness, and was settled at that rate. But the creditors came forward, now, and complained that inasmuch as through an error for which *they* were in no way to blame the false heir was not inventoried at that time with the rest of the property, great wrong and loss had thereby been inflicted upon them. They rightly claimed that "Tom" was lawfully their property and had been so for eight years; that they had already lost sufficiently in being deprived of his services during that long period, and ought not to be required to add anything to that loss; that if he had been delivered up to them in the first place, they would have sold him and he could not have murdered Judge Driscoll; therefore it was not he that had really committed the murder, the guilt lay with the erroneous inventory. Everybody saw that there was reason in this. Everybody granted that if "Tom" were white and free it would be unquestionably right to punish him—it would be no loss to anybody; but to shut up a valuable slave for life—that was quite another matter.

As soon as the Governor understood the case, he pardoned Tom at once, and the creditors sold him down the river.

THOSE
EXTRAORDINARY
TWINS

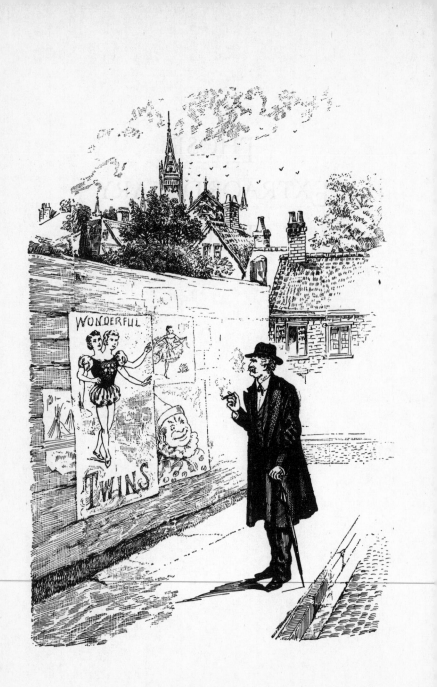

A man who is not born with the novel-writing gift has a trouble-some time of it when he tries to build a novel. I know this from experience. He has no clear idea of his story; in fact he has no story. He merely has some people in his mind, and an incident or two, also a lo-cality. He knows these people, he knows the selected locality, and he trusts that he can plunge those people into those incidents with inter-esting results. So he goes to work. To write a novel? No—that is a thought which comes later; in the beginning he is only proposing to tell a little tale; a very little tale; a six-page tale. But as it is a tale which he is not acquainted with, and can only find out what it is by listening as it goes along telling itself, it is more than apt to go on and on and on till it spreads itself into a book. I know about this, because it has hap-pened to me so many times.

And I have noticed another thing: that as the short tale grows into the long tale, the original intention (or motif) is apt to get abolished and find itself superseded by a quite different one. It was so in the case of a magazine sketch which I once started to write—a funny and fantastic sketch about a prince and a pauper; it presently assumed a grave cast of its own accord, and in that new shape spread itself out into a book. Much the same thing happened with "Pudd'nhead Wilson." I had a sufficiently hard time with that tale, because it changed itself from a farce to a tragedy while I was going along with it,—a most embarrassing circumstance. But what was a great deal worse was, that it was not one story, but two stories tangled together; and they obstructed and interrupted each other at every turn and created no end of con-fusion and annoyance. I could not offer the book for publication, for I was afraid it would unseat the reader's reason, I did not know what was the matter with it, for I had not noticed, as yet, that it was two stories in one. It took me months

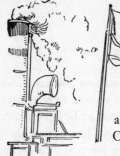

to make that discovery. I carried the manuscript back and forth across the Atlantic two or three times, and read it and studied over it on shipboard; and at last I saw where the difficulty lay. I had no further trouble. I pulled one of the stories out by the roots, and left the other one—a kind of literary Cæsarean operation.

Would the reader care to know something about the story which I pulled out? He has been told many a time how the born-and-trained novelist works; won't he let me round and complete his knowledge by telling him how the jack-leg does it?

Originally the story was called "Those Extraordinary Twins." I meant to make it very short. I had seen a picture of a youthful Italian "freak"— or "freaks"—which was—or which were—on exhibition in our cities—a combination consisting of two heads and four arms joined to a single body and a single pair of legs—and I thought I would write an extravagantly fantastic little story with this freak of nature for hero—or heroes—a silly young Miss for heroine, and two old ladies and two boys for the minor parts. I lavishly elaborated these people and their doings, of course. But the tale kept spreading along and spreading along, and other people got to intruding themselves and taking up more and more room with their talk and their affairs. Among them came a stranger named Pudd'nhead Wilson, and a woman named Roxana; and presently the doings of these two pushed up into prominence a young fellow named Tom Driscoll, whose proper place was away in the obscure background. Before the book was half finished those three were taking things almost entirely into their own hands and working the whole tale as a private venture of their own—a tale which they had nothing at all to do with, by rights.

When the book was finished and I came to look around to see what had become of the team I had originally started out with—Aunt Patsy Cooper, Aunt Betsy Hale, the two boys, and Rowena the light-weight heroine—they were nowhere to be seen; they had disappeared from the story some time or other. I hunted about and found them—found them stranded, idle, forgotten, and permanently useless. It was very awkward. It was awkward all around, but more particularly in the case of Rowena, because there was a lovematch on, between her and one of the twins that constituted the freak, and I had worked it up to a blistering heat and thrown in a quite dramatic love-quarrel, wherein Rowena scathingly denounced her betrothed for getting drunk, and scoffed at his explanation of how it had happened, and wouldn't listen to it, and had driven him from her in the usual "forever" way; and now here she sat crying and broken-hearted; for she had found that he had spoken only the truth; that it was not he, but the other half of the freak that had drunk the liquor that made him drunk; that her half was a prohibitionist and had never drunk a drop in his life, and although tight as a brick three days in the week, was wholly innocent of blame; and indeed, when sober, was constantly doing all he could to reform his brother, the other half, who never got any satisfaction out of drinking, anyway, because liquor never affected him. Yes, here she was, stranded with that deep injustice of hers torturing her poor torn heart.

I didn't know what to do with her. I was as sorry for her as anybody could be, but the campaign was over, the book was finished, she was sidetracked, and there was no possible way of crowding her in, anywhere. I could not leave her there, of course; it would not do. After spreading her out so, and making such a to-do over her affairs, it would be absolutely necessary to account to the reader for her. I thought and thought and studied and studied; but I arrived at nothing. I finally saw plainly that there was really no way but one—I must simply give her the grand bounce. It grieved me to do it, for after associating with her so much I had come to kind of like her after a fashion, notwithstanding she was such an ass and said such stupid, irritating things and was so nauseatingly sentimental. Still it had to be done. So at the top of Chapter XVII I put a "Calendar" remark concerning July the Fourth, and began the chapter with this statistic:

"Rowena went out in the back yard after supper to see the fireworks and fell down the well and got drowned."

It seemed abrupt, but I thought maybe the reader wouldn't notice it, because I changed the subject right away to something else. Anyway it loosened up Rowena from where she was stuck and got her out of the way, and that was the main thing. It seemed a prompt good way of weeding out people that had got stalled, and a plenty good enough way for those others; so I hunted up the two boys and said "they went out back one night to stone the cat and fell down the well and got drowned." Next I searched around and found old Aunt Patsy Cooper and Aunt Betsy Hale where they were aground, and said "they went out back one night to visit the sick and fell down the well and got drowned." I was going to drown some of the others, but I gave up the idea, partly because I believed that if I kept that up it would arouse attention, and perhaps sympathy with those people, and partly because it was not a large well and would not hold any more anyway.

Still the story was unsatisfactory. Here was a set of new characters who were become inordinately prominent and who persisted in remaining so to the end; and back yonder was an older set who made a large noise and a great to-do for a little while and then suddenly played out utterly and fell down the well. There was a radical defect somewhere, and I must search it out and cure it.

The defect turned out to be the one already spoken of—two stories in one, a farce and a tragedy. So I pulled out the farce and left the tragedy. This left the original team in, but only as mere names, not as characters. Their prominence was wholly gone; they were not even worth drowning; so I removed that detail. Also I took those twins apart and made two separate men of them. They had no occasion to have foreign names now, but it was too much trouble to remove them all through, so I left them christened as they were and made no explanation.

The Suppressed Farce

Chapter I

The conglomerate twins were brought on the stage in Chapter I of the original extravaganza. Aunt Patsy Cooper has received their letter applying for board and lodging, and Rowena, her daughter, insane with joy, is begging for a hearing of it:

"Well, set down then, and be quiet a minute and don't fly around so; it fairly makes me tired to see you. It starts off so: 'Honored Madam—' "

"I like that, ma, don't you? It shows they're high-bred."

"Yes, I noticed that when I first read it. 'My brother and I have seen your advertisement, by chance, in a copy of your local journal——' "

"It's so beautiful and smooth, ma—don't you think so?"

"Yes, seems so to me—'and beg leave to take the room you offer. We are twenty-four years of age, and twins——' "

"Twins! How sweet! I do hope they are handsome, and I just know they are! Don't you hope they are, ma?"

"Land, I ain't particular. 'We are Italians by birth——' "

"It's so romantic! Just think—there's never been one in this town, and everybody will want to see them, and they're all *ours!* Think of that!"

"—'but have lived long in the various countries of Europe, and several years in the United States.' "

"Oh, just think what wonders they've seen, ma! Won't it be good to hear them talk?"

"I reckon so; yes, I reckon so. 'Our names are Luigi and Angelo Capello——' "

"Beautiful, perfectly beautiful! Not like Jones and Robinson and those horrible names."

" 'You desire but one guest, but dear madam, if you will allow us to pay for two we will not discommode you. We will sleep together in the same bed. We have always been used to this, and prefer it.' And then he goes on to say they will be down Thursday."

"And this is Tuesday—I don't know how I'm ever going to wait, ma! The time does drag along so, and I'm so dying to see them! Which of them do you reckon is the tallest, ma?"

"How do you s'pose I can tell, child? Mostly they are the same size—twins are."

"Well then, which do you reckon is the best looking?"

"Goodness knows—I don't."

"I think Angelo is; it's the prettiest name, anyway. Don't you think it's a sweet name, ma?"

"Yes, it's well enough. I'd like both of them better if I knew the way to pronounce them—the Eyetalian way, I mean. The Missouri way and the Eyetalian way is different I judge."

"Maybe—yes. It's Luigi that writes the letter. What do you reckon is the reason Angelo didn't write it?"

"Why, how can I tell? What's the difference who writes it, so long as it's done?"

"Oh, I hope it wasn't because he is sick! You don't think he is sick, do you, ma?"

"Sick your granny; what's to make him sick?"

"Oh, there's never any telling. These foreigners with that kind of names are so delicate, and of course that kind of names are not suited to our climate—you wouldn't expect it."

[And so-on and so-on, no end. The time drags along; Thursday comes; the boat arrives in a pouring storm toward midnight.]

At last there was a knock at the door and the anxious family jumped to open it. Two negro men entered, each carrying a trunk, and proceeded up-stairs toward the guest-room. Then followed a stupefying apparition—a double-headed human creature with four arms, one body, and a single pair of legs!

It—or they, as you please—bowed with elaborate foreign formality, but the Coopers could not respond immediately; they were paralyzed. At this moment there came from the rear of the group a fervent ejaculation—"My lan'!"—followed by a crash of crockery, and the slave-wench Nancy stood petrified and staring, with a tray of wrecked tea-things at her feet. The incident broke the spell, and brought the family to consciousness. The beautiful heads of the new-comer bowed again, and one of them said with easy grace and dignity:

"I crave the honor, madam and miss, to introduce to you my brother, Count Luigi Capello," (the other head bowed) "and myself—Count Angelo; and at the same time offer sincere apologies for the lateness of our coming, which was unavoidable," and both heads bowed again.

The poor old lady was in a whirl of amazement and confusion, but she managed to stammer out:

"I'm sure I'm glad to make your acquaintance, sir—I mean, gentlemen. As for the delay, it is nothing, don't mention it. This is my daughter Rowena, sir—gentlemen. Please step into the parlor and sit down and have a bite and sup; you are dreadful wet and must be uncomfortable—both of you, I mean."

But to the old lady's relief they courteously excused themselves, saying it would be wrong to keep the family out of their beds longer; then each head bowed in turn and uttered a friendly good-night, and the singular figure moved away in the wake of Rowena's small brothers, who bore candles, and disappeared up the stairs.

The widow tottered into the parlor and sank into a chair with a gasp, and Rowena followed, tongue-tied and dazed. The two sat silent in the throbbing summer heat unconscious of the million-voiced music of the mosquitoes, unconscious of the roaring gale, the lashing and thrashing of the rain along the windows and the roof, the white glare of the lightning, the tumultuous booming and bellowing of the thunder; conscious of nothing but that prodigy, that uncanny apparition that had come and gone so suddenly—that weird strange thing that was so soft-spoken and so gentle of manner and yet had shaken them up like an earthquake with the shock of its gruesome aspect. At last a cold little shudder quivered along down the widow's meager frame and she said in a weak voice:

"Ugh, it was awful—just the mere look of that phillipene!"

Rowena did not answer. Her faculties were still caked, she had not yet found her voice. Presently the widow said, a little resentfully:

"Always been *used* to sleeping together—in fact, *prefer* it. And I was thinking it was to accommodate me. I thought it was very good of them, whereas a person situated as that young man is——"

"Ma, you oughtn't to begin by getting up a prejudice against him. I'm sure he is goodhearted and means well. Both of his faces show it."

"I'm not so certain about that. The one on the left—I mean the one on *its* left—hasn't near as good a face, in my opinion, as its brother."

"That's Luigi."

"Yes, Luigi; anyway it's the dark-skinned one; the one that was west of his brother when they stood in the door. Up to all kinds of mischief and disobedience when he was a boy, I'll be bound. I lay his mother had trouble to lay her hand on him when she wanted him. But the one on the right is as good as gold, I can see that."

"That's Angelo."

"Yes, Angelo, I reckon, though I can't tell t' other from which by their names, yet awhile. But it's the right-hand one—the blonde one. He has such kind blue eyes, and curly copper hair and fresh complexion——"

"And such a noble face!—oh, it *is* a noble face, ma, just royal, you may say! And beautiful—deary me, how beautiful! But both are that; the dark one's as beautiful as a picture. There's no such wonderful faces and handsome heads in this town—none that even begin. And such hands—especially Angelo's—so shapely and——"

"Stuff, how could you tell which they belonged to?—they had gloves on."

"Why, didn't I see them take off their hats?"

"That don't signify. They might have taken off each other's hats. Nobody could tell. There was just a wormy squirming of arms in the air—seemed to be a couple of dozen of them, all writhing at once, and it just made me dizzy to see them go."

"Why, ma, I hadn't any difficulty. There's two arms on each shoulder———"

"There, now. One arm on each shoulder belongs to each of the creatures, don't it? For a person to have two arms on one shoulder wouldn't do him any good, would it? Of course not. Each has an arm on each shoulder. Now then, you tell me which of them belongs to which, if you can. *They* don't know, themselves—they just work whichever arm comes handy. Of course they do; especially if they are in a hurry and can't stop to think which belongs to which."

The mother seemed to have the rights of the argument, so the daughter abandoned the struggle. Presently the widow rose with a yawn and said:

"Poor thing, I hope it won't catch cold; it was powerful wet, just drenched, you may say. I hope it has left its boots outside, so they can be dried." Then she gave a little start, and looked perplexed. "Now I remember I heard one of them ask Joe to call him at half after seven—I think it was the one on the left—no, it was the one to the east of the other one—but I didn't hear the other one say anything. I wonder if he wants to be called too. Do you reckon it's too late to ask?"

"Why, ma, it's not necessary. Calling one is calling both. If one gets up, the other's *got* to."

"Sho, of course; I never thought of that. Well, come along, maybe we can get some sleep, but I don't know, I'm so shook up with what we've been through."

The stranger had made an impression on the boys, too. They had a word of talk as they were getting to bed. Henry, the gentle, the humane, said:

"I feel ever so sorry for it, don't you, Joe?"

But Joe was a boy of this world, active, enterprising, and had a theatrical side to him:

"Sorry? Why, how you talk! It can't stir a step without attracting attention. It's just grand!"

Henry said, reproachfully:

"Instead of pitying it, Joe, you talk as if———"

"Talk as if *what?* I know one thing mighty certain: if you can fix me so I can eat for two and only have to stub toes for one, I ain't going to fool away no such chance just for sentiment."

The twins were wet and tired, and they proceeded to undress without any preliminary remarks. The abundance of sleeves made the partnership-coat hard to get off, for it was like skinning a tarantula; but it came at last, after much tugging and perspiring. The mutual vest followed. Then the brothers stood up before the glass, and each took off his own cravat and collar. The collars were of the standing kind, and came high up under the ears, like the sides of a wheelbarrow, as required by the fashion of the day. The cravats were as broad as a bank bill, with fringed ends which stood far out to right and left like the wings of a dragon-fly, and this also was strictly in accordance with the fashion of the time. Each cravat, as to color, was in perfect taste, so far as its owner's complexion was concerned—a delicate pink, in the case of the blonde brother, a violent scarlet in the case of the brunette— but as a combination they broke all the laws of taste known to civilization. Nothing more fiendish and irreconcilable than those shrieking and blaspheming colors could have been contrived. The wet boots gave no end of trouble—to Luigi. When they were off at last, Angelo said, with bitterness:

"I wish you wouldn't wear such tight boots, they hurt my feet."

Luigi answered with indifference:

"My friend, when I am in command of our body, I choose my apparel according to my own convenience, as I have remarked more than several times already. When you are in command, I beg you will do as you please."

Angelo was hurt, and the tears came into his eyes. There was gentle reproach in his voice, but not anger, when he replied:

"Luigi, I often consult your wishes, but you never consult mine. When I am in command I treat you as a guest; I try to make you feel at home; when you are in command you treat me as an intruder, you make me feel unwelcome. It embarrasses me cruelly in company, for I can see that people notice it and comment on it."

"Oh, damn the people," responded the brother languidly, and with the air of one who is tired of the subject.

A slight shudder shook the frame of Angelo, but he said nothing and the conversation ceased. Each buttoned his own share of the night-shirt in silence; then Luigi, with Paine's "Age of Reason" in his hand, sat down in one chair and put his feet in another and lit his pipe, while Angelo took his "Whole Duty of Man," and both began to read. Angelo presently began to cough; his coughing increased and became mixed with gaspings for breath, and he was finally obliged to make an appeal to his brother's humanity:

"Luigi, if you would only smoke a little milder tobacco, I am sure I could learn not to mind it in time, but this is so strong, and the pipe is so rank that——"

"Angelo, I wouldn't be such a baby! I have learned to smoke in a week, and the trouble is already over with me; if you would try, you could learn too, and then you would stop spoiling my comfort with your everlasting complaints."

"Ah, brother, that is a strong word—everlasting—and isn't quite fair. I only complain when I suffocate; you know I don't complain when we are in the open air."

"Well, anyway, you could learn to smoke yourself."

"But my *principles*, Luigi, you forget my principles. You would not have me do a thing which I regard as a sin?"

"Oh, bosh!"

The conversation ceased again, for Angelo was sick and discouraged and strangling; but after some time he closed his book and asked Luigi to sing "From Greenland's Icy Mountains" with him, but he would not, and when he tried to sing by himself Luigi did his best to drown his plaintive tenor with a rude and rollicking song delivered in a thundering bass.

After the singing there was silence, and neither brother was happy. Before blowing the light out Luigi swallowed half a tumbler of whiskey, and Angelo, whose sensitive organization could not endure intoxicants of any kind, took a pill to keep it from giving him the headache.

CHAPTER II

The family sat in the breakfast-room waiting
for the twins to come down. The widow was
quiet, the daughter was all alive with happy
excitement. She said:

"Ah, they're a boon, ma, just a boon! don't
you think so?"

"Laws, I hope so, I don't know."

"Why, ma, yes you do. They're so fine and
handsome, and high-bred and polite, so every
way superior to
our gawks here
in this village;

why, they'll make life different from what it was—so humdrum and commonplace, you know—oh, you may be sure they're full of accomplishments, and knowledge of the world, and all that, that will be an immense advantage to society here. Don't you think so, ma?"

"Mercy on me, how should I know, and I've hardly set eyes on them yet." After a pause she added, "They made considerable noise after they went up."

"Noise? Why, ma, they were singing! And it was beautiful, too."

"Oh, it was well enough, but too mixed-up, seemed to me."

"Now, ma, honor bright, did you ever hear 'Greenland's Icy Mountains' sung sweeter—now did you?"

"If it had been sung by itself, it would have been uncommon sweet, I don't deny it; but what they wanted to mix it up with 'Old Bob Ridley' for, I can't make out. Why, they don't go together, at all. They are not of the same nature. 'Bob Ridley' is a common rackety slam-bang secular song, one of the rippingest and rantingest and noisiest there is. I am no judge of music, and I don't claim it, but in my opinion nobody can make those two songs go together right."

"Why, ma, I thought——"

"It don't make any difference what you thought, it can't be done. They tried it, and to my mind it was a failure. I never heard such a crazy uproar; seemed to me, sometimes, the roof would come off; and as for the cats—well, I've lived a many a year, and seen cats aggravated in more ways than one, but I've never seen cats take on the way they took on last night."

"Well, I don't think that that goes for anything, ma, because it is the nature of cats that any sound that is unusual——"

"Unusual! You may well call it so. Now if they are going to sing duets every night, I do hope they will both sing the same tune at the same time, for in my opinion a duet that is made up of two different tunes is a mistake; especially when the tunes ain't any kin to one another, that way."

"But, ma, I think it must be a foreign custom; and it must be right too, and the best way, because they have had every opportunity to know what is right, and it don't stand to reason that with their education they would do anything but what the highest musical authorities have sanctioned. You can't help but admit that, ma."

The argument was formidably strong; the old lady could not find any way around it; so, after thinking it over a while she gave in with a sigh of discontent, and admitted that the daughter's position was probably correct. Being vanquished, she had no mind to continue the topic at that disadvantage, and was about to seek a change when a change came of itself. A footstep was heard on the stairs, and she said:

"There—he's coming!"

"*They*, ma—you ought to say *they*—it's nearer right."

The new lodger, rather shoutingly dressed but looking superbly handsome, stepped with courtly carriage into the trim little breakfast-room and put out all his cordial arms at once, like one of those pocket-knives with a multiplicity of blades, and shook hands with the whole family simultaneously. He was so easy and pleasant and hearty that all embarrassment presently thawed away and disappeared, and a cheery feeling of friendliness and comradeship took its place. He—or preferably they—were asked to occupy the seat of honor at the foot of the table. They consented with thanks, and carved the beefsteak with one set of their hands while they distributed it at the same time with the other set.

"Will you have coffee, gentlemen, or tea?"

"Coffee for Luigi, if you please, madam, tea for me."

"Cream and sugar?"

"For me, yes, madam; Luigi takes his coffee black. Our natures differ a good deal from each other, and our tastes also."

The first time the negro girl Nancy appeared in the door and saw the two heads turned in opposite directions and both talking at once, then saw the commingling arms feed potatoes into one mouth and coffee into the other at the same time, she had to pause and pull herself out of a faintness that came over her; but after that she held her grip and was able to wait on the table with fair courage.

Conversation fell naturally into the customary grooves. It was a little jerky, at first, because none of the family could get smoothly through a sentence without a wobble in it here and a break there, caused by some new surprise in the way of attitude or gesture on the part of the twins. The weather suffered the most. The weather was all finished up and disposed of, as a subject, before the simple Missourians had gotten sufficiently wonted to the spectacle of one body feeding two heads to feel composed and reconciled in the presence of so bizarre a miracle. And even after everybody's mind became tranquilized there was still one slight distraction left: the hand that picked up a biscuit carried it to the wrong head, as often as any other way, and the wrong mouth devoured it. This was a puzzling thing, and marred the talk a little. It bothered the widow to such a degree that she presently dropped out of the conversation without knowing it, and fell to watching and guessing and talking to herself:

"Now that hand is going to take that coffee to—no, it's gone to the other mouth; I can't understand it; and now, here is the dark complected hand with a potato on its fork, I'll see what goes with it—there, the light complected head's got it, as sure as I live!" Finally Rowena said:

"Ma, what is the matter with you? Are you dreaming about something?"

The old lady came to herself and blushed; then she explained with the first random thing that came into her mind: "I saw Mr. Angelo take up Mr. Luigi's coffee, and I thought maybe he—sha'n't I give *you* a cup, Mr. Angelo?"

"Oh no, madam, I am very much obliged, but I never drink coffee, much as I would like to. You did see me take up Luigi's cup, it is true, but if you noticed, I didn't carry it to my mouth, but to his."

"Y—es, I thought you did. Did you mean to?"

"How?"

The widow was a little embarrassed again. She said:

"I don't know but what I'm foolish, and you mustn't mind; but you see, he got the coffee I was expecting to see you drink, and you got a potato that I thought he was going to get. So I thought it might be a mistake all around, and everybody getting what wasn't intended for him."

Both twins laughed and Luigi said:

"Dear madam, there wasn't any mistake. We are always helping each other that way. It is a great economy for us both; it saves time and labor. We have a system of signs which nobody can notice or understand but ourselves. If I am using both my hands and want some coffee, I make the sign and Angelo furnishes it to me; and you saw that when he needed a potato I delivered it."

"How convenient!"

"Yes, and often of the extremest value. Take the Mississippi boats, for instance. They are always over-crowded. There is table-room for only half of the passengers, therefore they have to set a second table for the second half. The stewards rush both parties, they give them no time to eat a satisfying meal, both divisions leave the table hungry. It isn't so with us. Angelo books himself for the one table, I book myself for the other. Neither of us eats anything at the other's table, but just simply works—works. Thus, you see there are four hands to feed Angelo, and the same four to feed me. Each of us eats two meals."

The old lady was dazed with admiration, and kept saying, "It is *per-*fectly wonderful, perfectly wonderful!" and the boy Joe licked his chops enviously, but said nothing—at least aloud.

"Yes," continued Luigi, "our construction may have its disadvantages—in fact, *has*—but it also has its compensations, of one sort and another. Take travel, for instance. Travel is enormously expensive, in all countries; we have been obliged to do a vast deal of it—come, Angelo, don't put any more sugar in your tea, I'm just over one indigestion and don't want another right away—been obliged to do a deal of it, as I was saying. Well, we always travel as one person, since we occupy but one seat; so we save half the fare."

"How romantic!" interjected Rowena, with effusion.

"Yes, my dear young lady, and how practical too, and economical. In Europe, beds in the hotels are not charged with the board, but separately—another saving, for we stood to our rights and paid for the one bed only. The landlords often insisted that as both of us occupied the bed we ought——"

"No, they didn't," said Angelo. "They did it only twice, and in both cases it was a double bed—a rare thing in Europe—and the double bed gave them some excuse. Be fair to the landlords; twice doesn't constitute 'often.' "

"Well, that depends—that depends. I knew a man who fell down a well twice. He said he didn't mind the first time, but he thought the second time was once too often. Have I misused that word, Mrs. Cooper?"

"To tell the truth, I was afraid you had, but it seems to look, now, like you hadn't." She stopped, and was evidently struggling with the difficult problem a moment, then she added in the tone of one who is convinced without being converted, "It seems so, but I can't somehow tell why."

Rowena thought Luigi's retort was wonderfully quick and bright, and she remarked to herself with satisfaction that there wasn't any young native of Dawson's Landing that could have risen to the occasion like that. Luigi detected the applause in her face, and expressed his pleasure and his thanks with his eyes; and so eloquently withal, that the girl was proud and pleased, and hung out the delicate sign of it on her cheeks.

Luigi went on, with animation:

"Both of us get a bath for one ticket, theater seat for one ticket, pew-rent is on the same basis, but at peep-shows we pay double."

"We have much to be thankful for," said Angelo, impressively, with a reverent light in his eye and a reminiscent tone in his voice, "we have been greatly blessed. As a rule, what one of us has lacked, the other, by the bounty of Providence, has been able to supply. My brother is hardy, I am not; he is very masculine, assertive, aggressive; I am much less so. I am subject to illness, he is never ill. I cannot abide medicines, and cannot take them, but he has no prejudice against them, and——"

"Why, goodness gracious," interrupted the widow, "when you are sick, does he take the medicine for you?"

"Always, madam."

"Why, I never heard such a thing in my life! I think it's beautiful of you."

"Oh, madam, it's nothing, don't mention it, it's really nothing at all."

"But I say it's beautiful, and I stick to it!" cried the widow, with a speaking moisture in her eye. "A well brother to take the medicine for his poor sick brother—I wish I had such a son," and she glanced reproachfully at her boys. "I declare I'll never rest till I've shook you by the hand," and she scrambled out of her chair in a fever of generous enthusiasm, and made for the twins, blind with her tears, and began to shake. The boy Joe corrected her:

"You're shaking the wrong one, ma."

This flurried her, but she made a swift change and went on shaking.

"Got the wrong one again ma," said the boy.

"Oh, shut up, can't you!" said the widow, embarrassed and irritated. "Give me *all* your hands, I want to shake them all; for I know you are both just as good as you can be."

It was a victorious thought, a master-stroke of diplomacy, though, that never occurred to her and she cared nothing for diplomacy. She shook the four hands in turn cordially, and went back to her place in a state of high and fine exaltation that made her look young and handsome.

"Indeed I owe everything to Luigi," said Angelo, affectionately. "But for him I could not have survived our boyhood days, when we were friendless and poor—ah, so poor! We lived from hand to mouth—lived on the coarse fare of unwilling charity, and for weeks and weeks together not a morsel of food passed my lips, for its character revolted me and I could not eat it. But for Luigi I should have died. He ate for us both."

"How noble!" sighed Rowena.

"Do you hear that?" said the widow, severely, to her boys. "Let it be an example to you—I mean you, Joe."

Joe gave his head a barely perceptible disparaging toss and said: "Et for both. It ain't anything—I'd a done it."

"Hush, if you haven't got any better manners than that. You don't see the point at all. It wasn't good food."

"I don't care—it was food, and I'd 'a et it if it was rotten."

"Shame! Such language! Can't you understand? They were starving—actually starving—and he ate for both, and——"

"Shucks! you gimme a chance and I'll—"

"There, now—close your head! and don't you open it again till you're asked."

[Angelo goes on and tells how his parents the Count and Countess had to fly from Florence for political reasons, and died poor in Berlin bereft of their great property by confiscation; and how he and Luigi had to travel with a freak-show during two years and suffer semi-starvation.]

"That hateful black-bread! but I seldom ate anything during that time; that was poor Luigi's affair——"

"I'll never *Mister* him again!" cried the widow, with strong emotion, "he's Luigi to me, from this out!"

"Thank you a thousand times, madam, a thousand times! though in truth I don't deserve it."

"Ah, Luigi is always the fortunate one when honors are showering," said Angelo, plaintively, "now what have I done, Mrs. Cooper, that you leave me out? Come, you must strain a point in my favor."

"Call you Angelo? Why, certainly I will; what are you thinking of! In the case of twins, why——"

"But, ma, you're breaking up the story—do let him go on."

"You keep still, Rowena Cooper, and he can go on all the better, I reckon. One interruption don't hurt, it's two that makes the trouble."

"But you've added one, now, and that is three."

"Rowena! I will not allow you to talk back at me when you have got nothing rational to say."

CHAPTER III

[After breakfast the whole village crowded in, and there was a grand reception in honor of the twins; and at the close of it the gifted "freak" captured everybody's admiration by sitting down at the piano and knocking out a classic four-handed piece in great style. Then the Judge took it—or them—driving in his buggy and showed off his village.]

All along the streets the people crowded the windows and stared at the amazing

twins. Troops of small boys flocked after the buggy, excited and yelling. At first the dogs showed no interest. They thought they merely saw three men in a buggy—a matter of no consequence; but when they found out the facts of the case, they altered their opinion pretty radically, and joined the boys, expressing their minds as they came. Other dogs got interested; indeed all the dogs. It was a spirited sight to see them come leaping fences, tearing around corners, swarming out of every by-street and alley. The noise they made was something beyond belief—or praise. They did not seem to be moved by malice but only by prejudice, the common human prejudice against lack of conformity. If the twins turned their heads, they broke and fled in every direction, but stopped at a safe distance and faced about; and then formed and came on again as soon as the strangers showed them their back. Negroes and farmers' wives took to the woods when the buggy came upon them suddenly, and altogether the drive was pleasant and animated, and a refreshment all around.

[It was a long and lively drive. Angelo was a Methodist, Luigi was a Freethinker. The Judge was very proud of his Freethinker Society, which was flourishing along in a most prosperous way and already had two members—himself and the obscure and neglected Pudd'nhead Wilson. It was to meet that evening, and he invited Luigi to join; a thing which Luigi was glad to do, partly because it would please himself, and partly because it would gravel Angelo.]

They had now arrived at the widow's gate, and the excursion was ended. The twins politely expressed their obligations for the pleasant outing which had been afforded them; to which the Judge bowed his thanks, and then said he would now go and arrange for the Freethinkers' meeting, and would call for Count Luigi in the evening.

"For you also, dear sir," he added hastily, turning to Angelo and bowing. "In addressing myself particularly to your brother, I was not meaning to leave you out. It was an unintentional rudeness, I assure you, and due wholly to accident—accident and preoccupation. I beg you to forgive me."

His quick eye had seen the sensitive blood mount into Angelo's face, betraying the wound that had been inflicted. The sting of the slight had gone deep, but the apology was so prompt, and so evidently sincere, that the hurt was almost immediately healed, and a forgiving smile testified to the kindly Judge that all was well again.

Concealed behind Angelo's modest and unassuming exterior, and unsuspected by any but his intimates, was a lofty pride, a pride of almost abnormal proportions indeed, and this rendered him ever the prey of slights; and although they were almost always imaginary ones, they hurt none the less on that account. By ill fortune Judge Driscoll had happened to touch his sorest point, *i.e.,* his conviction that his brother's presence was welcomer everywhere than his own; that he was often invited, out of mere courtesy, where only his brother was wanted, and that in a majority of cases he would not be included in an invitation if he could be left out without offence. A sensitive nature like this is necessarily subject to moods; moods which traverse the whole gamut of feeling; moods which know all the climes of emotion, from the sunny heights of joy to the black abysses of despair. At times, in his seasons of deepest depression, Angelo almost wished that he and his brother might become segregated from each other and be separate individuals, like other men. But of course as soon as his mind cleared and these diseased imaginings passed away, he shuddered at the repulsive thought, and earnestly prayed that it might visit him no more. To be separate, and as other men are! How awkward it would seem; how unendurable. What would he do with his hands, his arms? How would his legs feel? How odd, and strange, and grotesque every action, attitude, movement, gesture would be. To sleep by himself, eat by himself, walk by himself—how lonely, how unspeakably lonely! No, no, any fate but that. In every way and from every point, the idea was revolting.

This was of course natural; to have felt otherwise would have been unnatural. He had known no life but a combined one; he had been familiar with it from his birth; he was not able to conceive of any other as being agreeable, or even bearable. To him, in the privacy of his secret thoughts, all other men were monsters, deformities; and during three-fourths of his life their aspect had filled him with what promised to be an unconquerable aversion. But at eighteen his eye began to take note of female beauty; and little by little, undefined longings grew up in his heart, under whose softening influences the old stubborn aversion gradually diminished, and finally disappeared. Men were still monstrosities to him, still deformities, and in his sober moments he

had no desire to be like them, but their strange and unsocial and uncanny construction was no longer offensive to him.

This had been a hard day for him, physically and mentally. He had
been called in the morning before he had quite slept off the effects of
the liquor which Luigi had drunk; and so, for the first half hour had had
the seedy feeling, and languor, the brooding depression, the cobwebby
mouth and druggy taste that come of dissipation and are so ill a preparation for bodily or intellectual activities; the
long violent strain of the reception had followed; and this had been followed, in turn, by
the dreary sight-seeing, the Judge's wearying explanations and laudations of the sights, and the stupefying clamor of the dogs. As a congruous
conclusion, a fitting end, his feelings had been
hurt, a slight had been put upon him. He
would have been glad to forego dinner and
betake himself to rest and sleep, but he held
his peace and said no word, for he knew his
brother, Luigi, was fresh, unweary, full of life,
spirit, energy; he would have scoffed at the
idea of wasting valuable time on a bed or a
sofa, and would have refused permission.

Chapter IV

Rowena was dining out, Joe and Harry were belated at play, there were but three chairs and four persons that noon at the home dinnertable—the twins, the widow, and her chum, Aunt Betsy Hale. The widow soon perceived that Angelo's spirits were as low as Luigi's were high, and also that he had a jaded look. Her motherly solicitude was aroused, and she tried to get him interested in the talk and win him to a happier frame of mind, but the cloud of sadness remained on his countenance. Luigi lent his help, too. He used a form and a phrase which he was always accustomed to employ in these circumstances. He gave his brother an affectionate slap on the shoulder and said, encouragingly:

"Cheer up, the worst is yet to come!"

But this did no good. It never did. If anything it made the matter worse, as a rule, because it irritated Angelo. This made it a favorite with Luigi. By and by the widow said:

"Angelo, you are tired, you've overdone yourself; you go right to bed, after dinner, and get a good nap and a rest, then you'll be all right."

"Indeed I would give anything if I could do that, madam."

"And what's to hender, I'd like to know? Land, the room's yours to do what you please with! The idea that you can't do what you like with your own!"

"But you see, there's one prime essential—an essential of the very first importance—which isn't my own."

"What is that?"

"My body."

The old ladies looked puzzled, and Aunt Betsy Hale said:

"Why bless your heart, how is that?"

"It's my brother's."

"Your brother's! I don't quite understand. I supposed it belonged to both of you."

"So it does. But not to both at the same time."

"That is mighty curious; I don't see how it can be. I shouldn't think it could be managed that way."

"Oh, it's a good enough arrangement, and goes very well; in fact it wouldn't do to have it otherwise. I find that the teetotalers and the anti-teetotalers hire the use of the same hall for their meetings. Both parties don't use it at the same time, do they?"

"You bet they don't!" said both old ladies in a breath.

"And moreover," said Aunt Betsy, "the Freethinkers and the Baptist Bible-class use the same room over the Market-house, but you can take my word for it they don't mush up together and use it at the same time."

"Very well," said Angelo, "you understand it now. And it stands to reason that the arrangement couldn't be improved. I'll prove it to you. If our legs tried to obey two wills, how could we ever get anywhere? I would start one way, Luigi would start another, at the same moment—the result would be a standstill, wouldn't it?"

"As sure as you are born! Now ain't that wonderful! A body would never have thought of it."

"We should always be arguing and fussing and disputing over the merest trifles. We should lose worlds of time, for we couldn't go down-stairs or up, couldn't go to bed, couldn't rise, couldn't wash, couldn't dress, couldn't stand up, couldn't sit down, couldn't even cross our legs, without calling a meeting first and explaining the case and passing resolutions, and getting consent. It wouldn't ever do—now would it?"

"Do? Why, it would wear a person out in a week! Did you ever hear anything like it, Patsy Cooper?"

"Oh, you'll find there's more than one thing about them that ain't commonplace," said the widow, with the complacent air of a person with a property-right in a novelty that is under admiring scrutiny.

"Well now, how ever do you manage it? I don't mind saying I'm suffering to know."

"He who made us," said Angelo reverently, "and with us this difficulty, also provided a way out of it. By a mysterious law of our being, each of us has utter and indisputable command of our body a week at a time, turn and turn about."

"Well, I never! Now ain't that beautiful!"

"Yes, it is beautiful and infinitely wise and just. The week ends every Saturday at midnight to the minute, to the second, to the last shade of a fraction of a second, infallibly, unerringly, and in that instant the one brother's power over the body vanishes and the other brother takes possession, asleep or awake."

"How marvelous are His ways, and past finding out!"

Luigi said: "So exactly to the instant does the change come, that during our stay in many of the great cities of the world, the public clocks were regulated by it; and as hundreds of thousands of private clocks and watches were set and corrected in accordance with the public clocks, we really furnished the standard time for the entire city."

"Don't tell me that He don't do miracles any more! Blowing down the walls of Jericho with rams' horns wa'n't as difficult, in my opinion."

"And that is not all," said Angelo. "A thing that is even more marvelous, perhaps, is the fact that the change takes note of longitude and fits itself to the meridian we are on. Luigi is in command this week. Now, if on Saturday night at a moment before midnight we could fly in an instant to a point fifteen degrees west of here, he would hold possession of the power another hour, for the change observes *local* time and no other."

Betsy Hale was deeply impressed, and said with solemnity:

"Patsy Cooper, for *de*tail it lays over the Passage of the Red Sea."

"Now, I shouldn't go as far as that," said Aunt Patsy, "but if you've a mind to say Sodom and Gomorrah, I am with you, Betsy Hale."

"I am agreeable, then, though I do think I was right, and I believe Parson Maltby would say the same. Well now, there's another thing. Suppose one of you wants to borrow the legs a minute from the one that's got them, could he let him?"

"Yes, but we hardly ever do that. There were disagreeable results, several times, and so we very seldom ask or grant the privilege, nowdays, and we never even think of such a thing unless the case is extremely urgent. Besides, a week's possession at a time seems so little that we can't bear to spare a minute of it. People who have the use of their legs all the time never think of what a blessing it is, of course. It never occurs to them; it's just their natural ordinary condition, and so it does not excite them at all. But when I wake up, on Sunday morning, and it's my week and I feel the power all through me, oh, such a wave of exultation and thanksgiving goes surging over me, and I want to shout 'I can walk! I can walk!' Madam, do you ever, at your uprising want to shout 'I can walk! I can walk'?"

"No, you poor unfortunate cretur', but I'll never get out of my bed again without *doing* it! Laws, to think I've had this unspeakable blessing all my long life and never had the grace to thank the good Lord that gave it to me!"

Tears stood in the eyes of both the old ladies and the widow said, softly:

"Betsy Hale, we have learned something, you and me."

The conversation now drifted wide, but by and by floated back once more to that admired detail, the rigid and beautiful impartiality with which the possession of power had been distributed between the twins.

Aunt Betsy saw in it a far finer justice than human law exhibits in related cases. She said:

"In my opinion it ain't right now, and never has been right, the way a twin born a quarter of a minute sooner than the other one gets all the land and grandeurs and nobilities in the old countries and his brother has to go bare and be a nobody. Which of you was born first?"

Angelo's head was resting against Luigi's; weariness had overcome him, and for the past five minutes he had been peacefully sleeping. The old ladies had dropped their voices to a lulling drone, to help him steal the rest his brother wouldn't take him up-stairs to get. Luigi listened a moment to Angelo's regular breathing, then said in a voice barely audible:

"We were both born at the same time, but I am six months older than he is."

"For the land's sake!"

"'Sh! don't wake him up; he wouldn't like my telling this. It has always been kept secret till now."

"But how in the world can it be? If you were both born at the same time, how can one of you be older than the other?"

"It is very simple, and I assure you it is true. I was born with a full crop of hair, he was as bald as an egg for six months. I could walk six months before he could make a step. I finished teething six months ahead of him. I began to take solids six months before he left the breast. I began to talk six months before he could say a word. Last, and absolutely unassailable proof, *the sutures in my skull closed six months ahead of his.* Always just that six months difference to a day. Was that accident? Nobody is going to claim that, I'm sure. It was ordained—it was law—it had its meaning, and we know what that meaning was. Now what does this overwhelming body of evidence establish? It establishes just one thing, and that thing it establishes beyond any peradventure whatever. Friends, we would not have it known for the world, and I must beg you to keep it strictly to yourselves, but the truth is, *we are no more twins than you are.*"

The two old ladies were stunned, paralyzed—petrified, one may almost say—and could only sit and gaze vacantly at each other for some moments; then Aunt Betsy Hale said impressively:

"There's no getting around proof like that. I do believe it's the most amazing thing I ever heard of." She sat silent a moment or two and breathing hard with excitement, then she looked up and surveyed the strangers steadfastly a little while, and added: "Well, it does beat me, but I would have took you for twins anywhere."

"So would I, so would I," said Aunt Patsy with the emphasis of a certainty that is not impaired by any shade of doubt.

"*Any*body would—anybody in the world, I don't care who he is," said Aunt Betsy with decision.

"You won't tell," said Luigi, appealingly.

"Oh, dear no!" answered both ladies promptly, "you can trust us, don't you be afraid."

"That is good of you, and kind. Never let on; treat us always as if we were twins."

"You can depend on us," said Aunt Betsy, "but it won't be easy, because now that I know you ain't, you don't *seem* so."

Luigi muttered to himself with satisfaction: "That swindle has gone through without change of cars."

It was not very kind of him to load the poor things up with a secret like that, which would be always flying to their tongues' ends every time they heard any one speak of the strangers as twins, and would become harder and harder to hang on to with every recurrence of the temptation to tell it, while the torture of retaining it would increase with every new strain that was applied; but he never thought of that, and probably would not have worried much about it if he had.

A visitor was announced—some one to see the twins. They withdrew to the parlor, and the two old ladies began to discuss with interest the strange things which they had been listening to. When they had finished the matter to their satisfaction, and Aunt Betsy rose to go, she stopped to ask a question:

"How does things come on between Roweny and Tom Driscoll?"

"Well, about the same. He writes tolerable often, and she answers tolerable seldom."

"Where is he?"

"In St. Louis, I believe, though he's such a gad-about that a body can't be very certain of him, I reckon."

"Don't Roweny know?"

"Oh, yes, like enough. I haven't asked her lately."

"Do you know how him and the Judge are getting along now?"

"First-rate, I believe. Mrs. Pratt says so; and being right in the house, and sister to the one and aunt to t' other, of course she ought to know. She says the Judge is real fond of him when he's away, but frets when he's around and is vexed with his ways, and not sorry to have him go again. He has been gone three weeks this time—a pleasant thing for both of them, I reckon."

"Tom's ruther harum-scarum, but there ain't anything bad in him, I guess."

"Oh no, he's just young, that's all. Still, twenty-three is old, in one way. A young man ought to be earning his living by that time. If Tom were doing that, or was even trying to do it, the Judge would be a heap better satisfied with him. Tom's always going to begin, but somehow he can't seem to find just the opening he likes."

"Well now, it's partly the Judge's own fault. Promising the boy his property wasn't the way to set him to earning a fortune of his own. But what do you think—is Roweny beginning to lean any towards him, or ain't she?"

Aunt Patsy had a secret in her bosom; she wanted to keep it there, but nature was too strong for her. She drew Aunt Betsy aside, and said in her most confidential and mysterious manner:

"Don't you breathe a syllable to a soul—I'm going to tell you something. In my opinion Tom Driscoll's chances were considerable better yesterday than they are today."

"Patsy Cooper, what *do* you mean?"

"It's so, as sure as you're born. I wish you could 'a' been at breakfast and seen for yourself."

"You don't mean it!"

"Well, if I'm any judge, there's a leaning—there's a leaning, sure."

"My land! Which one of 'em is it?"

"I can't say for certain, but I think it's the youngest one—Anjy."

Then there were handshakings, and congratulations, and hopes, and so on, and the old ladies parted, perfectly happy—the one in knowing something which the rest of the town didn't, and the other in having been the sole person able to furnish that knowledge.

The visitor who had called to see the twins was the Rev. Mr. Hotchkiss, pastor of the Baptist church. At the reception Angelo had told him he had lately experienced a change in his religious views, and was now desirous of becoming a Baptist, and would immediately join Mr. Hotchkiss's church. There was no time to say more, and the brief talk ended at that point. The minister was much gratified, and had dropped in for a moment, now, to invite the twins to attend his Bible-class at eight that evening. Angelo accepted, and was expecting Luigi to decline, but he did not, because he knew that the Bible-class and the Freethinkers met in the same room, and he wanted to treat his brother to the embarrassment of being caught in freethinking company.

CHAPTER V

[A long and vigorous quarrel follows, between the twins. And there is plenty to quarrel about, for Angelo was always seeking truth, and this obliged him to change and improve his religion with frequency, which wearied Luigi, and annoyed him too; for he had to be present at each new enlistment—which placed him in the false position of seeming to indorse and approve his brother's fickleness; moreover, he had to go to Angelo's prohibition meetings, and he hated them. On the other hand, when it was *his* week to command the legs he gave Angelo just cause of complaint, for he took him to circuses and horse-races and fandangoes, exposing him to all sorts of censure and criticism; and he drank, too; and whatever he drank went to Angelo's head instead of his own and made him act disgracefully. When the evening was come, the two at-

tended the Freethinkers' meeting, where Angelo was sad and silent; then came the Bible-class and looked upon him coldly, finding him in such company. Then they went to Wilson's house, and Chapter XI of "Pudd'nhead Wilson" follows, which tells of the girl seen in Tom Driscoll's room; and closes with the kicking of Tom by Luigi at the anti-temperance mass meeting of the Sons of Liberty; with the addition of some account of Roxy's adventures as a chambermaid on a Mississippi boat. Her exchange of the children had been flippantly and farcically described in an earlier chapter.]

Next morning all the town was a-buzz with great news; Pudd'nhead Wilson had a law-case! The public astonishment was so great and the public curiosity so intense, that when the justice of the peace opened his court, the place was packed with people, and even the windows were full. Everybody was flushed and perspiring, the summer heat was almost unendurable.

Tom Driscoll had brought a charge of assault and battery against the twins. Robert Allen was retained by Driscoll, David Wilson by the defense. Tom, his native cheerfulness unannihilated by his back-breaking and bone-bruising passage across the massed heads of the Sons of Liberty the previous night, laughed his little customary laugh, and said to Wilson:

"I've kept my promise, you see: I'm throwing my business your way. Sooner than I was expecting, too."

"It's very good of you—particularly if you mean to keep it up."

"Well, I can't tell

about that, yet. But we'll see. If I find you deserve it I'll take you under my protection and make your fame and fortune for you."

"I'll try to deserve it, Tom."

A jury was sworn in; then Mr. Allen said:

"We will detain your honor but a moment with this case. It is not one where any doubt of the fact of the assault can enter in. These gentlemen—the accused—kicked my client at the Market Hall last night; they kicked him with violence; with extraordinary violence; with even unprecedented violence, I may say; insomuch that he was lifted entirely off his feet and discharged into the midst of the audience. We can prove this by four hundred witnesses—we shall call but three. Mr. Harkness will take the stand."

Mr. Harkness being sworn, testified that he was chairman upon the occasion mentioned; that he was close at hand and saw the defendants in this action kick the plaintiff into the air and saw him descend among the audience.

"Take the witness," said Allen.

"Mr. Harkness," said Wilson, "you say you saw these gentlemen, my clients, kick the plaintiff. Are you sure—and please remember that you are on oath—are you perfectly sure that you saw *both* of them kick him, or only one? Now be careful."

A bewildered look began to spread itself over the witness's face. He hesitated, stammered, but got out nothing. His eyes wandered to the twins and fixed themselves there with a vacant gaze.

"Please answer, Mr. Harkness, you are keeping the court waiting. It is a very simple question."

Counsel for the prosecution broke in with impatience:

"Your honor, the question is an irrelevant triviality. Necessarily they both kicked him, for they have but the one pair of legs, and both are responsible for them."

Wilson said, sarcastically:

"Will your honor permit this new witness to be sworn? He seems to possess knowledge which can be of the utmost value just at this moment—knowledge which would at once dispose of what every one must see is a very difficult question in this case. Brother Allen, will you take the stand?"

"Go on with your case!" said Allen, petulantly. The audience laughed, and got a warning from the court.

"Now, Mr. Harkness," said Wilson, insinuatingly, "we shall have to insist upon an answer to that question."

"I—er—well, of course I do not absolutely *know*, but in my opinion——"

"Never mind your opinion, sir—answer the question."

"I—why, I *can't* answer it."

"That will do, Mr. Harkness. Stand down."

The audience tittered, and the discomfited witness retired in a state of great embarrassment.

Mr. Wakeman took the stand and swore that he saw the twins kick the plaintiff off the platform. The defence took the witness.

"Mr. Wakeman, you have sworn that you saw these gentlemen kick the plaintiff. Do I understand you to swear that you saw them *both* do it?"

"Yes, sir,"—with decision.

"How do you know that both did it?"

"Because I *saw* them do it."

The audience laughed, and got another warning from the court.

"But by what means do you know that both, and not one, did it?"

"Well, in the first place, the insult was given to both of them equally, for they were called a pair of scissors. Of course they would both want to resent it, and so——"

"Wait! You are theorizing now. Stick to facts—counsel will attend to the arguments. Go on."

"Well, they both went over there—*that* I saw."

"Very good. Go on."

"And they both kicked him—I swear to it."

"Mr. Wakeman, was Count Luigi, here, willing to join the Sons of Liberty last night?"

"Yes, sir, he was. He did join, too, and drank a glass or two of whisky, like a man."

"Was his brother willing to join?"

"No, sir, he wasn't. He is a teetotaler, and was elected through a mistake."

"Was he given a glass of whisky?"

"Yes, sir, but of course that was another mistake, and not intentional. He wouldn't drink it. He set it down." A slight pause, then he added, casually and quite simply: "The plaintiff reached for it and hogged it."

There was a fine outburst of laughter, but as the justice was caught out himself, his reprimand was not very vigorous.

Mr. Allen jumped up and exclaimed: "I protest against these foolish irrelevancies. What have they to do with the case?"

Wilson said: "Calm yourself, brother, it was only an experiment. Now, Mr. Wakeman, if one of these gentlemen chooses to join an association and the other doesn't; and if one of them enjoys whisky and the other doesn't, but sets it aside and leaves it unprotected" (titter from the audience), "it seems to show that they have independent minds and tastes and preferences, and that one of them is able to approve of a thing at the very moment that the other is heartily disapproving of it. Doesn't it seem so to you?"

"Certainly it does. It's perfectly plain."

"Now then, it might be—I only say it might be—that one of these brothers wanted to kick the plaintiff last night, and that the other didn't want that humiliating punishment inflicted upon him in that public way and before all those people. Isn't that possible?"

"Of course it is. It's more than possible. I don't believe the blonde one would kick anybody. It was the other one that——"

"Silence!" shouted the plaintiff's counsel, and went on with an angry sentence which was lost in the wave of laughter that swept the house.

"That will do, Mr. Wakeman," said Wilson, "you may stand down."

The third witness was called. He had seen the twins kick the plaintiff. Mr. Wilson took the witness.

"Mr. Rogers, you say you saw these accused gentlemen kick the plaintiff?"

"Yes, sir."

"Both of them?"

"Yes, sir."

"Which of them kicked him first?"

"Why—they—they both kicked him at the same time."

"Are you perfectly sure of that?"

"Yes, sir."

"What makes you sure of it?"

"Why, I stood right behind them, and *saw* them do it."

"How many kicks were delivered?"

"Only one."

"If two men kick, the result should be two kicks, shouldn't it?"

"Why—why—yes, as a rule."

"Then what do you think went with the other kick?"

"I—well—the fact is, I wasn't thinking of two being necessary, this time."

"What do you think now?"

"Well, I—I'm sure I don't quite know what to think, but I reckon that one of them did half of the kick and the other one did the other half."

Somebody in the crowd sung out: "It's the first sane thing that any of them has said."

The audience applauded. The judge said: "Silence! or I will clear the court."

Mr. Allen looked pleased, but Wilson did not seem disturbed. He said:

"Mr. Rogers, you have favored us with what you think and what you reckon, but as thinking and reckoning are not evidence, I will now give you a chance to come out with something positive, one way or the other, and shall require you to produce it. I will ask the accused to stand up and repeat the phenomenal kick of last night." The twins stood up. "Now, Mr. Rogers, please stand behind them."

A Voice: "No, stand in front!" (Laughter. Silenced by the court.) Another Voice: "No, give Tommy another highst!" (Laughter. Sharply rebuked by the court.)

"Now then, Mr. Rogers, two kicks shall be delivered, one after the other, and I give you my word that at least one of the two shall be delivered by one of the twins alone, without the slightest assistance from his brother. Watch sharply, for you have got to render a decision without any if's and and's in it." Rogers bent himself behind the twins with his palms just above his knees, in the modern attitude of the catcher at a base-ball match, and riveted his eyes on the pair of legs in front of him. "Are you ready, Mr. Rogers?"

"Ready, sir."

"Kick!"

The kick was launched.

"Have you got that one classified, Mr. Rogers?"

"Let me study a minute, sir."

"Take as much time as you please. Let me know when you are ready."

For as much as a minute Rogers pondered, with all eyes and a breathless interest fastened upon him. Then he gave the word: "Ready, sir."

"Kick!"

The kick that followed was an exact duplicate of the first one.

"Now then, Mr. Rogers, one of those kicks was an individual kick, not a mutual one. You will now state positively which was the mutual one."

The witness said, with a crestfallen look:

"I've got to give it up. There ain't any man in the world that could tell t'other from which, sir."

"Do you still assert that last night's kick was a mutual kick?"

"Indeed I don't, sir."

"That will do, Mr. Rogers. If my brother Allen desires to address the court, your honor, very well; but as far as I am concerned I am ready to let the case be at once delivered into the hands of this intelligent jury without comment."

Mr. Justice Robinson had been in office only two months, and in that short time had not had many cases to try, of course. He had no knowledge of laws and courts except what he had picked up since he came into office. He was a sore trouble to the lawyers, for his rulings were pretty eccentric sometimes, and he stood by them with Roman simplicity and fortitude; but the people were well satisfied with him, for they saw that his intentions were always right, that he was entirely impartial, and that he usually made up in good sense what he lacked in technique, so to speak. He now perceived that there was likely to be a miscarriage of justice here, and he rose to the occasion.

"Wait a moment, gentlemen," he said, "it is plain that an assault has been committed—it is plain to anybody; but the way things are going, the guilty will certainly escape conviction. I cannot allow this. Now——"

"But, your honor!" said Wilson, interrupting him, earnestly but respectfully, "you are deciding the case yourself, whereas the jury——"

"Never mind the jury, Mr. Wilson; the jury will have a chance when there is a reasonable doubt for them to take hold of—which there isn't, so far. There is no doubt whatever that an assault has been committed. The attempt to show that both of the accused committed it has failed. Are they both to escape justice on that account? Not in this court, if I can prevent it. It appears to have been a mistake to bring the charge against them as a corporation; each should have been charged in his capacity as an individual, and——"

"But your honor!" said Wilson, "in fairness to my clients I must insist that inasmuch as the prosecution did not separate the——"

"No wrong will be done your clients, sir—they will be protected; also the public and the offended laws. Mr. Allen, you will amend your pleadings, and put one of the accused on trial at a time."

Wilson broke in: "But your honor! this is wholly unprecedented! To imperil an accused person by arbitrarily altering and widening the charge against him in order to compass his conviction when the charge as originally brought promises to fail to convict, is a thing unheard of before."

"Unheard of *where?*"

"In the courts of this or any other State."

The judge said with dignity: "I am not aquainted with the customs of other courts, and am not concerned to know what they are. I am responsible for this court, and I cannot conscientiously allow my judgment to be warped and my judicial liberty hampered by trying to conform to the caprices of other courts, be they————"

"But, your honor, the oldest and highest courts in Europe————"

"This court is not run on the European plan, Mr. Wilson; it is not run on any plan but its own. It has a plan of its own; and that plan is, to find justice for both State and accused, no matter what happens to be practice and custom in Europe or anywhere else." (Great applause.) "Silence! It has not been the custom of this court to imitate other courts; it has not been the custom of this court to take shelter behind the decisions of other courts, and we will not begin now. We will do the best we can by the light that God has given us, and while this court continues to have His approval, it will remain indifferent to what other organizations may think of it." (Applause.) "Gentlemen, I *must* have order!—quiet yourselves! Mr. Allen, you will now proceed against the prisoners one at a time. Go on with the case."

Allen was not at his ease. However, after whispering a moment with his client and with one or two other people, he rose and said:

"Your honor, I find it to be reported and believed that the accused are able to act independently in many ways, but that this independence does not extend to their legs, authority over their legs being vested exclusively in the one brother during a specific term of days, and then passing to the other brother for a like term, and so on, by regular alternation. I could call witnesses who would prove that the accused had revealed to them the existence of this extraordinary fact, and had also made known which of them was in possession of the legs yesterday—and this would of course indicate where the guilt of the assault belongs—but as this would be mere hearsay evidence, these revelations not having been made under oath————"

"Never mind about that, Mr. Allen. It may not all be hearsay. We shall see. It may at least help to put us on the right track. Call the witnesses."

"Then I will call Mr. John Buckstone, who is now present, and I beg that Mrs. Patsy Cooper may be sent for. Take the stand, Mr. Buckstone."

Buckstone took the oath, and then testified that on the previous evening the Count Angelo Cappello had protested against going to the hall, and had called all present to witness that he was going by compulsion and would not go if he could help himself. Also, that the Count Luigi had replied sharply that he would *go*, just the same, and that he, Count Luigi, would see to that, himself. Also, that upon Count Angelo's complaining about being kept on his legs so long, Count Luigi retorted with apparant surprise, '*Your* legs!—I like your impudence!' "

"*Now* we are getting at the kernel of the thing," observed the judge, with grave and earnest satisfaction. "It looks as if the Count Luigi was in possession of the battery at the time of the assault."

Nothing further was elicited from Mr. Buckstone on direct examination. Mr. Wilson took the witness.

"Mr. Buckstone, about what time was it that that conversation took place?"

"Toward nine yesterday evening, sir."

"Did you then proceed directly to the hall?"

"Yes, sir."

"How long did it take you to go there?"

"Well, we walked; and as it was from the extreme edge of the town, and there was no hurry, I judge it took us about twenty minutes, maybe a trifle more."

"About what hour was the kick delivered?"

"At thirteen minutes and a half to ten."

"Admirable! You are a pattern witness, Mr. Buckstone. How did you happen to look at your watch at that particular moment?"

"I always do it when I see an assault. It's likely I shall be called as a witness, and it's a good point to have."

"It would be well if others were as thoughtful. Was anything said, between the conversation at my house and the assault, upon the detail which we are now examining into?"

"No, sir."

"If power over the mutual legs was in the possession of one brother at nine, and passed into the possession of the other one during the next thirty or forty minutes, do you think you could have detected the change?"

"By no means!"

"That is all, Mr. Buckstone."

Mrs. Patsy Cooper was called. The crowd made way for her, and she came smiling and bowing through the narrow human lane, with Betsy Hale, as escort and support, smiling and bowing in her wake, the audience breaking into welcoming cheers as the old favorites filed along. The judge did not check this kindly demonstration of homage and affection, but let it run its course unrebuked.

The old ladies stopped and shook hands with the twins with effusion, then gave the judge a friendly nod, and bustled into the seats provided for them. They immediately began to deliver a volley of eager questions at the friends around them: "What is this thing for?" "What is that thing for?" "Who is that young man that's writing at the desk? Why, I declare, it's Jack Bunce! I thought he was sick." "Which is the jury? Why, is *that* the jury? Billy Price and Job Turner, and Jack Lounsbury, and—well, I never!" "Now who would ever a' thought——"

But they were gently called to order at this point, and asked not to talk in court. Their tongues fell silent, but the radiant interest in their faces remained, and their gratitude for the blessing of a new sensation and a novel experience still beamed undimmed from their eyes. Aunt Patsy stood up and took the oath, and Mr. Allen explained the point in issue, and asked her to go on, now, in her own way, and throw as much light upon it as she could. She toyed with her reticule a moment or two, as if considering where to begin, then she said:

"Well, the way of it is this. They are Luigi's legs a week at a time, and then they are Angelo's, and he can do whatever he wants to with them."

"You are making a mistake, Aunt Patsy Cooper," said the judge. "You shouldn't state that as a *fact,* because you don't know it to *be* a fact."

"What's the reason I don't?" said Aunt Patsy, bridling a little.

"What is the reason that you do know it?"

"The best in the world—because they told me."

"That isn't a reason."

"Well, for the land's sake! Betsy Hale, do you hear that?"

"*Hear* it? I should think so," said Aunt Betsy, rising and facing the court. "Why, Judge, I was there and heard it myself. Luigi says to Angelo—no, it was Angelo said it to——"

"Come, come, Mrs. Hale, pray sit down, and——"

"Certainly, it's all right, I'm going to sit down presently, but not until I've——"

"But you *must* sit down!"

"*Must!* Well, upon my word if things ain't getting to a pretty pass when——"

The house broke into laughter, but was promptly brought to order, and meantime Mr. Allen persuaded the old lady to take her seat. Aunt Patsy continued:

"Yes, they told me that, and I know it's true. They're Luigi's legs this week, but—"

"Ah, *they* told you that, did they?" said the justice, with interest.

"Well no, I don't know that *they* told me, but that's neither here nor there. I know, without that, that at dinner yesterday, Angelo was as tired as a dog, and yet Luigi wouldn't lend him the legs to go up-stairs and take a nap with."

"Did he ask for them?"

"Let me see—it seems to me somehow, that—that— Aunt Betsy, do you remember whether he——"

"Never mind about what Aunt Betsy remembers—she is not a witness; we only want to know what you remember, yourself," said the judge.

"Well, it does seem to me that you are most cantankerously particular about a little thing, Sim Robinson. Why, when I can't remember a thing myself, I always——"

"Ah, *please* go on!"

"Now how *can* she when you keep fussing at her all the time?" said Aunt Betsy. "Why, with a person pecking at *me* that way, I should get that fuzzled and fuddled that——"

She was on her feet again, but Allen coaxed her into her seat once more, while the court squelched the mirth of the house. Then the judge said:

"Madam, do you know——do you absolutely *know,* independently of anything these gentlemen have told you—that the power over their legs passes from the one to the other regularly every week?"

"Regularly? Bless your heart, regularly ain't any name for the exactness of it! All the big cities in Europe used to set the clocks by it." (Laughter, *suppressed by the court.*)

"How do you *know?* That is the question. Please answer it plainly and squarely."

"Don't you talk to me like that, Sim Robinson—I won't have it. How do I know, indeed! How do *you* know what you know? Because somebody told you. You didn't invent it out of your own head, did you? Why, these twins are the truthfulest people in the world; and I don't think it becomes you to sit up there and throw slurs at them when they haven't been doing anything to you. And they are orphans besides—both of them. All——"

But Aunt Betsy was up again, now, and both old ladies were talking at once and with all their might; but as the house was weltering in a storm of laughter, and the judge was hammering his desk with an iron paper-weight, one could only see them talk, not hear them. At last, when quiet was restored, the court said:

"Let the ladies retire."

"But, your honor, I have the right, in the interest of my clients, to cross-exam———"

"You'll not need to exercise it, Mr. Wilson—the evidence is thrown out."

"Thrown out!" said Aunt Patsy, ruffled; "and what's it thrown out for, I'd like to know."

"And so would I, Patsy Cooper. It seems to me that if we can save these poor persecuted strangers, it is our bounden duty to stand up here and talk for them till———"

"There, there, there, *do* sit down!"

It cost some trouble and a good deal of coaxing, but they were got into their seats at last. The trial was soon ended, now. The twins themselves became witnesses in their own defense. They established the fact, upon oath, that the leg-power passed from one to the other every Saturday night at twelve o'clock, sharp. But on cross-examination their counsel would not allow them to tell whose week of power the current week was. The judge insisted upon their answering, and proposed to compel them; but even the prosecution took fright and came to the rescue then, and helped stay the sturdy jurist's revolutionary hand. So the case had to go to the jury with that important point hanging in the air. They were out an hour, and brought in this verdict:

"We the jury do find: 1, that an assault was committed, as charged; 2, that it was committed by one of the persons accused, he having been seen to do it by several credible witnesses: 3, but that his identity is so merged in his brother's that we have not been able to tell which was him. We cannot convict both, for only one is guilty. We cannot acquit both, for only one is innocent. Our verdict is that justice has been defeated by the dispensation of God, and ask to be discharged from further duty."

This was read aloud in court and brought out a burst of hearty applause. The old ladies made a spring at the twins, to shake and congratulate, but were gently disengaged by Mr. Wilson and softly crowded back into their places.

The Judge rose in his little tribune, laid aside his silver-bowed spectacles, roached his gray hair up with his fingers, and said, with dignity and solemnity, and even with a certain pathos:

"In all my experience on the bench, I have not seen Justice bow her head in shame in this court until this day. You little realize what far-reaching harm has just been wrought here under the fickle forms of law. Imitation is the bane of courts—I thank God that this one is free from the contamination of that vice—and in no long time you will see the fatal work of this hour seized upon by profligate so-called guardians of justice in all the wide circumstance of this planet and perpetuated in their pernicious decisions. I wash my hands of this iniquity. I would have compelled these culprits to expose their guilt, but support failed me where I had most right to expect aid and encouragement. And I was confronted by a law made in the interest of crime, which protects the criminal from testifying against himself. Yet I had precedents of my own whereby I had set aside that law on two different occasions and thus succeeded in convicting criminals to whose crimes there were no witnesses but themselves. What have you accomplished this day? Do you realize it? You have set adrift, unadmonished, in this community, two men endowed with an awful and mysterious gift, a hidden and grisly power for evil—a power by which each in his turn may commit crime after crime of the most heinous character, and no man be able to tell which is the guilty or which the innocent party in any case of them all. Look to your homes—look to your property—look to your lives—for you have need!

"Prisoners at the bar, stand up. Through suppression of evidence, a jury of your—our—countrymen have been obliged to deliver a verdict concerning your case which stinks to heaven with the rankness of its injustice. By its terms you, the guilty one, go free with the innocent. Depart in peace, and come no more! The costs devolve upon the outraged plaintiff—another iniquity. The Court stands dissolved."

Almost everybody crowded forward to overwhelm the twins and their counsel with congratulations; but presently the two old aunties dug the duplicates out and bore them away in triumph through the hurrahing crowd, while lots of new friends carried Pudd'nhead Wilson off tavern-wards to feast him and "wet down" his great and victorious entry into the legal arena. To Wilson, so long familiar with neglect and depreciation, this strange new incense of popularity and admiration was as a fragrance blown from the fields of paradise. A happy man was Wilson.

CHAPTER VI

[A deputation came in the evening and conferred upon Wilson the welcome honor of a nomination for mayor; for the village has just been converted into a city by charter. Tom skulks out of challenging the twins. Judge Driscoll thereupon challenges Angelo, (accused by Tom of doing the kicking;) he declines, but Luigi accepts in his place against Angelo's timid protest.]

It was late Saturday night—nearing eleven.

The Judge and his second found the rest of the war party at the further end of the vacant ground, near the haunted house. Pudd'nhead Wilson advanced to meet them, and said anxiously—

"I must say a word in behalf of my principal's proxy, Count Luigi, to whom you have kindly granted the privilege of fighting my principal's battle for him. It is growing late, and Count Luigi is in great trouble lest midnight shall strike before the finish."

"It is another testimony," said Howard, approvingly. "That young man is fine all through. He wishes to save his brother the sorrow of fighting on the Sabbath, and he is right; it is the right and manly feeling and does him credit. We will make all possible haste."

Wilson said—

"There is also another reason—a consideration, in fact, which deeply concerns Count Luigi himself. These twins have command of their mutual legs turn about. Count Luigi is in command, now; but at midnight, possession will pass to my principal, Count Angelo, and—— well, you can foresee what will happen. He will march straight off the field, and carry Luigi with him."

"Why! sure enough!" cried the Judge, "we have heard something about that extraordinary law of their being, already—nothing very definite, it is true, as regards dates and durations of the power, but I see it is definite enough as regards to-night. Of course we must give Luigi every chance. Omit all the ceremonial possible, gentlemen, and place us in position."

The seconds at once tossed up a coin; Howard won the choice. He placed the Judge sixty feet from the haunted house and facing it; Wilson placed the twins within fifteen feet of the house and facing the Judge—necessarily. The pistol-case was opened and the long slim tubes taken out; when the moonlight glinted from them a shiver went through Angelo. The doctor was a fool, but a thoroughly well-meaning one, with a kind heart and a sincere disposition to oblige, but along with it an absence of tact which often hurt its effectiveness. He brought his box of lint and bandages, and asked Angelo to feel and see how soft and comfortable they were. Angelo's head fell over against Luigi's in a faint, and precious time was lost in bringing him to; which provoked Luigi into expressing his mind to the doctor with a good deal of vigor and frankness. After Angelo came to he was still so weak that Luigi was obliged to drink a stiff horn of brandy to brace him up.

The seconds now stepped at once to their posts, half way between the combatants, one of them on each side of the line of fire. Wilson was to count, very deliberately, "One—two—three—fire!—stop!" and the duelists could bang away at any time they chose during that recitation, but not after the last word. Angelo grew very nervous when he saw Wilson's hand rising slowly into the air as a sign to make ready, and he leaned his head against Luigi's and said—

"O, please take me away from here, I can't stay, I know I can't!"

"What in the world are you doing? Straighten up! What's the matter with you?—*you're* in no danger—nobody's going to shoot at you. Straighten up, I tell you!"

Angelo obeyed, just in time to hear—

"One—!"

"Bang!" Just one report, and a little tuft of white hair floated slowly to the Judge's feet in the moonlight. The Judge did not swerve; he still stood erect and motionless, like a statue, with his pistol-arm hanging straight down at his side. He was reserving his fire.

"Two—!"

"Three—!"

"Fire—!"

Up came the pistol-arm instantly—Angelo dodged with the report. He said "Ouch!" and fainted again.

The doctor examined and bandaged the wound. It was of no consequence, he said—bullet through fleshy part of arm—no bones broken—the gentleman was still able to fight—let the duel proceed.

Next time Angelo jumped just as Luigi fired, which disordered his aim and caused him to cut a chip out of Howard's ear. The Judge took his time again, and when he fired Angelo jumped and got a knuckle skinned. The doctor inspected and dressed the wounds. Angelo now spoke out and said he was content with the satisfaction he had got, and if the Judge—but Luigi shut him roughly up, and asked him not to make an ass of himself; adding—

"And I want you to stop dodging. You take a great deal too prominent a part in this thing for a person who has got nothing to do with it. You should remember that you are here only by courtesy, and are without official recognition; officially you are not here at all; officially you do not even exist. To all intents and purposes you are absent from this place, and you ought for your own modesty's sake to reflect that it cannot become a person who is not present here to be taking this sort of public and indecent prominence in a matter in which he is not in the slightest degree concerned. Now, don't dodge again; the bullets are not for you, they are for me; if I want them dodged I will attend to it myself. I never saw a person act so."

Angelo saw the reasonableness of what his brother had said, and he did try to reform, but it was of no use; both pistols went off at the same

instant, and he jumped once more; he got a sharp scrape
along his cheek from the Judge's bullet, and so deflected
Luigi's aim that his ball went wide and chipped a flake
of skin from Pudd'nhead Wilson's chin. The doctor attended to the wounded.

By the terms, the duel was over. But Luigi was entirely out of patience, and begged for one more exchange of shots, insisting that he had had no fair
chance, on account of his brother's indelicate behavior.
Howard was opposed to granting so unusual a privilege, but the Judge took Luigi's part, and added
that indeed he himself might fairly be considered
entitled to another trial, because although the
proxy on the other side was in no way to blame
for his (the Judge's) humiliatingly resultless
work, the gentleman with whom he was fighting
this duel was to blame for it, since if he had
played no advantages and had held his head still,
his proxy would have been disposed of early. He
added—

"Count Luigi's request for another exchange
is another proof that he is a brave and chivalrous
gentleman, and I beg that the courtesy he asks
may be accorded him."

"I thank you most sincerely for this generosity,
Judge Driscoll," said Luigi, with a polite bow,
and moving to his place. Then he added—to

Angelo, "Now hold your grip, hold your *grip*, I tell you, and I'll land him, sure!"

The men stood erect, their pistol-arms at their sides, the two seconds stood at their official posts, the doctor stood five paces in Wilson's rear with his instruments and bandages in his hands. The deep stillness, the peaceful moonlight, the motionless figures, made an impressive picture and the impending fatal possibilities augmented this impressiveness to solemnity. Wilson's hand began to rise—slowly—slowly—higher—still higher—in another moment—

"*Boom!*"—the first stroke of midnight swung up out of the distance: Angelo was off like a deer!

"Oh, you unspeakable traitor!" wailed his brother, as they went soaring over the fence.

The others stood astonished and gazing; and so stood, watching that strange spectacle until distance dissolved it and swept it from their view. Then they rubbed their eyes like people waking out of a dream.

"Well, I've never seen anything like that before!" said the Judge. "Wilson, I am going to confess, now, that I wasn't quite able to believe in that leg-business, and had a suspicion that it was a put-up convenience between those twins; and when Count Angelo fainted I thought I saw the whole scheme—thought it was pretext No. 1, and would be followed by others till twelve o'clock should arrive and Luigi would get off with all the credit of seeming to want to fight and yet not have to fight, after all. But I was mistaken. His pluck proved it. He's a brave fellow and did want to fight."

"There isn't any doubt about that," said Howard, and added in a grieved tone, "but what an unworthy sort of Christian that Angelo is—I hope and believe there are not many like him. It is not right to engage in a duel on the Sabbath—I could not approve of that myself; but to finish one that has been begun—that is a duty, let the day be what it may."

They strolled along, still wondering, still talking.

"It is a curious circumstance," remarked the surgeon, halting Wilson a moment to paste some more court plaster on his chin, which had gone to leaking blood again, "that in this duel neither of the parties who handled the pistols lost blood, while nearly all the persons present in the mere capacity of guests got hit. I have not heard of such a thing before. Don't you think it unusual?"

"Yes," said the Judge, "it has struck me as peculiar. Peculiar and unfortunate. I was annoyed at it, all the time. In the case of Angelo it made no great difference, because he was in a measure concerned, though not officially; but it troubled me to see the seconds compromised, and yet I knew no way to mend the matter."

"There was no way to mend it," said Howard, whose ear was being readjusted now by the doctor; "the code fixes our place, and it would not have been lawful to change it. If we could have stood at your side, or behind you, or in front of you, it—but it would not have been legitimate and the other parties would have had a just right to complain of our trying to protect ourselves from danger; infractions of the code are certainly not permissible in any case whatever."

Wilson offered no remarks. It seemed to him that there was very little place here for so much solemnity, but he judged that if a duel where nobody was in danger or got crippled but the seconds and the outsiders had nothing ridiculous about for these gentlemen, his pointing out that feature would probably not help them to see it.

He invited them in to take a nightcap, and Howard and the Judge accepted, but the doctor said he would have to go and see how Angelo's principal wound was getting on.

[It was now Sunday, and in the afternoon Angelo was to be received into the Baptist communion by immersion—a doubtful prospect, the doctor feared.]

Chapter VII

When the doctor arrived at Aunt Patsy Cooper's house, he found the lights going and everybody up and dressed and in a great state of solicitude and excitement. The twins were stretched on a sofa in the sitting-room, Aunt Patsy was fussing at Angelo's arm, Nancy was flying around under her commands, the two young boys were trying to keep out of the way and always getting in it, in order to see and wonder, Rowena stood apart, helpless with apprehension and emotion, and Luigi was growling in unappeasable fury over Angelo's shameful flight.

As has been reported before, the doctor was a fool—a kindhearted and well-meaning one, but with no tact; and as he was by long odds the most learned physician in the town, and was quite well aware of it, and could talk his learning with ease and precision, and liked to show off when he had an audience, he was sometimes tempted into revealing more of a case than was good for the patient.

He examined Angelo's wound, and was really minded to say nothing for once; but Aunt Patsy was so anxious and so pressing that he allowed his caution to be overcome, and proceeded to empty himself as follows, with scientific relish—

"Without going too much into detail, madam—for you would probably not understand it anyway—I concede that great care is going to be necessary here; otherwise exudation of the aesophagus is nearly sure to ensue, and this will be followed by ossification and extradition of the maxillaris superioris, which must decompose the granular surfaces of the great infusorial ganglionic system, thus obstructing the action of the posterior varioloid arteries, and precipitating compound strangulated sorosis of the valvular tissues, and ending unavoidably in the dispersion and combustion of the marsupial fluxes and the consequent embrocation of the bicuspid populo redax referendum rotulorum."

A miserable silence followed. Aunt Patsy's heart sank, the pallor of despair invaded her face, she was not able to speak; poor Rowena wrung her hands in privacy and silence, and said to herself in the bitterness of her young grief, "There is no hope—it is plain there is no hope;" the good-hearted negro wench, Nancy, paled to chocolate, then to orange, then to amber, and thought to herself with yearning sympathy and sorrow, "Po' thing, he ain' gwyne to las' throo de half o' dat;" small Henry choked up, and turned his head away to hide his rising tears, and his brother Joe said to himself, with a sense of loss, "The baptizing's busted, that's sure." Luigi was the only person who had any heart to speak. He said, a little bit sharply, to the doctor—

"Well, well, there's nothing to be gained by wasting precious time: give him a barrel of pills—I'll take them for him."

"You?" asked the doctor.

"Yes. Did you suppose he was going to take them himself?"

"Why, of course."

"Well, it's a mistake. He never took a dose of medicine in his life. He can't."

"Well, upon my word, it's the most extraordinary thing I ever heard of!"

"Oh," said Aunt Patsy, as pleased as a mother whose child is being admired and wondered at, "you'll find that there's more about them that's wonderful than their just being made in the image of God like the rest of His creatures, now you can depend on that, *I* tell you," and she wagged her complacent head like one who could reveal marvelous things if she chose.

The boy Joe began—

"Why, ma, they *ain't* made in the im——"

"You shut up, and wait till you're asked, Joe. I'll let you know when I want help. Are you looking for something, Doctor?"

The doctor asked for a few sheets of paper and a pen, and said he would write a prescription; which he did. It was one of Galen's; in fact, it was Galen's favorite, and had been slaying people for sixteen thousand years. Galen used it for everything, applied it to everything, said it would remove everything, from warts all the way through to lungs— and it generally did. Galen was still the only medical authority recognized in Missouri; his practice was the only practice known to the Missouri doctors, and his prescriptions were the only ammunition they carried when they went out for game. By and by Dr. Claypool laid down his pen and read the result of his labors aloud, carefully and deliberately, for this battery must be constructed on the premises by the family, and mistakes could occur; for he wrote a doctor's hand— the hand which from the beginning of time has been so disastrous to the apothecary and so profitable to the undertaker:

"Take of afarabocca, henbane, corpobalsamum, each two drams and a half; of cloves, opium, myrrh, cyperus, each two drams; of opobalsamum, Indian leaf, cinnamon, zedoary, ginger, coftus, coral, cassia, euphorbium, gum tragacanth, frankincense, styrax calamita, celtic, nard, spignel, hartwort, mustard, saxifrage, dill, anise, each one dram; of xylaloes, rheum ponticum, alipta moschata, castor, spikenard, galangals, opoponax, anacardium, mastich, brimstone, peony, eringo, pulp of dates, red and white hermodactyls, roses, thyme, acorns, pennyroyal, gentian, the bark of the root of mandrake, germander, valerian, bishop's weed, bay-berries, long and white pepper, xylobalsamum, carnabadium, macedonian, parsley-seeds, lovage, the seeds of rue, and sinon, of each a dram and a half; of pure gold, pure silver, pearls not perforated, the blatta byzantina, the bone of the stag's heart, of each the quantity of fourteen grains of wheat; of sapphire, emerald and jasper stones, each one dram; of hazel-nut, two drams; of pellitory of Spain, shavings of ivory, calamus odoratus, each the quantity of twenty-nine grains of wheat; of honey or sugar a sufficient quantity. Boil down and skim off."

"There," he said, "that will fix the patient; give his brother a dipper-ful every three-quarters of an hour——"

—"while he survives," muttered Luigi—

—"and see that the room is kept wholesomely hot, and the doors and windows closed tight. Keep Count Angelo nicely covered up with six or seven blankets, and when he is thirsty—which will be fre-quently—moisten a rag in the vapor of the tea-kettle and let his brother suck it. When he is hungry—which will also be frequently—he must not be humored oftener than every seven or eight hours; then toast part of a cracker until it begins to brown, and give it to his brother."

"That is all very well, as far as Angelo is concerned," said Luigi, "but what am I to eat?"

"I do not see that there is anything the matter with you," the doctor answered, "you may of course eat what you please."

"And also drink what I please, I suppose?"

"Oh, certainly—at present. When the violent and continuous perspiring has reduced your strength, I shall have to reduce your diet, of course, and also bleed you, but there is no occa-

sion for that yet awhile." He turned to Aunt Patsy and said: "He must be put to bed, and sat up with, and tended with the greatest care, and not allowed to stir for several days and nights."

"For one, I'm sacredly thankful for that," said Luigi, "it postpones the funeral—I'm not to be drowned to-day, anyhow."

Angelo said quietly to the doctor:

"I will cheerfully submit to all your requirements, sir, up to two o'clock this afternoon, and will resume them after three, but cannot be confined to the house during that intermediate hour."

"Why, may I ask?"

"Because I have entered the Baptist communion, and by appointment am to be baptized in the river at that hour."

"Oh, insanity!—it cannot be allowed!"

Angelo answered with placid firmness—

"Nothing shall prevent it, if I am alive."

"Why, consider, my dear sir, in your condition it might prove fatal."

A tender and ecstatic smile beamed from Angelo's eyes, and he broke forth in a tone of joyous fervency—

"Ah, how blessed it would be to die for such a cause—it would be martydom!"

"But your brother—consider your brother; you would be risking his life, too."

"He risked mine an hour ago," responded Angelo, gloomily; "did he consider me?" A thought swept through his mind that made him shudder. "If I had not run, I might have been killed in a duel on the Sabbath day, and my soul would have been lost—lost."

"Oh, don't fret, it wasn't in any danger," said Luigi, irritably; "they wouldn't waste it for a little thing like that; there's a glass case all ready for it in the heavenly museum, and a pin to stick it up with."

Aunt Patsy was shocked, and said—

"Looy, Looy!—don't talk so, dear!"

Rowena's soft heart was pierced by Luigi's unfeeling words, and she murmured to herself, "Oh, if I but had the dear privilege of protecting and defending him with my weak voice!—but alas, this sweet boon is denied me by the cruel conventions of social intercourse."

"Get their bed ready," said Aunt Patsy to Nancy, "and shut up the windows and doors, and light their candles, and see that you drive all the mosquitoes out of their bar, and make up a good fire in their stove, and carry up some bags of hot ashes to lay to his feet——"

—"and a shovel of fire for his head, and a mustard plaster for his neck, and some gum shoes for his ears," Luigi interrupted, with temper; and added, to himself, "Damnation, I'm going to be roasted alive, I just know it!"

"Why, Looy! Do be quiet; I never saw such a fractious thing. A body would think you didn't care for your brother."

"I don't—to *that* extent, Aunt Patsy. I was glad the drowning was postponed a minute ago, but I'm not, now. No, that is all gone by: I want to be drowned."

"You'll bring a judgment on yourself just as sure as you live, if you go on like that. Why, I never heard the beat of it. Now, there,—there! you've said enough. Not another word out of you,—I won't have it!"

"But, Aunt Patsy——"

"Luigi! Didn't you hear what I told you?"

"But, Aunt Patsy, I—why, I'm not going to set my heart and lungs afloat in that pail of sewage which this criminal here has been prescri——"

"Yes, you are, too. You are going to be good, and do everything I tell you, like a dear," and she tapped his cheek affectionately with her finger. "Rowena, take the prescription and go in the kitchen and hunt up the things and lay them out for me. I'll sit up with my patient the rest of the night, Doctor; I can't trust Nancy, she couldn't make Luigi take the medicine. Of course you'll drop in again during the day. Have you got any more directions?"

"No, I believe not, Aunt Patsy. If I don't get in earlier, I'll be along by early candlelight, anyway. Meantime, don't allow him to get out of his bed."

Angelo said, with calm determination—

"I shall be baptized at two o'clock. Nothing but death shall prevent me."

The doctor said nothing aloud, but to himself he said:

"Why, this chap's got a manly side, after all! Physically he's a coward, but morally he's a lion. I'll go and tell the others about this; it will raise him a good deal in their estimation—and the public will follow their lead, of course."

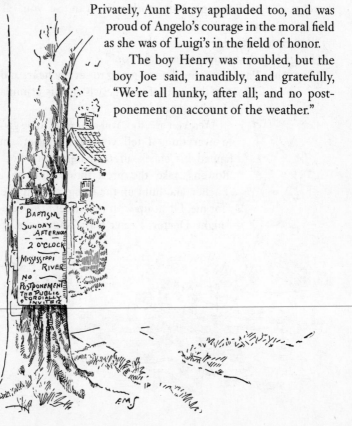

Privately, Aunt Patsy applauded too, and was proud of Angelo's courage in the moral field as she was of Luigi's in the field of honor.

The boy Henry was troubled, but the boy Joe said, inaudibly, and gratefully, "We're all hunky, after all; and no postponement on account of the weather."

BAPTISM
SUNDAY —
AFTERNOON
2 O'CLOCK
MISSISSIPPI RIVER
NO
POSTPONEMENT
THE PUBLIC
CORDIALLY
INVITED

FMS

Chapter VIII

By nine o'clock the town was humming with the news of the midnight duel, and there were but two opinions about it: one, that Luigi's pluck in the field was most praiseworthy and Angelo's flight most scandalous; the other, that Angelo's courage in flying the field for conscience' sake was as fine and creditable as was Luigi's in holding the field in the face of the bullets. The one opinion was held by half of the town, the other one was maintained by the other half. The division was clean and exact, and it made two parties, an Angelo party and a Luigi party. The twins had suddenly become popular idols along with Pudd'nhead Wilson, and haloed with a glory as intense as his. The children talked the duel all the way to Sunday-school, their elders talked it all the way to church, the choir discussed it behind their red curtain, it usurped the place of pious thought in the "nigger gallery."

By noon the doctor had added the news, and spread it, that Count Angelo, in spite of his wound and all warnings and supplications, was resolute in his determination to be baptised at the hour appointed. This swept the town like wildfire, and mightily reinforced the enthusiasm of the Angelo faction, who said, "If any doubted that it was moral courage that took him from the field, what have they to say now!"

Still the excitement grew. All the morning it was traveling countrywards, toward all points of the compass; so, whereas before only the farmers and their wives were intending to come and witness the remarkable baptism, a general holiday was now proclaimed and the children and negroes admitted to the privileges of the occasion. All the farms for ten miles around were vacated, all the converging roads emptied long processions of wagons, horses and yeomanry into the town. The pack and cram of people vastly exceeded any that had ever been seen in that sleepy region before. The only thing that had ever even approached it, was the time long gone by, but never forgotten, nor even referred to without wonder and pride, when two circuses and a Fourth of July fell together. But the glory of that occasion was extinguished, now, for good. It was but a freshet to this deluge.

The great invasion massed itself on the river bank and waited hungrily for the immense event. Waited, and wondered if it would really happen, or if the twin who was not a "professor" would stand out and prevent it.

But they were not to be disappointed. Angelo was as good as his word. He came attended by an escort of honor composed of several hundred of the best citizens, all of the Angelo party; and when the immersion was finished they escorted him back home; and would even have carried him on their shoulders, but that people might think they were carrying Luigi.

Far into the night the citizens continued to discuss and wonder over the strangely-mated pair of incidents that had distinguished and exalted the past twenty-four hours above any other twenty-four in the history of their town for picturesqueness and splendid interest; and long before the lights were out and burghers asleep it had been decided on all hands that in capturing these twins Dawson's Landing had drawn a prize in the great lottery of municipal fortune.

At midnight Angelo was sleeping peacefully. His immersion had not harmed him, it had merely made him wholesomely drowsy, and he had been dead asleep many hours now. It had made Luigi drowsy, too, but he had got only brief naps, on account of his having to take the medicine every three-quarters of an hour—and Annt Betsy Hale was there to see that he did it. When he complained and resisted, she was quietly firm with him, and said in a low voice:

"No—no, that won't do; you mustn't talk, and you mustn't retch and gag that way, either—you'll wake up your poor brother."

"Well, what of it, Aunt Betsy, he——"

"'Sh-h! Don't make a noise, dear. You mustn't forget that your poor brother is sick and——"

"Sick, is he? Well, I wish I——"

"'Sh-h-h! Will you be quiet, Luigi! Here, now, take the rest of it—don't keep me holding the dipper all night. I declare if you haven't left a good fourth of it in the bottom! Come—that's a good boy."

"Aunt Betsy, don't make me! I feel like I've swallowed a cemetery; I do, indeed. Do let me rest a little—just a little; I can't take any more of the devilish stuff, now."

"Luigi! Using such language here, and him just baptised! Do you want the roof to fall on you?"

"I wish to goodness it would!"

"Why, you dreadful thing! I've a good notion to—let that blanket alone; do you want your brother to catch his death?"

"Aunt Betsy, I've *got* to have it off, I'm being roasted alive; nobody could stand it—you couldn't, yourself."

"Now, then, you're sneezing again—I just expected it."

"Because I've caught a cold in my head. I always do, when I go in the water with my clothes on. And it takes me weeks to get over it, too. I think it was a shame to serve me so."

"Luigi, you are unreasonable; you know very well they couldn't baptise him dry. I should think you would be willing to undergo a little inconvenience for your brother's sake."

"Inconvenience! Now how you talk, Aunt Betsy. I came as near as anything to getting drowned—you saw that, yourself; and do you call this inconvenience?—the room shut up as tight as a drum, and so hot the mosquitoes are trying to get out; and a cold in the head, and dying for sleep and no chance to get any on account of this infamous medicine that that assassin prescri——"

"There, you're sneezing again. I'm going down and mix some more of this truck for you, dear."

Chapter IX

During Monday, Tuesday and Wednesday the twins grew steadily worse; but then the doctor was summoned south to attend his mother's funeral and they got well in forty-eight hours. They appeared on the street on Friday, and were welcomed with enthusiasm by the new-born parties, the Luigi and Angelo factions. The Luigi faction carried its strength into the Democratic party, the Angelo faction entered into a combination with the Whigs. The Democrats nominated Luigi for alderman under the new city government, and the Whigs put up Angelo against him.

The Democrats nominated Pudd'nhead Wilson for mayor, and he was left alone in this glory, for the Whigs had no man who was willing to enter the lists against such a formidable opponent. No politician had scored such a compliment as this before in the history of the Mississippi Valley.

The political campaign in Dawson's Landing opened in a pretty warm fashion, and waxed hotter every week. Luigi's whole heart was in it, and even Angelo developed a surprising amount of interest—which was natural, because he was not merely representing Whigism, a matter of no consequence to him, but he was representing something immensely finer and greater—to wit, Reform. In him was centred the hopes of the whole reform element of the town; he was the chosen and admired champion of every clique that had a pet reform of any sort or kind at heart. He was president of the great Teetotaller's Union, its chiefest prophet and mouthpiece.

But as the canvass went on, troubles began to spring up all around— troubles for the twins, and through them for all the parties and segments and fractions of parties. Whenever Luigi had possession of the legs, he carried Angelo to balls, rum shops, Sons of Liberty parades, horse races, campaign riots, and everywhere else that could damage him with his party and the church; and when it was Angelo's week he carried Luigi diligently to all manner of moral and religious gatherings, doing his best to regain the ground he had lost before. As a result of these double performances, there was a storm blowing all the time, an ever rising storm, too—a storm of frantic criticism of the twins, and rage over their extravagant, incomprehensible conduct.

Luigi had the final chance. The legs were his for the closing week of the canvass. He led his brother a fearful dance.

But he saved his best card for the very eve of the election. There was to be a grand turn-out of the Teetotaller's Union that day, and Angelo was to march at the head of the procession and deliver a great oration afterward. Luigi drank a couple of glasses of whiskey—which steadied his nerves and clarified his mind, but made Angelo drunk. Everybody who saw the march, saw that the Champion of the Teetotallers was half seas over, and noted also that his brother, who made no hypocritical protensions to extra temperance virtues, was dignified and sober. This eloquent fact could not be unfruitful at the end of a hot political canvass. At the mass meeting Angelo tried to make his great temperance oration but was so discommoded by hiccoughs and thickness of tongue that he had to give it up; then drowsiness overtook him and his head drooped against Luigi's and he went to sleep. Luigi apologized for him, and was going on to improve his opportunity with an appeal for a moderation of what he called "the prevailing teetotal madness," but persons in the audience began to howl and throw things at him, and then the meeting rose in wrath and chased him home.

This episode was a crusher for Angelo in another way. It destroyed his chances with Rowena. Those chances had been growing, right along, for two months. Rowena had partly confessed that she loved him, but wanted time to consider. Now the tender dream was ended, and she told him so, the moment he was sober enough to understand. She said she would never marry a man who drank.

"But I don't drink," he pleaded.

"That is nothing to the point," she said, coldly, "you get drunk, and that is worse."

[There was a long and sufficiently idiotic discussion here, which ended as reported in a previous note.]

CHAPTER X

Dawson's Landing had a week of repose, after the election, and it needed it, for the frantic and variegated nightmare which had tormented it all through the preceding week had left it limp, haggard and exhausted at the end. It got the week of repose because Angelo had the legs, and was in too subdued a condition to want to go out and mingle with an irritated community that had come to distrust and detest him because there was such a lack of harmony between his morals, which were confessedly excellent, and his methods of illustrating them, which were distinctly damnable.

The new city officers were sworn in on the following Monday—at least all but Luigi. There was a complication in his case. His election was conceded, but he could not sit in the board of aldermen without his brother, and his brother could not sit there because he was not a member. There seemed to be no way out of the difficulty but to carry the matter into the courts, so this was resolved upon. The case was set for the Monday fortnight. In due course the time arrived. In the meantime the city government had been at a stand-still, because without Luigi there was a tie in the board of aldermen, whereas with him the liquor interest—the richest in the political field—would have one majority. But the court decided that Angelo could not sit in the board with him, either in public or executive sessions, and at the same time forbade the board to deny admission to Luigi, a fairly and legally chosen alderman. The case was carried up and up from court to court, yet still the same old original decision was confirmed every time. As a result, the city government not only stood still, with its hands tied, but everything it was created to protect and care for went a steady gait toward rack and ruin. There was no way to levy a tax, so the minor officials had to resign or starve; therefore they resigned. There being no city money, the enormous legal expenses on both sides had to be defrayed by private subscription. But at last the people came to their senses, and said—

"Pudd'nhead was right, at the start—we ought to have hired the official half of that human phillipene to resign; but it's too late, now; some of us haven't got anything left to hire him with."

"Yes, we have," said another citizen, "we've got this"—and he produced a halter.

F.M. SENIOR

Many shouted, "That's the ticket." But others said, "No—Count Angelo is innocent; we mustn't hang him."

"Who said anything about hanging him? We are only going to hang the other one."

"Then that is all right—there is no objection to that."

So they hanged Luigi. And so ends the history of "Those Extraordinary Twins."

FINAL REMARKS

As you see, it was an extravagant sort of a tale, and had no purpose but to exhibit that monstrous "freak" in all sorts of grotesque lights. But when Roxy wandered into the tale she had to be furnished with something to do; so she changed the children in the cradle: this necessitated the invention of a reason for it; this in turn resulted in making the children prominent personages—nothing could prevent it, of course. Their career began to take a tragic aspect, and some one had to be brought in to help work the machinery; so Pudd'nhead Wilson was introduced and taken on trial. By this time the whole show was being run by the new people and in their interest, and the original show was become side-tracked and forgotten; the twin-monster and the heroine and the lads and the old ladies had dwindled to inconsequentialities and were merely in the way. Their story was one story, the new people's story was another story, and there was no connection between them, no interdependence, no kinship. It is not practicable or rational to try to tell two stories at the same time; so I dug out the farce and left the tragedy.

The reader already knew how the expert works; he knows now how the other kind do it.

Mark Twain

COMMENTARY

WILLIAM LIVINGSTON ALDEN (*THE IDLER*)

THE ATHENAEUM

THE NEW YORK TIMES

PUBLIC OPINION

THE CRITIC

WILLIAM LIVINGSTON ALDEN

Puddenhead Wilson [*sic*], Mark Twain's latest story, is the work of a novelist, rather than of a "funny man." There is plenty of humour in it of the genuine Mark Twain brand, but it is as a carefully painted picture of life in a Mississippi town in the days of slavery that its chief merit lies. In point of construction it is much the best story that Mark Twain has written, and of men and women in the book at least four are undeniably creations, and not one of them is overdrawn or caricatured, as are some of the most popular of the author's lay figures. There is but one false note in the picture, and that is the introduction of the two alleged Italian noblemen. These two young men are as little like Italians as they are like Apaches. When challenged to fight a duel, one of them, having the choice of weapons, chooses revolvers instead of swords. This incident alone is sufficient to show how little Italian blood there is in Mark Twain's Italians. But this is a small blemish, and if Mark Twain, in his future novels, can maintain the proportion of only two lay figures to four living characters, he will do better than most novelists. The extracts from "Puddenhead Wilson's Almanac [*sic*]," which are prefixed to each chapter of the book, simply "pizon us for more," to use Huck Finn's forcible metaphor. Let us hope that a complete edition of that unrivalled almanac will be issued at no distant day.

From *The Idler* (London: August 1894)

THE ATHENAEUM

The best thing in *Pudd'nhead Wilson,* by Mark Twain (Chatto & Windus), is the picture of the negro slave Roxana, the cause of all the trouble which gives scope to Mr. Wilson's ingenious discovery about finger-marks. Her gusts of passion or of despair, her vanity, her motherly love, and the glimpses of nobler feelings that are occasionally seen in her elementary code of morals, make her very human, and create a sympathy for her in spite of her unscrupulous actions. But hers is the only character that is really striking. Her son is a poor creature, as he is meant to be, but he does not arrest the reader with the same unmistakable reality: his actions are what might be expected, but his conversations, especially with Wilson and the Twins, seem artificial and forced. Wilson, the nominal hero, appears to most advantage in the extracts from his calendar which head the chapters, but as a personage he is rather too shadowy for a hero. And what has to be said about the book must be chiefly about the individuals in it, for the story in itself is not much credit to Mark Twain's skill as a novelist. The idea of the change of babies is happy, and the final trial scene is a good piece of effect; but the story at times rambles on in an almost incomprehensible way. Why drag in, for example, all the business about the election, which is quite irrelevant? and the Twins altogether seem to have very little *raison d'etre* in the book. Of course there are some funny things in the story, it would not be by Mark Twain if there were not, but the humour of the preface might very well be spared; it is in bad taste. Still, if the preface be skipped the book well repays reading just for the really excellent picture of Roxana.

From an unsigned review published in London on January 19, 1895

THE NEW YORK TIMES

This anonymous reviewer attributes the illustrations in the first American edition of *The Tragedy of Pudd'nhead Wilson and the Comedy of Those Extraordinary Twins* to a single artist. In fact, two illustrators, F. M. Senior and C. H. Warren, provided the numerous marginal illustrations for the American Publishing Company's 1894 edition.

MARK TWAIN'S NEW VOLUME

Thanks to an artist who, though he does not draw well, is clever in grasping ideas, the fun and drollery and the comedy and tragedy of two of Mark Twain's most interesting stories have been multiplied many times. Those who have enjoyed "Pudd'nhead Wilson," with nothing but their imaginations to help them picture what sort of man the hero of the story was and what the scenes were in which he acted his part, will be glad to run through the story again along with the artist, who, it may be assumed, has recorded in his marginal pictures the author's material conceptions of the things he has written about.

They may see that "well-fed, well-petted, and properly-revered" cat stretched at full length on the window ledge, "asleep and blissful with her furry belly to the sun and a paw curved over her nose." That was one of the sights of Dawson's Landing. They may see the tinmonger's pole standing on one of the chief corners of the village, "wreathed from top to bottom with tin pots and pans and cups," giving noisy notice to the world, when the wind blew, that the tinmonger was close at hand ready for business. They may look upon Wilson when, as he entered the village intent upon establishing himself in the law business, he made the remark that ruined him for the time being. "I wish I owned half that dog," said Wilson. "Why?" somebody asked. "Because," answered Wilson, "I'd kill my half." The villagers decided promptly that a man who did not know that to kill half a dog would be death to the entire animal was without that important requisite for a lawyer, a legal mind.

So all through the story the illustrator accompanies the text. He shows the village firemen drowning the old market house with water pumped through the little hand engine; he shows Wilson, when he had come to be somebody, addressing a mass meeting, a flag flying over him bearing the announcement that he is conducting a campaign for the Mayoralty, and in one of his best pictures he illustrates the text, "A devil born to a young couple is measurably recognizable by them before long; but a devil adopted by an old couple is an angel to them and remains so through thick and thin."

But it is in "Those Extraordinary Twins," which is the second part of the volume, that the artist has done his cleverest work. This undoubtedly is because the story is the funnier of the two. There is an almost infinite amount of suggestion for an artist of the humorous vein in the story of the two-headed man whom Twain persists in regarding as really two men—making one man sick while the other is well; making one fight a duel while the other protests against the performance; baptizing the good one while the other sputters curses; hanging the bad one while the other looks indignant, though he finally does consent to join in the kicking.

From a review published on January 27, 1895

PUBLIC OPINION

Mark Twain is an apostle of the unconventional, and he tells uncommon stories in uncommon ways. Being free from reverence for anything merely because it is customary, and being blessed with a fancy which knows no bounds, his readers are sure of meeting improbable situations, treated with a gravity beyond their deserts. It is one of the unexplained facts in the history of American literature that he has had no imitators. Possibly it is because his audacious extravagance has become so marked a characteristic that mimicry would be obvious at sight. Of late years his writings have shown a moral or social aim which, while it is sometimes overwrought and made to bear undue burden, is always of healthy tone.

In *Pudd'nhead Wilson* if we reflect upon the career—but lightly sketched—of the rightful heir, it seems to teach the greater force of education and habit than blood or heredity; certainly his pure white blood never taught him to feel his superiority over his surroundings. But the more minutely detailed behavior of his substitute appears to lead to the belief that antecedents and the inherited moral weakness of the slave were too much for training and environment. Perhaps the author would have smiled in his cynical way had he supposed that any attempt would be made at deductions of this nature, when his object, primarily at least, was to entertain. In this object, at least, he never fails, and while the story differs materially from the manner of his early works, it is as full as ever of his quips and shrewd jests on the weaknesses of human nature.

One of the most characteristically funny features is the absurd explanation in which he takes his reader into his confidence by explaining how this story got away from him and left some of his people stranded, so that he had to retrace his steps and drown them at different times in the same well. This proving unsatisfactory because it was not a large well and would not hold any more, and recognizing the fact that he had got two stories entangled, he gravely "cures the defect" by pulling out the the farce and leaving the tragedy. What he calls the tragedy is much the best piece of work—in many respects he has written nothing better—but the appended story or farce is extravaganza run mad without sufficient base. It would have been more amusing if it had been shorter, but *Pudd'nhead Wilson* is good and the irony of the calendar is delicious. In these days of authors' block calendars, Pudd'nhead's sayings will well bear amplification for 1896. The illustrations are remarkably abundant, being in the form of marginal sketches on every page, and are in the main very satisfactory.

From an unsigned review published in Washington, D.C., on February 14, 1895

THE CRITIC

The literary critic is often puzzled how to classify the intellectual phenomena that come within his ken. His business is of course primarily with *literature*. A work may be infinitely amusing, it may abound even with flashes and touches of genius, and yet the form in which it comes into the world may be so crude, so coarse, so erring from the ways of true classicism, so offensive to immemorial canons of taste, that the critic, in spite of his enjoyment and wonder, puts it reluctantly down in the category of unclassifiable literary things only to take it up and enjoy it again!

Of such is *Pudd'nhead Wilson,* and, for that matter, Mark Twain in general. The author is a signal example of sheer genius, without training or culture in the university sense, setting forth to conquer the world with laughter whether it will or no, and to get himself thereby acknowledged to be the typical writer of the West. He is the most successful of a class of American humorists whose impulse to write off their rush of animal spirits is irresistible, and who snatch at the first pen within reach as the conductor of their animal electricity. If we look at other national humorists, like Aristophanes, Cervantes, Molière or Swift, we find their humor expressed in an exquisite literary form, in which a certain polish tempers the extravagance, and annoying metrical (or it may be imaginative) difficulties have been overcome. What wonderful bird-rhythms and wasp melodies and cloud-architecture, so to speak, emerge from the marvellous choral interludes of the Greek comedian; what suave literary graces enclose the gaunt outlines of Don Quixote; in what honeyed verse are Alceste and Tartuffe entangled, and what new, nervous, powerful prose describes the adventures of Gulliver! When we turn our eyes westward we encounter Judge Haliburton, Hosea Biglow, Uncle Remus, Mark Twain—an absolutely new *genre* distinct from what we had previously studied in the line of originalities. The one accomplished artist among these is Lowell, whose university traditions were very strong and controlled his bubbling humor. The others are pure "naturalists"—men of instinctive genius, who have relied on their own conscious strength to produce delight in the reader, irrespective of classicity of form, literary grace or any other of the beloved conventions on which literature as literature has hitherto depended. This is true in a less degree of Uncle Remus than of Judge Haliburton and Mark Twain.

Pudd'nhead Wilson is no exception to the rule. It is a Missouri tale of changelings "befo' the wah," admirable in atmosphere, local color and dialect, a drama in its way, full of powerful situations, thrilling even; but it cannot be called in any sense literature. In it Mark Twain's brightness and grotesqueness and funniness revel and sparkle, and in the absurd extravaganza, "Those Extraordinary Twins," all these comicalities reach the buffoon point; one is amused and laughs unrestrainedly but then the irksome question comes up: What *is* this? is it literature? is Mr. Clemens a "writer" at all? must he not after all be described as an admirable after-dinner storyteller—humorous, imaginative, dramatic, like Dickens—who in an evil moment, urged by admiring friends, has put pen to paper and written down his stories? Adapted to the stage and played by Frank Mayo, the thing has met with immediate success.

From an unsigned review published in New York on May 11, 1895

Reading Group Guide

1. According to the writer Robert A. Wiggins, "Roxana represents a notable achievement on Twain's part. For the first time, the institution of slavery had been dealt with relatively objectively and realistically in American fiction. Uncle Tom and Uncle Remus are childishly artificial by comparison." Do you agree?

2. Drawing on examples from "Pudd'nhead Wilson," explain how Twain uses different points of view to depict slavery and miscegenation in the novel's pre–Civil War setting. How does he handle the theme of environment vs. heredity?

3. How does the author describe the residents and the physical setting of Dawson's Landing, Missouri? Which elements are the most vivid? Knowing that Twain grew up in Hannibal, a Missouri river town, do any particular descriptions strike you as being based on firsthand experience?

4. Critics have argued that some characters in "Pudd'nhead Wilson" are far more richly drawn than others. Do you agree? Do the Italian twins, taken from "Those Extraordinary Twins" and adapted for the longer work, belong in "Pudd'nhead Wilson"?

5. Leslie Fiedler is not the only critic to theorize that "Pudd'nhead is Tom Sawyer grown up, the man who has not surrendered with maturity the dream of being a hero." What do these two fictional characters have in common?

6. What do you make of the selections from Pudd'nhead Wilson's Calendar that open each chapter? What purpose do they serve in the novel?

7. Consider the original illustrations of 1894 that accompany the text of this Modern Library edition. Do they enhance or detract from your appreciation of the writing?

8. Twain explains in his "Final Remarks" at the end of "Those Extraordinary Twins," "It is not practicable or rational to try to tell two stories at the same time; so I dug out the farce and left the tragedy." Would you define "Pudd'nhead Wilson" as a tragedy?

9. Consider the text of "Those Extraordinary Twins," along with the author's accompanying commentary. What do they reveal about Twain's process as a writer?

MODERN LIBRARY IS ONLINE AT
WWW.MODERNLIBRARY.COM

MODERN LIBRARY ONLINE IS YOUR GUIDE
TO CLASSIC LITERATURE ON THE WEB

THE MODERN LIBRARY E-NEWSLETTER

Our free e-mail newsletter is sent to subscribers, and features sample chapters, interviews with and essays by our authors, upcoming books, special promotions, announcements, and news.

To subscribe to the Modern Library e-newsletter, send a blank e-mail to: **join-modernlibrary@list.randomhouse.com** or visit **www.modernlibrary.com**

THE MODERN LIBRARY WEBSITE

Check out the Modern Library website at
www.modernlibrary.com for:

- The Modern Library e-newsletter
- A list of our current and upcoming titles and series
- Reading Group Guides and exclusive author spotlights
- Special features with information on the classics and other paperback series
- Excerpts from new releases and other titles
- A list of our e-books and information on where to buy them
- The Modern Library Editorial Board's 100 Best Novels and 100 Best Nonfiction Books of the Twentieth Century written in the English language
- News and announcements

Questions? E-mail us at **modernlibrary@randomhouse.com**
For questions about examination or desk copies, please visit
the Random House Academic Resources site at
www.randomhouse.com/academic

APPLE SIGNATURE EDITIONS

The Classroom at the End of the Hall
by Douglas Evans

The Music of Dolphins
by Karen Hesse

Faith and the Electric Dogs
by Patrick Jennings

Afternoon of the Elves
by Janet Taylor Lisle

Somewhere in the Darkness
by Walter Dean Myers

The Fire Pony
by Rodman Philbrick

The Van Gogh Cafe
by Cynthia Rylant

Bad Girls
by Cynthia Voigt

The Mozart Season
by Virginia Euwer Wolff

APPLE SIGNATURE

Trout
Summer

JANE LESLIE CONLY

SCHOLASTIC INC.
New York Toronto London Auckland Sydney

For Paul, Mischa, and Sam —
may adventures and poetry fill your days.

ISBN 0-590-93975-0

12 11 10 9 8 7 6 5 4   8 9/9 0 1 2 3/0

Printed in the U.S.A.   40

First Scholastic printing, April 1998

Trout Summer

One

I'm waiting for Cody to come back. He's gone for the canoe so we can try to save the life of this old man, the one who's lying here on the riverbank by my feet with a great big puddle of blood around his head and his heart beating so fast it could give out any second. We thought we knew who he was, but it turned out we were wrong, that he's a damn crazy liar just like a lot of other people we know. But we can't watch him bleed to death, Cody says, so we're taking the boat toward the rapids: Dog's Breath and Horseshoe, Deerfoot and Blindman's Falls, where somebody died last spring. If we make it through, there are summer cabins on the other side. Somebody there will have a telephone.

I wipe the blood from the old man's head and I say my prayers: God, if there is a God, help us make it down the river. I'll do whatever you want from now on. And if there's any good to spare, could you save the old man, too?

Two

That's over now, but it's not where the story begins. I don't know if it starts when we found the cabin, or when Mama and Cody and I moved to Laglade, or when Daddy met the new waitress at the Peter Pan Inn, or even before that: twelve years ago, when Cody was born, or when I, Shana, was born thirteen years ago; or when Mama and Daddy met in the parking lot of the Superfresh Market in Warrensburg, Virginia, where he was selling a stringer of bass he'd caught that afternoon in the Castle River. I guess the best way to explain is like what Cody and I do when we're standing hot and sweaty on the riverbank: plunge in.

How would you feel if the members of your family were like dice and somebody stuck you in a shaker and tossed you around and threw you out any old way? The first time, you might land together in a heap, but the next throw would send the Dad dice flying off the table for a couple of months, and the one after that would sling someone else out of the way, once and for all. Over time the dice would get fewer, the shakes harder. Just as you thought you were used to it, you'd get swooped up and flung around again, knocking against people and places and feelings as if that's what they were meant for: to hurt you. If it happened to you enough, you might turn out like me: dreaming about a happy, smiling family like you see on television; holding in your hands the scraps from a family picture torn up because there was no family left.

My daddy was a big smiler. I've got pictures of him on the wall of my bedroom in the Laglade townhouse: Daddy on ice skates; in a cowboy hat and boots on top of Mr. Roy's horse, Dinah; sipping coffee with the regulars at the Peter Pan Inn, studying his book of Italian art. That picture ran in the Warrensburg paper last fall, in an article about the men who drop by the restaurant to talk about politics and weather, fertilizer and fish bait. The article allowed as how Daddy, with his interest in Leonardo and Raphael, was an oddball there. But we were proud of the picture. It was pinned on the cupboard door in the kitchen of the old house for a good long time.

Up until Easter, I'd lived in that house all my life. It

belonged to Mama's daddy, who lived with us till I was seven. Then cancer killed him. That was one of those shakes of the dice that sent me reeling, because somebody I loved every single day got carried away in an ambulance and never came back.

The house: It was white clapboard on the outside, faded and off-color like shingles get, with a big front porch and a little back porch and the Castle River running right through the back field, so you could look down anytime, day or night, and see the water. The rooms were small: the front room with an old black oil-burning stove and faded wallpaper; the kitchen with the hand pump still there, even though there'd been running water since Mama was a teenager; and lots of windows, and the vegetable garden right out behind where you could see if the weeds were starting to take over. On the left was Mama and Daddy's bedroom, with Daddy's notebooks lying here and there on the wooden book-shelves he'd made, and the big iron bed where Cody and I would bounce if they went out. Granddaddy's room was beside Mama and Daddy's. After he died, they moved the TV and a sofa bed in there, because the oil stove in the front room can be smelly when you first light it. Upstairs was my room, small and tucked under the back eaves, where I could see the river. Cody's was in the front, looking out on the lilacs with the road and the town just beyond.

It hurts to leave the place that's raised you. Losing

people is bad enough, although until they're dead, like Granddaddy, you dream you'll get them back. But the land will show you all its secrets, if you look. I must have known—still do—every little hollow in the ground that led down to the river, every gully or washed-out spot where a kid could curl up to hide or read or spy on someone else. I knew the clearings in the middle of the blackberry bushes, the space between tree trunks where I'd tried over the years to build lean-tos and playhouses. I knew—know—where the spring rises up, and how the ground smells just before you get there, that damp cool smell of wet earth, wet stone. I've lain on my stomach and seen the sun shine off the spring water, seen the moon and stars like the spring was a cup that held them, and you could put your face down in the darkness and swallow them up.

Most of all, better than I knew the house or maybe even the land out back, I knew the river. My memory begins there: sitting beside Daddy on the bank, clutching a bamboo pole, him saying to me, "Shana! Pull *now*!" I did, and up came a fish with blue and gold along her underside, wiggling to get back where she came from. I didn't want to kill her, so Daddy ran up to the house and got a bucket, and we filled it with water and carried her up and showed Granddaddy and Mama and Cody.

"You shouldn't have left Shana down there by herself while you got the bucket," Mama fussed. "What if she fell in?"

"She didn't fall in," Daddy said. "I knew she wouldn't."

"I'm naming her Fairy," I told them. I wanted to keep her in the bucket overnight, but they said she would die, so all of us took her down to the river and let her go.

I didn't free all my fish, not after I tasted what they were like rolled in cornmeal and fried up beside a couple of eggs, with potatoes on the side. I must have fed the family lots of those breakfasts, because after I caught Fairy I had Granddaddy take me down to the river almost every day to fish. We'd troop down together, him and Cody and me, because Mama'd already got her job as a telephone operator, and Daddy was either working or studying or looking for work. I got to know the river in all its seasons and all its times: morning, when the mist rose off it like magic breath; midday, with the dragonflies hovering and swirling and the muskrats leaving their water trails beside the banks; evening, when the deer came out of the woods on the other side to drink and spy on us two-legged ones before they turned tail-up and ran. Late at night we took our flashlights down and fished catfish on the bottom. That's Mama's favorite, because it's sweet, like chicken. Served up beside ripe tomatoes from the garden with a glass of ice tea, it makes a meal you can't buy at the Peter Pan.

Cody and I must have pulled hundreds of fish out of

the Castle: bluegills and perch, red-eyes and cats, willow bass and black bass. These last we caught mostly on lures: rubber worms, spinners, flatfish. We learned to fish the deep spots where the water stays cool even in July for largemouth, and to cast across the cobble bars, in and out of pools, for willow bass.

We didn't always catch fish. Some days we'd have everything perfect: the right bait, a good lunch in the backpack, a pair of old sneakers tied to our belts for wading the rocky shallows. As the hours passed, we thought our luck was bound to change with the next cast or around the bend. "There's a great place just behind that rock," Cody would say, not adding that you'd have to be an Olympic swimmer to reach it. Cody can pick the spots, I'll hand him that. As crazy as he is, he'll risk his life to get there, too.

What Cody lacked—and this balanced us out as a team—was patience. A snarl in his line would start him cussing so loud you'd hear him all the way across the river. Later he'd show up beside me, in tears from exasperation, his rod in his hand. Usually I can pick out a tangle, but sometimes I'd take my time before I agreed to do it. "Will you let me watch what I want on TV tonight?"

"Shana!" His eyes would turn dark, and he'd cross his arms and stare out over the water. Now and then he grabbed my bait and ran. Sometimes he did promise. Once the reel was working, he'd stalk off without saying thank you. But he stuck to his bargains, and he often caught a good one, to boot.

But he let his go. Cody's softhearted, though he tries to hide it. If he thought the fish was going to die anyway, he'd put it on the stringer, but he wouldn't look at it, after that; he said it made him feel bad, seeing it hurt and knowing he was the reason why. It didn't bother me. I told him, somebody kills all our meat. He didn't like that, and he said when he got older and cooked for himself, he planned to be a vegetarian.

The river wasn't just for fishing. Cody and I must have had a dozen places that were special to us: the rock we'd jump off where the current would swirl us around the bend on our way up; the place with the sand beach; the spot where sycamores grew out over the water, where we strung the swinging rope and the town kids would come watch us and ask: "Can I try it?" That was the only thing they ever envied us for, and we got what we could from it, making them share their Coke and chips before we'd climb up and unwind the rope from the high branches. Though they lived nearby, they didn't know the river like we did. You'd hear one of them say, "Look at that red flower. Ain't that pretty?"

"Cardinal flower," Cody would murmur to me, or "Bluebells," or "Trout lily." Granddaddy had taught us the trees and flowers, just like he'd taught Mama when she was little.

Daddy loved the river too. He grew up fishing and skating and swimming on the other side of Warrensburg. He went to high school at the regional. People said he was the smartest boy that school ever had. He qualified for the quiz show *I've Got a Question*, and they flew him to New York for an interview, but they didn't let him on because he had bad teeth. If he'd gotten on, he would have been the youngest contestant the show ever had.

Daddy was interested in art back then, too. He took every class the high school offered. But he didn't have the money to go to college, so he had to study on his own. He also loved to ice skate. He taught himself to do some of those fancy jumps you see on TV. And when I was born, he named me after his favorite skater: Shana LaPont. He watched her in the World Championships and the Olympics on TV, and when she came to Richmond to give an exhibition, he went to see her there, and took me, too. I can't remember it, but he said she made a fuss over me. Cody says she was probably faking, since I was bald and fat; but who knows?

By the time Cody was born, Daddy's interests had changed. He was doing long-distance trucking with a partner named Mel, and they'd made a pact to drive in every state in the Union. Daddy took pictures of them all. I loved to sit beside him and look at them: the red sands of New Mexico, the Chesapeake Bay country, the forests of the Ozarks in Missouri. He said one day he'd put them in a book and get it published. He'd been in twenty-two states when he passed through Wyoming and saw a rodeo. He named Cody after the town where he saw it, and for years after that he was desperate to get a horse. I was wild with hope that he would, but Mama put a lid on it, saying, "We can hardly afford the car, much less a horse."

"A horse doesn't cost that much. I'd fence the back field and it could feed on grass right up to the end of November. Save us having to cut back there."

"What about winter?" Mama was smiling, but she looked skeptical.

"It doesn't take much to feed a horse, honey. Twenty, thirty bales of hay. I could get that off Roy Haines. Hell, I could work for it, earn it in a weekend."

"Yes, yes!" I cried. I was running around in circles, dizzy with joy.

"You've got a job already," Mama said.

"I'm sick of it, Dot. I'm away from home, away from you and the kids, and it makes me lonely. And there's no excitement to it anymore, no romance." He paused. "I was thinking of putting my name in for work at the livestock market in Hopewell. In the meantime, if I have to, I'll work at the cement plant at Grove Hill."

Mama sighed. "Charlie, they're laying off down there."

"There's other places. Mel and I don't get along like we used to, and he drinks too much. And Cody's nearly three. I've missed seeing him grow. I want to stay home awhile."

"And get a horse!" I shouted.

Mama gave me a look that said be quiet.

"Money isn't everything," Daddy said.

"I thought you wanted to finish out your fifty states," Mama said. "You're just nine shy of the whole country."

"They're not going anywhere. When the kids are older, we'll take a trip and see them all."

He did what he wanted to. Not that Mama didn't like her job. She worked every week and every other weekend, and she got good pay. On Fridays we'd put her check in the bank and go to the supermarket, and if anybody needed something big like shoes or a coat, we'd buy it then, while Mama had the money in her account. Granddaddy's Social Security went for heating oil, or to repair the house if it was something he couldn't do himself. Daddy's money was used for emergencies or special times: birthdays and Christmas. Daddy loved holidays. He made sure the space under the tree was jammed with presents. The year I turned five, I remember coming down the stairs Christmas morning and seeing pink: dollhouse and snowsuit and stuffed animals and a brand-new pink two-wheeler. That day I must have been the happiest kid on earth.

Cody was born too late for the best times. He'd just turned six when Granddaddy died. He started first grade a month later, and he had to go to old Mrs. Reese for day care in the afternoons. Mama was worried about Cody, about all of us. Daddy was away a lot, looking for work. He'd call to say he'd be home Monday, but something would come up, and lots of times he wouldn't make it back till the weekend. I couldn't shut up about Granddaddy: Why did he die? Who gave him cancer? Why didn't the doctors have pills that would make him better?

Cody was just the opposite. When he wasn't in school, he stood at the window, looking out silently. I tried telling him what the grown-ups had told me: that Granddaddy was gone forever, that he was living someplace in the sky. Cody looked at me like I was nuts. "The sky is for birds," he said.

"Granddaddy isn't coming back," I repeated.

"He will, too," Cody said.

I wonder if that's where Cody lost his patience, because he stood waiting at that window for close to a year before he finally gave up. By then he'd turned into a nervous, fidgety kid who had a hard time sitting still or staying out of fights at school. Even at home, when he'd sit down to watch TV or read, he'd wriggle and squirm, as if there was something inside that wouldn't leave him alone.

But Cody always had friends, boys who laughed at his high jinks and called good-bye out the windows of the school bus. I was a loner. I didn't dislike the other kids; I just couldn't think of anything to say, and the more I tried, the more tongue-tied I got, until after a while I stopped trying. It was easier to live inside the books I read. I talked with Nancy Drew about her latest mystery, and rode Misty and Sea Star over the dunes at Chincoteague. Sometimes I read stories to Cody so that we could act them out. As he got older he liked being read to, especially books about animals, like *The Incredible Journey* and *Rascal*.

By then Daddy had taken a job at the sawmill at Landis. He hated that work, but Mama said he was lucky to get it, the way the economy was slumping. In the long run it may have been the steadiest job he ever had, because Uncle Mike worked there too, and he tried to keep Daddy going. They got into the habit of stopping at the Peter Pan for coffee and sweets on the way to the mill. Everybody liked Uncle Mike; he was big and loud and jolly, and the waitresses hurried to fill his cup and give him the biggest slice of pie. Daddy was quiet by comparison. I've wondered who it was that said, "Charlie, this is Paula Preston. She's an art student at the university, taking time off to save money 'cause she wants to go to Europe."

"Europe!" Uncle Mike probably roared. "What for?"

Maybe she was too shy to answer him. Maybe Daddy asked her later, quietly, and she talked to him about Michelangelo and Leonardo and Giotto and Raphael. All I know for sure is that summer Daddy started taking me to the Peter Pan for breakfast Saturday mornings. He said it was to make up for the Tuesday nights he spent with Cody at baseball, though I hadn't minded having Cody out of the house so I could pick my own TV shows or read in peace. Sometimes Mama and I talked. She told me about her friends at work, who were forever entering contests and sweepstakes. "Why don't you try too?" I asked. "We might win a new car or a trip to Hawaii. It only costs a stamp."

She shrugged. Her dark hair was coming free from the neat coil she fixed each morning. "I know I won't win."

"How come?"

"I've never won anything in my life, Shana. I had to struggle for what I got." She smiled. "Except for you and Cody, that is."

"The more you don't win, the better the chances that you will next time, Mama."

"You can't rely on luck."

"I want a Hawaiian vacation. . . ."

"Your grass skirt is on layaway. If you get lucky, I might have it paid off by Christmas." Mama brushed my straight brown hair back from my face. I snuggled into the pillows of the old sofa, its blue afghan warm around my shoulders. The comfortable buzz of the TV lulled me to sleep.

• • •

The waitress at the Peter Pan had blue eyes, and when she looked at you, you could tell she was *really* looking. I turned red when Daddy explained I'd been named for a figure skater, but she had an easy laugh that made embarrassing moments slip away.

"You should eat, honey," she said, as if she wanted to fill out my skinny arms and legs. "How about a pile of flapjacks?"

I nodded, but when she brought them I was still so flustered it was hard to swallow.

"Paula's only working at the Peter Pan a little while," Daddy explained on the way home. "She's saving her money to go visit the Sistine Chapel."

"What's that?"

"It's a church in Rome, Italy. Some of the world's greatest art is on the walls and ceilings there."

"I think I've heard of it."

Daddy nodded, as if he were sure I'd heard of it. "Paula showed me some pictures she keeps in her hand-bag. They're breathtaking."

"It'll take her a long time to save money working at the Peter Pan," I said.

Daddy looked at me with surprise. "You sound like your mama."

For the next month Daddy couldn't stop talking about Italy, and the artists who'd lived there in the 1500s. He took a day off work and went to the library to check out a stack of books on Renaissance art. He'd thumb through them in the mornings before Uncle Mike came to pick him up, showing us the paintings and sculpture he liked best. That got on Cody's nerves. He'd roll his eyes when Daddy wasn't looking, and once, down by the river, he said, "Do you realize we're named after Daddy's hobbies?" Before I could answer, he added, "If Mama got pregnant now, they'd call the baby Leonardo."

"Cody! You know Mama and Daddy aren't going to have more children."

He looked taken aback. "Why not?"

I had to stop and think. It wasn't anything I'd heard them say that made me so sure I was right. "They're too old. They hardly even kiss anymore. Anyway, we can't afford another child."

"We could if they wanted it. Daddy hasn't worked a full week this month. He stays home writing in those dumb notebooks."

"They're not dumb."

"They are too. Shana, those people he's studying have been dead four hundred years! They're not important now."

"They are to him."

"He needs to get his head examined."

"Cody, you're mean."

He shrugged his thin shoulders. "So what?"

◆ ◆ ◆

But when Daddy left before Easter, Cody was as upset as Mama and me. The note we found in the mailbox didn't tell us what we needed to know. I read the phrases over and over, as if they were pieces of a puzzle that would make sense if you got them in the right order: ". . . sorry to disappoint . . . time to study what I crave and figure out who I am . . . know that I have let you down . . ."

"It doesn't say where he's gone, or when he's coming back," I told Cody.

He shook his head. "He's dumping us like we're some boring TV show."

"Don't say that!"

"We should call Uncle Mike."

"Mama already did."

"What did he say?"

"He was shocked."

"This can't be true," I said, reading the note one more time.

"It is." Cody sounded tough, but I knew he was hurting too.

"Daddy's gone away before, when he was trucking or looking for work," I said finally. "He always came back, and he will again. It's just a matter of time."

Three

—

*E*verybody in Warrensburg heard about Daddy's leaving. We couldn't go anyplace without someone asking how we were doing or what we needed. Couples had broken up before, and some had gotten back together, but not before the town had the chance to hash over their problems. Now they couldn't stop putting Daddy down.

"I knew it would be hard for Charlie when he lost the chance to be a TV star," Mrs. Martin said, shoving our loaves of bread into a paper bag. "But I never thought he'd do you and the children like this. You asked so little. Why, that house came from your own daddy, didn't it, Dot? Charlie didn't have to pay a cent for it."

"Daddy offered us the house," Mama said. "He didn't like living alone."

"Charlie thought he was better than the rest of us," Mrs. Martin sniffed.

"That's why I married him," Mama said. She paid for the bread and let the screen door slam behind her.

When Mama brought up moving, it never occurred to any of us it would be permanent. I guess we thought we'd go someplace till the gossip died down and we could pull ourselves together. We'd never been any- where except camping in the state parks, so the idea of seeing another state was inviting, a little vacation we'd stay on until Daddy came back to his senses and found us there. Then we'd return to Warrensburg together, walking down Main Street and stopping at the Peter Pan for hot chocolate and pie.

But Cody didn't want to leave. He told Mama, "Base- ball's about to start. I'm supposed to pitch this year."

"Every place has baseball, Cody."

"But I know the hitters. I studied them last spring, to see what they swung at and where I'd have to keep the ball."

"Maybe you ought to wait a little while, Dot," Uncle Mike said. "Give the kids a chance to adjust to this before they have to make another change."

Mama shook her head wearily. "This town has such a hold on me. Ever since I was little, I've wanted to try something different. All the years Charlie traveled, he said we would. I was supposed to hold the fort until he had it figured out. We used to sit at night and look at his photographs: Florida would be nice, right between the bay and the ocean, but there's nothing like the Rockies. . . ." Mama's voice was worn out.

"Where would you go?"

"The phone company can transfer me. There's a pay increase when you move to a metropolitan area, and one suburb that needs operators has inexpensive town houses, too. I can rent this place out for extra money."

"Rent our house!" My eyes flew open, but Mama stayed calm.

"We wouldn't want it standing empty, Shana."

"There's worse places than Warrensburg," Uncle Mike said quietly.

"We'll be back," Mama said.

I was still in a daze when I first saw Laglade, Maryland. It looked like a picture from a magazine: row after row of pastel town homes, neat and clean, the grass cut and little trees planted every twenty feet beside the white sidewalks. The realtor who unlocked the door to our house and ushered us in must have guessed we were from the sticks, because she showed us the dishwasher and the sliding glass doors and the tiny back porch, which she called a deck. "The pool opens June first," she said. "And there are three malls within a ten-minute drive. King's Crossing has an A&P, and Havilland has a couple grocery stores too."

"We'll put things away and go stock up," Mama said cheerfully. "And tomorrow morning we'll get you registered at school."

Cody hated Laglade right from the get-go; maybe he would have hated anyplace, angry as he was then. But his complaints were right: Laglade was designed not for people but for cars. The sidewalks ended with the last town house, and after that came a snarl of expressways. He couldn't even get to a baseball diamond on foot.

The kids were different too. They all had Nintendo, and skateboarding was the in thing instead of baseball. They wore expensive sneakers and soccer shorts and cut their hair like bangs across the back. They weren't mean to us; they just didn't notice us at all. Cody made a fool of himself trying to get their attention. He borrowed a skateboard and rode it down a concrete drainage ditch until he crashed and had to get four stitches above his eye. He got into a fight on the playground, and he refused to do his homework because they did math a different way from how we'd been taught. Mama went through everything from begging to screaming. She hardly had time to ask how it was for me.

I'm not sure I could have answered her anyway. I was knocked dizzy by the latest tumble of the dice. Was Laglade ugly or beautiful? Did I like living in a house that looked like a picture in a magazine? Which of the girls at school liked to read and fish and swim, like me? A few of them giggled at my accent, but there were others that turned to shush them when they did. The kids didn't just repeat answers from the book, either—they spoke up about their ideas. One girl, called Catherine, wrote poetry so good that the teacher read it to the class. Mr. Thomas liked my writing too.

"You have talent, Shana," he said. "You should practice over the summer—keep a journal, and maybe try some poems. And when you get to high school, show them to Mrs. Kless. She teaches creative writing. Usually you have to be a junior to get in her course, but she makes exceptions. I'll mention your name next time I see her." He smiled. His eyes were blue, not brown, but they twinkled like Daddy's.

I dreamed about Daddy. I dreamed that he came back, bursting through the door of the town house, his arms filled with pink packages. He'd finished his studying, he explained happily. He'd brought little pictures for the stark white walls: a woman poised in a seashell, her red hair trailing over pale breasts; an old man plucking a thorn from a lion's paw; a king surrounded by his court, the picture all dark red and satins. . . . I woke dumbly, the images fresh in my mind, and realized Daddy wasn't here, and the pictures were ones he'd shown me at breakfast back in Warrensburg. What if I'd looked more closely? What if I'd stayed up to watch the art specials on public TV, so he'd had someone to share his interest?

I waited for a letter. I'd dawdle on the way home from school, deliberately granting the mailman more time to reach into the bottom of his bag and find the letter with the forwarding address scrawled on the front. I wouldn't look through the stack of mail until I got inside the house and made myself a snack. Then I'd go through the envelopes one by one, and then, when it wasn't there, again.

"What are you looking for?" Cody asked, watching my ritual one afternoon.

"None of your business."

"I'd like to know how the Cubs are doing," Cody said. That was the name of his baseball team in War-rensburg.

"Uncle Mike could find out."

"I guess." His head was down, so I couldn't see his eyes.

"How come you didn't sign up here?"

He shrugged. "I don't get along with the kids."

"If you had something in common, maybe you would."

"I doubt it." Cody paused, as if he wondered whether he should tell me this: "I've decided I don't like people."

"Thanks a lot."

He grinned suddenly. Cody's smile can light up a room. "You and Mama are okay, and Uncle Mike."

"What about your friends back home?"

"They were talking about us, just like everybody else. I heard them."

"They don't talk about us here. Nobody knows us."

"But they're creeps, and they're dumb, too. They don't even know their water tastes bad, and the air stinks."

"I hope you didn't tell them."

"As a matter of fact, I did."

"Cody . . ." I shook my head, but it was more because I thought I should than that I really disapproved.

The one thing about Laglade that was *good* was Mama's job. Somehow she'd ended up in an office full of nice people. A couple of them had gone through separations or divorces, and they seemed to care about us even though they hardly knew us. Barb, whose kids were in high school, sent me a bag of clothes that blended in with what the other kids had. She sent Cody her son's old skateboard and helmet. And she told Mama about some land her uncle owned along a river in southern Pennsylvania. She and her kids used to camp there when they needed peace and quiet. "Barb asked her uncle, and he says it's fine for us to go there too," Mama said. "It's only an hour away. We can drive up this Saturday."

"We'll go fishing," I told Cody.

"What about worms?"

"Try the backyard."

He shook his head. "I scratched around out there when I was thinking of planting some tomatoes. It's artificial dirt."

"There's no such thing as artificial dirt."

"Sure there is. They sell it at the mall."

"Liar."

"It's in the aisle behind the plastic Christmas trees." He started laughing at his own dumb joke. But he got out the fishing rods, so we knew he wanted to go.

The river was called the Leanna, but the map was vague after we left the superhighway. We turned on a dirt road and jounced over deep ruts. After a mile the road dead-ended, and a trail led off to the left, through the woods. I saw new leaves on the oaks and poplars, but most of the trees were evergreens with long, sloping branches. They shaded the trail and made the under-cover dark and mossy. The path turned and headed steeply down. We picked our way over outcroppings of jagged rock. I could hear the river in the gorge below. Then, through the branches, I saw water. I dropped my pack and slid the rest of the way down to the river. Cody tumbled after me. The trees thinned and we ended up on a big flat rock with sunlight all around us.

The Leanna was small—not even seventy feet

across—and so clear you could see the bottom in most places. It was scattered with boulders that divided the water into channels and pools. The current was swift, and the deeper spots were tinged black. In the shallows, the water bubbled up gold and pink over the sand and stones.

Though it was pretty, I was disappointed. "It's more like a creek than a river."

"It's not like the Castle, that's for sure." Cody stood arms akimbo, his gaze measuring depth and flow. He shook his head. "Most of our lures won't work here, Sha."

"How come?"

"The current's fast, and there's not much surface in the main channels. They'll be swept downstream before they start jigging."

"Maybe it's wider somewhere else."

Cody nodded. His face looked relaxed, like he was back in his element, and what it relaxed from, I realized suddenly, was anger. I studied his expression. Did Cody miss Daddy? Did he want him to come back?

"Come get these packs," Mama called. "I can't carry everything."

We scrambled up to help her. She was surprised too at how small the Leanna was. "But it's nice, with the firs around it. I didn't realize how much I'd missed seeing green."

We found a flat rock for our gear and baited up. I

used a worm (Cody'd been right—we'd had to buy them), but Cody tied on a Mepps spinner, a tiny silver spoon with two hooks on the underside. He headed upstream. I went down.

It was different, all right. The banks held a jumble of boulders; just beyond them, a narrow path followed the curve of the stream. Little gray birds with black caps were singing at me in the evergreen branches. At home they would have been red-winged blackbirds.

I found a likely spot and tossed my line into a pool. The little red float wavered for a minute, then drifted downstream. Suddenly it disappeared. I jerked but there was nothing at the other end. "Snagged already?" I have a habit of talking to myself when I'm fishing. I yanked, walked downstream, pulled again, and the hook came free. I adjusted the float and cast again. This time the hook stayed off the bottom. I watched it float down, the worm wriggling over the rocky riverbed. I waited.

The moment the fish strikes is my favorite time. It's always a surprise; your heart starts thumping, and your hand flies to the crank on the reel. Is it a big one? The biggest yet? You have to keep the line tight while you wait for the fish to surface. Some bass will jump, but others, even big ones, are sluggish, and easy to get into the net. I hummed a little tune under my breath, cast again, changed bait. After a while the smell of woodsmoke drifted down the river, and my stomach growled. I packed my gear and went to find Mama.

She'd started the fire on a flat rock; there were hot dogs sizzling on some green sticks she'd cut, and a pan of beans nestled to one side. I was about to call Cody when he appeared upstream. He was grinning.

"I've got a surprise."

"What?"

"I'm not telling."

"Come on, Cody—"

He shrugged like it was nothing, but I could see he was excited. "I'll show you after lunch."

It didn't take us long to polish off the food. Mama scattered the fire and poured water on the loose coals. We headed upstream.

I didn't know what to expect, and Cody wasn't giving any hints, either. Beside us the river tumbled between rocks and ledges. We came around a curve where the left bank rose high and wide. In the mud by the river I saw coon tracks, and the sharp cloven prints of deer. Cody led us up and across a path that smelled of pine needles. He pointed triumphantly: "There!"

The cabin was hidden among trees, set against a dark, rocky wall. It was shaped like the little houses kids build with log construction sets, except that the logs were darker, almost black, and there was a big stone chimney on one end. The door was sagging on its hinges, but Cody pushed it open and ushered us in as if he owned the place. "Ta-daaah!"

You could tell it had once been nice. The main room

had a couple of windows that looked out on the river, but the glass was missing and the wood around them smelled like rot. There were some shelves built up against the near wall, and an old table with benches that were green with mold. The fireplace took up most of the far wall. A broad mantel held the bottom of a kerosene lamp.

"There's more!" Cody exclaimed. He led us through a doorway into a small dark room where beds with chicken-wire springs were built into the wall. Beside them a single window looked out onto the rocky cliff.

Cody showed us another opening off the main room. It must have been the pantry, because it was lined with shelves and drawers. There was even a window looking out toward the trees, and an old woodbox with rotting logs still inside it. A second door led outside, but it was stuck shut. "You have to come through the front and walk around," Cody explained.

We followed him dutifully. There was a spring out back, with a chipped enamel pail to catch the water. And hanging from a nail in the tree next to the spring was a metal cup. Granddaddy had hung a cup near our spring back home. "It's a way of telling travelers the water's good," he'd explained, and now and then we'd see someone stop, take down the cup, and drink. I reached for it now, but Mama stopped me. "We're trespassing, Shana. We don't know anything about this place."

"Except that it's abandoned," Cody said. "Look how the spring is clogged."

He was right about that: It was filled with rotting leaves. He rolled up his sleeves and cleared it out. Then he cupped some water in his hands and tossed it in the air. The drops caught a ray of sun and gleamed like diamonds. Magic, I thought. I looked around for more, but there was only the back of the cabin and, beyond it, the outhouse.

We were about to leave when two things happened. The first was that Cody told us something so unbelievable that I actually thought, even then, that it might come true. "This is where we're going to live this summer," he said.

Mama stared at him like he was crazy. She started saying all the things you knew a grown-up would say: We didn't know who owned the cabin and it wouldn't be safe, and the roof leaked, and everything we owned was in the town house, and there wasn't even a road to get here. I was waiting for her to finish, so I could put in my own two cents, when the cat appeared.

Four

My granddaddy believed in spirits. He believed they lived under water with the fish, and in the air, and also in the deep pools of your mind. "They rise at night, while you're sleeping, and tell you their secrets," he said. "If you listen, you can hear them."

"Do they look white, like ghosts?" I remember asking.

"You never know what shape they'll take." He sat looking off toward the river, his arms crossed over his round belly. "But they're there. When you're least expecting it, they'll come to you."

I asked Mama about that. She whispered that Granddad was old, and sometimes old people want to believe that life goes on forever. "So they imagine things that make it seem that way," she said. "You shouldn't argue with him."

I told Granddaddy what she said. He shook his head and laughed. "I know I'm going to die, Shana," he said. "I didn't say I believed in ghosts."

"You aren't going to die, either." I said. I held his hand tight.

Later I mostly forgot about spirits. I was too busy playing and reading and fishing, and also missing him. The cemetery was too far to visit without a car, so I made a little shrine down by the river, just a board with his name printed on it in Magic Marker and some pretty stones arranged around it in a circle. I didn't tell anybody, but I used to go there and talk to him. I'd ask how he was doing, and what heaven was like. He never answered, and over time I went there less and less. Before we moved to Laglade, I went looking for the spot. I had to hack away at weeds and vines before I found it. The board was mostly rotted, but the circle of stones was still there. I sat down and told Granddaddy what Daddy had done. I told him we were leaving his house and that it felt like the good we'd once had was crumbling the way the old tobacco shed behind the house had rotted, tilted, and finally just fallen apart. I could hear the murmur of the river to my right. I waited to see if Granddaddy would speak to me, but if he did, I couldn't hear what he said. I felt like a book filled with blank pages, waiting for my story to be written by someone else.

On the other hand, Cody was certain about everything. He was sure that Daddy had betrayed us; if he came back, Cody didn't want to see him. Cody knew for a fact that Laglade was the worst place on earth, that nobody should have to live there, and that those who chose to were idiots. He was just as sure that the cabin was where we were meant to be: no people, no roads, just us and the river.

And the cat, who had emerged from a clump of rocks just as we were about to leave. He was an old orange tom, with a head the size of a softball and patchy fur covered with burrs. He was thin but proud; he didn't wheedle. Instead he leaped lightly into the empty window frame and stood peering out, as if to ask: Did I invite you in? He let me rub his head before he moved away and sat staring with yellow eyes.

"We can't just leave him here," I said.

"We can't take him, either. The lease says no pets." Mama was firm, but she looked concerned. "Where do you suppose he came from?"

"Who knows?" Cody was kneeling, holding out one hand. "But he's on his own, that's for sure."

"We can't leave him here," I said again. "He'll starve."

"He's not starving now. He probably catches mice in the cabin."

I didn't expect it, but I started to cry. I couldn't just walk away from him.

"We'll leave some food," Mama said briskly. "Cody, run back to the rock and look in my pack. There're some extra hot dogs there, and some cheese slices. When we get home, I'll ask Barb if she knows who owns the cabin, and if the cat is theirs."

Who owned the cabin was George Cosgrove, Barb's uncle, but he didn't know a thing about the cat. The cabin, he said, we could use in trade for the repairs it needed. He and his wife had moved to a retirement home, but they'd hated the thought of selling the place along the river 'cause they'd had good times there when they were young. Mama couldn't believe it when Barb told her. "Don't you and your children want to use it?" she asked.

"No, my kids don't want to leave their social life," Barb said. "Now that they're in high school, they have dates or parties almost every Saturday."

Not like us, I thought when Mama told me. I was still trying to figure out whether I wanted anything to do with that beat-up cabin. But Warrensburg was six hours away, and Uncle Mike didn't have a guest room in his tiny apartment. What would I do in La-glade once school let out? Wait for the mail to come? Watch TV? Go to the pool? The thought of the other girls looking at me pale and skinny in my bathing suit made me cringe. Maybe I'd be better off in the woods with Cody.

Then there was the cat—our cat, I called him in my mind. I'd worried about him ever since we'd left. Had he eaten the food we'd piled by the rocks where we'd first seen him? Was he waiting for us to come back?

Mama made Cody work for what he wanted. Before she'd consider the cabin, he'd have to show he'd done his homework every night for the last two weeks of school, and there couldn't be any pink slips from the teacher, either. Not only that, but he had to invite a friend for supper. Cody went down the row of desks in his class inviting kids until one girl said yes. She spent the whole evening talking about the day she met the star of *General Hospital* at the opening of Hillcrest Mall. Cody lied a lot. "Hillcrest's my favorite mall too," he told her. Mama nearly killed him after she left.

That weekend we sat down and talked about the problems with Cody's idea. We'd found a closer road in, but Mama'd still have to commute an hour, then walk the last half mile to the cabin. There was a house near where she'd park on the other side of the trail; the owner, Mrs. Burns, said we could use the phone for emergencies. But Mama still felt uneasy. "What if one of you gets hurt?" she asked. "You'd be left alone while the other one hiked to the phone. You could lie there for an hour."

"That's no different from back home," Cody argued. "We were gone all day when we went fishing. Sometimes we were miles from any house."

"That's true." Mama nodded. "But this is a strange place. There could be dangers we don't know about."

"Like what? Tigers? Quicksand?" Cody grinned.

Mama turned to me. "What do you think, Shana?"

I was pleased she'd asked my opinion, and I tried to sound grown-up and logical. "It'd be pretty boring being here all summer. You'd be gone all day, and there's not much to do without a car. I guess we'd just stay inside and watch TV."

"Some of those shows are so violent." Mama sighed. "Maybe you would be better off outdoors."

"We'd be careful," Cody said. "*Real* careful. I wouldn't do anything without asking Shana."

Mama didn't answer, but she looked right at me. "That's a lot of responsibility."

"I think I can handle it. I'll have some schoolwork— Mr. Thomas told me to keep a journal, and he gave out a summer reading list, too. I could work in the morning, and after lunch Cody and I'd go fishing."

"I'd want you to know exactly where Cody was," Mama said. "And the two of you'd have to be back in time to make supper. I couldn't get there before six, with the drive."

Cody could tell he'd almost won. "We'll make the

best food you ever tasted—fried chicken and ham and even broccoli, if that's what you want."

Mama smiled, but she kept looking at me. Cody kicked me under the table. I gave him a look that said, *You owe me.* "We'll be careful, Mama. It'll work out fine."

"I'm trusting you, Shana."

I nodded, like there was nothing to it.

Later that night she told us we could go. She'd written out some rules: no swimming alone; tell each other where you're going and when you'll be back; be at the cabin by five to fix supper. We'd have to boil the water from the spring until the state sent back test results from a sample Mama planned to give them. A week later I stood gazing at the loaded car, parked as close to the cabin as we could get it.

"Do we really need this much plastic?" Cody hoisted a thick roll over one shoulder. "Did you remember the staple gun? What about my box of Milky Ways?"

Mama was juggling a broom and a bag of potatoes. "For heaven's sake, Cody, be still." She frowned at me. "Shana, you have to carry something besides your library books."

"I am!" I grabbed a plastic grocery bag and picked up a bedroll, too. The pile sticking out of the trunk seemed bigger than ever. "This is going to take lots of trips."

"What did you expect? You're the one who kept adding stuff."

"Shut up, Cody." I started off. This trail approached the cabin from a different direction, angling across the gorge more gradually. When I saw the glint of water, I knew from the map to turn right. The path was choked with weeds. I beat them down with the grocery bag, wondering why I'd agreed to this. I shifted my books to the other arm and saw the roof of the cabin below me. I climbed down and stood in front of it. The doorway gaped, and I noticed a vine growing from the sagging gutter. I piled my load neatly in the yard and called the cat. I called again, but he didn't come.

Mama and I cleaned while Cody fetched our things. We started out sweeping, and once we'd cleared the leaves and sticks, we brushed the walls and ceilings, knocking down cobwebs, spiders, even a bird's nest. I scrubbed the shelves and table with vinegar and water, and Mama cut squares of clear plastic for the empty windows. We stapled the tops but taped the lower sections so they could be rolled up on hot days. Then Mama showed me how to cut screening, and we stapled that to the outside window frames. I built a little fire in the fireplace to dry out the damp, but Mama said until the roof was patched that smell was going to be there, and she hadn't had space to bring a pail of pitch.

What we had brought was piled outside now, and

Cody and I started to put it away: quilts and pillows in the back room; kerosene lanterns, one for the mantel, the other for the bedroom. Our propane camp stove went on the widest shelf, next to a water basin and a bucket. We hammered nails to hang our cast-iron frying pan and two cook pots, little and big; mess kits, matches, and a portable radio sat beside the stove. We'd brought two fruit crates for Cody's and my clothes, and a flashlight for each of us.

We sprayed the pantry for bugs, then washed it down before we put the food away. Mama had brought bread and peanut butter and honey, cereal and powdered milk, oranges and rice, baked beans and pretzel sticks. There were cans of soup, crackers, cookies, Vienna sausages, and beef stew. Mama would buy fresh meat or cheese on her way from work, since we had no way to keep them cold. A half-dozen eggs and a little tub of butter could rest in the stone alcove beside the spring.

I hung my nightshirt from a nail beside my bed and arranged my library books on top of the wooden box, which I'd painted blue the night before. On his crate Cody had piled his pocketknife, a compass, a bunch of comic books, and some string. Mama would sleep on a cot in the main room. She'd strung a rope with a curtain over it across one corner, for privacy.

"Shana—baby mice!" Cody found them nestled in a wad of sawdust under the eaves. Their pink bodies squirmed helplessly. He carried them outdoors and set them in a crevice between stones. "Have you seen the cat?" he asked anxiously.

"I called, but he didn't come."

"Hope he doesn't find these guys."

"I hope they stay out of our food!"

"There're metal boxes for the stuff that isn't canned."

"This is going to be like camping, isn't it?"

"It's going to be *good*," Cody said.

It was almost time to make supper. We walked through the house, inspecting our work. Mama'd spread a pretty cloth over the table; that and the curtain around her cot gave a touch of color to the front room. The lantern on the mantel, the pots on the wall felt cozy, even though there was no place to sit except the benches. The pantry, with its row of canned goods and metal grub boxes, was orderly, and though the bedroom was small, it was neater than Cody's or my room had ever been. We made a list of things we'd forgotten: another water bucket, caulk to patch the holes in the chinking between logs, extra batteries for the flashlights. Tonight, since it was Saturday, Mama said she'd make supper. "Why don't you go for a little walk, to shake the dust off?" she suggested.

We went down to the river. The light was different, because it was evening. The water gleamed; flecks of foam scudded like little boats down miniature rapids.

Cody lay on his stomach and threw sticks into the current, watching them twist and dodge. After a while he sat up and looked at me. "This is the first good thing that's happened since Daddy left," he said.

"Speak for yourself," I said, though I was happy too, partly because of the cabin but also for a reason no one else knew.

"I want to live here forever."

I laughed, feeling pleasure at his happiness. But I couldn't let him be.

"You can't spend your life hiding from people," I said.

"I can spend my life however I want to."

"Once you're grown, maybe . . . but you'll have to have a job, won't you?"

"Nope. I can fish and hunt, and have a garden for my vegetables. I'll have an apple tree, too, so I can make pies." Cody smacked his lips.

"I think I'll be a writer," I said. "That way I can live wherever I like. I could even live in Europe if I wanted to."

"Europe!" Cody's mouth turned as sour as a sour apple. I knew he was thinking of Daddy.

"For all you know it might be nice over there," I said. "Maybe it's nicer than here."

"No. Europe is full of people."

"And museums and castles and cathedrals."

"A river is better," Cody said.

We sat for a while, resting. I was waiting to hear Mama call, and finally she did.

We climbed the wall of the gorge, being careful because there was no path. Mama had heated stew and made bannock bread in the frying pan. The table was set with the metal plates and flatware from our mess kits. Though it was still light out, the front room was shadowed, so Cody lit the kerosene lamp and set it on the table. Mama said grace, and I let my lips move along with her words.

"The cat hasn't come back," Cody said suddenly.

"He's probably a wanderer," Mama said. "He may have a circuit he travels. And I'll bet this is one of his stops."

We boiled water and cleaned up the dishes. Then I sat at the table and read by lamplight, while Cody listened to the radio. I poured water from the bucket to wash my face and hands. Afterward, when I went outside to dump the dirty water, I saw that the swath of sky over the river was alive with glimmering stars.

I went to bed feeling lucky. Cody has chosen what was best for us. And in the pocket of my jeans, grabbed from the mailbox in Laglade before anyone else could see it, was a letter from Daddy.

Five

I read the letter when I was alone by the river. Before I opened it, I examined the envelope carefully, writing down the return address: 229 W. 79th St., Apt. 21B, New York, N.Y. The letter had been sent to Warrensburg; the postmistress, Mrs. Grubb, had printed our new address on the right side of the envelope just below my name: Shana Allen. Daddy had written to me, I knew, because I was the one who'd been waiting so patiently for his letter and who knew he would come back. *Shana darling*, the letter began:

What a wonderful day I've spent! I began at the Metropolitan Museum, only a fifteen-minute walk from my basement apartment. There I sat in front of a Raphael masterpiece, soaking in the rich colors and complex themes of that superb painting. Later I walked to the Frick Museum, which also contains several Renaissance paintings. Viewing the real art instead of the prints I saw in library books is wonderful. You can almost imagine the artist standing there in front of you, paintbrush in hand!

Shana, how are you and Cody and Dot getting along? I think of you all the time, and wish you could be here with me. My apartment is just one room, which I get rent free in exchange for being a security guard at night.

I'll write again soon.

> *Love and kisses,*
> *Daddy*

I read the letter a dozen times. I wished it was longer! There were a million questions I wanted to ask: What's your apartment like? How did you get a job? Where do you buy groceries? When will you come home? I fingered the single page. Why hadn't Daddy put his phone number? Then I could have found some change and gone to a pay phone. But maybe he didn't have money for a telephone. . . . I'll write to him, I decided.

My letter took up most of Monday. For some reason, I didn't want Cody to know about it, or about Daddy's letter: not yet. That meant I had to hide them every time he got near. I also had to think up an excuse for not doing whatever he wanted me to: going fishing, going for a hike, looking for the cat. Finally I told him I had a headache and wanted to be by myself. He looked at me like he didn't believe me, but he went off to explore the river farther up.

I rewrote my letter to Daddy four times. It ended up like this:

Dear Daddy,

It was great to get your letter!

Mama and Cody and I moved! We are mostly living in a town house in Laglade, Md. Our address is 219 Hamlin Way, Laglade, 21236. Our new phone number is 301-555-6742.

Even though we moved, we're not staying in the town house over the summer, because Cody hated it. So we're staying at a cabin in Pennsylvania, on the Leanna River. We don't have electricity, running water, or telephone, so it's like camping. You would love it—the river is pretty, with evergreens all around.

Please tell me: How did you get to New York? What's it like? Do you have another job besides security guard? Do you have a phone?

Daddy, I'm glad you're getting to see the artwork from the Renaissance. But Cody and I miss you very much.

Your loving daughter,
Shana

I read my letter over and folded it up. I had an envelope with a stamp on it stuck in one of my library books; I'd mail it over the weekend, when we went out to shop. I carried the letter up to the cabin and hid it in the book. Cody had boiled water and made Kool-Aid, and I drank a glass, feeling uneasy. Why didn't I want Mama or Cody to see Daddy's letter, or mine? Was I lying to keep it a secret? Why hadn't I asked Daddy the most important question of all?

"Shana, come quick!" Cody's voice was almost a scream. I ran out the door. He was standing partway up the path, his hands raised high. Below him, on a rock beside the river, stood an old man in a khaki uniform. It took me a second to see the gun in his right hand.

"Stop!" I shouted.

The man looked up, startled, and dropped the gun. It hit the rock and bounced somewhere along the bank. He cursed and bent over, looking for it. Cody scrambled up the slope and grabbed me, pulling me toward the cabin.

"He's crazy, Shana! Run!"

I turned, but as I did I glanced down and saw that the old man was on all fours, groping on the ground. His head bobbed as if he hardly had the strength to hold it up, and there was a naked pink spot in the middle of his thin white hair.

"Shana, come *on!*" Cody was yanking at my arm.

"Just a second."

The old man looked up and saw me watching. "You better get down here and help me, girl!" he bellowed. "That gun is worth eighty-three dollars, and if it's lost, it's your fault!"

"It's not my fault either! You were aiming it at my brother!"

"That's 'cause he's not supposed to be here, and neither are you. I'm giving you exactly one hour to get off this property before I arrest you for trespassing!"

"We aren't trespassing. We have the owner's permission to be here."

"What owner?"

"Mr. George Cosgrove."

The old man staggered to his feet. His empty hands clenched, like he was getting ready for a fight. "George Cosgrove has no right to give anybody permission to mess up this river, or to camp anywhere near it, or to stay in that old cabin of his. He should have told you that from the start."

"Why?"

"What do you mean, why? Don't you know anything?"

"I told you, he's *crazy*," Cody muttered from behind me.

"Why?" I repeated.

" 'Cause this is a trout stream, and the land around it is federally protected land. You can't walk here, you can't camp here, you can't do anything here."

"You mean nobody can come here?"

"That's right." The old man nodded as if finally I'd shown a grain of sense. "Nobody."

"What about you?"

He bristled again, and his chest swelled as if he'd swallowed something big. "I'm the ranger. I enforce the law."

"I bet you aren't supposed to be pointing your gun at people."

He turned red. "That boy is a bad boy. I told him to stop, and he kept on running."

"He isn't bad either. He just didn't know."

"Now he does." He crossed his arms. I could see printing over the left pocket of his shirt, but I was too far away to make out what it said. "Come help me find my gun!" he yelled.

"I will not! You could have hurt Cody, or me."

"I couldn't either. It isn't even loaded."

"Then you shouldn't aim it like it is!"

"You better help me. If you don't, I'm going to have you arrested."

"What for?"

He paused, as if I'd caught him. He licked his lips. "For insubordination. Not only that, but I'll tell your parents you were here."

"Not Mama," Cody whispered. "She won't let us stay if she finds out."

"How will you tell them?"

"How the heck do you think? I'll come up there."
He pointed toward the cabin.

"They're not here now."

"Later."

"But if I find the gun, you won't?"

He hesitated, thinking it over. "No."

"All right. But you better not point it at Cody or me
or anyone else."

He muttered something I couldn't hear.

"You stay here," I told Cody. I scrambled down the
rocky slope till I was only a few feet away from him.
Up close I saw he was even older than I'd thought; his
eyes were glassy, and the skin hung around his neck in
loose jowls, like an old bulldog. His shirt was worn and
so faded that it was hard to read the writing:

PA. F SH H   CH

"Over here," he growled.

I searched in the low underbrush near the rock while
he stood watching. It didn't take me thirty seconds to
see the black barrel of the pistol. I picked it up by the
handle and held it out at arm's length.

"You found it," he grunted. He stuck it in his pants
pocket and glared at me. "I'm not telling your parents,
but I am going to issue a citation," he said.

"What's that?"

"It's a notice of violation of the law. I send it to the
federal government."

"We haven't done anything wrong!"

"You should have known you can't stay in that cabin. Privies are illegal near the river. They pollute the water."

I stood there with my mouth open. "What are we supposed to do?"

"Get out," he said. He turned and limped away.

I practically dragged Cody into the cabin. I shoved him down on the bench and started yelling. "You better tell me everything that happened! What did you do to make him mad?"

"Shana . . ." Cody's face was white, and he looked like he was close to tears. "It's not my fault."

"Tell me everything, before Mama gets home!"

He sighed and started in.

"Since you wouldn't do anything, I figured I'd go upstream and find a good fishing spot. I hiked up about a mile and saw a couple nice, deep places. I cleared away the brush around them so they'd be easy to get to. Farther up, I came across a cliff with a little cave in it. I found some bones and hunks of fur, so I thought a wildcat might be living there. Then I thought I heard it! I scrambled up to the top of the cliff and ran along the edge. I could hear something crying upstream. Then I remembered the cat!"

Cody shook his head miserably. "I crossed the river to the other side. Around the bend I saw a canoe pulled up in the underbrush. I thought maybe it had swept downriver in high water—remember how that used to happen back home when there was a flood?"

I nodded.

"Well, I turned it over—I hadn't forgotten about the cat, I just thought I'd investigate the canoe first. Then somebody shouted. I stood up and waited, so I could explain, when that old guy came stomping through the trees screaming, 'Thief! Thief!' He wouldn't shut up. Finally I just took off running. I figured I'd outdistance him in a couple minutes, 'cause he's so old."

"You shouldn't have started running," I said. "That made him think you were guilty."

"Guilty of what? Touching his boat?" Cody shrugged, and went on: "Anyway, I hurried on back, thinking I'd tell you about the cat. I was just a hundred yards upstream from here when he came around the bend in the boat. As soon as he saw me, he beached it and pulled out the gun. That's when I started yelling."

I stared at Cody to see if he was lying, but he didn't blink or turn red. Instead he groaned and buried his face in his hands. "I heard what he said to you, Shana. What are we going to do?"

"I don't know. You start supper while I think."

I tried to sort it out. The old man had a gun, and probably bullets, wherever he lived. It made sense that a ranger would have a gun: You never knew when you'd come across a sick animal that had to be put out of its misery. Still, rangers weren't supposed to use their guns against people, especially kids. Had Cody really done anything that bad?

"What are you making?" I asked him, trying to slow the whirlwind of arguments in my head.

"Sausage and potatoes. There's a jar of applesauce we can have, too. Mama'll like that, won't she, Shana?"

"Mama," I muttered, nodding to Cody. On the hillside he'd whispered that she wouldn't let us stay. That was true—no parents would let their kids live near a lunatic. We'd move back to the town house. I'd hate that, and Cody would too. But if we stayed and he got shot, it would be my fault. . . .

"Shana, Mama'll be here soon." I knew what Cody was trying to ask, but I couldn't answer, not yet.

"Did you set the table?"

He nodded, his thin face twitching with nervousness. It would hurt him to go back, but it might kill him to stay.

"Did you decide?" he asked.

"Not yet."

"I won't go up there again if you don't tell. I swear."

"He knows we're here, Cody."

"He's old. Maybe he'll forget."

We heard footsteps outside, the door was drawn aside, and Mama came in.

Six

Dinner was quiet. We asked Mama about her day before she could ask about ours, and made small talk to fill in the spaces. Still, when she pushed back her plate and asked, "What happened today?" I wasn't sure what to say.

But Cody was. He told her about his walk, spreading it out as if it might have taken all day, and leaving out the cat noises and the ranger. When he finished, I couldn't help staring at him. I'd never known he was that good a liar.

"What about you, Shana?"

I took a deep breath, for my story'd have to cover up not only the ranger but Daddy's letter, and mine to him. "I spent most of the day reading," I muttered. "The book was just so good I couldn't put it down."

"What book was that?" Cody asked sharply, and I saw he'd realized I was hiding something from him, too.

I glared. "It's a suspense novel. The title is *Katie Spills the Beans*."

"I think I've heard of it," Cody said.

"I'll wash the dishes," I mumbled, and I got up and moved away.

We spent the next day hanging around the cabin. I helped Cody scramble up on the roof, where he poked around trying to find the leaks. The metal flashing near the chimney was rusty, he called. "Want me to bust it out?"

"Not till we have something to fix it with, dummy."

"The tarpaper's worn through up here too, Shana. You can see into the bedroom if you put your eye up close."

"Mama said she'd try to get some pitch at the hardware store."

"Remember that time Mama and Daddy patched the roof at home, and I got tar on my shoe and couldn't get it off?"

"That's 'cause you stuck your foot in the bucket."

"Yeah." Cody grinned from up above me. "I don't know how old I was, but I do remember thinking,

Should I? And before I could think it through, I did."

"You didn't want to think it through."

"When you think too much, you miss all the fun."

"Yeah, Cody—like yesterday."

His face got tight. "What would you have done?"

"I would have stood my ground and explained that I wasn't doing anything to his boat."

"He probably would have shot you on the spot. Only reason he didn't shoot me was 'cause there was a witness."

"I don't know about that. He said the gun wasn't loaded."

Cody slid to the edge of the roof, spun around, and hung from the overhang by his hands. He dropped. "Maybe it was, maybe it wasn't, but I'm not going back up there, I can tell you that."

"Good." For once, I thought, Cody has learned his lesson.

We built a fire outside and made hamburgers for lunch. There was a smooth patch of ground about fifteen feet from the cabin door where we built our campfire ring. While we were gathering stones, Cody found two salamanders: one with a blue streak and another with a gold body and black spots. We put some wet leaves in the washbasin, and they burrowed underneath them and wouldn't come out. We named them Shy and Spot. Cody was so busy playing with them that he didn't help me clean up the dishes, and when I said he'd have to do it after supper, he acted like he didn't hear.

Later, as if it had been listening when Cody was on the roof, thunder rumbled. We unrolled the windows and taped them down, hoping the dark clouds overhead would scud on by. Suddenly a wind blew down the side of the gorge, tossing dirt and stones in front of it. In the half-light the pines and hemlocks looked menacing, and lightning clattered in the strip of sky above the river. The cabin, on its shelf of dirt and rock, felt tiny and exposed. I lit the lamp and took a book from the crate beside my bed. Cody turned on the radio, but there was only static.

"The rain's coming," he said, standing by the front window. "Shana, look!"

Along the river a line of rain advanced like the steady silent march of an army. As it drew abreast of us, the storm hit the house. The plastic on the windows bulged, then tore loose; and rain hurtled through. "Quick, more tape!" Cody yelled.

"Where is it?"

"I put it right there!" He pointed to the mantel.

"If you had, it would be there!"

"Hurry, Shana . . ." Cody was trying to hold the plastic shut. I found the tape on the table, but by then the sill was too wet for it to stick. All we could do was stand there and watch the rain pour in.

"Oh my God—the roof!" The water must have pooled up there before the floodgates opened, and it began to stream down the wall beside the fireplace. In the bedroom, two spots were spouting like open faucets. We set a bucket and a pot under them. "At least it didn't get the quilts," I said.

"Not *yet*." Cody surveyed the ceiling there for drips. "This pot's full."

"Dump it in the washbasin."

"I can't—we put the salamanders in there."

He made a face. "The front room's flooded—you can empty it there."

"Maybe I'll dump it on *you*."

He grinned. "I wouldn't mind a shower, now that you mention it."

"Cody!"

But he was stripping off his clothes. A second later he ran into the big room in his underwear, a bar of soap in one hand. I lugged the water in after him, watching as he lathered up by the open window. "La . . . di . . . da . . ." Cody was hamming it up. He stuck his hands over his head and twirled around like a ballerina. "Hit me, Shana!" he shouted. I aimed the pot of water at his bony chest. *Splat!* He roared. I ran into the bedroom and got the bucket.

"Get my butt!" Cody yelled, spinning around.

I aimed and let fly. *Splat!* Cody screeched. He kicked up his heels and crowed like a rooster. The rain beat in through the windows, and thunder rumbled somewhere up the river.

The rain kept on for a half hour. By the time it slowed, Cody and I were trying to clean up. The cabin floor looked like a lake, and both of us were drenched.

Then Cody started shivering so bad his teeth chattered. I told him to get in bed while I made a fire. The wood was wet and wouldn't light, but then I remembered the dry stuff in the woodbox in the pantry. I managed to tear off some bark and twigs and get them started. The dry wood flamed right up, but when I added wet it hissed and steamed. By the time the fire was blazing, I was in no mood to tackle the wet floor. And we'd promised Mama we'd make supper, too.

"Cody, come help!" I called.

"I'm too cold."

"Then come in here and warm up."

He did, wrapping the quilt around him like a bathrobe. I moved a bench in front of the fireplace, and he stretched his bare legs toward the flames. I got the broom and tried sweeping the pools of water out the door. That cleared most of it up. The rest I soaked up with our towels while Cody watched.

"What if I need to dry off?" he asked.

"You should have thought of that before you took your clothes off."

"I can't think of everything," he whined.

I felt my face get red. When Cody was little, I used

to hit him and he'd hit me back, but we hadn't done that for a couple of years. Instead I slammed the broom down on the floor. "You better start helping!" I yelled. "What do you think I am, your damn servant?"

He grinned suddenly. "Servants don't cuss."

"Cody! Stop joking and help me!"

"What if I don't?"

It came out before I thought about it. "I'll tell Mama about yesterday."

He sat straight up. "You better not! Anyway, you lied too."

"To cover for you."

"No way. You said you'd spent the whole day reading."

I stiffened. "So what? I was down by the river writing. I told you I wanted to be a writer, remember?"

"Then why'd you lie?"

"I'm writing a poem for Mama, and I want it to be a surprise."

Cody stared sullenly. "You just thought that up this minute."

I crossed my arms and glared back. "Prove it."

We made the supper together, Cody doing what I told him but with a mean expression. Then when Mama got home he acted nice as pie. He showed her Spot and Shy and described the storm, pointing out the leaks and talking about how we'd get them patched. She had no idea how bad it had really been, and we didn't tell.

Because in the past few days, something had changed between the three of us. Cody and I had lied about the ranger so we could stay at the cabin. Whatever we faced, we faced on our own, and the outcome, good or bad, was up to us.

The next morning I did try to write a poem. I took a pencil and a book of poetry down to the river and sat leafing through the pages for inspiration. Back in my English class in Laglade, Catherine had said the poems she wrote came to her like songs. But my mind felt empty—dry and brittle as an autumn leaf.

"Shana?" Cody was standing on the little bluff above me. "Want to go fishing?"

"I'm writing," I lied.

"How about later?"

"Why don't you go by yourself?"

"I could. . . . It's just . . . I thought you might want to."

You're afraid of the ranger, I thought, but I didn't say it out loud. "I'll call you when I'm ready."

"Good! I'll get our tackle."

Once the idea of fishing was in my head, it wouldn't let go, and the blank paper in front of me began to seem like something that had drifted in on the wind. Still, I made myself wait a good ten minutes, holding on to the pencil to see if it would suddenly come to life. It didn't. I trudged up to the cabin and put my stuff away. Cody had made sandwiches: peanut butter on white bread. We wrapped them in a plastic bag with a couple of oranges and took off. I wanted to go down the river, but Cody said no: "The best spots are upstream."

"Are you crazy? That's where you saw the boat."

He shook his head. "The canoe was a half mile beyond the place I want to go. And there's plenty of spots to hide, if we hear him coming."

He was right about the fishing; the pools were deep and clear. We started out fifty feet apart, me working one bank and him the other. We'd cast into the eddies and let the lures drift down where the current could take them. I tried a Rapala minnow and then a rooster-tail. Then I changed to a size-five hook with a worm on it. That got me a hard swift tug. A minute later I pulled in a little sucker.

"Gross!" Cody yelled. He hates suckers. I flipped it off the hook and threw it back.

Cody thought we were doing something wrong. We sat on the bank eating sandwiches while he talked. "I think it's the bait," he said. "We're used to fish that live in slower water, like at home."

"Granddaddy would have known. . . . I bet he caught trout."

Cody shook his head. "I looked in the picture box, but I only saw bass and catfish."

"The picture box . . ." I'd forgotten about the bent-up cardboard box where we kept the family photo-graphs. Last time I'd seen it was back in Warrensburg, on the shelf beside Daddy's notebooks. Birthdays, Christmases, trophy fish, sunsets, the first flowers of spring, Granddaddy even after he got sick—they were all in the picture box. "Where is it?" I asked Cody.

"Under my bed."

"You snuck it up here?"

"I didn't *sneak* it—I brought it."

"How come?"

He looked embarrassed. "Because I like to look at the pictures."

"Is the picture of Daddy in his chaps and boots in there? The one Mel took at the rodeo?"

Cody nodded.

"I always loved that picture." I sat staring at the crust of my sandwich. Something inside me hurt, and I tried to steady it. "You miss Daddy too, don't you Cody?"

"I guess—I don't know. Why do you ask such dumb questions?"

"Because I've been thinking."

"What?"

"Mama really likes her new job, and she's making more money than she was. I'm afraid she won't want to go home when Daddy comes back."

Cody stared at me like he never thought about this stuff. "She did say the town house was easier to keep clean," he said.

"And they're training her so she can get a promotion. If she does, she'll be a manager. I heard her tell Uncle Mike on the phone."

"Managers can transfer."

"But not to Warrensburg. Remember old Mr. Weiss? He's been the manager there for a million years."

"I'll have to think about that." Cody sighed, wriggled, turned back toward me. "Know what, Sha? I keep hearing that cat."

"Now?"

He shook his head sheepishly. "In my mind. The thing is, it sounded hurt."

"No way am I—"

"I have a plan." Cody kept on. "Once we're near the canoe, we'll stay on the other bank and circle around till we're way upstream. If we don't hear anything, we'll come right back here. That cat's probably gone by now, like he left us. I just have to be sure."

"You don't know it's our same cat, Cody. You don't even know it is a cat."

"Nothing bad is going to happen," Cody said. "I swear."

We hid our fishing gear behind a log and went upstream. Cody pointed out the cave he'd found earlier. Farther on we saw the metal gleam of the canoe. We crouched, listened: nothing. We cut back like Cody'd planned, making a half-circle through the woods.

The place we came out was different: The river was

wider and calm, bordered by a grove of birches. Way back the gorge rose green and gray. We heard only the gentle riffling of the water between broad, low banks. "We'll go back," Cody whispered, and we did. From deep in the woods I still thought I could see the glimmer of metal against the other shore.

We'd gotten back to the cave when the cat cried out. I wanted to pretend I hadn't heard. Then it came again, a strange, hurt noise from the far side of the river.

We crossed downstream and headed north, bending low and running one at a time through clusters of broad-leafed shrubs—rhododendron, Mama'd called it. We took cover under a rock overhang. "I'll be back," Cody said.

"Wait!"

But he was gone. The cat cried again, a long thin howl.

"Cody!" I whispered.

His head appeared in a window of light in front of the rock. "I know where it's coming from. There's a cliff a couple hundred feet behind the canoe. It's there."

"The ranger's going to catch us, Cody." My heart was pounding.

"I have to find it," Cody said.

"Then I'm going with you."

We planned our route—from the rock to a clump of evergreens to another group of rocks beside the cliff—and we scrambled one at a time, Cody first, staying as low to the ground as we could. Besides the canoe there were no signs of people, and I began to think we might be all right. The cat howled again, somewhere close and to our right.

We had to pass a clearing between the cliff and the river. We went together, still crouched, hoping the cat would cry out to guide us. We looked along the cliff wall and in the high weeds and grass. A line of cedars blocked the view to our right. We darted behind the thick low branches of the closest one. On the other side, almost completely hidden by the trees, was a small cabin.

"His," Cody muttered. His voice rattled like dry leaves.

"Maybe he's not there."

The cat cried again. We sank to our bellies and crawled through the high grass, the tree trunks like a fence between us and the house. We could see his back-yard: a garden with flowers and a birdhouse. A couple of paddles leaned against a wooden shed. Beside them were some tools and a roll of chicken wire. A pump handle stuck up from a concrete cistern. An overturned bucket sat next to it on the bare earth.

The cat howled. We crawled along the tree line until we could see behind the shed, and there he was, our cat, his big orange head looking right at us.

He was in a metal cage, and on the door was a pad-lock.

Seven

When he saw us, the cat shrank against the far wall of the cage. Cody pulled on the lock, but it wouldn't budge.

I glanced toward the cabin. Had something moved there, in the window?

"He's got food and water," I said nervously. "The cage isn't against the law."

"This isn't his cat." Cody kept pulling on the lock.

"How do you know?"

His shoulders squared as if he was getting ready for a fight. "I just know."

I kept my eyes on the window. "Hurry up, Cody."

"I can't get it. We'll have to find the key."

"You want me to knock on the door and ask for it?

What do I say: This time we're here to steal your cat?"

Cody didn't answer me. He talked to the cat, to calm it down. He was rubbing its head through the bars.

"Come on." I gestured toward the line of evergreens. "We'll hide there and figure out what to do."

What we planned was this: I'd knock on his door, say we'd heard a cat and that ours was lost. If he got nasty, I'd put up my hands and walk away. If he wasn't home, I'd see if the cabin door was locked. Maybe the key to the padlock was hanging just inside. We could "borrow" it, free the cat, and carry him downriver. As long as we returned the key, there'd be no way to prove we'd done anything wrong.

"What if we can't find it?" Cody thought out loud. "Or what if he finds us?"

"Bang," I said. I flicked my index finger like it was a gun. Neither of us laughed. "Any other ideas?"

Cody shook his head.

"Then I'll go. You watch from here."

His cabin was smaller than ours but nicer, with big windows and a wide front porch. Peeking in, I saw that the main room contained a potbellied stove, a chair, a desk, and his bed. Against the back wall the kitchen table held a chipped pot filled with red geraniums. Books and papers were stacked beside it; next to them was a collection of dirty plates and mugs. There was no one home. I knocked, just to be sure. Then I tried the door. As if it were waiting for me, it swung open.

I didn't want to go in, and I don't know why I did, because usually I don't do crazy things. My whole life I've been the one who followed the rules. This is against the law, the voice in the back of my mind whispered. . . . There wasn't any key hanging on the wall near the door. I pushed through the clutter, toward the back. There was a bathroom and a pantry, like ours, stuck on the rear of the house, and the main room formed an L to accomodate an iron sink and dish cupboard. The log walls were hung with river maps and charts of fish, all of them grubby and covered with notes. A fishing rod and a couple pairs of waders slumped in one corner.

"Hurry," Cody called from outside.

"Is he coming?"

"No, not yet . . ."

Then I saw a key hanging from a nail in the back door frame. Please let it be the one, I prayed, and I took it out back, almost tripping over another pot of flowers set square on the steps there. The key fit. I opened the cage. Cody gathered the cat to him. "Run!" I said. "I'll meet you back at the cabin." He did run too, the cat's front legs draped around his neck like a baby's arms.

I returned the key and made sure the doors were closed. Before I left, I glanced through the front window. With its hodgepodge of dishes, charts, books, and flowers, the cabin drew me like a magnet; but this time common sense prevailed, and I hurried away, toward the river. The canoe was where we'd left it, pulled up and chained to an iron spike. I followed a path that led downstream. I was in such a hurry, I almost ran right into him.

The ranger didn't hear me coming. He was crouched over the riverbank, holding a plastic tube in both hands. I couldn't decide whether to back up or talk to him. Then he looked up and saw me.

"Seventy-one degrees, and the sedimentation is moderate," he said, as if we were friends. "I would have expected worse, after that rain Wednesday. I guess the low-pressure zone wasn't as big as the radio said." He wrote something down in a pocket notebook. Then he looked up, and I think it registered who I was, because he started to turn red.

"What are you doing here?"

"Taking a walk."

"Taking a walk! You can't take a walk here. It's private property!"

"I didn't see any signs."

"So what? I told you the other day, this land is federally protected!"

"I'm not doing anything wrong."

He struggled to his feet, glaring.

"You don't seem to understand: People aren't allowed here!"

"You're a person." I don't know why I said it; it just popped out.

He stopped as if I'd tripped him up. "I . . . I'm the *ranger*."

"What's your name?"

"I don't have to tell you that." He seemed flustered, and he'd turned red again. "I'm on special assignment—trout expert."

I took a deep breath. "*My* name's Shana Allen."

"Look, it's nothing personal, but the government doesn't want these fish bothered. They're supposed to be adapting, and they're not doing too bad, either. You come here, and I'll show you the fingerlings." He grabbed my shirtsleeve like I was a little kid.

"Let go."

"Come on. You only get to see this once in a lifetime."

"But you said—"

"They're in the pool, behind that rock. See how it's flowing upstream, against the current? We call that an eddy." He was pulling me and leaning on my shoulder at the same time. When I saw how badly he limped, I stopped being scared.

"I *know* that already. I've spent half my life fishing."

He glanced at me sharply. "Where?"

"In Virginia, on the Castle River."

He shook his head, as if the Castle was no good. Then he crouched down and patted the ground beside him. "Here."

"I don't want to."

"Then you won't see," he said crossly.

He took a plastic bag out of the pocket of his uniform, poured something into his palm, and flung it on the surface of the water. Right away three tiny fish jumped. He turned. "What did I tell you?"

I nodded, but he must have guessed I didn't know what they were, because he went on: "Fingerlings—two browns and a rainbow."

"What did you throw them?"

"Caddis larvae. I raise it for them—got a rain barrel on the side of my house. They love it."

"Is it good for bait, too?"

"I'm raising trout, not giving them away."

I thought of the fishing rod in the corner, but of course I didn't mention that. He went on: "This is a high-level assignment. You're not to mention my work to anyone, understand?"

I nodded. I guess I said what came next to knock the wind out of his sails. "We got our cat."

"What cat?"

"Felix." The name came out like I'd known it all along. "Our old orange tom."

He stared right at me. Something flashed in his watery

blue eyes, and I thought: He's measuring me up. Then he shouted, "No cats allowed near the river! If you don't keep that cat shut up, I'll issue a citation!"

I took a step back.

"I showed you the fingerlings. You know what's at stake."

"He doesn't like fish," I lied.

"There's a bluebird nesting in my yard. They almost died out, like the trout. I'm authorized to do what I have to to protect them. I have the gun!"

I left him shouting. I climbed partway up the ridge and sat for a while, to see if I could figure him out. I watched him pacing back and forth along the bank, scowling and muttering. Then he disappeared up the path. I was about to leave when he came back in his canoe. He swung it around so he was facing upstream, then slid from one side of the river to the other. He glided partway back and pushed the bow of the boat into the current. It stood still, letting the water foam around it. Then with a flick of the paddle he turned it sideways and shot into the little eddy below the rocks. He got out, took another plastic tube out of his pocket, and dipped it in the river. He threw out more larvae and wrote down what happened. Afterward he paddled back into the current and pivoted the boat so that it plummeted downstream. Before he left, he looked up as if he knew exactly where I was.

♦ ♦ ♦

The cat was under Cody's bed, and it wouldn't come out. He'd shoved a can of tuna under there, but maybe Felix had heard what I told the ranger, because he wouldn't touch it. He howled as if we ought to know better.

"Felix?" Cody frowned. "Is he the cat from Uncle Mike's cartoons?"

Uncle Mike watched old cartoon shows each Saturday morning. He'd taught me Felix's theme song when I was little. I sang it for Cody. He nodded. "I could use a bag of tricks myself."

"Felix?" I held out my palm, and he slapped it. We didn't worry much about what Mama would say. We knew she'd let us keep Felix at the cabin, and we had no plans beyond the end of summer anyway. I told Cody I'd run into the ranger, and what he'd said. "Afterward he came back in the canoe. I've never seen anyone handle a boat like him. He's better than Eddie Brent."

"Better than Eddie?" Cody didn't believe me, I could tell. Eddie was a kid from Warrensburg who'd become a raft guide in the Cheat River Canyon. Every year someone dies in the rapids there. Cody shook his head. "You're nuts, Sha."

"Uh-uh. He can turn that boat on a dime, even in the middle of the current."

Cody changed the subject. "Why'd you tell him about the cat?"

"I didn't really think it through. I guess I wanted to shock him. He's just so . . . arrogant."

"He didn't say Felix was his, did he?"

"No. It's more like he has a right to do whatever he wants."

"He acts like he owns the river," Cody said.

We told Mama we'd found the cat in the woods—lie number who-knows-what for us, and her smiling and calling the cat and not paying much attention to the story because she had news too: They'd set a date for the accounting exam she'd have to take to get her promotion. "It's August twelfth," she said, stroking Felix. "I've got a lot of studying to do." She hated how thin he was. "We'll take him to the vet this weekend," she said. She didn't even mention the fall.

Eight

Saturday we drove to Laglade, carrying Felix in a cardboard box. Mama and Cody took him to the vet while I hung around the town house, watching TV and looking at the mail. There was nothing from Daddy, but a course list had come from Laglade High School, where I could have been enrolled come September. I thumbed through it, thinking I'd be back in Warrensburg by then. Still, I couldn't help noticing the electives they offered: not only creative writing, but photography, ecology, history of ideas, and a whole course of Shakespeare plays. Where Warrensburg had Latin and Spanish, Laglade offered those and French, Russian, and Japanese. In your junior or senior year you could go abroad, or you could take all advanced-placement courses if your grade-point average was high enough. That saved you money if you went to college, which most of the graduates did—eighty-four percent, the letter said. They had counselors who could help you get financial aid, too. I made a mental note to ask if Warrensburg High had them.

Later I took a walk and mailed my letter to Daddy. Laglade was hot, because of all the asphalt, and the car fumes stayed low in the air, so you felt like you were choking from pollution. I could hear the kids screaming at the pool from a mile away. I went past the chain-link fence, noticing a couple of girls my age. Just as I'd suspected, they had real figures and bathing suits that showed them off. They were reading magazines and chatting, while a horde of little boys ran around throwing wet towels. Nobody recognized me, and I was glad.

I went home, turned on the central air, and poured myself an iced tea. With my feet resting on the polished coffee-table, I felt like someone's guest. Then the phone rang. I expected a wrong number, but instead Uncle Mike boomed into the receiver: "Shana, you catch any fish?"

"Just a little sucker."

"Daag, I thought you and Cody could do better than that."

"The river's different." Uncle Mike made me smile without trying. "It's small and rocky, and it's got trout in it."

"You ain't gonna be outsmarted by trout, are you?"

"I hope not."

"Where's your mama? She said she'd be around today."

"She and Cody took our cat to the vet." I told him our story about Felix.

"Girl, you're telling some tales," he said at the end.

My face got red. "I'm not, either."

"Listen, tell Dot to call me, all right, sweet-pea? And Shana—"

"What?"

"The other girls are asking for you. I miss you kids myself. And I love you, too."

My eyes filled up; I couldn't help it. Mama and Cody came in just as I was hanging up the phone. Cody was full of news about the cat.

"Felix has scars from lots of fights. Even the vet says he's one mean cat."

"How come?"

"He tried to scratch him. I had to hold Felix still."

"He would have let me." I said it just to rile Cody.

"No, he likes me better. He's my pal." Cody rolled the cat on his back and scratched his belly. Felix grabbed his arm, but his claws were pulled in.

"Uncle Mike called." I told them our conversation, and Mama called him back right then. Cody and I played with Felix. If you pulled a string, he'd hide and jump it. In the background Mama said, "I haven't heard anything." "Is that so?" she said later. I could tell Mike was asking when we'd come to see him; but Mama didn't say. "You come up here, Mike. I'm having a barbeque at the cabin for everybody in the office in a week or so. Come on then. They'd like to meet you."

Mama laughed. "Just get on up here. If you don't trust the truck, I'll meet you at the bus station."

"Is he coming?" I asked when she hung up. She made a face.

"He's got more excuses than a dog has fleas."

"I miss him," I said suddenly. "And Daddy, too."

"Oh, Shana." Mama put her arms around me.

"Why can't things go back the way they were?"

Mama shook her head as if she didn't know, but when she walked away, I saw her face was tight, like a mask.

On the way back to the cabin we stopped and bought supplies: food, flashing and tar and nails, a flat of impatiens to plant by the cabin door. I got a couple of paperbacks: *Bleak House* and *A Guide to Pennsylvania's Trees and Flowers.* Cody got *Fishing for Trout* and *Rascal,* which he'd read before.

It was dusk when we hiked in. Mama cooked spaghetti while Cody made extra trips to bring back all our stuff. I lit the lantern and set it on the table. Felix circled Mama's legs, crying. "He's hungry," I said, but when I set the cat chow on the floor, he looked the other way.

"He wants Cody, I guess," Mama said.

"That's not fair. How come he likes Cody best?"

She shrugged. "Love doesn't know fair."

"What do you mean?" I asked; but she shook her head and didn't answer.

Sunday we spent the day together, just the three of us. In the morning we worked: Mama cut the flashing, Cody nailed it in, and the two of them painted pitch around the edges, then over the seams in the tar paper where the roof had leaked, Cody cleaned out the gutters while Mama and I made a bird feeder out of a slab of wood and hung it up where Felix couldn't reach.

Later I lay out on the rocks by the river and read. Mama was still working; she likes that, I think: Back home she rarely sat down, except at night. When I came up, I saw the flower garden was laid out with pretty stones, and the house smelled like pickles. Mama had made the brine and put it in a crock. She planned to bring back cucumbers the next evening. Granddaddy made pickles too. We kids used to go with him to the root cellar to check them every day. Sometimes he'd add a hot pepper or some dill on our say-so. When he finally brought the crock up, we'd have a special dinner: ham and potato salad and homemade cheese rolls, and all the pickles you could eat. We canned what was left, for winter, but they're never quite as good. I wondered if Daddy missed pickles.

That night I set the table and lit the lamp. We had macaroni with grated cheese on top, and sliced tomatoes.

Cody scorns tomatoes he didn't grow himself, but these, which came from Amish farmers off the highway, were almost as good as his. Afterward there was a shoofly pie from the same stand. We polished the whole thing off and squabbled over the crumbs. Mama's face was soft in the lamplight—pretty, I thought suddenly. What did she look like when she was thirteen? I wanted to ask, but it was safer to keep to the present, letting the past and the coming autumn stay suspended in some other place.

Monday morning Cody bugged me to go fishing. He'd read in the trout book that worms and corn are good bait on spinning tackle, and he'd managed to find a few red wigglers under rocks by the cabin foundation. He'd changed his hook size, too: down to a ten, which is tiny compared to what we're used to. The book said trout are smarter than normal fish. I wondered about that, but Cody was impatient when I brought it up: "Are you coming or not?"

"No, there's something else I want to do."

He made a face.

"Stay away from the ranger," I said.

I read for a while and then started my journal. I described the Leanna and its banks, naming some of the trees and making sketches of the ones I couldn't find in the nature guide. There were birds I'd never seen either, and I promised myself I'd learn their names over the summer. Then I told about how we'd ended up here. Writing about Daddy was hard, but later I felt relieved, as if I'd had the chance to talk to a good friend. Afterward I found raspberries on the other side of the river. I picked my fill, then waded back through the current. Cody returned with big news: He'd caught two good-sized smallmouth. He'd let them go, but it made me nervous anyway: "The ranger thinks those fish belong to him," I said.

"I was way downstream—he doesn't go that far."

"How do you know?"

"We'd see him paddle past the cabin."

I nodded, but inside I felt Cody was bound for trouble.

The week and the weekend after flew by. One day, trailing Felix through a thicket of rhododendron by the river, I came upon a hidden spot perfect for reading and writing. Where the bushes ended, an overhanging stone formed a shallow cave with a sandy floor. On sunny days I could sit on the rock ledge outside and dangle my legs in the water, but the cave sheltered me from wind and rain. I found a piece of driftwood for a shelf, and kept my books and journal there, along with a towel and a sweatshirt for cool evenings. I didn't tell Cody, and if he wondered where I was, he didn't ask.

Mama didn't either. She was busy planning the cook-out for her friends the next Sunday. We helped her get the place ready, trimming the brush on the trail down the ridge and gathering wood for an outdoor fire. We even got in the river and pulled away some rocks to make a shallow pool for the little kids. Mama had invited everyone in the office and a traveling supervisor, too. Cody shook his head. "Do you think they'll bring their alligator pocketbooks?"

"Barb used to camp here when her own kids were small," Mama reminded him. "She knows what it's like, and we've told the others."

"They won't like it," Cody said. "There's snakes, and poison ivy, and you have to leave your car back near the road."

"You just don't want to share the place," I said. I thought of the ranger.

"I haven't had a party since your granddaddy's birthday, when he was seventy." Mama pushed the hair back from her face. "Then I had Mike and Charlie to help me. Ralph Emmet butchered a hog, and they dug a pit to roast it in."

"He had a big cake, didn't he?" Cody rubbed Felix between the ears. "That's the thing I remember, seeing it and hoping I'd have a cake like that when I got old."

Mama laughed. "Alma made that cake. She always loved Daddy, because he snuck her on the train a couple times when they were young—took her up to Washington and all the way down to Atlanta, so she claimed."

"Did he take you and Mike, too?"

"No, he was stricter with us kids than he was with you all. We had to stay home and help with the place."

"He didn't take you even once?" Cody turned his head from the window.

"Not once." Mama's face clouded just a little.

"Did you want to go?"

"Sure I did. But back then people didn't pay much attention to what children wanted. You did what you had to just to live. Daddy was a teenager during the Depression. His family lost their farm, and they had to camp out all winter by the river. So we were always ready for hard times: We kept the garden, and he wouldn't let Mother sell the cow or chickens even when they built the town road past the house. 'We'll have milk and eggs and potatoes no matter what,' he'd say. But when the other kids walked by and saw that cow staked in the front yard, I felt like hiding my head for shame."

"Did Uncle Mike, too?"

"No, he just laughed it off." She smiled, remembering. "He'd call out to the kids, 'Ya'll want to pat my cow? You can even milk her, if you'd like.' I was so embarrassed, I'd run ahead and pretend I hadn't heard."

"Maybe Daddy walked by," I said. "He might have walked right by and you didn't know."

"Daddy grew up on the other side of town," Mama

said. "His folks weren't much better off than us. The new shoes he got for school had to make it all the way to summer, when he could go barefoot."

I remembered Daddy's old work boots, the steel toes scraped bare of color. He laced them last thing every morning before he left the house. I wondered if he'd wanted new shoes, shoes we couldn't afford to buy.

Nine

The party turned out well. I met the people Mama had been talking about: Barb and her boyfriend, Ed; Julie; Rita and Fred; Philip the supervisor; Marilyn, Debbie, and Bob. Barb I liked especially, 'cause she'd sent me clothes for school and helped us get the cabin. She was a short round woman who was so warm you felt you'd known her a long time. She made herself at home and started serving up cole slaw and potato salad, which she'd brought in ice-cream tubs. She cut Cody a slice of cherry pie for an appetizer. She wasn't afraid of his silence, either. "I hear you haven't exactly fallen in love with Laglade," she teased, and he smiled despite himself.

There was no one our age. Barb's kids hung at the mall on weekends, and Marilyn's girls were only one and three. I helped look after them down by the river. They splashed and giggled and didn't want to come out of the water. I found a green-backed frog to lure them up the bank. Marilyn wrapped them in towels and put the baby to her breast to feed. I turned red, but Philip, an older man who was sitting with us, chatted on as if nothing special was happening. He was wearing brand-new jeans, and his leather shoes didn't look right for the outdoors. He saw me looking at them.

"You can tell I'm a city slicker," he said. "I told Dot I'd like to have you three come to Baltimore to eat with me. I love to cook, and it would be fun to show you the sights."

"Do you live right in the city?" I asked. The TV news always talked about people being murdered there.

"Yes, I've lived there all my life, and I love it." Philip smiled at me as if he could read my mind. "My apartment overlooks Mount Vernon Place. There's a Thai restaurant on the first floor, so I get to smell their food every time I open my windows."

"Food from Thailand?" I wasn't even sure where Thailand was.

"Pad Thai, green curry, chicken with lemon grass— I know their menu by heart. And next door there's a club where my neighbor plays jazz on weekend nights."

"Doesn't that keep you awake?" I thought of the sounds of the gorge, the river murmuring and the tree frogs' calls. They seemed more soothing than music. But Philip shook his head.

"When I visited my daughter in the country, I had a hard time sleeping in the quiet and the dark."

Marilyn's baby slurped her milk. You could hear her swallow: *gulp, gulp, gulp.*

"I like to hear the train whistle blow, before I fall asleep," Marilyn said. "Sometimes I lie awake waiting for it."

"Ma, I'm hungry!" Little Laura pulled her arm.

Philip held out his hand, and she took it. He extended the other one to me. "Let's go feed Laura."

I took it for a second, then pretended I had to tie my shoe. "I'll be up in a minute," I said. My face burned, and I ducked my head away so they wouldn't see. I'm not holding hands like a little kid, I thought. Still, seeing Laura scrambling up the path so happily in front of him, I wished I could.

Before the cookout ended we had ice cream with fresh raspberries on top. People were talking and laughing. Cody'd slipped away. Somebody'd brought a tape player and some tapes, old-fashioned ones like Glen Miller and Benny Goodman, and a couple of women were showing each other how to dance in the clear space outside the cabin door. Mama tried, too, first with Barb, then Philip. In the middle of the song she threw her arms up in the air and burst out laughing: "I'm hopeless."

"You were getting it, Dot," Barb said. "I was watching your feet, and you had it right."

"They have fall classes at the community center," Marilyn said. "I was thinking of signing up. Why don't we do it together?"

Mama hesitated: You could see her mind going back and forth between the pleasure of the idea and our plans to go back home. She smiled. I spoke up for her. "We'll probably be gone by then."

We walked them out, carrying Marilyn's sleeping kids and the bowls and platters the food had come in. By the parked cars people hugged Mama and said how much fun they'd had. We stood together, she and I, as the headlights disappeared into the twilight. Fireflies lit our way down the trail. We sat out front on a couple of folding chairs someone had forgotten to take. Dark settled in the gorge, flowing softly down the ridges.

"Did you like them?" Mama asked.

"They seem nice." Something pulled at me, making me say less than I should have.

"Barb's treated me like a sister—the sister I never had." Mama smiled at me. "And Marilyn, Julie, Philip; all the same."

"Philip's old," I said. "I guess he's so old his wife is dead."

Mama shook her head. "He's divorced. He used to be an alcoholic, and his wife left him because he couldn't stop drinking. Since then he's pulled himself together."

"What happened with Barb?"

"You mean her divorce?" Mama looked over at me. I nodded.

"She never told me the whole story. She started, but it's still so painful she can hardly talk about it."

"Maybe they should have gotten back together—Philip and his wife, too. Now they might be happy."

"I don't think it's that simple," Mama said.

"It's always worth one more try—that's what this counselor on TV said."

"Sometimes you can't try anymore," Mama said. "You're just worn out."

Cody came in late, picking up Felix and slinging him around his neck. Mama fussed at him for leaving the party, but you could tell her heart wasn't in it. He told me he'd gone down to the river to sit. Later he beckoned me outside. We went back beside the spring.

"I was about to come back when the ranger came down the river in his boat," he said.

"What happened?"

"I hid behind a rock. I was afraid he'd hear the music from the party—you know how sound carries on the water. . . . Then he *did* hear it. He jerked upright, spun the canoe into an eddy, and sat there listening. I was trying to figure out how to stop him when he took off upstream."

"Upstream?"

Cody nodded. "You were right about the way he handles the canoe—he's the best I've seen. He leapfrogged from eddy to eddy like the current didn't exist." He paused. "I waited around a while, thinking he might be back with one of those citations, or his gun, but he never came."

"That's weird."

"I know." He shrugged and rolled his eyes. "How was the rest of the party?"

"Good. They're nice people, all of them. Only I wish Mama didn't like them so much."

"How come?"

"What I said before—she won't want to go back."

Cody sighed. Wisps of his long hair glinted in the moonlight. "September's a ways off."

"When Daddy comes back from New York . . ."

He looked startled. "What'd you say?"

I faltered just a second. "I got a letter."

"You what? When?"

He was mad. I put my hand out toward him, but he knocked it away.

"I was going to tell you—"

"Liar!"

"Cody, I was. I was trying to figure out the right time."

"You haven't even told Mama—I'll tell her," he said fiercely, but I caught hold of his arm and pulled him back.

"We have to do this right. We could end up in Laglade for good."

"You can't keep that from her!"

"I'm not going to!"

He clenched his fists, unclenched them, looked at the backs of his hands. His mouth was a tight line. "Why'd he write *you*, anyway?"

"He knew you'd be mad. He must have reckoned I'd forgive him."

"He doesn't deserve it."

"That's what I mean."

"I'll call him," Cody said. "Did he send a number?"

"No, just an address."

"Then I'll write."

"Cody . . ."

"He doesn't belong to you, Shana. Just 'cause you shared this little secret—"

"Calm down!"

"Shut up!" Cody said, and he stalked off into the dark.

When I went inside, Mama was in bed behind the curtain. She sounded half asleep: "You and Cody go on to bed; it's late."

But I couldn't sleep. Felix prowled in and out of the room, wanting Cody, and I wondered where he'd gone. No wonder I didn't tell him things, the way he'd exploded, then run off. I wondered if he'd tell Mama about the letter before I got the chance.

＊ ＊ ＊

When I woke up he was back, wrapped tight as a mummy in one of Gram's threadbare quilts. I heard Mama rattle around the big room, getting ready to leave for work. Before she left she peeked in, but I closed my eyes as if I were asleep.

Later I went down to my secret place beside the river. I wrote in my journal about the party, and the fight I'd had with Cody. A blue jay shrieked as if he didn't want me there. I put him on paper too, trying to capture the harshness of his cries. Then Felix appeared, and I realized it wasn't me the jay was screeching at after all. "I thought you'd stay with Cody," I murmured, but maybe Felix could tell I was upset, because he rubbed against me, just once, before he disappeared into the thicket. "Don't go upstream," I called after him.

I wrote to Daddy, telling him about the party and how Mama seemed to like it here. *Come back, before it's too late!* I put. I told him I'd let Cody know about his letter, and that he should expect one in return—not a nice one, either. Daddy had always been good at listening to Cody, had known he didn't mean everything he said. "Better for him to get it out than keep it trapped inside," he said. "That can make you crazy."

"But why does he have to be so mean?"

"Those are words on the way to something else. In the long run no one's more loyal than Cody."

Not you? Or Mama? But those questions were silent, so Daddy didn't have the chance to answer them.

When I got back to the cabin, Cody was sitting on the bench with his face over a basin of water. He dunked himself, then shook like a dog.

"Here's Daddy's address." I handed it over.

He looked at it, then up. "Did you tell Mama?"

"I will tonight."

He didn't say anything.

"When you write him, try to be nice," I said.

"Don't tell me what to do, Sha."

"I'm not, really. It's just that . . ." I broke off when he glared.

"If you don't tell Mama, I will," he said coldly.

Later we made up. We put on old sneakers and half-waded, half-swam down the river. We floated on our backs where it flattened out, splashing like little kids. In the narrow spots we kicked and jostled, each of us trying to slide through the rapids first. Once Cody won and ended up piling into a big rock. The river's so full of twists, you have to watch it every minute—even the deep pools have jumbles of boulders on the bottom. "This is the kind of place people drown," Cody said. "They get one foot wedged between rocks. The current pulls them down, and they can't get up again."

"That's morbid."

"It's true. Eddie told me. As long as you keep your legs up and float downstream, you're all right. It's getting your foot caught that will do you in."

"I'll remember that," I said, letting the toes of my old sneakers poke up through the current in front of me.

"Fish don't have feet. That's why they never drown."

"Wisdom of Cody," I told the river. "Listen up now."

"Birds don't drown either. They have oily feathers, so they pop up to the surface like corks."

"They'll get zits," I said.

"Better zits than drowned."

"What's the worst way to die?" Cody asked suddenly. He'd turned serious.

"I don't know. I never thought about it."

"What kind of cancer did Granddaddy have?"

I had to think back. "Lots of kinds, I guess, because he didn't go to the doctor till he was real sick. They didn't even bother to give him treatments."

"Why'd he go to the hospital, then? Why didn't he stay home?"

"Nobody was there. We were in school, and Daddy was working at Grove Hill."

"Still . . . don't you think he'd rather've been with us?"

"I never thought about it."

"You ought to, if you want to be a writer. They're

96

supposed to *contemplate*." He pronounced it slowly, as if the word tasted good in his mouth.

"I'll start tomorrow."

"Mind you do, then." He nudged my sneaker with his foot, trying to spin me back so he could go through the tongue of current and over the drop before me.

It was late afternoon when we left the river. Where we got out, the water flowed fast and deep. "Could be big rapids farther down," Cody said.

"The ranger knows. He's got survey maps on his walls."

"I wish we had one."

"Maybe he has extra."

"For us? Ha!"

"He did talk to me that time, about the trout."

"That was before he knew we had Felix."

"If he'd been mad about that, he'd have come after us."

Cody thought about that. "Maybe he was glad to be rid of him. Felix can howl. He probably kept him awake at night."

"I think he's lonely. With the trout, it was like he had to tell someone the good news."

"Dream on, Shana. He's crazy as a loon. It's a wonder he hasn't been fired."

"I might go by his cabin anyway."

"Don't."

"I'd just leave him a note . . . or maybe some raspberries. He's in such bad shape, I doubt he could walk down to pick them. Did you notice how he limps?"

Cody nodded.

"His face is odd too—kind of crooked. The two sides don't quite fit together."

"I think you should stay away," Cody said.

Mama was home when we got back to the cabin, which was bad, because we were supposed to be there in time to cook supper. She didn't seem mad, though; she'd been studying, and she said we'd eat leftovers from the picnic. Cody clammed up and stared at me, waiting to see when I'd tell about the letter, so after I set the table I plunged in.

"I've been meaning to tell you, I got a letter from Daddy," I said.

Mama was silent for a minute. It was like she was composing her response. "I knew a letter had been sent," she said. "Mrs. Grubb at the post office recognized Charlie's handwriting, and told Mike. It wasn't her business, but that's how things are in Warrensburg."

"He's in New York City, studying art and working as a security guard. He said he misses us a lot." I stumbled on. "I wrote him back, saying you'd been transferred to Laglade and we'd ended up here at the cabin." My face burned, but Mama didn't interrupt or try to help me out. "I told him to come back so we can be a family again," I finished lamely. To my left I saw Cody standing like a statue, small and pale.

"I'm glad you told me about the letter," Mama said softly. "But it was sent to you. If you get more, you can tell me or not, as you like."

"Do you want the address?"

"Yes." Mama nodded. I started to go into the bedroom to get it, but she caught my arm. "Listen, Shana," she said. "Families change, just like people."

I was afraid to ask what she meant. I glanced at Cody, but he was staring out the window.

"He'll be back," I murmured. It was something I used to tell myself when I was little and Daddy was off trucking. He wouldn't be around to kiss me good night or tell me a story, but Granddaddy or Mama would help me count the days until his rig came flying down our road and pulled into the field beside the house. I was usually out there before he had the chance to open the cab and call that he was home. I'd climb up, sit in his lap, and pull the horn just to make sure the world knew he was back. Mama would come out, if she was home from work, and Granddaddy and Cody would wander up from the garden or the spring. If he'd been away long, we'd have a celebration: chocolate milk and cookies. Mama was always glad to see him, too: They hugged, back then, and sometimes he took her face in his hands and kissed it like it was something he wanted to hold on to for a long, long time.

Ten

I stuck to my plan about the ranger. I picked two quarts of raspberries and took one up to his cabin in a plastic box. I went in the middle of the day, when I thought he'd be out working, but as I approached I saw his canoe on the bank and not long after he shouted at me from the side of the house, where he stood holding a hoe: "Hey, girl! You stop right there!"

"I brought you some raspberries!" I called, but he was already limping toward me, scowling fiercely.

"What the hell do you think—"

"I brought you these," I said, holding out the box. "Do you like them?"

His mouth fell open and he looked taken aback, as if no one ever gave him anything.

"Of course I like them! Why wouldn't I?"

He snatched the box like it was his from the start. I turned and left. I looked back once and he was standing there staring as if he couldn't believe his eyes.

I hadn't expected anything different, I told myself, but I was ticked off anyway, and I thought I wouldn't go back.

I don't know why I did. Trouble's been a magnet for Cody, not me; but our roles were changing. After Mama left in the morning, Cody would start fussing.

"Shana, you aren't going to mess with that old man today, are you?"

"Don't know what I'll do," I'd say, kind of flip. "What's it to you?"

"What if he chases you up here and sees Felix?"

"That cat won't let the ranger within a hundred feet of him. Soon as he hears him, he'll take off."

"Not Felix." That got Cody's goat. "He's not scared of nobody."

"Not like you, huh?"

He crossed his arms and looked in the other direction. "You're turning, Shana."

"What are you talking about?"

"Turning bad. Since Daddy left you've gotten hardheaded. It's all got to be your way—you won't listen to anything else."

"I do too listen!" I could feel the blood rise to my face. "I've been listening to you all my life!"

"Maybe I'm not perfect." Cody's voice was measured. "Specially back in Laglade. But since I've been up here, I've been trying. And what I hear from you is 'I'll do whatever I want.' Or else it's 'Leave me alone, I want to write.'"

For a minute I couldn't think of what to say. The writing part was true, and hard to explain. All I knew for sure was that the pages in the journal couldn't pass judgment on what I had to say. But Cody wasn't done.

"You're starting to remind me of Daddy," he said. "You think your journal's more important than real people—even your own family."

"I don't! I was just trying to sort things out, and the writing seemed to help."

"You've hardly been fishing," Cody said.

"I'll go tomorrow—I promise."

He nodded, and we let it go at that.

I went back to the ranger's. Something about the old man was drawing me there, I don't know what. This time I went in the morning, carrying some leftover potato salad and a couple of our fresh pickles. He was sitting at his cluttered table. When I knocked on the door, he was so startled he practically fell out of his chair. "Who is it? What do you want?" he hollered. Then he saw it was me.

"You again!" He didn't look friendly.

"I brought you more food—potato salad, and these pickles. We made them ourselves."

He stared at the containers in my arms, then reached out and took them. His hands shook.

"You can give me back the other box—the one I brought the berries in."

"The berries—I liked those." He nodded. "There's something else I need too."

"What?"

"Some powdered milk, and more flour. I'm almost out of flour." He put the food in an old refrigerator—the kind that's rounded on top. It didn't have much in it—there were some vegetables from his garden, and a few cans and bottles. The box I'd brought the berries in was sitting on the drain board. There was a bowl of brown soap beside it—the kind that gets soft and gloppy when it's wet.

"Flour and powdered milk—I'll write it down for you," the ranger said. He limped over to the table and cleared a space among the plants and dirty cups. He had to steady one hand with the other so he could write. He saw me watching that. "There's nothing wrong with me," he said angrily.

"I didn't say there was."

"You were looking at my hands." He thrust the paper at me. "Here."

"I'll get these soon as I can. I don't have a car." I

hurried on. "My brother and I wondered if we could borrow a map."

"What kind of map?"

"That kind." I pointed to one of the survey maps on the wall.

"You have to get those from the federal government," he said brusquely. "You *order* them."

"Could I just look at it, then?"

"For a minute." He acted like it was the world's biggest favor.

The map was hard to read. The few roads had no route numbers, and the banks of the Leanna were marked with wavy lines and red dots. Someone had drawn heavy black lines through the south section of the river. DANGER! the scrawling print beside it said. I tried to figure out where our cabin was, and the ranger's. He got a pair of heavy glasses off the table and looked through the bottoms of the lenses.

"Here." He rested his thumb on one of the dots.

"Is that your cabin?"

"What else would it be?"

"Then where's ours?" I ran my finger along the curve of the river. I figured that the brown lines marked the gorge—they were close where it was steep, farther apart where the land rose gradually. I found a dot set to the south of the ranger's. "This must be it."

"George Cosgrove's place." He said the name as if it

were a curse. "I told him to put in a septic when he built it. Now he's got people there for the summer."

"That's Cody and me! We're not doing anything wrong, either."

"Come fall, that cabin'll be torn down." The ranger turned back to the map, put his finger on another spot. "Over here's where I check the fingerlings. There's three kinds of trout spawning here—rainbows, browns, and palominos. Used to be they'd stock all three."

It took me a minute to stop him. "What do you mean, it'll be torn down?"

"Just what I said," he answered gruffly.

"You can't tear down someone else's house!"

"Won't be me. Federal government'll do the job."

I stared. "I don't believe that."

"Don't then." He turned his back and limped away.

I stood there for a minute, my hand still resting on the map. I took a deep breath. "I'm not bringing you the flour," I said. "You're too mean."

He didn't answer at first, so I went on: "You knew Cody wasn't going to steal your canoe, and putting that cat in a cage was wrong too. Seems like you hate everything that isn't part of your plan for the river." I was mad now. "You don't own the Leanna," I said. "You just pretend you do, to drive everyone else off."

"I didn't invite you here," he muttered.

"But you took the food I brought!"

"Course I did. I can't hardly get to the store, the way my leg's been acting. Can't even get up the hill to the car." He was looking out the window into the back garden.

"If you'd asked for help, we would have given it. Instead you're hateful. And now you claim they're going to tear down our cabin."

"It isn't yours anyway. And you've got another house—a year-round house. The cabin's just a summer place for you."

"You don't know about our house! It's in a development, and Cody and I hate it! If we had to stay there, we'd go nuts!"

For the first time that day he really looked at me. "What's wrong with it?"

"It's stuck in the middle of blocks of houses, with highways all around. There's nothing to do but go shopping or watch TV. It doesn't even have a real yard."

"Everybody wants that. What's wrong with you?"

"Nothing's wrong with us!" I spat out the words. "But we grew up in the country, by the river—"

"Come here," he interrupted, pointing out the window. His tone was gentler. Something blue flashed in the garden, and he nodded as if he were answering my question. "Bluebird. She's nesting in the box I made for her."

Seeing the pretty little thing made me remember Granddaddy, and I swallowed my anger. "We had those down home when I was little. My granddaddy showed me one. Later it left and never came back."

"Years ago they were common, like the trout. Now they're rare. If no one cares, they'll die out."

I watched for a minute. The bird with her bright wings and rust-colored belly seemed to be showing off just for us. She perched on a fence post, fluttered close, then went into the birdhouse.

"I'll show you something else," the ranger said. He opened his desk drawer, took out a rock, and held it out to me.

I examined it carefully. The surface was gray, but one side of the rectangular stone was honed to a fine edge. A picture was scratched on the flat surface. I ran my finger over it: an animal like a deer, but heavier.

"A bison." His voice was soft for the first time, but still urgent. "I found this along the river twenty years ago. It's Algonquin—they had settlements all along the Leanna. They lived off trout and freshwater salmon—and these."

"I thought buffalo lived on the Great Plains."

"They were driven there by civilization—and slaughtered. Them, the salmon, the trout, the bluebirds—all victims." The hard edge returned to his voice. "You can't trust people. They'll ruin everything, if they have the chance."

"Is that why you tried to chase us off the river?"

He nodded. I stared at him.

"Not everyone's like that," I said. "Cody and I care about the outdoors—we grew up in it. Anyway, you can't protect the river by yourself."

He glared. "I have the canoe."

"But they ought to send more rangers. Don't they know you need help?"

"I *don't* need help."

I tried to reason with him. "You said you can't go to the store. And what if you need medicine—"

"I don't *want* medicine!" He slammed his fist on the table. "Doctors are fools! The stuff they gave me made me sicker than I was before!"

"Calm down . . ."

"I can't calm down!" The ranger's face turned red, and he was shaking. "I don't have to listen to any damn doctor."

"I didn't say you did."

He shook his head wildly. "You probably hope I drop dead. But let me tell you something—I'm not kicking the bucket till I have this river in good hands. You and your brother and that cabin—you'll be long gone before I am."

"I'm leaving now!" I snatched my box off the drainboard.

"What about that flour?"

I turned, furious. "What about the map?"

He snorted, pulled open a desk drawer, and tossed

something on the table to my left. It was a brand-new survey map.

"You can borrow it for a few days," he said. "That's all."

I kept my promise to Cody. We went fishing that afternoon, down at the pool where he'd had luck before. On the way there I told him about the Indian ax. His eyes opened wide. "They lived along here?"

"That's what he claimed."

"I want to look for arrowheads."

"Me too. There must be books about where to search."

"We can go to the library Saturday, when we pick up supplies." Cody was excited. "Maybe the ranger's not so bad after all," he said.

I didn't answer, but I couldn't help remembering the threat about the cabin. I kept that to myself, thinking that in the long run I'd figure out what to do.

The fishing was good. The pool Cody'd found was lined with marsh grass, unusual for the Leanna, and a downed tree gave cover for bass. We started off with worms. Then I tried a plastic twister grub, bouncing it off the bottom and reeling in slow. A fish took the lure gently, then began to run. Line was pouring off my reel. I screamed for Cody to get the net.

"Keep your rod up—he'll jump!"

The fish broke water, shook; but the hook held, and I reeled like crazy now. Cody was knee deep in the water, one hand cupped around my line. I could see the shape of the fish dashing back and forth. My rod bent low. Then Cody scooped deep with the net and brought him up. "Nice one, Sha!" I clambered down to take a look.

The fish was sixteen inches, green and black, still fighting. I kept him in the net whlie I hooked him to the stringer. "Smallmouth." Cody ran a finger down his mottled side. "Will you let him go?"

"Nope." Cody and I'd had this talk lots of times. "He's dinner."

"Sha . . ." He looked at me pleadingly, but I was resolute. "You let yours go. It's been a long time since I've had fresh fish."

"I wouldn't have brought the net if I'd known . . ." Cody said, but I could tell he was pleased I'd caught a good one. We kept trying after that, and pulled in a couple of breakfast-sized bass, which we put back. By the time Mama got home, the fish was sizzling over the campfire, and we'd boiled squash and green beans, too.

"My goodness," she said. "A party."

"For Felix, too." Cody pointed.

Felix was prancing among the trees, the fish head in his mouth. We ate out front. Afterward Cody put his hands on his stomach and groaned with pleasure.

I couldn't help thinking how much Daddy would have loved that meal. He always said, "There's nothing better than fresh fish." I wondered what he ate up in New York. I decided to write to him again. There was so much I didn't know; so much that he was missing. It felt like if we didn't catch up soon, maybe we never would.

Eleven

———

*F*riday evening Mama brought the mail she'd picked up at the town house. There was nothing from Daddy, but Cody had a letter from his friend Pete back home, telling about the Cubs' season and how some boys caught a four-foot cottonmouth in a hole by the bridge where the river cuts through town. Cody must have read that thing five times.

The next day we went to the grocery store for supplies. I got the flour and the powdered milk with my own money, and tucked them behind the backseat where Mama wouldn't notice. Cody and I went to the library, too. It was tiny, but the librarian was great. She showed us how to do a computer search on local Indians, whom she called Native Americans. The program showed a couple of book titles, and we found them and checked them out. I got some poetry books, a bird guide, and another novel.

That evening we begged Mama to let us camp by the river. She hemmed and hawed, but in the long run she couldn't think of a good excuse, so we carried our blankets and quilts down to a flat spot not too far from the cabin. We built a fire on a rock jutting into the water. Cody threw on some hemlock branches, and the sparks flew. "Fireworks!" he shouted. He gathered more. The little green needles fizzled and popped. Then he came back with a whole armful.

"Cody! That's too many!" It was just like him to get carried away, after we'd promised Mama we'd be careful.

"It's not!" He threw them all on. Sparks shot everywhere. I grabbed our bedding and yanked it back. Beyond the fire, like a backdrop, fireflies spotted the dark. The river gleamed under flickering stars. We wrapped the quilts around us and watched. Then Cody fell asleep. The fire settled to a red glow, and the air turned cool and damp. I shivered, and decided to fetch a sweater before the night got colder.

I thought Mama would be asleep, but instead she sat by the lamp, a book in front of her.

"Are you studying?" I asked.

"No, I'm taking a break. I borrowed one of the poetry books you got from the library. I used to love poems when I was in high school."

"You did?" I'd hardly ever heard Mama talk about books, or high school, either.

She nodded. "I wanted to teach English back then. I still remember some of the poems I memorized. Sometimes I used to tell them to you when you were small." She recited one that started, "How do I love thee? Let me count the ways . . ." and suddenly I recalled sitting on her lap, hearing those words like a lullaby. Then I remembered another poem, about daffodils. She nodded when I mentioned it, and said it out loud. "You can see them so clear in your mind, can't you, Shana? I picture them under the willow tree near Ned Gwynn's barn."

"There's a girl in my class at Laglade who writes poems, and they're good, too." I told Mama about Catherine. "I tried to write some too. I might want to be a writer, or a poet."

"That's a good hobby, but you have to learn things that will help you get a job, like marketing, or computer programming. If I'd learned more about computers in high school, I'd have had more choice about the work I wanted."

"I'm not interested in that." I kept my tone mild, so we wouldn't get into an argument.

"If you go to college, you'll have time to study lots of things." Mama kept her voice neutral too.

"How come you didn't?"

"Didn't what?"

"Go to college." I was surprised I'd never asked. Mama seemed like the kind of person who'd get a scholarship if she wanted it. I said that.

"I did get one, to Radford," she admitted. "But I couldn't take it."

"Why not?"

She shrugged, as if it didn't really matter. "Family problems."

"What kind of problems?"

There was a stillness when Mama was deciding what to say. She pushed her hair back from her face. "Daddy wouldn't let me go."

I couldn't believe it. Granddaddy'd always talked about how Cody and I would be doctors or lawyers or engineers. "Why not?"

"It's a long story. . . ."

"I want to know!"

She sighed. "Remember how I told you Daddy worried about money, because of the Depression?" I nodded. Mama went on: "It took us years to convince him to get indoor plumbing, even though he had that good job on the railroad. Finally he saved up, and we did. Mike and I were in heaven when we got that faucet— we turned it on and off all day. Of course, my girlfriends didn't know—I hadn't told them we still used the outhouse and the pump." Mama's voice was strained.

"What happened?"

"When the bill came, it was more than what they'd said—more than we had, too. Daddy was in debt to the plumber. They took a lien on the land, just till he paid it back. He couldn't stand that. He was convinced we were going to lose the farm.

"We tried to tell him it would all work out, but he wouldn't listen. He'd planted the back fields in tobacco, but right away he signed on extra hours at the railroad. That left Mike and me to work the crop—you know my mother had a bad heart, so she couldn't do anything heavy. Just about then I got the letter from Radford."

"You turned down a scholarship to work tobacco?"

"I had no choice. I was seventeen, and Daddy forbade me to take it. He was afraid we'd lose the farm, afraid the scholarship meant he'd owe money he didn't have. Mother tried to talk to him. She said she'd sell her rings to pay the plumber's debt if he'd let me go. But it turned out they weren't worth what we owed."

"How long did it take you to make the money?"

"We did it, Mike and I, with that one crop. We broke our backs on it." Mama's voice was dark with anger. "That old tobacco—it's not just the smokers it hurts. Even when I wore gloves, the juice seeped onto my hands and wrists and burned so bad I thought I'd go crazy."

Her bitterness shocked me. "Why didn't you go to college later?"

"Once I turned eighteen, I wrote to them, but the scholarship was gone."

"That's not fair!"

She shrugged. "A couple of months later I met Charlie and we decided to get married. He was kind. My dreams were gone, but he had his, and they carried me for a long time."

I was aware of a rising in my stomach, like a good meal turned sour. "I thought Granddaddy was the nicest man who ever lived."

"By the time you were born, things were different. The debts were settled, and he'd even managed to pay off the mortgage on the house. He was at ease."

"Did you forgive him?"

"I tried," Mama said.

I stood there feeling lost. Then Mama looked up. "It's okay, Shana," she said softly. "I'm grown now, and I decide things for myself."

I started to shiver, and remembered the sweater in the bedroom. I put it on and headed out, into the dark.

Granddaddy said the spirits have voices: happy or sad, mad or lonely. That night the crickets seemed to groan in the underbrush, and the twigs snapping under my feet reminded me of broken bones. Mama had been a teenager, with her own dreams. What was it like, when a dream died? Did you cry as you watched it slip away?

I stumbled to the campsite and lay down. Cody sputtered in the dark. His breathing seemed unreliable, like a candle that might flicker and go out. Behind me the river gnashed stone on stone, washing down the ledges. When sleep came, I tumbled between bad dreams like a leaf scudding in a dangerous wind.

Twelve

I didn't tell Cody about my talk with Mama, not that morning, anyway. We cooked bacon over the fire, and I boiled water and made hot chocolate. Cody was looking through one of the Indian books. It said their camps were common along the Susquehanna and its tributaries, especially on the islands and river deltas. Cody started combing through a heap of stones along the gravel bar below our camp. I remembered the survey map, still neatly rolled in my backpack. I spread it on the quilt. After a bit he lost patience with his sorting and came up to see what I was looking at.

"You got a map!" He bent over. "Did the ranger give it to you?"

I nodded.

"Let me see."

I showed Cody the dots that stood for our cabin and the ranger's, and he figured out where we were, and where we'd floated that day we went so far downstream. "We were right above the rapids," he said. "Look here, Sha."

He pointed to a section of river seven or eight miles down. There the banks were steep, and the elevation—between three and four hundred feet—meant that the gorge was more like a canyon than a valley. An abandoned rail line ran for a couple miles upstream but veered north before the riverbed started to drop. After that there was no access until the Leanna merged with Tom's Creek, where a cluster of dots stood between the river and a gravel road. "Summer cottages," Cody said. "Barb told me there's a boat launch down there too. Most people who fish in the Leanna start there." Cody traced the river with one finger. He stopped at the canyon entrance. I knew what he was thinking.

"That's a long walk, even if you use the train bed partway, and once you get there, there's no trail."

"How do you know?"

" 'Cause trails are marked by dotted lines. See, even the path from the dirt road to our cabin is here. It's just so tiny you wouldn't notice unless you looked for it."

Cody nodded. "So once you enter the rapids, you're stuck."

"The ranger's map said 'Danger' all through there."

"I wish Eddie could come up, with his raft," Cody said. "We'd have fun."

"We don't know how to paddle in white water."

"You worry too much," Cody said.

I spent more time at the cave that week, thinking about Mama's scholarship. She'd never seemed to mind working for the phone company, though she'd always worried about money. I wondered if Daddy thought about Mama's dreams. Maybe he figured she was happy with her job; or maybe he spent so much time on his own dreams that he didn't have the energy for hers. I didn't like that thought, and I put it out of my mind as quickly as I could.

I wrote in my journal, imagining what Mama was like when she was young. Had she sat beside the river to learn the poems she loved?

I went to see the ranger, carrying the flour and powdered milk in my backpack. For once he didn't scowl when I showed up, and he took the supplies with shaking hands. He put everything in the refrigerator.

"Mice," he explained, frowning. "They think the cupboard belongs to them."

"What about mousetraps?"

He sighed. "I don't have time to get any. Sometimes I even wish I had that evil cat back."

"What evil cat?"

"The one you claim is yours." He looked at me sharply. "I wasn't fooled by that. But I figured if you wanted him, that was up to you, as long as you keep him away from the river."

"Felix isn't evil."

"He howled like the devil, that's for sure."

"Cody loves him."

"Cody . . . is that the boy?"

I nodded.

"Tell him to come up here," the old man said.

"How come?"

"I want to show him something."

"What?"

He glared. "Is it your business?"

"He's my brother. Last time you saw him, you were waving a gun."

He grunted angrily. The sound reminded me of a mangy old bear, and I almost smiled. Then I remembered his threats. "I won't bring Cody unless you tell me why."

"I want to teach him to paddle the canoe." He turned his back as soon as he said it.

"You want to teach Cody?"

"You've got ears, don't you?"

"We saw the canyon on the map. Will you teach him down there?"

He looked at me like I was a fool. "People die on

the flumes—good paddlers, not just kids. You stay away from there."

"We don't even have a boat."

"One time I caught some boys about to go through the falls on rubber rafts. The undercut rocks can shear your head clean off, and there're holes in the canyon that can pull you under and hold you there for weeks. What do you think they would have looked like when the river was through with them?"

I didn't back off. "How come you want to teach Cody?"

"If he's not interested, he doesn't need to come."

"He's afraid of you."

The ranger laughed harshly. "Tell him to look harder."

"Why?"

"Can't you do anything besides ask questions?"

"I brought the flour, didn't I?"

"Tell your brother to come" was all he said. I went back to the cabin as fast as I could.

Cody couldn't believe it. "Why does he want to teach me?"

"Don't ask me."

"Maybe it's a trap."

"What kind of trap?"

"I don't know—it just doesn't make sense."

"I'll go with you, if you want to talk to him."

"Couldn't hurt, I guess."

"We'll go tomorrow," I said.

That night, when I was alone, I pulled the picture box from under Cody's bed. At first the pictures seemed as jumbled as the changes we'd been through these last six months; but I dumped a bunch in my lap and sorted through them. The babies were hardest: bright beady eyes in bald heads, arms and legs as thick as hams. But here was Cody: I remembered the cowboy shirt and the fringe of light hair on his temples. I'd been fatter, but I smiled more than Cody even then. Mama and Mike were usually posed together: sitting on the galvanized washtub turned upside down, or clutching some terrified kitten. As they got older, their thin legs trailed out of baggy shorts, and thick, dark hair framed their shy faces. Sometimes Gram stood behind them. She died when I was three, so I'd hardly known her, but Mama said she'd grown up poor in North Carolina. She'd worked so hard raising cotton and tobacco that her heart was bad by the time she was forty. I remembered her propped up in bed, sewing, in her flowered nightdress. She kept a Mother Goose book beside her pillow to read to me. She'd hold out her arms, and I'd run to get in bed with her.

There weren't many pictures of Daddy as a child.

Two showed him sitting astride the mule teams that his father raised; in another, he was posed on the front porch of their old brick farmhouse. He was an only child, and people said his mother pampered him, but she died when he was twelve, and two years later his father's tractor turned over on a hillside, killing him, too. After that Daddy lived from family to family, helping out in exchange for board. At night he'd study, then read from an old set of encyclopedias his mother'd given him before she died. Maybe being on his own so young made him more eager to get married when he got the chance.

The wedding pictures were in a white album in Warrensburg; but I knew them by heart. When I was six, I'd planned my wedding to be just like theirs. Mama wore a long white dress and carried white roses, and Daddy, with his slicked-back hair, looked like a singer for a country band. They smiled for the camera as they cut the cake and stood in line with Mama's family. Now I tried to remember those smiles. Was Mama happy, or pretending? Did Daddy know she'd wanted something else? Was Granddaddy sorry for what he'd done?

I passed the beam of my flashlight over the pictures spread out on my bed, lighting up people whose lives I thought I knew. Here were Daddy and Granddaddy side by side with stringers of bass; Mama talking on the telephone in the front room; Uncle Mike posed beside his old truck, Bess. Cody and I stood on the running board of Daddy's rig in cowboy hats brought from a trip out west; in another picture he held us in his lap, smiling down as if we were a gift too good to be true.

I let the light play on those paper faces for a long time. Then I gathered them into the box and stuck them back under Cody's bed.

Thirteen

The poplar leaves turned yellow and began to fall. I'd refused to look at the calendar, and I was fooled at first, and frightened, till Cody reminded me that poplars shed early. "Summer's not over till the sourgum leaves turn red."

"Maybe there aren't any sourgums here," I said.

Cody was whittling a bird from a pine block. "Then it won't end. We'll have to miss school. We'll stay till Christmas, cutting wood and hiking and paddling on the river."

I nodded. "I'm getting to like the Leanna. I'll bet it's pretty when there's snow on the hemlocks."

I expected Cody'd want to stay too, but he wavered.

"I wouldn't mind a few days with Pete and Jimmy, just to see what's new."

"Do you think they're still talking about us back home?"

He shrugged. "There was only so much to say, wasn't there?"

"Somebody said the whole thing had to do with that waitress at the restaurant—did you meet her, Cody?"

"Yeah." His face darkened, and he looked at the wood in his hands as if he hated it. "She was still there when we left."

"She was saving money to go to Italy. She never said anything about New York."

"Lighten up, will you?" Cody snapped his knife shut.

"Coming to see the ranger?"

"I guess." He stood up reluctantly. I reached out fast and tickled him, and he slapped my hand away, laughing. We patted Felix good-bye and headed up the river.

Like last time, the ranger was almost civil. He was on the bank when we approached, a plastic tube in his hand. He eyed Cody sternly. "So you want to learn?"

Cody nodded.

"The first thing you do is look in my shed for a life jacket."

"I can swim." Cody's eyes snapped.

"Doesn't matter. State law says you have to have one on."

"I'll come with you," I said.

We went into the back, behind the cabin. The metal cage stood open, like we'd left it; morning glories and wild chickory made splashes of blue and pink among the bars. The garden had changed too: red geraniums bloomed beside the Swiss chard, and the greens had died in the potato patch. There was a fork sticking out of the ground there; but few holes. I wondered if the ranger was strong enough to dig potatoes. "Come on," Cody said.

The shed was cluttered with tools and scraps of wood. We had to brush spiders off the life vest that looked to be Cody's size. He zipped it, and it fit. I looked for one for me.

"Why?" he asked.

"I'll learn too."

"He would have told you if he'd wanted you."

"So?" I didn't want to admit that was true. I walked back with Cody. The old man was in the stern of the canoe. "Get in."

Cody waded out. He balanced his weight by leaning one arm on the far side of the boat—Eddie had taught us that. The ranger seemed disappointed. He showed Cody how to hold the paddle.

"Going forward, your stroke looks like this." The old man dug the blade of the paddle into the water, and the boat shot forward so fast Cody almost lost his balance. "Try it."

Cody did. Before he finished the stroke, the ranger yelled, "You have to push harder than that. Watch me."

Again he stroked, his shoulder leading forward and down. The canoe lunged ahead.

Cody tried again. This time his paddle went so deep he had trouble finishing the stroke.

"Better—but you have to lean forward and extend your arm. Then you pull like you're parting the water with the paddle blade. Keep the stroke going till it's opposite your leg."

Cody tried five of them. He was pulling so hard, his face turned red.

"You're weak," the ranger said.

"I'm not."

"Then pull harder. Use the muscles in your trunk."

Cody tried again. The canoe pulled to the left, moved forward smoothly. The old man ruddered with his paddle to straighten them out. "That's a little better. You need to practice that—three hundred strokes a day, sitting in the stern. I'll supervise. But if I see you doing it wrong, or not working hard, you're done."

"Thanks." Cody's face was grim.

"Now I'll teach you the draw." The ranger demonstrated a technique that moved the boat from side to side. "You try."

I stopped watching then, but I could hear the ranger yelling as I wandered up to his cabin. The flowers on the side of the house looked dry. I remembered a bucket near the pump. I set it under the spout and pulled the handle: down, up down. It was so stiff, my arms ached by the time the water started running. I lugged the bucket over to the flowers and emptied it. Then I went inside to get myself a drink.

I knew I shouldn't do that, not without asking. The cabin was still cool and dark from evening; facing north and sheltered by ridges, its windows caught the late-day sun. There was a jar of water in the refrigerator, and I rinsed out a mug and drank. I couldn't help looking around. Without the ranger, the room seemed quiet and settled, a cross between a study and the messy bedroom of a little boy. Some of his uniforms hung from pegs, but a bunch of dirty ones had been tossed in a heap by the closet door. Old sneakers and boots poked out from under the bed, where the sheets looked stained and crumpled. An open dresser drawer showed a tangle of socks and underwear.

"You should wait outside," I told myself. I looked out the window and saw the canoe still on the river. I went over to the ranger's desk and poked around.

His books, mostly about trout, lay on the desktop, along with his pocket notebooks. The top drawer held a mix of papers, some rubber-banded together: fishing regulations, something from Social Security, what looked like a health-insurance bill, and a bottle of pills.

"Take three times daily for high blood pressure," the directions said. The script was dated two years ago, in the name of Henry Luck, but the bottle was almost full. *You're a snoop,* Cody's voice whispered in my ear, but I shook my head to chase it away. I turned to the table.

That was the worst: a clutter of books, half-filled cups of coffee, plates stained with egg yolk and dried baked beans. Two dented pans held water: for the flowers, I supposed, which bloomed in cracked clay pots in the middle of the mess. I picked up a book; bookmarks fluttered out like falling leaves. I gathered them up and stuck them hastily in the front.

They were coming off the water. I went out the back door and around as if I'd spent the whole time in the yard. Cody looked awful: red and walking like he hurt all over. The ranger was yakking it up behind him: "Don't forget about the left side when you practice. If you don't build your strength there, you'll be good for nothing."

Cody didn't answer.

"Same time tomorrow."

"Right."

"Wait a minute," I said. "Do you want to, Cody?"

"I can speak for myself," he said wearily, and when I started to open my mouth again, he shook his head.

At home Cody soaked in the river for a long time. Then he rolled himself in his quilt and lay on the floor. He was so tired, he could hardly talk.

"Why didn't you tell him you were worn out?"

"I don't know."

"Why's he doing this?"

"I asked him. All's he said was 'I have to.'"

"That sounds like someone told him to."

Cody shrugged.

"He lives by himself. I looked around the cabin. There's no sign anybody even comes to visit."

"He's got something wrong with his left hand. After a while he had to tape his fingers to the shaft of the paddle. He used duct tape." Cody winced.

I didn't mention the blood-pressure medicine in the drawer. I asked, "Why is he so mean?"

"I learned a lot."

"Why you? I could learn to paddle." But the truth is I'm not as strong as Cody. I'd last about three minutes practicing those strokes. I wondered if the ranger knew that.

The next day we went back. This time the old man took me aside. "I need meat and eggs," he said. "I have to keep up my strength."

"Meat and eggs cost money."

He opened a side drawer in the desk, took out a twenty-dollar bill, and handed it to me.

"I'll get them when Mama goes to the store. What kind of meat do you want?"

"I don't care—anything."

"What if she sees?"

"She better not see—I told you, this assignment is secret."

"I'll do what I can. If you're nice to my brother, I'll get more."

"I don't have time to be nice."

"That's silly—you can be nice in the same amount of time you can be mean."

He looked at me. "Not if you don't know how."

He put Cody through the mill. I couldn't stand to watch after a few minutes, so I went back to his house and sat on the front porch. His cabin was better built than ours—the edges of the logs were carefully caulked, and the mortar was pointed up where it had started to crumble. The windows were real, and were lined with wood storm windows and screens. Blue curtains and a hooked rug by the cast-iron stove, a pretty pillow in the rocking chair, a bedspread: color could have made this place nice. . . . I wondered if the ranger had been married. If he had, there was no sign of it. On the other hand, who would put up with him?

He was yelling now—at Cody.

"Can't you do anything right? I told you, *draw stroke*!"

Cody changed grips, but the ranger wasn't satisfied. "You have to pull! Put your weight behind it!"

Cody mumbled.

"I don't care how much you weigh! If you can't do better than that, you're weak!"

Later he softened. He got out of the canoe and stood on the bank, directing Cody in and out of an eddy that lay to one side of a small rapid. "Keep the boat at the same angle all the way across—paddle steady—steady now! Straighten out her bow! Now cross over and bring her around!"

Cody knelt in the middle of the canoe. At times the front end twisted in the current. Then the stern would stray, and he'd have trouble getting the boat back in line. The ranger warned him about pinning if you let the canoe swing sideways: "It'll hit a rock and fill up with water. That's a thousand pounds you never bargained on. If you get caught between the boat and a downstream rock, you can be crushed like this." He crunched his heavy boot on the riverbank.

I pulled on his arm. "We've got to go. We're supposed to make supper, and Mama gets home at six."

"Mama!" He sneered. "We can't disappoint Mama."

"If we're not on time, she'll ask where we've been." My voice was icy.

"Better get in here, Cody. Sis says you've got to go."

Cody paddled in. His face was flushed. He pulled the boat up and chained it.

"Come tomorrow, at the same time," the ranger said. "And remember the meat."

"I told you, I'll try to get it Saturday."

"Then Saturday."

"I'll do it when I can."

"You seem tired, and your face is red," Mama said to Cody later. "Are you getting sick?"

"No, it's sunburn."

"Wear a hat tomorrow," Mama said. "Or stay inside. You said you'd make frames for the plastic in those windows. The boards have been standing in the corner for two weeks."

"I'll do it this weekend."

"This weekend? What's to keep you from doing it tomorrow?"

"Nothing, really. I just had something else planned."

"What?"

"Nothing much . . ."

"I can do the windows, if Cody draws the angles for the corners," I said.

Mama looked from one of us to the other. For the first time she seemed to notice there was something odd. She took her dirty dishes to the stove and started heating the wash water. She didn't say anything, but a couple of times that evening I caught her looking at us, and I knew she was wondering what was going on.

The next day rain saved us. We stayed inside and worked on the windows, and played with Felix. I read to Cody from the Indian book, about how their camps were set up and what they ate. Then I read his favorite part of *Rascal*, which we'd read a hundred times before: where Sterling goes out in the canoe and sets the raccoon free. When I finished, Cody sighed. "Do you think that's how it really was?"

I pondered that. "I doubt it. In real life your shoelace breaks, or you have to pee in the middle of what you're doing."

Cody was using the mitre box, lining up the corners of the window frames. "Would you have let him go?"

"Who?"

"Rascal."

"I don't know. I might have built a bigger pen, so he'd be happier at home."

"What if he wasn't?"

"I would have tried things till I figured out what worked."

"What if nothing worked?"

He was making me edgy. "I don't know."

Cody squinted at the wood in his lap. "Remember Richie Bird?"

"What about him?" I turned red. Richie was a high-school junior who rode the bus with us back home. Last winter I started getting flustered whenever I was around him. But I didn't think anyone noticed, and even though he was good-looking and nice, I stayed away so I wouldn't have to face my own confusion.

"You had the hots for him," Cody said.

"Shut up! I didn't, anyway."

He shook his head in disgust. "You're pretending, Shana."

"You don't know!"

"Everybody knew!"

"Brat!" I slapped his face. Cody drew back. He broke the piece of wood in two. Then he went out, into the rain.

Fourteen

Cody and I stayed apart after that. Mama could tell we'd had a fight. She didn't ask what happened, but she did say it was hard to get along when you spent so much time together. After breakfast I'd slip down to the cave and sit. If I was still enough, the water snake that lived upstream would crawl from under its rock and hunt for minnows in the pools along the bank. Another time a sleepy-looking possum trundled through the under-brush and stared as if I were a visitor from another planet. One rainy day a huge bird dropped into the river right in front of me. He went under water, came back up, and flew away with a fish dangling from his yellow talons. The ranger said that was an osprey, and that he'd better leave his trout alone; but he smiled when he said it, as if he knew he were no match for a hawk that big.

Cody started going to the ranger's by himself. It wasn't something we agreed on; it was more like we weren't talking, and neither of us asked the other, Are you coming?

I took the old man meat and eggs. I bought them Saturday while Mama and Cody were at the hardware store. Soon as I got the chance, I took them to his cabin. He wasn't home, so I put it all in his refrigerator. Then he came in and surprised me. He looked sick: His eyes were glassy, and he wobbled like he might fall down.

"What are you doing?" he demanded.

"I brought the food."

He looked so bad I made him a platter of eggs and sausage. He ate them like he was half starved, bending his face down and shoveling the food in with his right hand. When he finished, he closed his eyes for a second. "Cody's doing all right," he said.

I didn't want to hear about Cody, but he went on: "He says you're a writer."

I was taken by surprise. "I'm just learning."

"He thinks you'll be good."

"He does?"

The ranger nodded. He kept his water supply in gallon jugs under the drainboard and in the bathroom; I poured some into a pan and set it on the stove. "What's that for?" he asked.

"The dishes."

"I can wash them," he said gruffly.

"I know you can. What I'm saying is, this time you don't have to."

We were quiet for a while. I saw the bluebird fluttering in and out of her house. The afternoon sun began to slant through the window, lighting up the table and the iron sink where I stood. The ranger nodded off in his chair. The water boiled, and I put the dirty plates in the sink with a glob of hand soap. Usually I don't like washing dishes, but the view out the window—the bluebird, the flowers, the ridge with its fringe of pine and hemlock—was soothing. Then the ranger startled and woke up. He looked around.

"Who are you? What are you doing here?"

For a second I thought he was joking. "I'm Shana— I brought the meat."

"What year is it?" He looked upset. He gripped the edge of the table.

I told him.

"You're lying." He looked down at his hands, stared at them. "I thought you were Edna, but she's gone. Gone and good riddance."

"Who's Edna?"

"Now I remember—you're the one with the brother, the one who's always asking questions."

I nodded.

"She's none of your concern." His voice was cold.

"I didn't bring her up."

"No, I don't guess you did." He wiped one hand across his face. "I've been having this trouble," he said suddenly. "Not all the time, just now and then . . . this trouble remembering." His voice quavered. I couldn't help staring.

"I know some things: I was born in 1918 in Williamsport. We lived at Forty-three Sumner Place. My mother was Rose Green and my father was William Henry Luck. I went to St. Michael's Primary School." He looked up, and his voice trailed off. "The rest comes and goes."

I'm not sure why, but I wanted to change the subject. "The bluebird's in the house you made for her," I said.

"I don't want anyone to know. . . ." He went on. "They have cages for people like me, old people who can't remember. You lie in bed and eat pablum."

"Pablum's for babies."

"It's a way of life, for them."

I stirred the dishes in the sink.

"Have you ever been afraid?" He looked right at me now. "Not just a little bit, but really afraid?"

"I don't know." I was afraid right then.

"I have." He went on, but he was staring at his hands instead of me. "The first time I went through the canyon I was that afraid. I saw the first drop coming, and I thought: 'This is it, Henry. You're going to die.' " His hands clenched and unclenched.

"I gripped the paddle. The boat slammed into a wave and started to flip. Somehow I knew to brace on the right: Maybe there was an angel watching, whispering what to do. . . . I was crying, praying to get through it. Every cell in my body wanted life. I paddled like a madman, and in the end, the river shot me out alive." He looked up now. "Beginner's luck. You get that once or twice."

I didn't move.

"After that I told myself I'd change: treat people good. For a year or so I tried. But it was too hard. I was rough leather to their silk. There was a few put up with me, just a few, and after a while they gave up too. I told myself I'd marry the river, and I did. I learned her ways, even the flumes; and I gave her children, too."

"The fingerlings . . ."

He nodded.

"I'm sick, but I'm holding on, just like I did in the canyon that first time. Old as I am, I still want life." His voice broke then.

I was afraid to speak, afraid to move. He must have know that.

"Go on," he said roughly. "Go on home."

I went back to the cabin. I wanted to talk to Cody so bad, but he wasn't there. I sat a bit with Felix, feeling the warmth underneath his fur. He purred and licked one paw. I saw where the space between his ribs had filled out over the summer. I'd grown too: There were new muscles in my arms and legs, and the beginning of roundness in my chest. I'd wanted things to go back the way they'd been, or even stay the same; but it was starting to seem like nothing stopped you growing.

I went down to the cave and got my journal. My mind was so full of the ranger I felt choked, and the words wouldn't come. I picked up a rock, then another, and flung them into the water. I thought of Cody searching for arrowheads, thought of the Algonquin families that lived along this shore hundreds of years ago. I imagined a girl my age standing as I was then, throwing stones because she was too full of feelings to do anything else.

Later—all of a sudden—I heard a poem. It came so quietly that it seemed as if it must have been there all along, like a sleeping cat that wakes, stretches, and shows itself. I wrote it down, holding my breath so that it wouldn't disappear before I got the words on paper. Later, I thought, I'll read it to somebody—maybe.

That evening Mama had something serious to say: "I'm taking the state accounting exam a week from Saturday. It's in Baltimore, and it takes four hours. I'll be gone the whole day."

She looked at us hard. "Philip has invited you to stay with him while I take the test. He plans to take you out to lunch at a restaurant near his apartment, and to see the Orioles play that afternoon." She paused. I wondered if she'd told Philip how bad Cody wanted to go to Camden Yards. He was so wild to see it, he would have gone there with the devil himself. Now he sat across from me with his mouth hanging open.

"You mean Philip has tickets to the ball game?"

She nodded.

Cody clenched his fists over his head. "Wait till Pete hears about this!"

"I'd rather stay here." The words felt thick in my throat.

Cody gaped. "Rather stay here than go to the ball game? What are you, crazy?"

"I just don't feel like going." I glared at him.

"Don't you know how hard it is to get tickets? It's impossible!"

I shrugged as if I didn't care.

"You're crazy!" Cody said.

Mama talked to me later. "I'm not sure I want you here alone, Shana. We won't get home till after dark."

I didn't answer, but I was thinking: You can't make me go. Mama asked, "What if you fell and broke your leg?"

"I'll stay around the cabin. I won't even go fishing, if you don't want me to."

She looked right at me. "I think you'd enjoy this, Shana, if you'd let yourself."

I didn't answer.

"Philip is my friend, just like Barb and Marilyn. There's nothing else between us, if you're wondering." She got mad then. "But if there were, that would be my choice, not yours."

My face burned. "Cody and I are stuck with what you want! You didn't even ask before you decided to move! We had to come along whether we wanted to or not!"

She nodded, but her lips were tight. "I made the decision I thought was best."

"Best for you! What about us?"

Mama looked away. My eyes filled up. I went into the bedroom and slammed the door. Cody was in there reading a comic, but he slipped out without looking me in the face.

That night I wrote to Daddy:

Mama has a friend in the phone company, and he's got tickets for the Orioles for Saturday. Remember how you used to say we'd go see them play? Now it's going to happen, but with someone else.

Why don't you write to us? Why don't you tell us when you're coming back?

I almost signed the letter then, but after I addressed the envelope, I decided to add another line.

I've met a ranger, and I wrote this poem.

I copied it, folded it with the letter, and stuck them both in the envelope.

Fifteen

After Mama left for work, I talked to Cody.

"Those baseball tickets are a lure, and you're the fish who's dumb enough to bite."

He looked at me blankly. "What do you mean?"

"Philip wants you—or us—to like him, because he likes Mama. And this is a sure way to get you to."

"If you think I'm going to miss that ball game, you're nuts," Cody said.

"You need to think about what it means, Cody."

He rolled his eyes. "I think Philip's trying to be nice."

"How do you know?"

"Because Mama said he's just a friend. Anyway, she can't spend her life waiting for Daddy to come back."

"It's been six months! That's only half a year!"

Cody sighed, and for a moment I thought I saw tears in his eyes. He shook his head. "I'm not missing that ball game."

"You're selfish."

"*You're* not my boss, Shana." That was all he had to say.

The next few days were awful. Cody'd told Mama yes about the day with Philip, and she was leaning toward making me go too. It didn't help that she was nervous about the test; every spare moment she was bent over a book or a sheet of figures. I felt so alone. I wanted to see the ranger, but I was afraid he'd be weak and sad, like before.

I also worried I'd find Cody there. He disappeared each morning without telling me where he was headed. When I tried asking him, he wouldn't answer. "You're supposed to let me know where you're going," I said. "That's what we agreed to do."

"You just want to bug me," Cody said.

"What if you drown? I won't know where to look for your body."

"Ask the ranger."

"He might drown too!"

Cody grinned. "You'll hear his ghost cussing me out: 'Don't you know how to paddle, boy? Call that a draw stroke? If you can't do better, I'll have to issue a citation!'"

We both laughed then, and Cody headed up the river.

• • •

Later I went up myself. I wondered if he'd still be there, but the canoe was chained and the old man was stomping around upstream, yelling at a couple of guys in a flatboat.

"You can't fish here! There's a state boat launch down the river at Tom's Creek."

One of the men said something to him.

"If you don't turn back, I'll write you a citation. I'm the ranger here, and this part of the river is federally protected. You can't fish here—you can't even walk here."

The guy answered.

"I'm not telling you again," the ranger said. "Listen to me, or face the consequences in court!"

Slowly, reluctantly, the men turned their boat and poled upstream. The ranger stood there, hands on hips, watching them go. Then he came down to the bank, clucking like an old hen. He didn't even say hello.

"They act like fishing is a right! Said they didn't see any signs! I should have asked to see their licenses. Fishing without a license carries a one-hundred-dollar fine!"

"I'm surprised we don't see more people around here."

He turned like I'd threatened him.

"There's no public access. They can go to Tom's Creek. That's where they're supposed to fish!"

We turned and walked up toward the cabin. He was mumbling under his breath as if I weren't there. Then out of the blue he asked, "Will you dig some potatoes?"

I nodded.

"Let's do it now," he said.

I've dug potatoes lots of times back home, so I know what I'm doing, but of course the ranger didn't think so. "You'll cut them up if you dig that close to the stem," he fussed. I ignored him and did what Daddy had shown me, pulling back the dried-up stalk and then digging around it till I could lift the mass of tangled roots. He had a good crop: I pulled two dozen potatoes from three plants.

"Where do you want them?"

"In the bucket. They have to be scrubbed."

I wondered if he'd ask me to do that, but he was too stubborn. He could barely prime the pump without losing his balance, and when the water finally ran into the bucket, he picked it up and swished it around as if that was all it took. He poured off a stream of mud, stared dolefully at the potatoes, then thrust the pump handle up and down until the bucket filled again. He rinsed the potatoes and dried them on his shirttail. I was poking around the garden. He had a bed of wildflowers, and there were some I'd never seen before, tall with dark-pink petals.

"What are they?"

He grunted.

"What?"

"Wild phlox!"

"They'd be pretty at our old house, next to the porch."

"Come back like weeds every year, no matter what." He shrugged as if he didn't care about them, but I could see he did, 'cause they'd been tended.

"Where'd you get the seeds?"

"I didn't. She planted them." Before I could ask more, he went into the house and slammed the door. I followed him in. Before long the pungent smell of sausage filled the room. He cut up some potatoes and threw them in with the meat. Then he cracked an egg over the whole mess. He glanced at me.

"Want one?"

"No thanks."

He poured the food onto a plate and shoveled it down. Afterward he said, "Forget about what I told you the other day."

"Okay." I'd wanted to, but suddenly I regretted it. He'd talked to me like a friend. Now his voice was harsh, like I was used to. He looked out the window as if there was something more interesting than me out there. "Winter squash is coming in."

"My daddy used to make squash pie."

"I didn't think you had one. You all talk about Mama."

It took me a minute to figure out what he meant. "He's away."

"Where?"

"New York."

"How come?"

His coolness bugged me. "What do you care?"

"I don't." He pushed his fork around his plate, then struggled to his feet. His head was bent over the sink. "Only I had a kid once."

"You did?"

He shrugged, as if it wasn't important. "She's grown now. Last I saw her, she told me to drop dead."

"What's her name?"

"Daisy . . ." He was looking out the window, but his eyes seemed far away. "I named her that."

"Was Edna your wife?"

He turned angrily. "Where'd you hear Edna?"

"You said it yourself, the other day."

"I never say that name out loud."

"You'd just waked up, remember? And you asked what year it was, and then you said—"

"All right!" he snapped. He smacked the dishes against each other so hard I thought they'd break. "You can count on people to let you down," he said.

At first I thought he meant me, and I bristled, but he went on: "Her, Daisy, your daddy . . . there's always someplace better, or somebody."

"Daddy's not like that."

He didn't look at me. "You're making excuses for him."

"I'm not! Everyone deserves a chance to follow their dreams! Look at you—you're here, with the river."

"That's different," he grunted. "They left me."

"You said you were miserable to be with!" I couldn't let up. "Daddy's nice!"

The old man stiffened, breathed deep. "I'm here listening—he's not!"

"He'll be back."

"I'll look out for him." He laughed abruptly.

"Shut up!" I would have run away, but my eyes were full of tears.

"You don't get it," he said slowly. "I'm trying to tell you what it took me years to learn."

"What's that?"

He leaned over. "Don't count on anybody."

I should have asked him then and there what he wanted with Cody. Instead I came back to our place and pulled the weeds that had sprung up in Mama's flowers. Afterward I went to the cave and wrote in my journal. I tried to imagine the ranger's daughter. What had she looked like? Did she love her father, despite everything? Or had she finally given up?

Later, back home, Cody came up the bluff. He had two fishing rods in one hand, and his old sneakers were oozing water.

"Catch anything?"

It was a good thing I asked. His face lit up. "A twelve-inch brown trout."

"Let's see!"

"I threw him back."

"You're making it up."

"I'm not. Got him on a spinner down near the fallen tree. He took it and ran."

"Lucky!"

So Cody had caught the first trout.

Sixteen

Phillip told Mama I shouldn't have to go if I didn't want to. He offered his dog Nina for protection, since I'd be alone. Mama looked sheepish when she showed up Friday with the dog in tow. We'd thought it would be a German shepherd or a Doberman, but instead a fat old bulldog came trundling down the trail behind her.

"Philip claims she barks at strangers," Mama said. Just then Cody appeared from behind the house. He stared.

"That's the ugliest dog I've ever laid eyes on."

Nina wagged her tail.

"Take her with you wherever you go," Mama told me. "Philip says she gets nervous when she's left alone."

Cody grinned. "Sounds like you'll be baby-sitting her."

"You can still change your mind, Shana. We'd be happy if you came with us."

For some reason I actually considered it. "No, thanks."

Nina whined and rubbed her head against my knee.

They got up early. I managed to tell Mama good luck before they left; but when I got back in bed, the trouble started. Felix had been outside all night. When he saw Nina, he freaked out and started spitting. She acted like she'd never seen an angry cat. Her eyes got big, and she began to howl. I grabbed her collar and pulled her into the main room. A cascade of hisses exploded behind us. Nina stared dolefully at the bedroom. Then she climbed onto Mama's cot and fell asleep.

We'd had dogs before, back home: coon dogs and mutts and a Labrador retriever named Andy. But they lived outside, in doghouses, and were mostly used for hunting, though Cody and I sometimes took them off their chains and played with them. After Granddaddy died, Mama gave the dogs away, and I can't say that I missed them much. Daddy didn't either. Though we'd told him over and over, he'd never even learned their names.

I thought about Daddy. He didn't like animals, except for horses; they were too much work, he said. He'd had to muck out stalls when he was little, and after that he hated cleaning up, even after himself. Mama'd get mad at him for leaving dishes in the sink. He said she should buy paper plates, so no one had to wash them. "What's money for, anyway?"

"Charlie . . ." Mama'd pick up a stack of envelopes, hold it in front of him. "Do you know what these are?"

"Let's go," Cody'd whisper. He hated it when they argued. We'd slip outside and climb the apple tree. If it was fall, Cody'd throw rotten apples at the wreck of the tobacco shed. He loved it when they splattered on the crumbling wood.

I shifted on the bench, scratched Nina's head. Mama'd be bent over her test now, and Cody and Philip on their way to Camden Yards. I could almost hear them laughing as they strolled the city streets. They're having fun, I thought. Nina sighed, as if she felt sad too. "Come on," I said, "we're going for a walk."

I had to coax her out and down the ridge. I knew a place where a brook came into the river over a series of waterfalls. I showed Nina a mess of Christmas ferns I'd found there. Then I decided to build a dam where the banks were close. We used to love that, when we were kids; sometimes Cody and I would spend a morning piling rocks and mud and wet leaves into a wall. But by myself, it wasn't as good as I remembered. The dam leaked, and rushing to patch it I broke my fingernail on a stone. Then I stumbled into the water and got a hotfoot. Usually I don't mind that, but I wasn't expecting it, and the wet shoe rubbed against my sock and felt like it was starting a blister. I went back to the cabin to change.

Maybe Nina was smarter than she looked, because as soon as I started toward the house, she trotted happily behind me. She scurried through the door and flung herself onto Mama's cot with a snort of relief. I fixed myself a sandwich and some Kool-Aid. I couldn't help wondering, What are Cody and Phillip doing now?

I got the idea after lunch. I was thinking about Uncle Mike, and how good it felt talking to him that day at the town house. I thought suddenly: I'll call him! Then, replacing that idea before it even took hold, came another: I'll call Daddy. He may not have a phone, my mind argued—after all, he didn't send a number. "But that was a while ago," I answered out loud. "I bet he's got one now. I'll call information in New York and get the number. I can use our card, so there won't be any reverse charges."

I wanted to leave Nina, but I was afraid to after what Mama'd said. So I pulled her up the trail. Poplar leaves fluttered around us. I came to the end and followed the road to Mrs. Burns's house. I'd met her only once, when Mama'd introduced us and explained that we could use the phone or go to her in an emergency. As soon as she opened the door, I told her, "There's nothing wrong. I was just wondering if I could make a call."

"Of course." She beckoned me in, then noticed the dog.

"Stay," I said. I closed the door.

"The telephone's here." Mrs. Burns pointed to a little table by the couch. "I'll leave you alone, for privacy." But she paused on her way out. "Are you sure everything's okay?"

"It's fine—I just want to call a friend I haven't seen for a while."

She went out then, and I got the New York City area code from information. I phoned it and asked for a new listing for Charles Allen on West Seventy-ninth Street. The operator seemed to take forever. Then a recording said the number before I realized I didn't have a pen. I'll have to remember it, I thought; and I listened one more time.

"212-555-6655," I said under my breath. My fingers trembled as I dialed and gave the billing information. Another operator put the call through. I heard the familiar clicks of phone lines connecting. Then it began to ring: *veeeeeep, veeeeeep, veeeeeep.*

He isn't home, I thought, and I almost hung up; but I wanted so bad to talk to him, so I held on one more minute. Then, amazingly, the ringing stopped, and someone said, "Hello?"

"Hello, Daddy?"

"Hello?"

I stopped, the phone still in my hand. I willed my fingers to push, and the line went dead. Mrs. Burns must have been listening in the other room, 'cause she stuck her head in. "Did you get through?"

"Yes, thanks." I put the receiver down and went outside. Nina was waiting for me, but I shoved her away and took off down the ridge. I could hear her behind me, chugging along like an old steam engine. *Hello? Hello? Hello . . .* the voice repeated. "Daddy?" I'd said, before it had even registered, so he would know I'd called, but not because I'd talked to him. The voice on the phone, soft and Southern like Daddy's, was a woman's.

I took it out on Nina. I closed her out and shouted, "Go away!" I lay on Mama's cot with the pillow over my head. If I'd been able to cut it off, maybe I would have then: to stop the thoughts and undo the phone call. Maybe I'd undo the last six months of my life. From the bedroom Felix cried piteously, but I knew he liked Cody better than me, and I yelled, "Shut up!"

I wanted to disappear. I imagined myself shrinking slowly back in time: getting smaller, smaller; back to the moment I was born and then beyond—a fetus, an embryo, an egg. If I'd had an eraser I could have erased that tiny dot and saved myself a lot of disappointment. *Don't count on anybody,* the ranger said. I hated him, too: hated him for telling me something so mean and so true.

• • •

I pretended I was sleeping when they got back. Mama came over to the bed to check on me. She put her palm on my cheek. "We're home, honey," she said softly.

Next morning Cody wouldn't shut up. "You don't know what you missed, Shana!" he babbled. "The Orioles won six to three, and we had seats along the first-base line. We could see everything!"

I didn't answer. Mama asked, "What did you do?"

"Nothing, really. How was the test?"

"Hard, but I think I did okay." She smiled at me. "Anyway, it's over. In three weeks they'll announce the scores."

"What then?"

"I'll turn them over to the phone company, with my request for promotion. They'll decide what to do."

"What if they turn you down?"

"I'll try again next year." She stirred her coffee.

"Old Mr. Weiss might be dead by then," Cody said. "You could run the office back home."

"You never know." Mama hummed to herself.

But I knew, and I wished I didn't, something about her husband, my daddy: something that felt like a punch, or a slap, or a throw so hard that the dice this game is played with might be gone for good. I had a family once, but the word is cracking into pieces. Some of them may even disappear.

Seventeen

―――

"You could have dialed the wrong number," Cody said when I told him. "You said you didn't write it down."

"I think I recognized her voice."

"Whose voice?"

"That waitress—Paula."

Then Cody got snide—maybe because it hurt him, too. "He's there by himself—he can do what he wants, can't he?"

"Maybe he won't come back after all," I said.

Cody stared at me. I guess he knew I felt bad, 'cause he took a Milky Way out of his pocket and broke it in two. It was squishy, but I ate it anyway. When I was done, my insides still felt empty.

"What if they get a divorce?" I asked. "What about those promises?"

"What promises?"

I knew the words by heart because of the times I'd played wedding when I was little. " 'For better or worse, in sickness or health'—all that."

Cody shrugged. "I guess they lied."

We sat for a while. Felix came along, and Cody rubbed his fur the wrong way, then smoothed it back into place. "The ranger was married once," I told him. "He and his wife had a little girl. She's grown now, and she hates him."

"He can be nasty."

"Do you think he's gotten worse?"

"His yelling?"

"No, the way he limps, and how weak he seems."

"I think so. The minute we come in from paddling he sits down and falls asleep." Cody stretched. "I'm going up there in a half hour. He's going to show me how to run a Class Three rapid."

"What's Class Three?"

"Whitewater's rated one to six according to how dangerous it is. A one is easy, and a six is impossible—like Niagara Falls. Threes and fours are serious rapids."

"You might get hurt."

He shook his head. "There's a big drop, but if you flip, there's nothing down below to bang you up. That's why it's a good one to learn on."

"I want to see."

"I'll ask if you can come tomorrow."

"Why not today?"

But Cody shook his head. "I want to try it on my own."

"I don't see why I can't come," I muttered, but Cody'd made his mind up, and he didn't bother to answer.

After he left, I went to the cave, but all I could write was the word *Hello*. I filled a half page with that before I put the journal away and lay on the ledge on my stomach. I could see water striders putt-putting in the pool beside me. I wondered if there was a pattern in what they did; if they made choices: Left or right? Forward or back? Did they have minds, feelings, dreams? A chickadee noticed me from the low branches of the hemlock across the river and flew closer, staring curiously. "I'm new here," I explained. The little bird twittered as if it understood.

Later I went to the ranger's. I saw Cody on my way: He'd made it through the rapids twice, but the third time he got stuck in a reversing wave and flipped. He was soaked, but happy. "You've got to try it, Sha. It feels like flying."

"What good is flying if you get pneumonia?"

"Wait till you try it," Cody said.

I'd made up my mind not to talk about Daddy, but the ranger was so beat he couldn't pay attention anyway.

He was sitting in his desk chair with wet boots on his feet and his mouth half open. When I came in, he snapped it shut.

"Your brother's wearing me out," he mumbled. "He doesn't know when to quit."

"I saw him on my way here. He said he made it through the rapid."

"Of course he made it! He's a natural. I guessed it the first time I saw him."

I didn't argue. I cooked him a hamburger and a pan of beans, and he slurped them down. Then I helped him get his boots off and gave him a cup of tea. It must have been in that cupboard for years, it was so musty; but he didn't care. After he drank it, he sighed and closed his eyes.

"I wrote a poem," I told him.

He wheezed in his sleep, and I left him in the chair and headed home.

When I got back to the cabin, Cody had made a fire and was sleeping beside it. It was his night to make supper, but I decided to start it myself. That meant I got to pick the meal, and I chose spaghetti and garlic bread. The whole time I was working, I kept thinking of that phone call. What if I hadn't hung up? Then I'd know what was going on, instead of imagining the worst. What a jerk I was, to panic like that! Like Cody said, I didn't even know if I'd got the right number.

• • •

That night the three of us went fishing. We bundled up in sweaters and windbreakers and climbed down to stand by a quieter stretch of the river. Maybe because we'd come on impulse, we'd brought only one rod and a few lures. We took turns casting over the water and reeling in slow. Bats dove for insects in the dusk, and the dark ridges on both sides of the Leanna framed the fading light. Cody talked about the ball park, and Philip's apartment.

"You can hear his neighbor Marvin practicing his saxophone right through the wall. We went over, and he let me try a few notes. Philip said when I come back we'll go hear him play at his club."

"Did you feel . . ." I searched for the right word. "Crowded?"

He shook his head. "The apartment has a balcony and there's a square across the street with a fountain. People sit beside it and play chess. I even saw some jugglers there."

"I wouldn't want to live in the city," I said carefully. "Would you, Cody?"

He shot me a look. "Shana, I'm talking about one day."

I shrugged it off. Beside me, Mama tensed, then gave the rod a little tug. She said. "I believe I've got something."

"Reel!" We were both watching the line, seeing the end of the rod go down. Her hands moved fast and easy against the pull of the fish. We hadn't brought a net, but Cody waded into the stream.

"It's too cold for that," Mama fussed. The fish jumped, and she jerked the line to set the hook. It jumped again, this time close to the bank. Cody followed the line with one hand, grabbed, and came up holding it through the gill.

"A rainbow!" The fish was silver, long and slim. It was too dark to see the pattern on its side. Mama was beside herself.

"It's a nice one too. What do you know about that?"

"Are you going to let it go?"

"I don't think so. This is my first trout, and I want to see how it tastes."

"You ought to put it back," Cody said nervously.

But Mama wouldn't budge. "I'm having it for breakfast."

"Trout are endangered," Cody argued.

"Nonsense. I see them in the grocery store every week."

"Those are farm-raised. That's different."

Mama shook her head. "I'm not going to change my mind."

Cody shrugged then, and gave up.

She fried the fish in butter. The smell got me up, and she cooked a couple of eggs alongside it and gave me half. The flesh was pink, different from bass or bluegill, and the taste was sweet.

"I could go for more of these," Mama said. "I wonder if they're stocked."

I was surprised she asked. "They stock them down the river at Tom's Creek," I said. "Up here they're trying to grow them naturally."

"How'd you know that?"

I colored. "Cody and I met a ranger, and he told us."

"A ranger! You all never mentioned that. I didn't know you saw anybody down here."

"We hardly do."

Mama watched me. "I wondered if you were lonely. Are you glad you spent the summer here?"

I scraped the last bit of fish off my plate. I thought of my secrets: the phone call, the ranger, the cave. "It *was* lonely, but I learned a lot. There're all kinds of birds and flowers that we don't have back home. The gorge is peaceful, too." I shifted uneasily, knowing my answer was mostly a lie, but she didn't seem to notice.

Mama looked at her hands. She had on her wedding ring, and the two rings she'd gotten from Gram: silver rings brought from Scotland by her grandparents, who had settled in North Carolina. "It was true what you said before: that I didn't ask you before I moved us all. That was a mistake. I was so upset by Charlie's leaving that I didn't think things through."

I held my breath.

"I'm not sorry I moved—it was the best thing for me. But as far as you two, I'm not so sure."

She looked right at me. "I want to stay in Laglade a while longer. But that doesn't mean you and Cody have to. I talked to Mike on Tuesday, and he said he'll move back into the old house if you children want to go home for school. I'd come down on the weekends. . . ."

"We wouldn't be together." My voice faltered.

"Not during the week, no. I'd miss you a lot, but I don't want you suffering just so I can feel good about myself." She looked away. "I meant to talk to you together. I'll tell Cody tonight, same as I told you."

"Do you want us to go?" I was thinking of Philip. Maybe Mama guessed that, 'cause she met my eyes.

"No, I'd rather be with you."

"Couldn't you come home, too?"

"Not yet."

"How come?"

"Too many memories, I guess. And moving gave me the chance to meet people with different lifestyles and ideas. I want to take some courses in the fall, and learn new things. If I get the promotion, we'll be able to save some money, too. Maybe next summer we can take a real vacation—you know we always talked about going to Yellowstone, or the Great Lakes."

"Or Hawaii," I said. Mama smiled, but I went on: "What about Daddy?"

She hesitated. "I'm not sure what he wants."

"Have you talked to him?"

A shadow crossed her face. "I have. We're trying to sort out what's best for everyone."

"We used to have so much fun," I said.

She put the back of her hand against my cheek, but she didn't answer.

That whole day I was shook up. On the one hand, Cody and I could finally go home. On the other, Mama wouldn't be there, and what was home without her or Daddy?

But Cody didn't hesitate. That night, as soon as Mama gave him the choice, he said, "Warrensburg."

He couldn't believe I wavered. "You've been talking about going back for months."

"Not as much as you, Cody. Anyway, that was all of us, not just you and me."

"Think about Laglade, Shana—think about what it's like!"

I nodded, but the course directory with its choices stuck like an itch in the back of my mind. Warrensburg was safe, and the house and the river were home. But since Daddy left, Mama wanted something more. Even I'd begun to think of possibilities. I'd met the ranger, explored the gorge, written a poem. At the same time I ached for what had been, and wanted it back.

Eighteen

---

*T*he next day Cody took me over the Class Three flume. The ranger didn't like the idea, but the two of us stood our ground, and he gave in. There was another life preserver, lumpy and covered with spiderwebs, in the shed; I brushed it off and tied the strap around my waist. Cody paddled upstream, then dragged the canoe over the rocks to the head of the rapid. All I was supposed to do, he explained, was paddle on my right. The ranger stood on the bank below the drop with a throw rope, in case we had problems.

The thing that got me, by hindsight, was the sound. We approached around a curve lined with hemlock, the ripples in the water showing underlying ledges. Fifty yards ahead of us, a flat line marked the edge of the river, which seemed to disappear. An ominous rumble came from below, low at first, then louder.

"When I say paddle, paddle hard," Cody said. "We'll be cutting right, around a set of rocks, then straight down the middle till we hit the pool at the bottom."

"What if we miss?"

"If we miss the right, we'll spin out and go over backward. Most likely the boat will tip, and we'll end up washing through beside it."

"I don't think I want to wash through," I said. Something about the phrase reminded me of the old wringer washer that used to sit on our front porch. You could mash your fingers in it if you weren't careful.

"It's not that bad—I've done it three times. If you fall out, keep your feet up and in front of you."

"What if I bang my head on a rock?"

"Are you chickening out?" The line across the river grew steadily closer.

"I guess not." My heart was thumping. I could see white spray rising somewhere down the drop, and the noise was almost deafening.

"Get ready! Paddle *now*!"

My hands were shaking. I dipped the paddle in the river, took a stroke, tried to lean into it like Cody had showed me. We shot past a rock, then headed toward another outcropping. I felt fear clutch at my throat. I wanted to paddle, but my hands grabbed the sides of the canoe and held on.

"Shana, *paddle!*" Cody's voice came over the roar of

the water, but I wouldn't let go of the boat. I wanted to close my eyes.

"Shana!"

Cody was furious. I grabbed the paddle and thrust it in the water just as we hit the drop. The boat bounced and flew. Spray hit me in the face. I could feel Cody maneuvering from the rear. We slid past a boulder and hit thunk on the pool below the flume. Big waves pushed us to one side. Cody tilted the boat in the other direction, laying his paddle blade almost flat on the water. The boat straightened and pushed into an eddy right below where the ranger stood. He looked at me and shook his head.

"Big baby," Cody said later.

"I didn't know what it was like. You never told me!"

"What do you mean, I never told you? I said it was great!"

"Great?" I faced him. The ranger looked from one of us to the other. "I could have drowned," I said coldly.

"You couldn't either. You had on a life jacket, and Henry was standing right there with a rescue rope. And it's shallow just beyond the pool. He could have waded in and pulled you out."

That just made me madder; but the ranger thought the whole thing was funny. For the first time ever, he laughed out loud.

"Be quiet!" I snapped; but he only laughed harder.

What got to me, besides how scary it was, was the way they acted together: like they were friends. The ranger never treated me like that. Furthermore, Cody had called him Henry. Wasn't I the one who'd gone to see him first? Wasn't it me who'd bought him food and washed his dishes? How could he treat Cody better than he treated me?

I went and saw him on my own. He wasn't so uppity then; he whined for me to dig more potatoes and carry in a couple buckets of water. "Why don't you ask Cody?" I said.

"He's too light to work that pump."

"So you teach him canoeing, and I'm supposed to do the work."

The ranger fingered his stubbly chin. "I hadn't thought of it like that."

"And he calls you Henry." I knew it sounded childish, but I didn't care.

"You should too. I meant to tell you that. And if you like, I'll give you a few paddling lessons."

I was too disgusted to answer. I thumped myself down and looked at his books. They showed the trout catches from stream to stream in Pennsylvania. I looked up the Leanna, but the tables were confusing.

"These figures represent fly fishing areas, and the others are where the river's stocked," the ranger explained. "But the numbers aren't accurate, because lots of fishermen don't report catches till the season ends September first—that's next week."

I wished I'd had my hands over my ears. He must have seen that on my face. "I guess you'll be starting school," he said.

I nodded. "Cody's going back to Warrensburg."

"And you?"

"I don't know yet. I haven't made up my mind."

"You didn't seem to like that town house."

"I don't. But Mama's staying, and the schools in Laglade are better, too. My English teacher got me started keeping a journal. And the high school has lots of stuff they don't back home."

"Like what?"

"Languages, writing courses . . ." My voice faded.

"You said you wrote a poem."

"I thought you were asleep."

"I'm a light sleeper." The ranger shut the book. "I wouldn't mind hearing it."

I turned red. I'd been carrying the poem folded up in my back pocket, but I was scared to read it out loud. "It isn't any good."

"How do you know?"

A lump came in my throat.

"Read it," he said.

I stumbled through the poem, but when he asked me to do it again, I read it better. Afterward the old man stared at me. "That poem's about me," he said.

"It isn't either. I wasn't thinking of you one bit when I wrote it."

He grunted like he didn't believe me.

"I ought to know who I was thinking of," I said.

He turned cold then. "You're better at poems than canoeing."

"I'm sorry I read it to you."

"I'm not. I liked it."

"You can pump your own water, Henry," I said coldly. I went out and shut the door behind me.

On the way home I took the crumpled paper out of my pocket. I read the poem as if it were something I was proud of:

> *In the grove of the laurels,*
> *In the sound of the rushing stream,*
> *In the patterns of the rainbow trout*
> *   I will seek my name;*
>
> *In the tongues of the river,*
> *In the camps of the Algonquin,*
> *On the green tips of the hemlock branches*
> *   I will seek my name.*

"But you know your name," I told myself. "It's Shana Allen."

The paper stared up at me like an unblinking eye.

Nineteen

I got a letter from Daddy. Mama brought it to me a few nights later, while I was still trying to make up my mind about where to live. I took it down to the cave and tore it open.

Darling Shana,

Thank you so much for the beautiful poem. It reminded me of the river and forest that I don't get to see here in New York, and made me homesick.

I think I know what you mean when you say you're seeking your name. Though I named you for someone I admired, everyone has to find their own name. I feel like, at my late age, I'm doing that too!

I've been taking an art course at night, and I still enjoy the museum, but I miss you and Cody and Dot more than ever. I plan to complete my studies and come home by Christmas.

Paula Preston, the art student from the Peter Pan, visited me on her way to Italy—she finally saved up enough for a one-way ticket! Once I get home, I'm determined to start saving for the four of us.

> *Love and kisses,*
> *Daddy*

I read the letter twice. I felt limp, worn-out. I wondered if Mama'd got a letter, too, and when I went back to the cabin I asked her. She shook her head. "Daddy says he'll be home by Christmas," I told her.

She didn't answer.

"Families are stronger than people on their own," I said. "Remember how Granddaddy used to drive in four stakes when he planted a tree? If the wind blew one stake down, the others would hold."

"I remember," Mama said.

After that my veins felt electric. Daddy was coming home. All Mama had to do was forgive him. She'd forgiven Granddaddy, or at least tried; and Daddy was her husband. But thinking about that, I was uneasy. Something had grown in Mama since we moved; each thing she did without Daddy—patching the roof, taking the accounting test, even catching the trout—seemed to raise her chin a little higher. Before this summer I'd never heard her talk about poetry, or going to college; and her friends from work seemed to encourage her to try new things. Would she be ready to come home by Christmas? I asked Cody, but he was mad at Daddy and didn't pay that much attention.

"What makes him think he can come back as if he'd never left?" he asked.

"Don't you want him to?"

"Of course. Only . . ."

"Only what?"

"It doesn't even sound like he's sorry."

"I bet he is. He just didn't put it in the letter."

"Furthermore, he should have written to all of us." Cody's fists were clenched. I tried to tickle him but he yanked himself away.

"We'll work it out," I said.

Cody glared as if it was my fault too.

And he was upset about the ranger. "You shouldn't have left him without water, no matter how mad you were," he said. "That was wrong."

"I'll bring some in today."

He nodded. "We got a little, but the pump's hard to work."

That brought up something that was bothering me.

"Cody, how's he going to get along once we're gone?"

"I don't know. I've been thinking about that too." He frowned. "He was okay before we came."

"If what he's got comes and goes, like arthritis, then he might get better. As it is, he can't get to his car to buy food. And he doesn't have a phone. If he did, he could call for help."

Cody rested his chin between his fists. "I don't think it's arthritis. For one thing, his weakness is on one side—his left. That's where he stumbles, and he tapes his left hand to the paddle, too. Remember back in June, when you said his face seemed crooked?"

I nodded.

"I think he'd had a stroke. I looked in a book in the library, and that's a symptom. Since then he's gotten weaker. For all we know, he could have had another one."

"He won't go to a doctor. When I brought it up, he had a fit."

"He has fits over lots of things, but that doesn't mean he can't change. Look how he screamed at us that first time."

"That's true."

"We could ask Mrs. Burns to help him."

I made a face. "She's pretty old herself."

"There isn't anyone else," Cody said.

• • •

That night Mama brought up leaving the cabin.

"I talked to Mike on the phone, and he's going to come up and get Cody and his things," she said. "And you, Shana, if that's what you want."

"When?"

"Not this Sunday, but the following one. School starts Wednesday in Warrensburg, so that'll give you a few days to settle in."

"What about my stuff in Laglade?"

"I can bring it up in my car."

He nodded, like it was all so easy.

Mama looked at me. "Have you figured out what you're going to do?"

"Not yet."

"You need to make up your mind, honey."

"I know." But I kept hoping, if I held out long enough, that I wouldn't have to decide.

Now that Mama'd mentioned leaving, each day along the river was more special. Hidden flowers blooming in a cup of dirt behind a ledge; a row of tiny orange mushrooms; a hummingbird; the murmur of the water by the cave; the first flock of geese, headed south; even the cold air that waked me in the mornings and made me snuggle deeper into my quilt—all fragments of a summer that wouldn't come again. I took long walks and fished the shallow pools, and the deep ones, too. The water had turned colder, so if you snagged your line you cut it instead of wading in to get it back. I caught some suckers and a couple smallmouth, but nothing to brag about.

Cody came back from the ranger's with strange news. "He keeps talking about the canyon. He wants me to paddle him down there and walk back by myself."

"What did you say?"

"No way." He raked the evergreen needles into a pattern with his shoe. "I talked to him about our leaving and said we'd ask Mrs. Burns to help him, but he started yelling, 'I don't want help! All I want is to go through the canyon!' " He looked up at me. "What are we going to do about him, Sha?"

"We'll talk to her anyway. And if she won't help, we'll tell Mama."

Cody reddened. "Tell her we lied all summer?"

"I don't know. I don't know what to do."

I went to see the ranger myself, hoping I could talk some sense into him. He gave me a short paddling lesson and showed me how he checked the fingerlings. He had lists of water temperatures and sediments, which show how muddy the river is. "The cloudier the water, the harder it is for trout to naturalize. They need clear, cold water." He wrote something down. "Every time land gets cleared near a river, especially if it's farmed, that's a death knell for the trout. The rain washes dirt and fertilizer down into the water. To them, that's poison."

"I thought the river was protected."

"It's supposed to be. But I can't be everywhere, and the rules are easy to break. People think if they own the land, they can do whatever they want."

"The Indians knew better than that."

"I'll say they did." He grunted angrily. I tried to help him up, but he brushed me off. Afterward he seemed exhausted. "There's something I want to show you," he said. "You and Cody together."

"What?"

"It's a surprise. Come tomorrow and I'll take you there."

"Is it near the canyon?"

"*No!*" He was so snappish, I didn't have the nerve to ask about Mrs. Burns. I figured Cody and I would do it together, the next day.

Cody was nervous about the surprise. "He asked me to practice more Class Threes. Do you suppose he'll try to trick us into taking him down there?"

"I thought the canyon was Class Four."

"Three, four, and one five: the falls. A guy died there last year. His helmet strap broke on an undercut rock, and his head got bashed in."

"That's horrible."

"You can portage the falls, if you get out soon enough. Even the ranger does."

"How do you know?"

"He's described the rapids. I even know how the river curves, and which way you have to lean."

I groaned. "He has a way of getting what he wants," I said.

We went to his cabin the next day. He was sitting on the bench on the front porch, sound asleep. I was afraid to wake him, but Cody took his arm and gave it a good shake. "We're here, Henry." He startled, stared, shook his head. "It's Cody and Shana."

"You . . ." he mumbled, but he knew who we were. "We'll have to take the boat."

Cody and I looked at each other. "Which way?"

"Upstream," he said. That's why we agreed to go.

They stuck me in the middle, between the thwarts. I wondered how hard it would be, pulling against the current with three of us in the boat; but the ranger started out strong, and Cody's strokes were deep and long. We traveled near the banks and through the eddies, where the current was weaker. I'd never been farther than the flume beyond the ranger's cabin; now Cody and I portaged that, the thwarts digging into our shoulders. The ranger carried the paddles, leaning on them like crutches as he stumbled over the rocky ground. Once around the drop, we launched the canoe from a weedy bank. Wild asters and orange touch-me-nots trailed down to the water. We snaked our way upstream, passing forested banks of hemlock and laurel. Chickadees and titmice twittered in the trees, and a kingfisher flew ahead of us over the water, warning others of our coming with his harsh cry.

"To the right," the ranger murmured. Cody changed his stroke. We sidled along a steep bank laced with roots. "Here," the old man said. But he slipped getting out of the boat, wetting both feet, and that made him mad. He acted like it was our fault. "Both of you can go to hell," he muttered.

"What do you want to show us?"

"I changed my mind." He went and stood by himself. But later he headed upstream, through the thickets. A creek divided the shelf of land that ran along the river, and a rock ridge rose almost perpendicular behind it. He went back there, with us following from a distance. We saw him scrabbling against the wall, pulling back vines. He rubbed his hand across the stone, feeling for something. "You have to promise not to tell," he said. He looked right at us.

"Okay."

"Give me your hand." He took Cody's first, and put it on the rock. Cody traced something with his fingers.

"It's a fish," he told me. "Feel."

I came closer. The picture was outlined on the dark surface of the wall. It reminded me of the Indian ax, and I said so. The ranger nodded. "It's Algonquin," he said. "It's the sign for good fishing. They left it for whoever came along."

I remembered the cup Granddaddy hung beside our spring, so travelers would know the water was safe. But the old man wasn't finished. "Follow me."

He led us up the creek. Abruptly it disappeared among boulders fronting the cliff. We squeezed through a gap between them and stood on a ledge above a pool six feet across. The rock bowl that held it was smooth as silk, and almost white; and the water was pale green.

"A limestone spring." The ranger spoke so softly, his words sounded like prayer. He pushed back through the boulders, but Cody and I stayed. I dipped one hand in the ice-cold water.

"Where does it come from?"

"Somewhere under the ridge," Cody said.

Above us a gust of wind tumbled leaves down the cliff. A bunch cascaded into the spring, rimming the green water with yellow. "We'd better follow him," Cody said.

He was standing arms akimbo on the point where the creek and the river came together. His expression was hard, but I knew by then how frail he really was: so weak that if you bumped him the wrong way, he would fall. I remembered what he'd said before: *I'm holding on. . . .* I thought of the fall leaves with their brittle stems, clinging to the darkening branches. The ranger stared out over the river.

"That spot is sacred," he said. "The Algonquin worshipped it, because its waters multiplied their crops, and grew big fish. The limestone does it. Best fishing in the whole river, right below this creek. . . ."

"The limestone?"

"It neutralizes acids in the water and soil." His eyes were veiled, as if his mind had wandered to another time. "I caught a nineteen-incher on a midge fly right down there. . . ." He pointed to a pool beside a stand of birches. "Don't know what year it was, but I had a fly rod. I wondered if I'd ever bring him in, but I took my time and let him run himself out. I cooked him over hickory chips. . . ." He wet his lips, kept looking down the river. I wasn't sure he remembered Cody and I were there.

"Their wildness settles in you, when you eat them," he said. "They put the river in your bones."

"How do you catch them?" Cody asked.

I thought he'd be mad, but he wasn't. "Worms, minnows—whatever's here naturally. In springtime they like grubs and maggots."

"I thought no one could fish here," I said uneasily. "I thought the government forbid it."

"I'm giving you permission," he said. "Not over and over, but once or twice a year."

I stood there with my mouth hanging open, but Cody said, "Thank you."

I paddled back, with the ranger in the middle. He gave me my second lesson, and by his standards I didn't do well. He fussed at me until he got tired and shut up. When we got to the flume, the ranger and I got out so Cody could run it on his own. He went right through without faltering. When he hit the pool at the base of the drop, the boat landed light and steady as a dancer.

"He's good," the old man said. "One day he'll run the canyon."

"Why'd you ask him to take you there?"

But the ranger wouldn't answer.

Twenty

I think now that the ranger wanted to show us magic. He wanted us hooked on the Leanna, so that wherever we were—in Laglade or Warrensburg, in the house watching TV, reading a book, sitting in the classroom listening to a teacher teaching or droning on and on— our minds, our hearts would be whispering: *River.* He wanted to make sure we'd be back—not just once, but over and over, because the ones who come back are the ones who'll make sure it's treated right: guarded and watched over as zealously as the fingerlings; as carefully and lovingly as the mother cat tends her kittens or the human mother her newborn child.

But he made mistakes. He didn't realize—couldn't, maybe—that we had other loves pulling us too: home and Mama and Daddy and learning new things like writing and paddling a canoe. And he lied: not just once, but lots of times. Maybe you could say he was living a lie. We lied too, about what we'd done all summer, but later we set the record straight, because we had to. There was no one who could force him to come clean.

"He says if I don't take him, he'll go alone," Cody said. We were on our way to Mrs. Burns's house, to talk about the ranger. "He's dead set on going through the rapids one more time."

"That's crazy—he'll never make it."

"He blew up when I said that. He said stay out of his business once and for all."

"He'll change that tune quick enough," I said. "Wait till his food starts running low."

"I guess . . ." Cody looked worried. "Do you think Mrs. Burns will help?"

"We'll have to ask, and see if she says yes. Then we have to get him to accept the help."

"He took ours. . . ."

"I kept going back," I reminded Cody. "And he was still mean about it."

Mrs. Burns seemed glad to see us, and I realized she was probably lonely too, living by herself at the end of that rutted dirt road. She made us chocolate milk. I tried not to look at the telephone while we were waiting. Had

Paula stayed with Daddy as a friend before she left to catch her plane? Or was there more to it? Did he love her, even for a little while? I trembled, sitting there, but Mrs. Burns came back in and Cody gave me a look that meant begin.

"There's a ranger living a few miles up the river in a cabin with no phone or running water," I said slowly. "He works for the federal government, raising trout. Over the summer he's been sick. Now he's too weak to get to his car, or pump his own water."

Mrs. Burns nodded, and I thought she wanted me to go on, but instead she said, "Maybe I should have warned you about Henry. But he hasn't been bothering people like he used to, so I hoped he'd stay away."

Cody and I stared.

"He's not a ranger," she explained. "That's a story he made up. His uniforms come from the fish hatchery where he used to work. They fired him because he couldn't get along with anyone. Things had to be done his way or not at all."

She shook her head. "The sheriff threatened to arrest him three years ago for harassing fishermen. After that he swore he'd stop. He pretends he's in charge of the river, but he only owns that little cabin and the land it sits on." Mrs. Burns sighed. "I knew his wife," she said. "She was a nice girl, and she cared about him too. But she got lonely down there by herself. She couldn't even watch TV."

"Are you sure he's not a ranger?" Cody asked. Then Mrs. Burns realized we'd been duped.

"I should have warned you," she said.

"But he *is* sick," Cody said. I had to admire him for not giving up.

"I'll call the sheriff—they'll bring him out," Mrs. Burns said. "They tried to put him in a nursing home last year. They think he's getting senile. I laughed when the sheriff told me that. 'You don't know Henry,' I said. 'He's been nuts for forty years. Not just crazy—mean, too.'"

Cody and I just sat there.

"You're not the first to try to help him," she added. "A social worker went there in April, and he threatened her with a gun."

I stood up. "You don't need to call," I said. "Thanks, anyway."

"He didn't threaten you, did he?"

"No, ma'am."

"Have you had a good summer?"

I had to answer, 'cause Cody had his hand on the doorknob and I could tell he wasn't looking back.

"Very good," I said. "Thanks again."

Mama had news for me the next morning before she left for work. "I saw an old man in a canoe when I got up. He was heading down the river a mile a minute."

Soon as she started up the ridge, I woke Cody and

told him. He whipped the quilt off and grabbed his pants. "He's going for the canyon."

"I thought he wanted you to take him."

"He knows I won't."

"That's crazy. Weak as he is, he'll never make it through."

"I know." Cody was tying his sneakers. He stuck a knife and some string in his jeans pocket. "I'm going after him."

I stood there for a minute, not sure what to do or say. "He lied to us, Cody. Most of what he said was lies."

"Once I stop him, I'll tell him we found out."

"I'm coming too."

We grabbed a couple oranges and a hunk of cheese and took off down the river.

The first part was easy. We knew where the trails went and, after they stopped, how to scramble over the rocks without hitting a dead end. We went a couple of miles that way, though it was slow going staying on one side of the river. Chilly as it was, we didn't want to cross unless we had to.

There were no signs of him, though I don't know what we were looking for. We hustled between thickets. Briars tore at my shirt, and my socks were covered with hitchhikers. Once I had to stop and rest. "Why don't we say to hell with him?" I asked Cody.

"Would you?"

I faltered then. "I don't know."

"We wouldn't know what happened, or why he went," Cody said. "And he did teach us things. He showed us the Indian picture, and the spring."

"Why did he lie?"

"Shana—look!" Cody pointed. The tail of a red fox disappeared around a fallen tree not forty feet away.

"There might be kits!"

"We don't have time to look," Cody said.

After a while the south side of the river got too dense for bushwhacking. Cody thought the north looked better, and I did too. We found a shallows, took off our shoes and socks, rolled our pants, and waded over. The cold water was a shock, but at least we had dry socks when we got to the other side. "Hypothermia," Cody muttered as we put them on.

"What's that?"

"Exposure to cold air or water drops your body temperature. If it stays low, you die."

"I'm not *that* cold."

"I'm not talking about you."

The thought of the ranger in the water moved us faster. We pushed through high weeds until the old rail line swooped down from the north for us to follow. That made walking easier, though trees between the water and the track hid parts of the riverbed. Every few minutes we climbed down the bank onto some rocks and looked around. But there was only the river, quiet in some stretches, other places rushing and foaming like a rabid animal. My legs felt like sticks about to break. "What if he's already in the canyon?" I asked.

"We'll have tried to stop him." Cody peeled the skin back from a piece of orange, swallowed it down.

"What if he's . . ." My voice dried up before I finished the question.

"Come on," Cody said.

This time we kept our shoes on and waded downstream on the left, where the riverbed was shallow. It only took us a few minutes to find him. He must have crawled out of the river, 'cause he was lying on a gravel bar with his feet still in the water and his head covered with blood. There were flies buzzing around like he was dead, and for a moment I thought he was. Then I pulled off his life preserver and saw his chest moving. I put my fingers on the inside of his wrist while Cody hauled his feet out of the water. His skin felt clammy, and the pulse was so fast and weak, I thought it might stop any second. I didn't want to look at his head, but after a bit I turned it toward me. His eyes were shut, and the left side of his face was thick with blood. A deep wound from temple to eyebrow was still bleeding. I took my bandanna out of my pocket and pressed it there. Within a half minute it was soaked.

"He hit his head on a rock," Cody muttered. "He must have lost control of the canoe—maybe there." He pointed. "The boat flipped, but he managed to make it to shore."

"He's lost a lot of blood."

Cody was pale himself. Suddenly he turned and retched. I remembered, when we were little, how he used to cover his head with a blanket if someone got shot on TV. I felt my stomach rising too, but I closed my eyes and willed it down.

We sat there for a moment. I couldn't help thinking how ridiculous that was, the two of us sitting while his head was pumping blood like a piston. But it was pointless to call for help: There was no one to hear us. Cody must have been thinking the same thing.

"There's cabins at the junction with Tom's Creek," he said. "I saw them on the map."

"There's no way to walk around the canyon." We both knew that. My heart was hammering against my ribs.

Cody said, "He told me I was good."

"We can't trust anything he said."

"Shana . . ." Cody was calm now, as if he'd thought things through. "It's three hours back to the cabin, and then we'd have to walk to Mrs. Burns's. The route downstream is a half hour at the most. There're phone lines and a paved road. I'd be talking to a doctor in forty minutes."

"They can't get here anyway."

"They can send a helicopter—they'll lower a stretcher and a medic, like they do on television."

"You'd never make it alone." I stared at Cody. "I'm older, and I'm telling you: You can't go."

He wouldn't look at me. "I won't sit here and watch him die."

"You're not going down that river by yourself."

"Shana—" He was practically begging.

That was when I figured it out. Maybe I was afraid to see someone die, or maybe I was trying to protect Cody, though if you think it through, there was no sense to that. "I'm going with you," I said.

"You?"

I nodded. I read the thoughts that crossed his mind, knew he wouldn't speak them because if he did we wouldn't go. Finally he said, "This time you'll have to paddle."

"I will."

"If you paddle, we might make it." His voice was thoughtful, considering.

"I'm not afraid." My voice quavered.

He looked at me and shook his head. "I'll go find the canoe," he said. "It's probably swamped somewhere downstream." He took off down the river.

I sat beside the ranger while I waited for Cody. I kept the bandanna pressed against his cut. Now and then I rinsed it, wrung it out, and put it back. After a little while the bleeding slowed, but his heartbeat raced, and it seemed to me his breathing grew faster and more shallow. I tried to tell him everything would be all right, but he didn't seem to hear. Then I remembered that he'd lied to us, and how mad and hurt we'd been. That's when I decided to tell the truth.

"You may die," I said, forcing the words out one by one. "You've lost a lot of blood, and who knows whether we'll make it down the river to get help." Flies buzzed around his eyes, and I swished them away.

"I want you to know that Cody and I found out you aren't a ranger after all. You tricked us and made it stick for the whole summer. You didn't need to do that. We would have listened to what you had to say whether you were a ranger or not. We would have been *interested*. Instead, we don't know what to believe, except one thing, and that is, you're a fake."

Horribly, like a ghost in a dead man's skin, the ranger stirred. I'd thought he couldn't hear me, but I went on:

"You put us in danger," I said. "You knew if you came down here Cody'd follow you. He's looking for your boat. When he comes back, we're going through the canyon to get help. You said not to count on people, and that's fair, I guess; but if I get through and Cody dies, I'll blame you forever."

A breeze stirred up and down the river, soft as baby's breath. I was glad no one would know how I'd treated the ranger when he was hurt. I thought of my granddaddy then: lying in a strange bed, sick with cancer, away from the people and places that he loved.

That softened me, I guess, or maybe I just felt I'd had my say. I took his pulse again and touched his hand. It was only faintly warm. Down the river a buzzard drifted in slow circles, so high his wings were smaller than a postage stamp. I'd seen them before, circling like that: waiting for some suffering squirrel or muskrat to give up the ghost. The ranger gasped, then kept breathing. Beside him the Leanna droned and murmured. I wiped away the blood and put my mouth close to his ear.

"What you did to us was wrong, and you shouldn't have put Felix in that cage, either," I said. "But you did it for the river. And it's here, with you. If you listen, you can hear it."

He nodded. I started crying then. I thought of Granddaddy and Daddy, and now Henry.

"People leave," I mumbled. "I hate that."

I watched to see if he would nod again, but he didn't.

Twenty-one

Cody came around the bend, pulling the canoe. He'd had to go almost to the mouth of the canyon to get it back. The good thing was, there was another life jacket in the ranger's gear bag, and a helmet, too. We knew he kept an extra paddle duct-taped to the inside of the boat. Cody fumbled with the helmet straps, muttering, "Why didn't he wear it?"

"'Cause he's a stubborn old fool." I was crying. I put on the life jacket, cinched it tight. We argued about the helmet, but Cody said since I'd be in the bow, I should wear it. My hands were shaking so bad, he had to fasten it. He pulled the canoe out from the bank and looked at me. "Are you sure you want to go?"

I nodded. He patted the ranger's shoulder, got into the boat. I bent over the old man.

"I'll be back," I whispered. "Wait for me."

I climbed into the canoe and pushed off. I only looked back once. I could see his legs and brown rubber boots sticking out from behind the curve of the gravel bar. I felt queasy, like I might faint, but Cody stared at me hard. "You can't panic like you did before."

"I won't!"

"Then paddle hard."

I knelt and dug the blade in deep, pushed the water back like I was shoveling earth in a garden. To my surprise the boat leaped forward.

"That's where it starts." Cody nodded toward a spot ahead of us where the ridges rose high and the river narrowed. There was a little space to pass through, like a door. My heart began to slam against my ribs. A muffled booming came from the canyon, like the engine of Uncle Mike's old truck. "Get ready—*now*!"

I pushed with all my strength. We passed through the door, into white water. We caught the downside of a wave and the boat took off like it had wings.

"*Right!*" Cody shouted. I paddled hard. The noise was deafening. Pale tongues of water lapped the sides of the canoe, and a boulder slipped by, then another, both of them close enough to touch. The current twisted left, and we went with it, down a narrow chute into calmer water.

"We did it!"

Since Cody was behind me, I couldn't see his face, but he sounded cautious. "Four more to go, Shana . . ."

"Four more!" I echoed, but I couldn't help feeling proud. I wished the ranger could have seen me paddle! I sat back on the seat for just a minute. My knees were wet and clammy. Water sloshed back and forth in the bottom of the canoe, but there was nothing to bail with. Cody used his paddle blade to splash some of it over the side.

"Dog's Breath's next," he said. "There'll be standing waves as we approach it, but if we head straight into them, they won't upset us."

I looked ahead. The high walls of the canyon shaded the river most of the way across, but I could see moving hills of water—the standing waves, I guessed—and, beyond them, an outcropping of rocks.

"Which way do we go?"

"Right. Look for an eddy above those boulders where we can pull up and look the rapid over. The ranger said there's a clear diagonal path across the current, but I'd like to see it before we get started, so we can plan our route."

"What if we miss the eddy, or there isn't one?" I looked back.

He shrugged his thin shoulders. "We'll have to do the best we can."

I got back on my knees. We started paddling hard just before we hit the standing waves, and though they looked big, we cut through them without a hitch. The noise was picking up, so that it was hard to talk. The rapid approached fast, as if it were rushing toward us. I tried to guess where Cody wanted us to pull over. "To the *right*!" he yelled, and I saw a pool there, but the current was pushing us the other way. I stabbed my paddle in and swung wide; the bow hit the eddy, but Cody's end was sliding away. *"Dig!"* he screamed, and I dug like some cartoon creature, like Woody Wood-pecker or the cat in *Tom and Jerry*, paddling so fast and hard my arms seemed like a windmill. Ever so slowly the canoe slipped into the pool. Below us, boulders big as the cab of Daddy's truck stood shoulder to shoulder, water crashing off them in sheets. "I'm so scared," I said; but Cody couldn't hear. He shrieked over the noise: "Remember what I said?"

My mind went blank. *"What?"*

"We're paddling on a diagonal—there to there." He showed me with one arm. "You paddle on the left unless I tell you to switch." He paused, took a deep breath. "When I say go!"

I closed my eyes for just a second.

"Ready, set, go!"

I opened them and dug the paddle in. We shot like an arrow across the current. Below us the rocks stood like a wall, but I kept paddling, and just as I thought we'd be swept upon them, Cody turned the boat and we slid by. A wave caught the bow and soaked me.

"Two down!" Cody yelled.

I couldn't stop shaking. After a minute he noticed. "You cold, Sha?"

Not just cold, I thought; but I nodded.

"We've got another half mile before Deerfoot. If we move over, we can paddle in the sun."

To our left a narrow band of sunlight played among the waves. The river had calmed now, and was rocking us gently. My heart stopped pounding, and I had time to look around: Scraggly trees sprouted from the sides of the canyon, and the dark shapes of deer moved along the crest of a high ridge. The sun felt good on my back and shoulders.

Cody began to review what lay ahead. "Deerfoot's a Class Four, but the ranger said for a four it's not too bad. Then comes Blindman's Falls—there's a portage going off to the right just before it, so we'll beach the boat and carry it around. The last rapid's an easy Class Three. The cottages are a half mile beyond that."

"What's Deerfoot like?" I tried to keep my voice steady.

"Two oblong chutes go around a rock island—they say from above it looks like a cleft hoof. The hard part's that the current piles into the rock. You can either hug the wall on the far right or else cross to the eddy just above the island and then shoot off to the left."

"What do you want to do?"

"Hug the right wall." Cody had to shout, because the canyon was starting to echo the roar of white water. Up ahead spray hung like mist over the Leanna. "Remember the pry stroke?"

I showed him, sliding the paddle perpendicular, to the left side of the boat and pushing away. The canoe slid to the right.

"You'll have to do it harder than that."

"You sound like Henry," I muttered, but of course Cody didn't hear.

We pulled closer to the rapid. Deerfoot didn't seem worse than the others, but the river had a dark, boiling look, like the surface of a witch's cauldron. I noticed that the swirling currents made it hard for the paddle to grab hold. We stayed to the far right, but like before, the current tried to push us toward the middle. Twenty feet before the island Cody started yelling: "Pry!" I pushed the paddle with all my strength, but it didn't make any difference. *"Pry!"* he screamed again, but terror gripped me, and I couldn't move. We were sliding away from the right wall. Then he must have given up, 'cause I heard his voice faintly through the roar of the rapid: "Center eddy, Shana—*paddle hard*!"

"Left or right?" I wondered vaguely. The water

crashed around me. I chose left and started pushing The island was coming at us like a bus in the wrong lane of a highway. Before, Cody had turned us at the last minute. I took a deep breath and paddled like crazy. Then we were grabbed by a huge wave. I hoped we'd slide off into the eddy, but instead it dropped us smack into the center of the island. *"Hold on to your paddle!"* Cody screamed. We hit the rock with a horrible grinding sound. The boat flipped to the right. We hung in midair for a split second; then the river rose to meet us and the canoe heaved onto its side like a dying whale. I was pulled under by the current, tumbled upside down, back up, all under the crushing weight of water. It was cold and dark, and I was running out of air. I pushed for the surface, pushed again. Pictures tumbled through my mind: a bird, a book, the ranger's brown boots. I kicked again; then I was gulping air, but the bottom dropped from under and I was flung like a fish into brightness. Looking down, I saw that I was going over a drop. I hit the pool with a splash, went under, came back up. I stuck my feet up, like Cody had told me to. *Cody!* Where was Cody? Then I saw him, clinging to a rock near the right bank. I was flooded with relief.

"Cody, I'm here! I'm all right! Cody!"

He looked up. His face was white. He said something I couldn't hear.

"I'm keeping my feet up, like you said!" I shouted.

He gestured toward the right bank, spoke again.

I tried to paddle toward him, but I couldn't. Drifting past, I finally heard what he was shouting: *"Get out, Shana! The falls! The falls!"*

If you've ever lived a nightmare, you know it doesn't end when the action's over. It hovers in the back of your mind, emerging when you least expect it; so that coming upon some ordinary place you're suddenly frightened, and you have to summon courage to go on. Recalling Cody's shout, I tremble even now. The water spun me like a twig; the right bank was close, but beyond my reach. "Keep trying, Shana!" I heard from behind, and I pushed and kicked. Then the paddle, clasped in my right hand, scraped something, and I shoved it down and felt the riverbed. I pushed off the bottom toward the right, then again. Cody was up now, splashing along the edge, his arm toward me: "The paddle! Here!" I managed to hoist it toward him. He grabbed the blade and pulled: "Hold on!" My legs touched rock. He dragged me to a shallows, hovering beside me as if he still thought I might get swept away. I was shaking all over.

"You okay, Sha?"

I couldn't say yes, not then; but after a minute I said, "Thanks."

Cody nodded. "Can you stand up?"

I tried. To my surprise, my legs held me.

"The ranger," Cody murmured. We could see the

swamped canoe above the portage, twenty feet downstream. "Come on," Cody said. "Let's go."

It turned out Cody'd wrenched his wrist in the river, so I did most of the work, snagging the boat, emptying it, dragging it over the path. I could hear Blindman's Falls roaring on my left. Cody looked at it, but I didn't want to. Later he told me it was bad.

This time I sat in the stern, since Cody could hardly paddle. For some reason that didn't throw me. We shoved off, with the rapid crashing behind us.

"Only one more," Cody said. The walls of the canyon started to recede. I must have got a second wind, because my paddling was shooting us forward. Cody noticed too.

"Henry wouldn't believe it was you," he said.

The last rapid came then: a set of boulders with a chute right down the middle. Cody ruddered from his side, grasping the paddle by the blade with his good hand. I paddled hard, and we swooped over the drop and right on through. A great blue heron, fishing behind a rock, turned and rose on wings that stretched taller than me. Somewhere in the distance a car ground over pavement. After a while we saw three houses clustered on the bank like comfortable old friends.

"I'm going to write this down," I told Cody. "The whole summer, but starting with today."

"No one will believe you." He pointed suddenly. "Look—phone lines. And there's a man, chopping wood."

We pulled up the canoe and went toward him. My legs were shaking so bad. I could hardly walk.

"Someone's hurt up the river. We'd like to use the phone to call for help."

He held out his hand. "Come inside."

He called the shock/trauma unit at the hospital in Harrisburg. They said the helicopter would pick me up so I could show them where the ranger was. The stranger promised Cody a ride home.

The helicopter trip was noisy and fast, with me sitting up front beside the pilot. He gawked over the canyon, asking how we'd made it through, but I was so nervous about Henry I could hardly speak. He looked tiny and still on the gravel bar, and I thought for sure that he was dead. They lowered me down in a harness, with a medic and a stretcher right behind.

"He's alive," she shouted over the din of the helicopter. "What's his name?"

"Henry Luck."

"Did you see it happen?"

I shook my head.

"How do you know him?"

"He lives up the river."

She'd taken his pulse by then and given him a shot. She taped the head wound quickly. "He's lost a lot of blood. Tell his family to come fast. . . ." She hesitated, then looked around nervously as if she'd never seen a wild place before. "Can you get home?"

"Yes."

She strapped him down. "Is he a friend?"

I don't know why, but I nodded.

"He's lost a lot of blood," she repeated. She looked at me to see if I understood. I held his hand for a second. "We made it through the canyon," I said. I tried to let go, but he clung on. I knew then he was scared.

"Henry," I said, "good-bye."

He was holding on, clinging on. The medic moved impatiently. "We've got to go."

"Henry . . ."

He gripped my hand like it could save him. His mouth moved, but nothing came out. Suddenly I knew what he wanted. For a second I was angry. "I can't do it," I said.

The medic looked confused.

"I'm going back to school," I tried to explain. "I won't be here, except maybe a few weekends."

Henry held on. I remembered saying to Cody he has a way of getting what he wants. I shook my head, but he looked so frightened. I couldn't stand for him to leave like that.

"I'll try to take care of it," I said.

That was when he let me go.

Twenty-two

We found out the ranger died. The medic told Mama he didn't even make it to the hospital. He died in the helicopter, with all that noise. I wonder if he opened his eyes and looked out at the patchwork of rocks, trees, and river. Maybe he saw what the wild geese see when they swoop low over the ridges on their way to some-place else.

Cody and I grieved his death. We sat together under the hemlocks and said we'd miss him no matter what Mama thought. I showed Cody a new poem:

> *I dream of Henry,*
> *standing fit and strong*
> *at the edge of a river;*

He does not see where the black bear
   laps water
   or the mountain lion, with full belly,
      suckles her cubs in a den on the hemlock ridge;

But songbirds bright with color
   flutter around him,
   and every flower—phlox, violet, touch-me-not—
      has chosen this day to bloom.

The fish are thick in the water
   as he snaps his rod:
   the line rolls back,
   comes forward in a perfect arc;

And the largest trout
   in the clear, deep pool
   prepares to rise.

Cody had his own way of remembering Henry. He claimed he was going to keep paddling till he was good enough to do Class Fours. When he turned eighteen, he'd run big rivers: the Cheat, the Gauley, and the Tygart. "And I'm going to learn the saxophone," he said.

"What's that got to do with rivers?"

"Nothing, except I heard it this summer, and it sounds so cool, Shana—like a waterfall, only it's music."

"Do you think you'll find a teacher back home?"

He shrugged. "I bet Uncle Mike will drive me to Oldtown. I know there'll be somebody there."

I felt like saying, There'd be someone in Laglade. That's where I'd be starting high school. When Mama found out how much I'd lied over the summer, she said she didn't trust me on my own. Cody stood right there and heard her say it, and he didn't stick up for me, either. I guess he was afraid she'd change her mind about him, too. Mama knew what we were thinking—she said I was the one in charge. When I tried to explain what happened, she shook her head and said she didn't even want to know.

The day the bandage came off Cody's wrist, he went out fishing. After he left, someone knocked on the cabin door. I thought it might be Uncle Mike, come early; but when I looked out, two men in uniforms were standing there. The older one, fat and with a mustache, tipped his broad-brimmed hat: "I'm Sheriff Cooper, looking for Mrs. Allen."

I called to Mama, and she went to the door with a face that said *What next?*

The sheriff introduced himself and his deputy. "We been over to Henry Luck's cabin yesterday. We knew he kept a gun, and we didn't want it lying around where somebody could walk in and take it. Turned out there weren't any bullets, but we picked it up and cleared out the food, and burned the trash and dirty clothes." He cleared his throat and looked at Mama kind of funny.

"It's the second time I've been there this month. Some fishermen complained about him, and I went by a couple weeks ago to say he'd better stop that nonsense. Then I saw how bad he looked. I asked him if he didn't want to visit the senior home in town, just to see what it's like. He didn't blow up like he did last time, but he took this paper off his desk and asked me to witness it; and so I did.

"I said I'd come back Tuesday and drive him into town. To my surprise he said okay. Said he had a couple things to take care of first. Next thing you know, I heard that he was dead.

"I found this on his desk." The sheriff held out a piece of paper. "You're Shana Allen, aren't you?"

She pulled back like the words stung. "That's my daughter."

My heart started banging, but he didn't hand the paper to me. He gave it to Mama, and she read out loud:

"*To whom it may concern:*

I, Henry Luck, being of sound mind, do hereby declare this to be my last will and testament. I bequeath my land, my house, and its contents to Shana Allen and her brother, Cody.

"It's signed and dated last week." Mama stared at the paper. "Is it legal?"

The sheriff cleared his throat. "Reckon so. Hope you don't mind, but I took the liberty of telling his ex-wife and daughter about it, being as they're from around here. It's no contest far as they're concerned."

"Shana's just thirteen."

"I don't think anyone's going to make a fuss over it. The cabin's just one room, and there's no road access to the place; no utilities, either—the stove and refrigerator run on propane. I checked the taxes, and they're eighty dollars, paid up last spring."

"Shana?" Finally Mama spoke to me. "Did you know about this?"

I took the paper in my hands. His old scrawly handwriting reminded me of him: wobbly but stubborn. I wondered when he'd done it. Was that what he was trying to tell me on the riverbank, before they took him away?

I swallowed. "No."

"Why would he leave it to you?" Mama asked.

"He wanted us to care for certain things," I tried to explain. "The river, and the trout. Maybe he thought we needed a place to work from. He didn't approve of this one, 'cause of the outhouse."

"You're children," Mama said. "How could you care for a river?"

I didn't answer. The sheriff smiled.

"He wasn't right in the head, ma'am. But Ada Burns said the youngsters helped him out, and maybe he was thinking of that. He never did anything regular; wasn't that sort of person. He was as ornery as any man I ever met."

I looked at the sheriff, and he smiled, and I saw that he knew Henry. Maybe he even liked him a little. He nodded at me.

"Not many have their own place at your age, young lady. Maybe that's what you get in return for a kindness."

My eyes filled up then, and he looked embarrassed.

"File the paper in the probate court," he told Mama. "They'll stamp it in a month or two; then it's hers. In the meantime I locked it up, but it's awful messy, so here's the key." He handed it to me.

Twenty-three

The only good thing about Cody's leaving was seeing Uncle Mike. He hadn't heard about the ranger, so he wrapped his arms around me and asked, "Coming home, Sha?"

"I can't." He must have seen from my face there was something wrong.

"How come?"

I didn't want to tell, so I went outside while Mama was explaining. When I came back in, he still looked baffled. But he must have decided not to question Mama's judgment, 'cause he hugged me and said, "We'll see you at Thanksgiving, if not before."

We showed him around the river and the woods. He wanted to see the ranger's cabin, but Mama said there wasn't time. She hadn't even gone up there to see it herself, though I'd asked her to. Maybe she couldn't accept that something good had come out of the whole thing.

We ate our lunch together, hamburgers cooked outside on the fire ring Cody and I had built. I remembered how we'd found those salamanders and played with them. Then we realized Uncle Mike hadn't met Felix. Cody ran around looking for him. We'd agreed he'd go to Warrensburg, 'cause Laglade was no place for an outdoor cat.

But Felix didn't come, or wouldn't; he could be perverse, especially if he knew you wanted him to do something. We checked the top shelf in the pantry, a hole in the foundation of the house, the tall hemlock where warblers and jays attacked and tried to drive him down. Cody was getting upset. It seemed like he'd be able to leave us if he had Felix, but he couldn't go without him.

"Damn cat," he said. His voice was half dried up.

"I'll start toting your stuff to the truck," Uncle Mike said. "Maybe if he sees you're really leaving, the rascal will come out."

Mama walked with Mike. I guess she was telling him more about the rotten stuff I'd done, and how I couldn't be trusted. Cody was trying not to cry.

"You went through all those rapids," I told him. "Now you're falling apart over a cat."

He shook his head and looked away.

"We'll bring him down on a weekend," I said.

Cody didn't answer. I got the feeling there were things between us, things besides Felix, that needed to be said.

"I wouldn't have gone home with you, even if I'd had the choice," I told him. "I thought about it a lot, and I want the school in Laglade. They care about what you think, instead of just the right answers. And most of the kids go on to college. They even have an office to help with scholarships."

"Won't you miss being outdoors?"

"I can come up here on weekends, or even after school. And it won't last forever—Mama said she just wanted to stay a while longer."

Cody wouldn't look at me. Maybe he didn't believe me, or maybe he was hurt I wouldn't have gone with him. "You shouldn't have gotten all the blame," he muttered.

"You told me not to go back to the ranger's."

"At first I did. But I went up there myself, when he offered the canoeing."

I shrugged.

"Anyway, Mama's wrong," Cody said suddenly. "And I was too. Because if you hadn't gone, we wouldn't have known him. They can say he's crazy—maybe he was; but he knew what kind of life he wanted, and when to end it. He couldn't have lived in that old folks' home."

I nodded. I felt like throwing my arms around Cody when he said that, but I knew he'd get mad.

"They don't know certain things," Cody said. "Like the fish carved in the cliff, and the limestone spring."

"Keep secrets," I told him; and we hooked our pinky fingers around each other's like we used to when we were small.

Felix came out while we were talking. If there was ever an animal that wanted to know your secrets, it was that cat. We grabbed him fast. He guessed that something was up, and he hissed and spat, but we held on for dear life.

"Next time you come home, bring the canoe," Cody said once he was in the truck.

Mama looked at him and shook her head. I could tell she didn't want him running any more rapids.

"Take good care of our cabin," Cody told me. He was holding Felix up to look out the window.

"Good-bye!"

I felt like running along behind him, grabbing on, but I held myself back and watched as they pulled away.

We stayed five more days on the Leanna. I was counting down: days and family—four, three, two. Mama'd taken vacation that last week, and she kept a tight rein on where I went and what I did. I asked to go to the ranger's, but she always had some reason to say no. Maybe she thought keeping me away would lessen what had happened. But I felt shackled, after the freedom of those months with Cody.

We couldn't get along. She was cold, because of what I'd done, and I was mad she wouldn't listen to my explanations. When I mentioned the ranger, she got this look like he was an ax murderer. After a while I gave up. I missed Cody like crazy. Thinking of him back at the house, sitting on the front porch or walking through the field toward the river, made me shiver with longing and regret.

Twice, at night, I slipped out the bedroom window and went to the cave. I balanced my flashlight on the shelf and wrote in my journal, explaining the things Mama wouldn't listen to. I wrote another poem, and started the story of the summer, a story it would take me years to finish.

I was so lonely I was desperate. One day Mama took me with her to the grocery store. I said I'd stay in the car and read, but the truth was I'd noticed a pay phone in a corner of the parking lot, and as soon as she got inside the store, I dialed the New York operator and told her Daddy's number. This time I was prepared: If a woman answered, I'd ask to speak to him as if she wasn't even there. The phone started ringing, and I rehearsed what I wanted: to have him hear about the ranger, and be sad that he was dead. Daddy could grieve a mouse or even a flower. He used to help us bury dead pigeons, and say prayers over their graves. The phone rang four times. Then a voice said, "The number you have dialed has been disconnected. . . ." I asked the operator to check it for me. She couldn't find another listing for Daddy. I kept asking and asking, and she seemed glad when I gave up.

I didn't tell Mama about the call. What was the point in telling her? 'Cause Mama was unhappy too. At night, when she thought I was asleep, I heard her crying. It was such a lonely sound, in that lonely cabin, and I had to lie there and listen. Sometimes I tried to hold my ears to keep it out. But later the wind blew down the ridge, and the trees moaned, and it seemed as if the whole world was grieving.

Star light, Star bright,
Take me home. . . .

Lift me like mist over the ridges
to the farmhouse by the field;
Carry me like foam on dark water
rushing to the place
where I was born;

Let me rise from the riverbank
where honeysuckle fills the air with sweetness
and crickets sing my name;
And find the light in the back-room window
softly glowing;
shining
for me.

The fourth day I started packing. I got out my duffle bag and threw in shorts and T-shirts, socks and underwear, the holey sneakers I used for fishing, a couple pairs of worn jeans. I got my journal from the cave and the nature guides I kept down there. My tackle box went into the crate I'd had beside the bed, along with the map, knife, flashlight, and some pretty stones I'd found by the water. I put Daddy's letters on top.

I cleaned up the room, too. I swept out the dead leaves and bits of bark from the whittling I'd told Cody to do outside. The broom hit something hard under the bed. I got down on my knees and saw the picture box! Had Cody left it for me? I dragged it out and opened the flaps. He'd looked through it last, because the snapshots on top were his favorites: our family sitting at the table at Thanksgiving, or posed on the running board of Daddy's rig. Here we were by the river, holding stringers of fish we'd caught on a float trip; and by the Christmas tree, with Granddaddy in his nightshirt, a Santa Claus hat on his head. Under that was a picture I'd forgotten: an old woman looking down at an infant, her face wreathed with smiles. The baby peered back with solemn eyes. Those are my eyes, I realized; and that's Gram, holding me. I thought I remembered her voice, reading out loud; and I'd been told how, in the year before she died, when she was too sick to walk, I'd try to climb into her lap. She'd move her quilting first, so I wouldn't get stuck by pins. I traced the squares in the quilt in my bed: mostly dark colors, greens and blues and browns, with a few stripes and patterns. Mama'd said Gram made it from old clothes. A patch covered with purple flowers came from the overalls I'd worn when I first learned to crawl. They were so full of holes, Daddy'd thrown them in the trash; but Gram had made him fish them out again. She'd searched until she found a square that was salvageable. "She made stuff from other people's castoffs," Granddaddy told me once. "Good things: rugs and quilts from rags; feather pillows; apple jelly from the peels I would have thrown away. . . ."

I put the picture box in my crate and wandered into the big room. Mama was sitting at the table reading papers. When I came in she set them aside.

"Are you done packing?"

"Almost."

"I've got most of the pots and dishes put away." She showed me a cardboard box. "We'll have to make lots of trips to the car."

"I'll make one now." I half expected her to say she'd go along; but she didn't, and as I walked back down the trail, I felt a little better. The cabin looked neat and tidy on its perch partway down the ridge: We'd sealed the windows with plastic; the roof was patched and tarred; downed wood was chopped and stacked along one wall. We'd helped the place along, and it had sheltered us. I went into the house. Mama was bent over papers—the ones she'd put aside before, I thought.

"Are those your scores from the accounting test?"

She shook her head, but for the first time in what seemed like days, she smiled. "No, but I passed. In fact, I did well. Philip thinks I'll get the promotion."

"That's good." I tried to sound enthusiastic. Mama picked up on that.

"I know things have been hard between us, Sha, but they'll get better. I was just so shocked by what happened, and how little I knew about what was going on. I've thought about it, and I realize how you got sucked in. You must have thought I'd take you back to Laglade if I found out about the ranger. There's some truth to that. . . ." She nodded as if I'd said it and she was agreeing. "I don't condone what you did, but I blame myself, too. I was so preoccupied making a life for myself that I didn't pay enough attention to you and Cody."

"The ranger was strange, but he was interesting, too," I told Mama.

"Interesting?" She blinked as if we'd gotten off course.

But I persevered. "Cody liked him once he got to know him. He could be childish, but he wanted what was best for the river. And he wanted us to love it, like he did."

"Oh." The look on Mama's face told me she couldn't

imagine loving a river; or maybe she just thought loving people was hard enough. She changed the subject, asking about school clothes and what I thought I'd need. But I wasn't ready to move forward, not yet.

"Over the summer I kept a journal," I told her. "I started a story, and I wrote three poems."

"You'll have to read them to me." Mama was smiling.

I don't know why I said the next thing, it was so stupid; and maybe, if I hadn't, the whole summer would have ended only halfway rotten, though I doubt it. "I read one to the ranger, and I sent it to Daddy, too. He said it reminded him of himself."

Mama's face must have changed, but I didn't notice that yet, because I was rushing blindly ahead, letting my hopes hang out like bright-colored laundry on a clothesline. "When he comes back, we'll sit around the oil stove after supper and read poetry," I said. "We'll have popcorn, and Cody'll pick something dumb like 'Casey at the Bat,' and Daddy can read one from the Renaissance, and you choose one of your favorites, the 'Daffodils,' or something new. I'll read the poems I wrote myself. You all will be the first to hear them."

I stopped suddenly, because by then I *had* noticed Mama's face. It was so sad, she looked like someone else.

"It's not going to be like that," she said. "When Charlie comes back, we're not going to live together."

I thought she meant he'd go to Warrensburg, but she and I'd still be up here. "He can come to Laglade," I said. My tongue was skipping ahead. "He'll get used to it. And Cody will too, once we're together. That's what counts, for Cody."

"No. That's what counts for *you*, Shana." Mama shook her head slowly. "Cody's accepted the truth. I didn't tell him—he brought it up himself."

"Brought what up?"

She handed me one of those papers, the ones I thought were her test scores. I didn't want to look at it, but she was sitting there watching me, so I had to. The top said *Allen* v. *Allen*.

"What's this?"

"We're getting a divorce." She said it just like that.

"How come?"

"Because I can't go back with him. I thought I could, and I've tried to talk myself into it, but I can't."

"He'll come here," I said again.

"I love Charlie more than anyone, but we can't go on together."

"You have to. You have Cody and me. You can't ruin things for us."

"You'll have to accept it," Mama said.

"I won't!" I stared at her so hard she shrank back, and I guessed that this part—the divorce—was her fault.

"Have you told Daddy?"

"I talked to him before he left for Italy."

I guess she could tell I didn't know. "He flew there last week," she explained.

I couldn't believe it. My face turned red. "He said we'd all go," I mumbled. "He wrote me that."

Mama barely heard. "It's not just the waitress," she said, not looking at me. "I really don't think it is. He said he had to see the Sistine Chapel." Her voice broke then. I felt like tiny shards of glass were falling around me. If I moved or opened my mouth, I'd get cut.

I sat there for a while. She was crying, but I was already so hurt, nothing could make it worse. They had betrayed us, each of them, and there was nothing we could do about it.

Twenty-four

That night I waited till Mama went to bed, then climbed out the window, carrying the quilt, a flashlight, and the crate with my belongings. A full moon lit my way along the path to the ranger's. I felt drained and empty, like a ghost. I thought I'd known the people I loved best, but one by one—Granddaddy, Daddy, Mama—I'd found pieces that turned them into strangers. Even Cody: *He's accepted the truth*, Mama'd said. I wanted to believe she was lying, but I knew she wouldn't lie about that.

The padlock gleamed on the cabin door. I unlocked it and went in. The room was cold, but there was kindling in the woodbox, so I started a fire in the cast-iron stove. I went out to the woodpile for logs. Moonlight outlined the shed, the pump, the garden. An owl called shrilly, and I thought of the little bluebird, trying to survive against the odds. Was it safe in its birdhouse? Or had it chosen this night, this moon, to fly?

Whooooo . . . The owl's cry echoed from the ridge as I carried wood through the back door. Darkness piled deep in the corners of the room, blotting out the shapes of table and chair, desk and bed. I put two logs in the stove and left the metal door open to help them catch. The flames made shadows on the cabin walls. My foot touched the crate, and I sat down, took out the picture box, and put it in my lap. In the wavering light I sorted the snapshots. Cody's favorites went into the top drawer of the desk; mine I held close, as if they were alive. My fingers traced faces, memories. I ripped them up, one by one, and threw them in the fire.

I cried then, because I knew the family was gone, and nothing would bring it back. Daddy wanted something we didn't have, wanted it so bad he'd crossed the ocean to find it, and Mama was tired of waiting for a man she couldn't count on. I'd dreamed we'd go home together, but it didn't make any difference. Birthday wishes, pennies in the well, the wishbone from Sunday's chicken dinner didn't have magic enough to heal us.

Gram used to read me this nursery rhyme:

Humpty Dumpty sat on a wall.
Humpty Dumpty had a great fall.
All the king's horses and all the king's men
Couldn't put Humpty together again.

"What about Band-Aids? Or glue?" they say I asked. "Shana likes happy endings," Daddy said. "Like me."

But Gram shook her head. She and Granddaddy'd been through hard times too. I guess she knew how fragile some things are, like love and promises and hope.

I went to bed with the quilt wrapped around me. The mattress had the ranger's old-man smell: sweat and woodsmoke and muddy clothes, and I sucked it in, knowing it wouldn't last. When I woke up, dawn had broken to the south. Gray light hung timidly at the front window, like a stranger afraid to knock. I thought of Mama, who would get up and find my empty bed. She'd guess where I was, but she'd have to ask Mrs. Burns for directions. That meant I'd have a few more hours to myself.

I built up the fire in the woodstove and put the kettle on top, to boil water for tea. Then I put my things away: the nature guides upright on the desktop, my knife and flashlight on the kitchen shelf. I copied my poems and stuck them on the wall next to the ranger's maps. My tackle box went by the back door, and the crate next to the bed, with the pretty rocks on top. I tucked the quilt in neatly. Then I washed the big front window, so you could see the river like you were outside.

I decided to go fishing. I headed upstream with the ranger's old fly rod under my arm. I'd found his net hanging on a nail, and I took a bait box and extra hooks. Daddy'd had a fly rod years ago, and he'd showed me how to use it on the Castle. I'd liked the way the thick yellow line hung in midair when you cast it out, and the rod was so limber even bluegills seemed enormous. I passed a rotten log and rolled it over: There were some grubs in the soft, thick bark, and a black beetle. I put them all in the bait box. Mist hung heavy on the river. I passed the flume, with its cascade of water, and dodged through thickets of laurel and rhododendron. After a while I found the pool below the limestone spring. Pale birches overhung the water there, and a shelf of rock offered space to stand and cast. I baited up and looped some line around one hand, then flicked the rod back to put it in the air. It took me a dozen tries to land the grub where the current met still water. Nothing. I reeled in and tried again.

I almost lost track of the time, fishing there; but the mist rose and when I looked upstream there was sunlight winnowing through the tangle of trees and brush. From somewhere on the ridge a sourgum tree cast wine-red leaves on the surface of the river. Something rattled in a thicket up the bank, and I tensed, wondering if someone was coming. But there was only a deer mouse scuttling by; leaves drifting on the wind; the murmur of water winding through the gorge.

I changed my bait and decided to try one more cast. The line hung lazy in the air, and I held my breath as the little beetle landed light and easy by a sunken log. Like slow motion a fish rose to the bait. Set the hook! my mind screamed, but I just stood and stared. The ranger used to say you can tell the wild trout by their colors. This one gleamed green and brown, with bright orange spots. It shook its head, and I came to life, snapping the rod back and to the side. The fish jumped again and found spare line to move in, dancing across the pool on its tail. "Wait!" I said out loud, and I grabbed the line and jerked, but there was nothing left but bubbles and a ring of circles and a leader with an empty hook.

Granddaddy said some moments come to us as gifts. I remember walking with him in the field beyond the spring, finding spider webs so hung with dew they looked like silver chains. I wanted to take them home and save them for the Christmas tree, but he said they'd break, so we left them swaying in the tall grass. The memory of the trout was brighter, more alive, but it was also special: one salvageable moment from an awful summer. But standing by that pool, I thought of other moments too: times with the ranger; drifting down the river on my back with Cody; Felix; the cave; a baby slurping milk. I thought of my journal. Gram had used thread to bind what could be saved, but I had words. My quilt would be written: spoken, rhymed, sung, whispered, but also shouted, because anger was a part of it too.

I headed back, pushing through weeds along the riverbank. Mama'd be mad at *me*, I knew. I'd have liked to tell her that my leaving out the window was the last bad thing I'd do; but everything was pared down and turned around. We'd probably fight more. The last two dice on the table, I thought; and I pictured a giant arm sweeping us off in opposite directions.

But maybe, like she'd said, things would get better. I imagined Mama walking from downstream, passing the line of evergreens and seeing the ranger's cabin suddenly, like Cody and I had. She might smile and think: So this is Shana's place. If we were feeling friendly, I'd invite her in; show her my poems; add wood to the stove, so she'd be good and warm after that long walk.

What about Daddy? Would he ever see the ranger's cabin? He'd gone so far away, his face seemed small and faded in my memory, but I spoke to him anyway. *You left us,* I whispered. *You didn't even say good-bye.* He tried to answer but the words were too soft to hear.

Then something pricked my ankle, and I started from my daydream and looked down. My socks were thick with seeds: hitchhikers, sticktights, little brown cockleburrs. I cleared a space on the ground and got down on one knee to pick them off. They clung to the fabric, then to my hands. A tiny drop of blood welled on one finger. It made me think of people I'd lost: Granddaddy, Daddy, Gram, Henry. For some reason I pictured that boy on the school bus, Richie Bird. I brought my hands up close and stared at those burrs. If I ever have a family—my own family—this is how tight I'll hold to them, I thought. I'll cling to them this tight, and never let them go.

ABOUT THIS APPLE SIGNATURE AUTHOR

JANE LESLIE CONLY is the author of *Crazy Lady!*, a 1994 Newbery Honor Book, an ALA Notable Book for Children, and a YASD Best Book for Young Adults. She is also the author of *Rasco and the Rats of NIMH*, a *Booklist* Editors' Choice, and *R-T, Margaret, and the Rats of NIMH*, which received an Honorable Mention from *Parenting*'s Reading Magic Award.

Ms. Conly lives in Baltimore, Maryland, with her husband and two children.

Books to Treasure

Apple
Signature

Start a library of your very own! Each Apple Signature Edition comes with a special bookplate for your name, a short biography of the author, plus the author's photograph and signature.

❏ BCV43944-6 *Afternoon of the Elves*
    by Janet Taylor Lisle $3.99

❏ BCV60135-0 *Bad Girls*
    by Cynthia Voigt $4.50

❏ BCV02570-8 *The Classroom at the End of the Hall*
    by Douglas Evans $3.99

❏ BCV34186-3 *Somewhere in the Darkness*
    by Walter Dean Myers $3.99

❏ BCV90717-4 *The Van Gogh Cafe*
    by Cynthia Rylant $3.99